KU-437-894

Betrayal at Cleeve Abbey

Anita Davison

W F HOWES LTD

This large print edition published in 2017 by
W F Howes Ltd
Unit 5, St George's House, Rearsby Business Park,
Gaddesby Lane, Rearsby, Leicester LE7 4YH

1 3 5 7 9 10 8 6 4 2

First published in the United Kingdom in 2016
by Aria

Copyright © Anita Davison, 2016

The right of Anita Davison to be identified as
the author of this work has been asserted by her
in accordance with the Copyright, Designs and
Patents Act, 1988.

All rights reserved

A CIP catalogue record for this book is available
from the British Library

ISBN 978 1 51006 539 0

Typeset by Palimpsest Book Production Limited,
Falkirk, Stirlingshire

Printed and bound by
T J International in the UK
Printforce Nederland b.v. in the Netherlands
Ligare in Australia

For my Mum and Dad, wherever you are now,
Tom and Eileen, I hope it's together

We must not look at goblin men,
We must not buy their fruits:
Who knows upon what soil they fed
Their hungry thirsty roots?

from Goblin Market by
Christina Rossetti

CHAPTER 1

RICHMOND, SURREY, AUGUST 1902

Flora shifted the weight of her wicker basket from one arm to the other, her lower lip jutted to blow a breath upwards, stirring the stray damp curls on her forehead. A trickle of sweat worked down between her shoulder blades, plastering her muslin dress to her skin.

The landlord of The Cricketer's swept the pavement in front of his public house on the edge of the green. He looked up when he saw her and paused, righted his broom and crossed his hands on the top.

'Beautiful day again, Mrs Harrington, eh?'

'A little too hot for me, Mr Brace.' Flora raised her free hand in a wave and winced as her leather boot rubbed her right ankle. The sting there told her a blister would form soon to add to her discomfort. The basket dragged against her hip, causing her to regret her offer to fetch the provisions the grocer had failed to deliver that morning; an omission that had sent her mother-in-law into a barrage of complaints about tradesmen in general.

An occasional click of leather on willow accompanied by a languid shout drifted across the green

1

enclosed by trees that had been saplings before Queen Elizabeth's time. Cricketers in white trousers and shirts loped across the field, too indolent to run in the oppressive heat. The weather had been stiflingly hot and dry for the past week, the exhausting humidity worsened by the constant dust thrown up from horses and carts on the roads that clung to buildings, clothes and damp skin.

Flora turned into Old Palace Lane, whose row of neat town houses thinned out into larger properties set behind shoulder-high manicured hedges; the River Thames at the far end of the road shimmered like glass in the sunlight. Even the river looked too languid to move as starlings and blackbirds flew low enough to dip their beaks in the cool water.

Flora quickened her stride in anticipation of a cool drink as the house where she lived with her husband and mother-in-law came into view on her left.

At the gatepost she slowed, frowning. Something wasn't right. A sharp bonfire smell caught the back of her throat, where a minute before the air had been laden with the scent of summer flowers and cut grass. While she ruminated on where it came from, the distinctive sound of breaking glass reached her, followed by a female scream.

Flora's head filled with grim possibilities that swirled and collided just as a thick cloud of grey smoke wafted over the hedge that shielded the house from the road.

Dropping the basket, she broke into a run across

the gravel drive where sharp stones cut through the soles of her boots, but she pounded on toward the house where orange flames licked round the window frame on the lower ground floor.

Flora froze a few feet away, watching in horror as the paint bubbled, wrinkled and turned black. Vein-like cracks appeared in the glass, spread outwards and exploded into a thousand glittering shards that rained down onto the area steps. She threw up an arm as searing heat surged toward her, then sucked back again into the basement as the fire roared like a live creature consuming the room.

Fear she could almost taste gripped her as she went through a mental list of who might still be inside the house. Bunny was at the motorcycle factory in Penge and wouldn't be back until early evening, though just then she didn't know if this was a good thing or not. He would have known what to do.

Should she go inside to ensure there was no one left in the house? Or run to a neighbour's and summon the fire brigade?

Apart from the crackle and spit of the flames, the front of the house remained ominously silent. Her mother-in-law had been inside the house when Flora had left to fetch the groceries a half-hour before. Had she got out, or was she inside and too frightened to try and leave?

Flora gathered her courage and sprinted for the front door, just as the side gate flew open and crashed against the wall.

3

Mary, the kitchen maid burst through from the rear garden, her face streaked with soot that had settled in unsightly smuts on her cap and apron.

'Miss Flora! Miss Flora! The 'ouse is on fire!' She twisted her apron between her hands, wavered and took a step back the way she had come, then changed direction, only to hesitate again, her eyes clouded.

Flora caught her upper arms and brought her to a halt as curls of ash floated from the ruined window like grey snowflakes and settled onto their hair and shoulders.

'Who screamed?' The thought her mother-in-law being trapped filling her with dread, but the voice she had heard was surely too high and young to have come from her.

The maid didn't reply, so she gave her a small shake. 'Mary!'

'What?' Her eyes cleared and she blinked. 'Oh, that was me, Miss. The window blew out and—'

'Never mind.' Relief flooded through Flora. 'Is everyone out of the house?'

'I think so, Miss.' Mary frowned. 'Crabtree ordered us all into the back garden.'

Flora nodded, and headed for the gate relief allowing her to think. 'Go to the fire house and alert them. Run! As quick as you can.'

A door slammed somewhere, bringing Flora's gaze to an upper floor where a filmy white curtain fluttered from an open window but no one appeared. Mary halted beside her and stared upwards.

'Mary go, now!' Flora gave her a shove.

Mary flinched but seemed to come to her senses, turned and took off down the road in the direction of the Green.

Four female servants huddled together on the lawn at the rear of the house, all staring wide-eyed at the plumes of smoke and flames that erupted from the lower ground floor. They all had smuts on their faces and clothes, but as far as Flora could make out, no one was hurt, although there was no sign of Beatrice.

'Where's your mistress?' Flora demanded, joining them.

'She was in her sitting room when it started.' Mrs Barrett, the housekeeper stood twisting her apron in her hands much like Mary had.

'She's still inside?' An image of Beatrice, lying unconscious on the floor propelled her towards the steps that led to the terrace.

A work-hardened hand clamped on her upper arm, pulling her roughly backwards.

'You can't go in there, Miss Flora,' Mrs Bennett pleaded. 'It's too dangerous. The flames might have spread to the upper floors by now. Crabtree and a footman went to find her. They'll get her out.'

Renewed clouds of choking smoke drifted up from the basement, a hint of flames behind it that drove them all back a pace.

'Has anyone gone for help?' Flora asked, uncertain she could trust a simple creature like Mary to do what she was told in a crisis.

'Crabtree sent the boot boy to raise the alarm before it got out of control.' Mrs Bennett adjusted her disarranged cap on her greying curls.

'What happened?' Flora shifted her feet, helpless to do anything but wait, debating whether she should have gone inside after all.

'I don't know Miss Flora.' Mrs Barrett shook her head. 'Mary said something smelled funny and when she opened the cellar door, there was this whoosh and a terrible heat. It were awful.'

A low boom of an explosion sent broken glass and bits of wood and debris through the lower window. One of the maids screamed and the others covered their ears and issued distressed sobs.

'What was that?' Nancy grabbed hold of Flora's arm, shaking.

'I don't know, the gas, maybe?' Worry bunched beneath Flora's ribs as she offered silent promises to a higher power for future good behaviour if Beatrice could be got out in time.

A loud bang brought Flora's head up to where the French doors that led from the terrace flew open, most likely from a kick, followed by a wisp of smoke that drifted out through the gap.

'Look, there they are!' Mrs Barrett shook a plump arm in the direction of the terrace. 'They've got the mistress!'

Crabtree shouldered through the door, head down one arm wrapped round Beatrice Harrington's waist while the other shielded both their heads. A footman assisted from her other side as they half-carried, half-dragged her down the stone steps onto the lawn.

Flora darted forward as they lowered Beatrice into a peacock backed garden chair someone had dragged from the terrace. Her mother-in-law's eyes were closed, her breathing laboured as if she had been running.

'Was she anywhere near the fire?' Flora demanded, making a rapid examination of Beatrice, who appeared uninjured.

Crabtree bent at the waist, his hands braced on his knees as he hauled deep breaths into his lungs. The footman stood nearby, enduring similar discomfort.

'No, Miss,' the butler gasped when he could finally speak. 'She didn't believe me at first. Then smoke started coming through the door and she just froze and refused to move. I'm afraid I had to insist, Miss Flora.'

'You did well, Crabtree.' His face and hair was streaked with soot, one sleeve of his livery scorched and torn revealing a livid red mark. 'You're hurt!'

'Nay, Miss Flora, it's nothing.' He straightened, easing his arm from her grasp. 'My jacket took the worst of it.' He pushed his other hand through his wavy silver hair, a characteristic that deceived most people into believing he was older than he was.

'Even so, you must get that burn dressed before you do anything else.'

'I will, Miss Flora. When I know the fire is out.'

He stepped away, his uninjured arm gripping the other one.

'I'm so relieved you're all right, Mother.' Flora took Beatrice's free hand in hers, the other still held by Mrs Barrett.

'Of course I'm not all right, girl.' Beatrice's strident voice snapped. 'I was almost killed!' She yanked her hand from Flora's grip and flapped the other to fend off the housekeeper.

'I understand it must have been frightening for you, but that isn't quite true.' Flora took in Beatrice's emerald green silk dress, which was barely creased, her hair still immaculately coiffured. 'We must be thankful no one was hurt.'

'Not hurt?' Beatrice shrieked, all signs of her previous near faint gone. If one had been there at all. 'My nerves are shattered, I'll have you know.' She patted her immaculate hair and fanned her face with a handkerchief. 'My beautiful house is being destroyed and no one's doing anything about it.'

Flora was about to remind her it was also Bunny's beautiful house, but this was not the time. An image entered her head of all their furniture and belongings consumed by the flames, but she pushed it away. None of that mattered if Beatrice was safe.

'The fire brigade will be here soon.' Flora returned to practicalities, the fingers of both hands behind her back. The smoke seemed to be getting thicker and red flames had filled the now exposed kitchens. If it wasn't put out soon, the whole house would be engulfed.

'And how did it start, I should like to know?' Beatrice demanded, drawing all eyes to her. 'Who allowed this to happen?' She raked each one of the servants with an uncompromising look; the same one she used to enquire after vanishing leftover apple pie or a stray pork chop. 'One of you must have neglected to extinguish the stove properly.'

'I hadn't even started the dinner, Mrs Harrington.' Mrs Barrett coughed and covered her mouth with the end of her apron. 'The range was damped down, so it can't have been that.'

'It weren't my fault, Missus. Truly,' Nancy pleaded, twisting her hands in front of her. 'Everything happened so fast, we couldn't do nothing.'

'Hush, Nancy. No one's blaming you.' Mrs Barrett gestured the girl away.

Beatrice looked about to continue her questioning when the harsh clang of a bell from the road drew their attention, accompanied by the rhythmic clop of hooves and the firemen's shout of 'Hi! yi!' warning pedestrians and traffic to stand aside.

'Thank goodness,' Flora exhaled a relieved breath.

'They took their time.' Beatrice huffed and smoothed back a strand of iron grey hair. 'Fetch my smelling salts, would you Nancy?'

'Stay where you are, Nancy!' Flora's voice halted the maid in mid stride. 'What can you be thinking, Mother? No one can go back inside until the firemen tell us it's safe.'

Nancy threw a fearful look at Beatrice, but stayed where she was.

'I'll go and speak to them.' Flora had got as far as the side gate before Beatrice called her back.

'Where are you going, Flora? I need you here.'

'The firemen will need to be told no one is still inside, Mother. They might also need directions to the nearest standpipe.' She kept her voice level and her face bland, a skill she had learned to acquire at will during the fifteen months of her marriage to Beatrice's son.

'I'm sure they're perfectly capable of doing their job.' Beatrice sighed. Her head flopped against the rounded chair back as if she were unable to hold her neck upright. 'Leave them to it, they won't want your interference.'

Flora gave her a polite, though insincere smile, before ignoring her, she carried on to the front of the house, where a group of about eight firemen crowded around the basement steps. More had ventured inside, their brass hats visible through the ruined window.

Someone had propped the basket of groceries she had abandoned earlier against a gatepost; the contents undamaged apart from one egg which oozed yellow yolk through its brown paper packaging.

The firemen had taken charge, located the standpipe without help and set one of their number to order the curious crowd back behind an invisible line. The others moved quickly and efficiently through the house, having already dampened down the flames, then set to bringing out destroyed furniture and clearing debris to ensure the fire was out.

The ruined kitchen window bore scorch marks around the bare stonework where no trace of the wooden frame remained, but for a pile of cinders on the flagstones. The inside of the room was unrecognizable as a kitchen, with dripping black walls and a jagged black hole where part of the ceiling had fallen down.

It would take a while to clear up this mess.

She stared round in dismay, her attention caught by two magnificent grey horses being guided into the shafts of the pump engine that stood in the road.

One of the firemen saw Flora watching and smiled, an open attractive smile of someone who enjoyed his role in life. 'Beautiful aren't they?' Taking her nod as encouragement, he went on, 'Sixteen hands these two and strong, which is just as well when the engine weighs three tons fully loaded.' He patted the nearest one on its solid neck. 'But they don't like fire much.'

'Few animals do. What do you do with the horses while you deal with the fires?'

'We unhitch them and take them somewhere quiet. It's easy enough with these snap harnesses.' He flicked a finger at the nearest trace. 'There's always someone around to feed them treats while we work.' He indicated the small crowd gathered on the road, their necks stretched to see what all the activity was about.

'All right then, Miss?' The head fireman brushed soot from his shoulders as he approached. He tipped his gleaming brass helmet that bore the letters MFB on the front below a curled comb that sported a dragon. 'Nasty mess in there, I suggest no one go in for a while. Let the air settle a bit.'

He was unusually tall, with craggy tanned features which made his age hard to determine. His high leather boots and navy blue double-breasted uniform and stand-up collar faced in scarlet must have been uncomfortable in this heat, though he gave no sign of it.

'Thank you, I won't. I'm grateful our butler got everyone out of the house straight away,' Flora replied. 'And thank you for arriving so promptly.' *Despite what Beatrice said.*

'Glad to be of service.' He retrieved a sturdy axe from the ground and tucked it into a thick leather belt at his waist, nodding toward the lower floor. 'It could have been worse though, what with all that oil.'

'Bad enough,' Flora murmured, staring with dismay at the untidy pile of kitchen furniture that had been thrown to one side of the steps. Stools, wooden shelves, rugs and pots and pans sat in a broken, scorched heap. Flattened hosepipes lay criss-crossed over the gravel between the truck and the house, still dripping pools of water over the basement area, forming puddles on the gravel.

'At least we didn't need the ladder for this one,' the fireman went on. 'The flames were confined to the lower floor.' At Flora's enquiring frown, he continued, 'There's an escape ladder beside a sentry-type box at the end of the road. Sometimes we have to wheel it to the fire to help victims escape.'

'Ah yes, I see.' Flora nodded, recalling the contraption she passed most days without noticing. 'I don't have much experience of house fires, I'm afraid.' She hefted the basket in both hands, then recalled something he had said and turned back. 'What was that you said about oil?'

'A roll of old carpet in the cellar was soaked with it.' He lifted his helmet and wiped his forehead with a rag as he spoke. 'Burned straight through and spread to the stairs and up into the kitchens. Despite you being so close to the river here, the steps and floorboards were bone dry, so it caught fast. Another few minutes and it would have reached the main rooms.'

'I see. I believe the servants keep oil down there to light the lamps with.' She hefted the basket into her arms. 'I'm glad you managed to put it out in time.'

'I suggest you make sure your servants take more care with that stuff in future, Miss. Should be kept in sealed containers as it can be lethal.'

'I will do that, thank you.' Flora nodded absently and glanced round to where Mary hovered beside the open front gate, talking animatedly to an

13

entranced audience of curious passers-by, her story embellished no doubt with dramatic details.

When she saw Flora, she flushed, ducked her head and hurried towards her.

'I was halfway to the fire house when the engine came past me with Jimmy on board.' Mary swiped a grubby sleeve beneath her nose. 'He must have run all the way. I came back here and then the neighbours—'

'Thank you, Mary. You did the right thing.' Flora cut off her excited chatter, though she didn't blame her for making the most of a rare drama in her life. 'Would you find somewhere to put these, please, Mary?' She handed her the basket. 'Though I doubt there will be any cooking done in the kitchen tonight. By the way, where's Jimmy now? I hope he didn't try to go back inside?'

'No, Missus. He's been out here the whole time feeding Mrs Barrett's carrots to the horses.'

By the time Bunny returned home that evening, the house was almost in normal order again, apart from a destroyed lower level, the pile of broken kitchen furniture and crockery on the drive.

'I had quite a shock when I turned the corner, I can tell you.' Bunny came through the front door and gathered Flora into his arms, rubbing her back with one hand. 'Are you all right? Is Mother?'

'No one was hurt, at least not badly.' Flora wrapped her arm round his waist and together

14

they walked through a hall that stank of smoke, with black stains on the walls and a ruined carpet.

At the sight of Beatrice on a chaise in the sitting room, a limp hand raised to him like royalty accepting homage, Bunny released Flora and went to her side.

'I'll have you know, I've experienced a dreadful ordeal today.' Beatrice adjusted the rug over her knees despite the heat, dislodging her copy of *London News Illustrated*, which fluttered to the carpet. 'I could have been a charred corpse on the floor for all anyone cared.'

'Judging by that mess outside, it's a miracle everyone was unharmed,' Bunny said. 'And thank goodness the flames hadn't reached the mews.'

'I might have known your uppermost concern would be for that filthy contraption.' Beatrice sniffed.

'Bunny's concern was most likely for the carriage horses, Mother, not his motor car.' Flora retrieved the magazine and replaced it on a side table before returning to the sofa.

Bunny dropped a swift kiss on his mother's forehead on his way to the sideboard. He poured a generous glass of sherry and handed it to her, rolling his eyes at Flora over her head.

'Ptolemy, is that grease on your fingers?' Beatrice wrinkled her nose as she took the glass from him. 'When will you realize that motorcycles are hardly a proper mode of employment for a gentleman? Why don't you stick to practising the law? Such a waste of your qualifications.'

Bunny inhaled, as if about to say something, then let it go again in a sigh.

Flora shot him a sympathetic smile as she took the glass he handed her, aware neither of them wanted to open up that particular debate again. Nor the one about Beatrice's insistence she call him by his given name.

Bunny loved nothing more than spending his time tinkering with engines, his beloved Panhard-Levassor Landaulet motor car tucked up under canvas in the mews attested to that. Had the automotive manufacturing industry been more lucrative, Beatrice wouldn't have been quite so scathing. The only reason he had turned to building motorcycles was because they sold where motor cars did not. Not that his mother made the distinction. In her world anything which required physical labour left her despairing in comparison with a genteel profession like the law.

'I hear Crabtree did a sterling job getting everyone out of the house.' Bunny said, indicating he too wished to change the conversation. He joined Flora on the sofa, one arm laid across the back in line with her shoulders.

'He suffered a badly blistered arm for his heroism, which he tried to shrug off, but I sent for the doctor,' Flora said. 'The rest of the staff are unharmed apart from a few bruises when they scrambled for the doors.'

'You were all most fortunate. Don't you agree, Mother?'

'I suppose so.' Beatrice took a large gulp from her glass she held in one hand then sniffed theatrically into a handkerchief in the other. 'If you believe Flora's version of events, who, incidentally, was gallivanting in town when it happened.'

'I would have been here,' Flora insisted. 'I normally am at that time, but this afternoon I went out to fetch the groceries that weren't delivered this morning.' She instantly regretted the apology in her voice, but somehow Beatrice always made her feel the need to justify herself.

'Does anyone know how it happened?' Ignoring his mother, Bunny addressed the question to Flora.

'According to the fireman, one of the servants must have spilled lamp oil onto an old piece of carpet in the cellar. Somehow it caught alight.'

'Lighting lamps in the daytime?' He consulted his watch. 'It won't get dark for hours. Seems a bit odd.'

'That's what I thought,' Flora straightened.

'Listen to you both, wittering on about lamps and oil despite the state of my nerves.' Beatrice huffed a breath and set down her empty glass with a click. 'I've questioned the servants already but got no sense out of them at all. No one will admit to anything.'

'Probably because they had nothing to admit to, Mother,' Bunny offered. 'It sounds like an accident, pure and simple.'

Beatrice threw off the rug and climbed awkwardly

to her feet. 'I cannot stand the lingering smell of burning.' One hand fluttered at her chest as if to bring attention to her suffering. 'I'm going upstairs to pack my things, it's not quite so bad up there. Let me know what accommodations you intend to arrange for us until the damage is repaired, will you, Ptolemy? And wherever it is, I expect an exceptional dinner after what I have been through.'

'She's calmer than I would have thought.' Bunny observed as Beatrice's footsteps receded up an unseen flight of stairs. 'I would have expected more hysterics from her.'

Flora exhaled slowly, tempted to remind him that the fire was confined to the kitchens in which Beatrice never set foot, but decided against it. The tension had left the room with her going so she chose not to invite it back again. 'She didn't even ask what the servants would do while the house is being repaired. Nor did she come out to thank the firemen.'

'And address a tradesman directly? What can you be thinking, Flora?' He rolled his eyes behind his spectacles in mock horror. 'She's a second cousin to the Earl of Ashley you know, with a position to maintain.'

'As she keeps reminding me.' Flora took another sip of sherry, though only to hide the slight acrid taste that clung to her tongue. Sherry was not her favourite drink, being too viscous and sweet, but Beatrice liked to maintain this pre-prandial ritual.

Bunny chucked, misinterpreting her grimace and

crossed one leg over the other, easing backwards with a sigh. 'Has she been too awful?'

'Not really,' Flora replied, warmed by his sympathy. She could stand everything his mother threw at her provided Bunny continued to support her. His calm tolerance of Beatrice's more unreasonable behaviour was something Flora did her best to emulate, aware confrontation only resulted in more dissent. Allowing her mother-in-law's sharp remarks to go unchecked was a hard lesson to learn but one she was prepared to endure when Bunny's love proved more than adequate compensation.

'Don't worry about the servants,' Bunny added, again misunderstanding the reason for her silence. 'They can hardly do their jobs at the moment. While we are away, I'll pay for them to visit their families for a short holiday. Crabtree has a brother in Kingston he can stay with, but he can come over each day and supervise the workmen.'

'I must remember to speak to Nancy.' Flora leaned against the chair back and closed her eyes.'

'Who's Nancy?' Bunny's fair eyebrows lifted into his hairline.

'Really, Bunny, she's the new housemaid. She was eager to insist the fire wasn't her fault. Which makes me think either it *was* her fault, or she expects to be blamed on someone else's behalf.'

'You're doing it again, aren't you?' Bunny peered at her over his spectacles like a disgruntled schoolmaster. 'Looking for villains where there aren't any. From what I've heard it was a freak accident.'

'Maybe. And your mother's right about the smell.' She echoed Beatrice's observation, thus acknowledging a thought that had struck her earlier. She had had no time to ponder on it then but what with Bunny's comment about lamps in the daytime her unease resurfaced. How *did* the blaze start, and why wasn't it noticed until it became almost beyond control? 'We've closed all the inner doors and stuffed blankets into the gaps, but it made no difference. Perhaps a hotel is the best place for us for the next few days?'

'I suspect it will be considerably longer than that, Flora. Have you seen the state of the kitchen floor? It's a foot deep in water.' Bunny wrapped his arm round her shoulders and leaned closer, nuzzling her neck. 'Actually, I'm sorry I missed all the fun.'

'Fun?' Flora's eyes snapped open. 'It wasn't much fun at the time. I thought the whole house was going up. Fortunately, the firemen arrived promptly and had the flames under control in minutes.'

'And very relieved I am too.' He crossed one leg over the other and lazily swung his ankle. 'The Metropolitan Fire Brigade is an impressive organization. Did you know, that Massey Shaw, the original chief fire officer, would only recruit former sailors into the fire service?'

'No, I did not know that.' She leaned into the comfort of his one-armed hug, inhaling the spicy scent of his *Floris* cologne, overlaid with a tang of motor oil. 'Where do you unearth all these fascinating facts? Not that I'm complaining, as I learn so much from you.'

'I have an enquiring mind, much like yours, though I'm not quite so fixated on solving crime.'

'It was only that one time on the SS Minneapolis, hardly a fixation.' Though she had to admit that it had fostered a hearty curiosity. Her voyage on the steamship from New York two years before had been a seminal one. Not only had she met Bunny, but she'd been involved in solving the case of two murders alongside a Pinkertons detective. She would be lying if she claimed the excitement of the chase hadn't piqued her interest, but there was little call for female detectives in deepest Surrey. Anyway she was perfectly happy with her lot, if Beatrice did sometimes get under her skin. She nudged Bunny gently with an elbow. 'Now, tell me about these sailors.'

'Well.' He took a sip from his glass and licked his lips as if preparing to give a lecture. 'It makes a sort of sense. Seaman's training made men physically strong, accustomed to working at heights and likely to obey orders without question. It's a hard life at sea.'

'Says a man whose only experience of such is a First-class passenger on an Atlantic steamship.' Flora puckered her lips and he ducked his head to receive her kiss.

'And,' he added, 'were you aware that terms like "aloft", "avast", and "the deck" are common parlance for firemen?'

'Why you thought I might be aware of that, I had no idea.' She eased sideways and twisted to face him. 'Although I might have done had I hung around watching them like young Mary did this afternoon. Incidentally, aren't you supposed to be organizing a hotel?'

'Well remembered,' he replied, just as the door clicked open and Crabtree appeared, immaculate in a clean uniform, his face scrubbed and pink, his damp hair slicked back behind his ears.

'Ah Crabtree, excellent timing. Would you send a message to the Coach and Horses and book a couple of rooms for us for an indefinite stay. Oh, and have our luggage sent over. Pack what you think suitable for me. Mother's maid will see to hers and Flora's.

He pushed the bridge of his spectacles further up his nose with a middle finger and lowered his voice for Flora's benefit. 'Oh, and Crabtree, should the occasion arise, you don't need to mention the venue to the senior Mrs Harrington.' He lowered his voice and addressed Flora. 'She will only question my choice, then demand an alternative.'

Flora smiled at his diplomacy, wishing she could learn such tactics instead of letting Beatrice irritate her.

'How's the arm, Crabtree?' Flora asked, spotting the outline of a bandage under his shirt that went from wrist to elbow.

'Sore, but not serious, Miss Flora.' His eyes twinkled conspiratorially, then coughed into a fist, bring their attention to the silver tray he held in his outstretched hand.

'What do you have there, man?' Bunny belatedly noticed the tray. 'It's a bit late for the postman.'

'A telegram, sir,' Crabtree replied with all the gravitas of his post at such an important event.

'Goodness, I don't often receive one of these.' Bunny reached towards the tray.

'Sir,' Crabtree's sharp tone halted Bunny's hand in mid-air, 'it's addressed to Miss Flora, sir.'

CHAPTER 2

CHELTENHAM, GLOUCESTERSHIRE, AUGUST 1902

The town coach rumbled through countryside Flora had once found achingly familiar, but which now she barely recognized. How had her whole world become so distorted in a single day?

The telegram in her pocket crackled as Bunny's arm encircled her hip, her cheek pressed against the rough fabric of his jacket.

'How can Father be dead?' she asked for the tenth time since they had set out from Richmond that morning. 'He was only in his forties and was never ill. What could have taken him so suddenly?'

'Has Lady Vaughn said nothing about how it happened?' Bunny rested his lips against her forehead, his breath warm on her skin.

'I can't bear to look at it again, here please you read it.' She withdrew the paper from her pocket and thrust it into his free hand and huddled closer, drawing comfort from the fresh linen and sandalwood smell on her husband's clothes, her eyes squeezed shut to prevent welling tears.

Bunny retrieved his arm and repositioned his

horn-rimmed spectacles. 'Brief and to the point. I expect all our questions will be answered when we get there.'

He handed the slip of paper back, then smoothed her damp hair back from her brow, squashing the rim of the unflattering black hat Flora hated on sight but had hurriedly purchased to complete an outfit suitable for deep mourning.

'I imagine so, although this reads more like an instruction than an invitation.' She thrust the crumpled page back into her pocket. 'Father's twenty-five-years of loyal service as their butler reduced to a smattering of words on a sheet of cheap paper.'

'That's a little harsh, Flora. By their very nature telegrams do that.' Bunny stretched his legs in the space between the buttoned seats. 'It's a pity we have no telephone, or we might have discovered more. Instead, you've allowed your imagination to make everything worse overnight.'

'How could it be worse?' she snapped, then clamped her lips shut. 'I'm sorry, Bunny. None of this is your fault and I've been snappy ever since that telegram arrived. Besides, Lord Vaughn has yet to install electric lights at Cleeve Abbey, let alone a telephone.'

'When the National Telephone Company installs an exchange in Richmond,' Bunny pointed a finger at his chest, '*I* shall be among the first to subscribe. No more relying on boot boys being fast runners to deal with future crisis.'

'I don't doubt it.' Flora hoped there wouldn't be any more crises but chose not to voice the thought. She angled her head and smiled at him with bemused affection. 'Modern innovations don't move fast enough for my husband, do they?'

Bunny's chuckle vibrated against her forehead, making her smile, though the ache in her chest remained as Lord Vaughn's hot and airless carriage, which he had sent to collect them from the station, moved through the Gloucestershire landscape, where straggly grass-covered verges dotted with blood-red wild poppies rushed by. Fields of wheat stretched into the distance and rippled in a heat haze beneath the late afternoon sun.

'It will be harvest time soon,' Flora murmured into his shoulder. A trickle of perspiration slid between her shoulder blades beneath her gown as images of her childhood returned. In weather too hot for stockings and encumbered by earthenware pitchers of lemonade and sandwiches wrapped in waxed paper, she had run through waist-high wheat stalks to where the harvesters worked. Her hair had always frizzed in the moist, heavy air, while wheat grains rubbed the skin raw between her toes. Endless days that seemed utter perfection now.

The weight of Bunny's look made her fidget. 'You're staring at me again. Do I have soot smuts on my cheek? Not that it would surprise me, it was stifling in that train.'

'You're lovely as always.' Bunny pushed his

spectacles further up his nose with a middle finger. 'I like to remind myself on occasion that you're mine, though I knew we would be married the first moment I saw you on the deck of the *SS Minneapolis*.'

'Did you really?' Flora asked, enjoying their physical closeness. In the train they had shared a carriage with a sour-faced couple and their miserably silent brood of children, unable to exchange more than a brief handclasp, leaving Flora to endure her raw misery in solitude.

'Really,' Bunny insisted. 'When you stroked Matilda's engine, cowling as if it were a favourite dog, I took one look and everything slotted into place.'

'I still cannot believe you named your motor car.' Flora nudged him gently with an elbow. 'We hadn't spoken at that point.'

'When I finally plucked up the courage to speak, you were so startled you banged your head on a support.'

'You required courage in order to approach me? Surely not?' she teased. 'It was your motor car after all and I presumed to examine it without permission.'

'Then you chastised me like a schoolmarm and laughed at my name. From that second, I was lost.' He laced the fingers of his free hand into hers and squeezed. 'I still am.'

Flora recalled her first sight of the handsome, blond young man with the devastating smile, so

27

eager to show off his horseless carriage. She hardly listened to what he was saying, fearful that he would discover she was a governess whose employer had bought her a ticket on a first-class ship as guardian to her thirteen-year old son. That would have been enough for most young men of his class to avoid her for the rest of the voyage, but it had not taken long for her to discover Bunny was not like that at all.

'I didn't want you to take fright and leave,' he continued. 'That would have given me no excuse to engage you in conversation.'

'You're trying to make me feel better about Father, aren't you?' His ability to fill awkward silences with fascinating snippets was one of the endearing qualities she loved about him.

'Yes, but every word is true. I hope I've distracted you slightly. I cannot bear to see you so distressed.'

'You have, honestly.' She squeezed his hand again. 'I appreciate your coming with me. It means so much to me to have you here when I know how busy you are with Mr Batson and your motorcycles. It's a bad time for you with the opening of his new factory.'

'Sam was very understanding, and most of my work is complete now. Besides, where else would I be?'

'At The Coach and Horses in Kew with your mother, perhaps? You could have supervised the rebuilding work as she wanted.' She slanted a look up at him, conscious her hair had slipped from its pins and sat in a heavy, damp bun at the back of her neck. 'She was quite angry about you leaving her wasn't she?'

'Don't underestimate her competence. She likes to play the helpless female in case I expect too much of her. In truth she'll enjoy holding court at the hotel to every builder, decorator and furnishing emporium in West London.'

He planted a brief, warm kiss on her cheek, then straightened as something caught his eye through the window. 'I think we've arrived.'

Easing upright, Flora looked past him to a grey stone Jacobean mansion squatted on a rise and surrounded by a bank of ancient hedgerows manicured into submission by generations of gardeners. Wide, undulating lawns dotted with oak and elm trees that had probably been saplings during the Civil War, stretched down a gentle incline to a brook.

The horses swept through a pair of wrought-iron gates and down a tree-lined drive onto a circular forecourt in front of the house where they rolled to a gentle halt. A series of bangs and thumps followed by a scrabbling above was followed by a tilt of the bodywork, and then the footman opened the door.

Bunny unwound from Flora's side and alighted, then turned to help her down. 'Are you ready?'

'No, and I don't think I ever will be.' The tensions that had twisted Flora's gut for the last twenty-four hours increased, and she fought an urge to turn and run.

She wanted to go home, forget the awful tele-gram and imagine her father as she always thought of him; issuing curt and half amused orders to saucy footmen and chivvying maids like a benevo-lent headmaster.

Her hand trembled as she placed it in Bunny's firm one. They approached the familiar double front door with its row of studs big as half crowns, the long iron bell pull attached to the stonework on one side.

'Whatever happens, I'll be here,' Bunny nodded to a solid façade with its row of mullioned windows. 'We'll face it together.'

Unconvinced, though more confident, Flora allowed him to lead her up the short flight of worn steps, where one half of the double doors had swung open silently as if of its own accord.

A small, vestibule opened into a wide hall, its walls panelled with pale oak linen-fold. A curved, cantilevered staircase wound up two stories to where a glass lantern ceiling spread daylight onto a marble tiled floor. The Tudor solidity of the exterior gave way to pastel-painted walls favoured by the early nineteenth century.

'Quite a mixture of architectural styles,' Bunny whispered at her shoulder.

'You ought to see the kitchens. I think they still roast whole oxen on the fire down there,' Flora replied.

She caught sight of a man in Vaughn livery who stood in the hall and her breath hitched, unprepared for the sharp pang of disappointment that he was not her father.

This man was of about the same height, but at least twenty years younger, a lanky, soft eyed man with thick blond hair darkened by pomade. His eyes were set close together and his nose was asymmetrical, as if he had broken it at some point.

His unremarkable face held none of the stoic politeness concealing private amusement her father had mastered. This man returned her look with an almost sullen expression. His clothes were the standard black for a butler but did not quite fit him. The material at the shoulders wrinkled as if the jacket was designed for a larger man and his shoes were dull, the laces loose.

Had they bought him new ones, or did he quite literally occupy a dead man's shoes?

'Lord and Lady Vaughn are in the sitting room, sir, madam.' He threw open a door to his right without looking at either her or Bunny.

Flora couldn't bring herself to respond, though her practical side told her she was being unreasonable, yet her throat burned with emotion as she stepped into the room.

Venetia, Lady Vaughn rose slowly from a gold brocade sofa and glided forward on a whisper of silk. 'I'm so dreadfully sorry about Maguire, my dear.' She took both of Flora's hands in hers, her head tilted on one side in sympathy. 'I never imagined this would be the reason for your return to Cleeve Abbey.'

Tall for a woman, she topped Flora's own five foot five by at least two inches, her back ramrod straight, her waist as tiny as Flora remembered. Her ebony hair was now streaked with steel grey, while tiny lines creased the corners of her intelligent grey eyes.

Her papery complexion sagged a little around her jawline; changes which should not have been a surprise as she must be in her early fifties.

'And dear Ptolemy.' She transferred one delicate hand to Bunny's shoulder. 'How nice to see you again, although the circumstances are regrettable.'

Flora's carefully prepared greeting came out almost unintelligible.

'We're delighted to be here, Lady Vaughn,' Bunny answered for her. 'Bearing in mind the circumstances.' He dropped a kiss onto the lady's knuckles while his steady gaze behind his spectacles held hers, making her blush like a schoolgirl.

Flora couldn't help but smile as she observed the effect Bunny had on Lady Vaughn, the same effect he had on women of all ages.

'We'll all miss Maguire dreadfully.' Lady Vaughn sighed, then intercepted the glance Flora threw the man who stood in the door frame, his eyes cast down, white gloved hands clasped in front of him. 'Ah yes.' She gave a discreet cough. 'I see you have already met Scrivens.'

An awkward silence ensued, then she dismissed the butler.

'I confess to a mild surprise myself whenever

32

Scrivens answers the bell.' Their hostess urged Flora toward a Wedgewood blue sofa. 'It will take a while to get used to.'

The sitting room greeted Flora like an old friend; a feminine haven decorated in blue, white and cream where painted shelves in alcoves sported Meissen figurines in regimental rows and gilt-framed mirrors that rose to a bossed plaster ceiling; all Georgian additions commissioned by Lord Vaughn's grandfather. Flora's reflection confronted her at every turn, and she groaned inwardly. The heavy black bombazine dulled her bright chestnut hair and leached colour from her already pale skin, made worse by the matronly hat that wouldn't sit right.

'Do sit down, my dears.' Lady Vaughn indicated an intimate arrangement of three sofas set in a horseshoe before an Adam fireplace. 'I'll send for some tea, and—'

'Oh, not for us, Lady Vaughn,' Flora interrupted her. 'It's almost six and the kitchens must be busy with preparations for dinner.'

'As you wish.' Lady Vaughn stepped away from the bell-pull handle beside the fireplace. 'You always were a considerate girl where the staff were concerned.'

'I used to be one of them,' Flora said, sotto voce, aware she sounded arch when Bunny gave a minute shake of his head.

'Flora's a little on edge, Lady Vaughn.' He took a seat on the camelback sofa. 'Your news came as something of a shock.'

'I don't mean to reject your hospitality,' Flora said in an attempt to compensate for her lack of manners. 'I'm simply eager to know exactly what happened to my father.'

'Of course you are, that's quite understandable.' Their hostess lowered herself onto the sofa opposite, her knees inches from Flora's and her hands clasped demurely in her lap. 'I'm afraid there isn't much to tell you, my dear. The day before yesterday, Maguire took one of the horses from the stables.' At Flora's sudden start, she lifted a hand. 'With permission of course, I don't mean to imply otherwise. No one thought it strange, being as it was his day off. However, some hours later, the horse came back alone. A search was organized, but he wasn't discovered until it was almost dark.'

'Discovered?' Flora pounced on the word. 'Was he still—'

'I'm afraid not, my dear.' Lady Vaughn cut her off. 'He was already dead when he was found, and had apparently been for some time.'

'What happened? Flora croaked, tears perilously close.

'The doctor said his injuries suggested a fall from the horse.'

'Something must have caused it.' Flora twisted her hands in her lap that felt clammy inside her gloves. 'Did the horse panic? Did a carriage come past and unbalance him?'

Bunny plucked one of Flora's hands from her

lap and held it between both of his. She left it there, drawing comfort from his touch.

'I'm afraid we don't know. As far as everyone was aware, he was out riding alone.' Lady Vaughn threw Bunny an anguished look. 'No one witnessed the incident.'

'I see.' Flora exhaled in a rush, her hope flowing with it. 'Had he been located sooner, might he have survived?'

'Flora,' Bunny dragged out the word in warning.

She turned and glared at him, then snatched her hand away from his. 'I have to know.'

An image of her father lying hurt and with no one to help while the strength drained slowly from him flashed into her head. Her gut twisted and a tiny cry issued through her lips, suppressed at the last second.

'We cannot be sure.' Lady Vaughn's eyes misted with emotion. 'I'm so sorry, Flora. I wish the outcome had been better.'

'Where was he going?' Flora asked when she trusted her voice not to crack. 'Whenever he went out on personal errands, he always used the dog cart.' Her voice trailed off into memory. 'Messages he called them.'

'I don't know.' Lady Vaughn cast a vague look at the door as if the answer would magically appear. 'Perhaps one of the servants might answer that question. He certainly wasn't on estate business. There'll have to be an inquest, of course.'

Flora's head jerked up to stare at her hostess. 'Inquest?'

'It was a sudden death.' Lady Vaughn lowered her voice. 'The reasons for which must be decided by law.'

'Yes, yes of course, I didn't think.' Flora's nose began to run and she fumbled in a pocket for a handkerchief. 'Where was he found?'

'In Bailey Wood.' Lady Vaughn's brow creased in mild confusion. 'At least that's what I was told.'

'Why would he go there?' Flora crumpled the handkerchief in her fingers. 'It's several miles in the opposite direction to either the village or the town. From what I can recall, there are only a few houses out that way.'

'Is it really important where he was going, my dear?' Lady Vaughn held both palms upwards in a gesture of surrender, then left her seat and reached for the bell pull again. 'You must be tired after your journey. Perhaps a rest before dinner would be beneficial.'

Flora was about to say it mattered her, but the door clicked open and the butler appeared like a silent ghost at the door.

'Ah Scrivens.' Lady Vaughn bestowed a cold smile on him. 'Take Mr and Mrs Harrington's luggage upstairs, would you?'

'We appreciate the gesture, Lady Vaughn,' Bunny began, rising. 'We didn't want to intrude, I'm sure there will be enough to sort out without worrying about us. If I might impose upon you again for the use of your carriage to take us into town later, we would be quite comfortable at the Queens Hotel.'

'I won't hear of it, you'll stay here with us, naturally.' Her tone brooked no argument. 'I thought the blue room would be the most suitable.'

Flora's stomach lurched at the thought of the suite with its Italianate furniture, the canopied bed draped in sapphire velvet and the trompe l'oeil walls. The thought of the lavish suite with its Adam fireplace, antique porcelain ornaments and crystal chandelier where duchesses had slept made her feel inadequate. What she craved just then was the familiar and comforting. Somewhere she could mourn her father among the trappings of his life, surrounded by their joint and more personal memories.

'If-if you don't mind, might we stay in my old apartment in the attic?' At her hostess's surprised start she rushed on, 'I'll need to sort out Father's things in any case and—' she trailed off, unable to think of a way to refuse the offer without insult.

'Very well.' Lady Vaughn's smile wilted round the edges. 'If you feel that would be more comfortable.'

'I'm sure the apartment will be more than adequate,' Bunny said.

Flora threw him a grateful smile. Bunny was born into wealth and privilege, where meals appeared by magic, and laundry was some vague concept, but despite that, he understood how Flora might feel out of place in her former employer's home.

Scrivens was dispatched to retrieve their luggage and as Flora climbed to the third floor, albeit via the ornate grand staircase and not the plain wooden servants' stairs at the back of the house, Flora had time to ponder the question of what Riordan was doing on horseback in the middle of a wood miles from anywhere.

He was a creature of habit, whose inherent consideration for others would never have allowed him to go anywhere without telling someone where he was going and why. As for riding, she had never in her life seen him astride a horse.

Nothing about his death made sense.

CHAPTER 3

'What a charming room.' Bunny discarded his jacket on a wheel back chair as he strolled the green and gold attic room. 'Not like a servants' quarters at all.'

Flora clamped her lips together, nodding as the rooms closed in on her and images from her childhood rushed back and threatened to break her fragile self-control. She knew coming back would be sad, but the strength of her nostalgia was almost painful.

Set beneath the eaves on the second floor, two dormer windows overlooked the grounds, which gave the room the impression of a cottage. A semi-circular rug sat before a tiny fireplace, the black grate bordered by ceramic tiles in a Morris design of red lilies.

She wanted to explain that the Strawberry Thief Morris wallpaper was her choice, the cushions on the twin armchairs her own work on cold winter evenings, the polished brass candlesticks on either side of the mantelpiece had been kept shiny by her own hands.

'Our bedrooms open onto this room,' she said

at last, her throat burning. 'The bathroom is across the hall.' She pulled the hatpin from the hated hat and tossed it onto a chair. 'The other servants sleep on the far side of the house, so it is like being in our own little world up here.'

Her eyes welled as she inhaled lavender and furniture polish which evoked so many memories. The handmade rag-rug, a china shepherdess on the mantle, the twin wing-back chairs in front of the fire where she and her father had sat together and shared their day.

Everywhere she looked, from the dent in the cushioned chair back where her father's head rested, to the cracked tile beside the fireplace she had once damaged with a badly aimed foot when she was in a temper; memories crowded the room making tears well. She fought them down, hearing his voice in her head saying, 'Cease yer greeting, lass.'

An invisible string pulled her to the door of her father's bedroom, but she could not bring herself to venture inside – yet. Instead she strode to the opposite side of the room and her own childhood bedroom. Inside, she halted, frowning at the sight of a high double brass bed that took up most of the space she had never seen before. She pushed a hand into the deep mattress, the other caressing the knob on the nearest bedpost, the metal cold to her touch.

The dormer window stood open, drawing her towards the expansive but remote view of the gardens. A waft of honeysuckle-laden air flowed in and cooled her face and she might have been ten years old again. 'I used to imagine myself as the Lady of Shalott in this room.' Disturbed by how close to the surface her emotions were, she turned away as tears threatened.

'Ah, so this is where you read Tennyson as a girl?' Bunny lounged against the door frame, his hands in his pockets.

'I'm still a girl,' she narrowed her eyes at him. 'And definitely not! I've never seen this bed before, it must be new. I had a low single one as a child which creaked with each movement so it practically played a tune.'

'This looks solid enough not to creak.' Bunny grasped the bottom rung of the brass bed with both hands and gave the frame a vigorous shake. 'It hardly moves, see?' He caught her look and his grin dissolved. Sighing, he drew down onto the bed and sat beside her, plucked her hand from her lap and brought it to his cheek. 'I'm sorry, that was insensitive. I shouldn't make risqué jokes at a time like this.'

'I like your jokes.' She leaned sideways against him. 'And risqué or not. You always know the right thing to say to make me feel I'm not alone.

'Does that mean I'm not in disgrace for my suggestion we try out this bed?' He tucked in his chin and aimed a teasing look at her.

'You're never in disgrace with me.' She contemplated their twin trunks that had been set by the door with dismay, I suppose I had better unpack.'

41

'I doubt it. We might be in the servants' quarters, but I'll wager a maid will be up to do that presently. Guests of a lord aren't required to do their own unpacking.'

'There you see. You always know how things should be.' She pushed the idea to the back of her mind. 'What puzzles me,' she said after a moment, 'is why Father was on horseback in Bailey Wood at all?'

'Was that unusual?'

'It was, and whenever he left the estate he took the gig or sometimes the governess' cart. Riding astride for more than a short time was too painful, a legacy from an accident when he was young.'

'What sort of accident?'

'He never spoke about it other than to say he had suffered some sort of injury to his hip. On my sixth birthday he bought me a doll in a midnight blue velvet coat I had seen in a shop window in Cheltenham. I was so delighted, I threw myself into his arms. My booted foot caught his hip and he gave this gasp of sheer agony that I have never forgotten. The colour drained from his face and seeing him in such pain, I burst into tears. He said the 'old hurt' only occurred when he bent at a certain angle, which was why he never rode astride.'

'Injuries heal, Flora. Which follows if he never referred to it again.'

'Then why did he never ride? He wasn't afraid of horses. He liked them.'

'In which case that does seem odd. We'll likely some answers at the inquest.'

'Official ones maybe,' she murmured. 'He was young still, and strong, with so many years ahead of him. I wanted him to be so proud of me, of us.' She leaned her hot forehead against the cool metal bedstead.

'He *was* proud of you, I know he was.' He leaned closer and lowered his voice. 'Flora?'

'Yes?' Her back went rigid, alerted by a change of tone that warned he was about to broach a difficult subject.

'This may seem precipitous, but have you given any thought to where you intend to have him buried?'

'I would like to lay him to rest beside my mother of course, but—'

'You don't know where her grave is,' he finished for her.

'Ridiculous I know.' She relaxed against him, relishing the quiet of the attic room where few sounds penetrated and even birdsong seemed distant. 'She died when I was small, and Father never talked about her. If I asked questions, which was rare, his eyes took on a pained, haunted look and he would distract me. I didn't want to cause him any more pain, so I stopped asking.'

'You cannot hurt him anymore, so this might be the perfect time to seek answers to those questions? It might also put a stop to those dreams you've been having for so long.'

The thought sent a shiver of relief up her spine and she returned his smile. 'Where do I begin?'

'As Lady Vaughn's personal maid, did she never mention your mother to you?'

'I never dared ask her. Lady Vaughn and I weren't on the kind of terms where secrets were exchanged. I was a governess to her son, and she was my employer.'

'Were any of the staff here during your mother's time?'

Flora pondered for a moment. 'The estate manager has been here more than twenty years, as has the housekeeper, Hetty Farmer. She might remember my mother.'

'Then maybe that's where you should start. And Flora?'

'Yes?'

'Can we hear the dinner gong from up here? I'm starving.'

'Flora!' a lanky youth with wayward curly hair in black tie and dinner jacket crossed the hall in long strides and threw his arms round her in an exuberant hug.

'Mama told me you were here, though she insisted I wasn't to disturb you while you rested.' He rolled his eyes as if conceding defeat to a higher power, thrust out his hand and gave Bunny's an enthusiastic shake. 'And good evening to you too, Mr Harrington, how marvellous to see you.'

Eddy, Viscount Trent's features had become

44

more chiselled in the year since she had last seen him. At fifteen and about to begin his third year at Marlborough College, he had grown several inches with the loose limbed, unco-ordinated build of a bolted plant. His curly hair was badly in need of a cut, something Flora wouldn't have overlooked had he still been in her charge.

'Goodness, Eddy, you've grown so tall.' Flora held him away from her in order to appraise him properly. 'You look thin though, and very pale. Are you sure you are quite well?' Her governess instinct rose to the surface and she realized with a pang that she had missed him.

'I wish everyone would stop asking me that.' He flushed and eased his collar away from his neck with a finger. 'Papa keeps me busy with estate business even though it's the hols. I might as well have stayed at school.' His eyes widened suddenly. 'Oh, I almost forgot. I'm so sorry about Maguire, Flora. It was such an awful thing to happen.'

'Thank you, Eddy.' A shiver ran through her at this reminder of why they were at Cleeve Abbey. 'His death was a dreadful shock, but your parent have been most kind.' She found the compassion in everyone's eyes when they spoke of her father's passing difficult to get used to. Repeatedly robbed her of her composure she floundered as she tried to conceal the rush of emotion their kindness elicited. Mentally, she checked her pocket for her handkerchief, suspecting she would need it before long.

45

Flora wrapped an arm around Eddy's shoulders as they entered the sitting room, a feat not easily accomplished when he topped her by several inches. 'I want to hear about everything you've been doing since I last saw you. How is school?'

'The end of term exams were quite tough and—'

Lord Vaughn turned from the sideboard, a glass in each hand. 'Flora, my dear girl.' He paused, gave the glasses a perplexed look before he returned them to the tray and enveloped Flora in a fatherly hug. Eddy faded into the background with a benevolent smile as he allowed his father to monopolize their guests.

'Please accept my sincerest condolences. Flora dear.' The scratch of Lord Vaughn's moustache against her cheek brought childhood memories flooding back, threatening her fragile control.

He released her, and held her away from him, his face creased beneath a thatch of sandy hair in comical anguish as his chocolate-brown eyes bored into hers. 'Awful business. Terrible shock for everyone.'

'I'm still in shock, my lord,' Flora replied, her voice scratchy in response to the genuine warmth of his greeting. 'It's very kind of you to have us here while we make the arrangements.'

'This is your home, Flora. Where else would you come at such a time?' Despite his only having met Lord Vaughn once, Bunny's back received an enthusiastic slap that threatened to throw him off balance. Lord Vaughn retrieved the glasses from the tray and handed one to each of them. 'Another for you, Venetia?' he asked over Flora's shoulder.

'I still have mine, thank you, George.' Lady Vaughn, serene in sage green trimmed with grey, occupied a sofa set next to the empty fireplace, her half-full glass held aloft.

'I'm jolly glad you put the guests off tonight, Mama,' Eddy said with the thoughtlessness of youth. 'Much nicer with just us than all those stuffy old folks.'

'You had a dinner party scheduled for tonight?' Flora gasped, mortified as she lowered herself into a camelback sofa. 'Had we known we wouldn't have intruded. We would have been quite comfortable at the hotel.'

'Which is precisely why I didn't mention it.' Lady Vaughn glared at her son, who, chastened, ducked his head. 'Under the circumstances we thought it best,' she continued. 'Besides, Eddy is quite right, we would prefer to spend the evening with you and Bunny than with a room full of neighbours. Don't you agree, George?'

'Absolutely.' Lord Vaughn removed the sherry decanter from Eddy's hand and returned it to the tray. 'Only one glass for you, my boy.'

Resigned, Eddy curled his lip and straddled the arm of the sofa where Bunny sat. 'How are your plans going, Harrington?' Lord Vaughn asked. 'Last I heard you intended on a venture into the motor manufacturing business.'

'Um, well, not so well, I'm afraid.' Bunny coughed

47

into a fist. 'The industry as a whole isn't moving as fast as I hoped. At the moment I'm involved in some work with Sam Batson in Penge. His motor-cycles have rapidly gained in popularity as they are less expensive than motor cars.'

'Is there a reasonable living to be made from such things?' Lord Vaughn's brow rose, openly sceptical.

'If so, it will be in the long term,' Bunny replied. 'For the moment I've fallen back on my qualific-ations as a solicitor to pay the bills.'

'A more sensible mode of employment for a married man,' Lady Vaughn murmured into her glass, the sentiment as well as her raised eyebrows reminding Flora of Beatrice.

She glanced at Bunny, whose mouth twitched, indicating his thoughts ran along the same lines.

'The Automobile Club's time trial passed through Cheltenham in 1900 on its route to London.' Lord Vaughn grinned with boyish enthusiasm. 'I missed it, unfortunately, Venetia and I happened to be in the United States at the time.'

'I would have liked to have seen that too, but if you recall I was at the Duryea Motor Company at the time.' His private smile as he dipped his nose to his glass told Flora he also recalled they had been aboard the *SS Minneapolis* on their way home to England at the time – where they had first met.

'Molly Freeman gloated for weeks about how divine the luncheon was at the Queens Hotel on the day,' Lady Vaughn said with only a trace of envy.

'The winner was Charles Rolls, Lord Llangattock's boy, a daring adventurer by all accounts. He drove a Panhard Levassor, not unlike yours, Bunny,' Lord Vaughn said. 'He got his up to over thirty-seven miles an hour. Can you imagine? I thought only trains went that fast.'

'You haven't given up on motor cars altogether, have you, sir?' Eddy straddled the arm of the sofa where Bunny sat, his ankle swinging. Despite having gotten taller, and older, Flora could see clearly the wide-eyed little boy still lurked inside.

'Never.' Bunny grinned, caught Flora looking at him and winked. 'I would no more part with Matilda than I would Flora.'

'I should hope it won't come down to you having to make a choice then,' she said.

'Lady Vaughn,' Flora ventured, when the conversation turned into an enthusiastic discussion on the merits of de Dion engines over Daimlers. 'There's a rather handsome brass bed in my room I've never seen before. If you mean to use those rooms for another purpose, I'm happy to remove my father's belongings—'

'Oh my dear, of course not.' Lady Vaughn cut her off with a motherly pat of her hand. 'Your father bought it especially in preparation for when you and Bunny came to stay. He said your old one was woefully inadequate.'

'He never mentioned it.' Flora swallowed the

lump that formed in her throat. 'He came to see me in Richmond three times during this last year, yet not once did he intimate he wanted me to come home.' Flora blinked back welling tears. She and Bunny had always intended to visit the Abbey, though the opportunity simply hadn't presented itself, what with Bunny's work and settling into life as newlyweds.

'The first year of marriage is always a time of adjustment. Maguire knew you would come home again when the time was right,' Lady Vaughn said gently. 'He was prepared to wait.'

A stone settled in Flora's chest. Her father would never have complained that she had failed to visit him. The fact he had prepared her old room so she and Bunny would be welcome when they chose made her want to cry again.

While she fought for composure, the door opened to reveal a young woman in a peacock-blue gown, her glossy dark hair piled on top of her head in loose sausage curls.

Bunny rose to his feet, and Eddy slid off the sofa arm as the girl hurried towards Flora in a stride that still managed to look graceful.

'I'm so sorry I wasn't here when you arrived, Flora dear.' Her pretty, mobile face exhibited both apology and delight. 'I was at the station seeing Jeremy off back to London.'

Lady Jocasta Vaughn was the closest Flora had to a friend at Cleeve Abbey. They had shared a schoolroom until the three Vaughn daughters had attended the Ladies' College in Bayshill Road, leaving Flora to complete her education on her own with the help of Lord Vaughn's extensive library.

Flora returned her sherry glass to a low table just in time to avoid it being spilled as she was enveloped in a cloud of heady spice and citrus fragrance of Penhaligon's, *Blenheim Bouquet.*

'I'm so dreadfully sorry about dear Maguire.' She held Flora away from her, raking her from head to toe as if debating whether to mention the unflattering dress, finally releasing her with a tiny sigh as if she thought better of it. Instead, she bussed Flora's cheek before accepting the sherry glass her father held out.

'Who's Jeremy?' Flora asked, retrieving her untouched sherry.

'My fiancé, darling.' Jocasta sank onto the sofa beside Flora and waggled her left hand on which sat a large solitaire diamond that sparkled in the light.

'Of course, it had quite slipped my mind,' Flora said. 'I saw your photograph in *The Tatler.* You looked lovely, Jocasta, and Congratulations.'

'It was rather adventurous of us wasn't it?' Jocasta hunched her shoulders in a girlish gesture. 'Mama wasn't sure it was quite the thing, but everyone who is anyone has their engagement announced in *The Tatler* now.'

'I still have reservations about that rag,' Lord Vaughn said. 'It's lauded as an illustrated journal of both society and the stage. Ah well, I suppose if Jocasta doesn't qualify for the first she might revert to the second.' He delivered a slow wink in Flora's direction, ignoring his wife's startled frown.

'You don't shock me at all, Papa.' Jocasta pulled a face at him. 'The stage is quite a respectable profession these days.' She inclined her head flirtatiously up at Bunny who was still standing to attention. 'And how lovely to see *you* again, Mr Ptolemy Harrington. He of the Greek name and matching looks. Why do you only visit us on such solemn occasions?'

'Jocasta! Don't be so forward!' Lady Vaughn's eyes rounded in horror.

'I assume you remember our youngest daughter, Lady Jocasta?' Lord Vaughn heaved a sigh.'

'Lady Jocasta,' Bunny murmured and dropped a brief kiss on the hand which did not sport an oversized diamond. 'I'm delighted to make your acquaintance again.'

'I distinctly remember asking you to call me Jo when we last met.' She fluttered her long lashes while giving Bunny a slow, appraising look. 'I only mentioned the name thing because my own is also from Greek mythology. Jocasta was Oedipus' mother, you know.'

'I do, actually.' Bunny ducked his head to hide the smile he exchanged with Flora, who knew better than to take offence. Jocasta was the rebel in the family, who refused to be demure in company and said whatever outrageous thing which jumped into her head.

Bunny's total lack of vanity meant the overt attention he received from most women only embarrassed him. He would never give Flora a reason to be jealous.

'A teacher at school,' Jocasta went on, unabashed. 'Told me Jocasta married Oedipus, which I thought was decidedly odd at the time.' She slapped his forearm gently. 'That's the entire sum of my classics knowledge, I'm afraid.'

'Humph, a pity.' Lord Vaughn sniffed. 'Had I known, I wouldn't have wasted all that money on the Ladies' College fees.'

With the sofa now fully occupied, Eddy had retreated to one of the hard chairs against one wall. 'Don't worry, Jo,' he said. 'Married ladies aren't expected to know about Greek mythology.'

Jocasta narrowed her eyes at him over the rim of her sherry glass. 'Don't tease, little brother. As the troublesome one in the family, I take the pressure off you no end.' She ran a manicured finger round the top of her glass before bringing it to her mouth.

Lady Vaughn looked as if she was about to say something, but broke off at the sharp click of the door opening again.

'Not dinner already, Scrivens?' She frowned at the butler who stood expectantly on the threshold. 'It's not yet ten minutes past the hour.'

'No, my lady. Mrs Caroline Mountjoy has arrived – to dine.' He dragged the last two words out meaningfully.

'To dine? Oh really!' She placed her glass on the table with a loud click and rose. 'I sent a note round to Beaumont Place this morning that said quite specifically the dinner was off. She *must* have received it.'

Jocasta released a low chuckle, and leaned closer to Flora. 'Wait until Uncle William finds out she came anyway, despite Mama cancelling, which I know for certain she did.'

Flora lowered her glass. 'Lady Vaughn's brother is here?'

'Indeed he is.' A feline smile crept across Jocasta's face, while an enquiring one appeared on Bunny's.

Flora summoned an image of a handsome, always smiling man, attached to memories of long, hot sunny afternoons; picnics on the grass, impromptu cricket matches and games of hide-and-seek.

'Tell her the entire household has come down with the chicken pox or something, Scrivens,' Lord Vaughn impatiently waved him away, though the butler did not move.

'I cannot do that, George.' His wife looked stricken. 'She's already here, and—'

'Good evening everyone.' A flame-haired woman in an oyster silk gown swept past the immobile Scrivens and halted in the centre of the room. 'Oh!' She performed an exaggerated double take. 'I thought it was going to be a party.' Her parted lips and the way she held one hand splayed against her revealing décolleté struck Flora as contrived.

'There's been a change of plan, Caroline.' Lady Vaughn directed the newcomer to an empty sofa, rolling her eyes at her husband behind the newcomer's back. 'Scrivens,' she addressed the butler who still hovered by the door. 'Would you arrange to have a place laid at the dinner table for our new guest?'

'As you wish, my lady.' The butler raised a sardonic eyebrow as he withdrew.

'Do introduce me, Venetia, darling.' The newcomer swept the company with an assessing gaze. 'I don't think I know everyone.'

'Mrs Mountjoy, this is Flora Maguire, as was. She's Flora Harrington now.' Lady Venetia waved a gracious hand. 'And her husband, Ptolemy Harrington.'

'Of the Surrey Harringtons?' Her sharp eyes raked Flora's black gown with distaste before turning a speculative look on Bunny that instantly sparkled with interest.

'At one time, I believe, but we're somewhat depleted now.' Bunny took her outstretched hand but released it abruptly.

Flora allowed herself a smile at his show of solidarity, delighted he had not kissed it.

'Ah, yes of course, you're the governess,' she drawled, taking a seat with a cat-like smile which did nothing to minimize the implied insult. 'I gather you're here for the butler's funeral?' Her tone held a hint of contempt reminiscent of Flora's mother-in-law.

'My *father's* funeral.' Flora met the woman's steady stare. If Beatrice Harrington didn't possess the ability to unnerve her, the hard-eyed stranger with her cat-like smile stood no chance at all.

'I heard Maguire fell from a horse.' Mrs Mountjoy sniffed as if the incident was of no interest, dismissing Flora with a deliberately turned shoulder, but offered no apology. 'Such dreadful things happen to people when out riding. Not that I ride myself, I was brought up in a city and prefer my carriage. Much safer.'

'Didn't you receive my note, Caroline?' Lady Vaughn's voice held something close to suspicion. 'It specifically said the dinner was cancelled.'

'What note would that be, dear?' The lady's blue eyes rounded in innocence, her attention shifting to Lord Vaughn as she removed the full glass from his hand. 'Oh, thank you, George, that's just what I need.'

Lord Vaughn blinked, his lips parted to issue a protest, but instead, he frowned as his requisitioned glass was borne away. Giving a resigned shrug, poured himself another.

'Where's your charming brother this evening, Venetia?' Mrs Mountjoy gave the room a sweeping glance, then turned a frown on her hostess. 'Is he not joining us?'

'Uncle William will be down in a moment, Mrs Mountjoy,' Jocasta's lips twitched mischievously.

In answer to Bunny's inquisitive look, Jocasta whispered, 'He's Mama's younger brother who has come to stay for the summer. He always turns up after months away on some ranch in South Africa or a sheep farm in Australia. When we were children he stayed long enough to spoil us outrageously, get us into all sorts of scrapes, then disappear again until the next time. Needless to say we adored him.'

'Ah, and does he happen to be a wealthy bachelor by any chance?' Bunny directed a knowing look at their latest guest, who now gossiped animatedly with Lady Vaughn.

'Funny you should say that,' Jocasta replied, just as the door opened again and a tall muscular man entered, his intelligent green eyes sparkling with some private good humour above symmetrical features that evidenced his close kinship to Lady Vaughn.

His thick, conker-coloured hair bore the beginnings of silver wings at his temples, the only characteristic which attested to the fact he was in in his early forties. A pair of earnest brows were offset by a boyish grin, the beginnings of tiny lines beside his eyes and a deeply tanned skin which told of a life spent in warmer climes.

Murmuring apologies for being late, he went straight to where Flora sat, lifted her hand from her lap and pressed it to his clean-shaven lips. 'Dearest, Flora. Allow me to offer my condolences for Riordan's passing. If there is anything I can do, anything at all—' he trailed off, as if struck by the inadequacy of this remark.

'I appreciate the sentiment, Mr Osborne. Thank you.' Flora's face warmed, keenly aware that Bunny had broken off his conversation with Jocasta to stare at them.

'Mr Harrington, I don't believe you know my brother, William Osborne,' Lady Vaughn said, coming to Flora's rescue.

Bunny rose and shook William's hand, though the way they eyed each other reminded Flora of two stags prepared to fight for possession of the herd.

'My brother is what they call a free spirit,' Lady Vaughn added. 'He tends to drift in and out of our lives leaving chaos in his wake.' Her musical laugh implied this fact had caused her some anguish in the past.

'I love Uncle William,' Jocasta interjected. 'He made being a child exciting, and fun.'

'Thank you, dearest Jo.' William saluted Jocasta with his sherry glass. 'Flora here was always the fourth hoyden. She was never one to turn down a dare, were you?'

'You, a hoyden, Flora?' Bunny's chin jerked backwards. 'That does surprise me.'

'No more than the others.' Flora stared straight ahead, pretending not to see the bemused look on her husband's face.

'She certainly was.' Jocasta rapidly swallowed a mouthful of sherry. 'Do you remember when she took that row boat out onto the river and dropped the oar in the water? You had to wade out and save her?'

Flora dipped her head to her glass, recalling the day with embarrassing clarity.

'Ruined my favourite blazer, if I remember.' William took a mouthful from his glass and winked at Flora.

'Do sit here, right beside me, William.' Mrs Mountjoy pouted, her hands spread on the sofa next to her in open invitation.

'A kind offer, dear lady.' William eyed her with a wary smile that did not reach his eyes. 'I need a firmer chair, I'm afraid. Back problems, you know from my days spent on horseback rounding up cattle in the Veldt.'

Her expression hardened into an angry grimace, which disappeared so quickly when Lord Vaughn offer her more sherry, Flora thought she had imagined it.

William took an upright chair beside the sofa where Flora sat with Bunny and Jocasta. 'Marriage suits you, Flora.' William's eyes roamed her face.

'Thank you, sir, I'm very happy. Well, that is I was, until—' She broke off, uncomfortable beneath his penetrating look, made worse by the way Bunny shot an occasional hard one of his own towards him.

'I understand,' he murmured, then louder. 'And don't call me "sir". You're not a governess any longer, you're a guest. It's William, please. When you were a child you used to call me Uncle William.'

'That's right, I did.' Her life at the Abbey was

different when she was a child; she didn't fully understand the servant hierarchy, let alone adhere to its strictures. It was only as she got older and her role changed once she became Eddy's governess did their lives split into different directions. Less than two years before, Flora had dipped curtseys at the door and hovered like a ghost on the fringes of the Vaughn's lives. To be taking pre-dinner sherry with the family as a guest made her feel slightly out of place, though proud too that she was welcome.

At the sound of the dinner gong, fans and shawls were hurriedly gathered as the company left their seats in preparation to relocate to the dining room along the hall.

Jocasta nudged William, nodding over his shoulder to where Mrs Mountjoy sat like a sphinx on her sofa. 'I think our unexpected guest would like you to escort her into dinner.'

'Stop goading me, minx.' William downed half his sherry in one gulp, took Flora's hand and tugged her gently to her feet. 'You don't mind, do you, old man?' he addressed Bunny. 'After all, you have her company all the time.'

'Of course not.' Bunny's tight smile told a different story, but he graciously gave way and offered his arm to Jocasta.

Lord Vaughn offered Mrs Mountjoy his cocked elbow. 'Allow me to claim the right as host and escort you into dinner myself.'

The lady dimpled her acceptance, then shot a

sharp glance at William over her shoulder as they took the head of the line.

'I take it you're not entranced by her charms, sir – ah, William?' Flora nodded to Mrs Mountjoy's swaying rear end as she they took their place in line behind Bunny and Jocasta.

'Suffice it to say,' William dropped his voice, 'the woman's too predatory for my taste.'

'You make her sound like a fox eyeing the chickens,' Jocasta turned her head and grinned. 'Whereas I see her more as a snake.'

'Hush, Jo, she'll hear you.' Flora bit her lip to prevent a laugh.

The small procession filed down the hallway beneath portraits of past Vaughns, accompanied by the gentle hiss of gaslight from the wall sconces.

'Papa,' Eddy's voice drifted backwards along the hall. 'Mr Harrington says anyone can ride a motorcycle. May I have one?'

'Whatever for?' Lord Vaughn snorted. 'There's a stable full of horses here on which you could happily break your neck.' He nodded at Scrivens who held open the dining room door, and disappeared inside.

Flora came to an abrupt halt as a roaring sounded in her ears, her knees buckled and she staggered. Had William not had a tight grip on her arm, she might have crumpled to the floor.

'Oh, Papa!' Jocasta gasped, though he had moved too far ahead to hear her. 'He didn't mean anything by it, Flora, truly. He simply didn't think.'

'I know.' Flora smiled at her. 'I'm fine, truly.' She took a deep breath and fought for control, aware of the combined concerned looks Bunny and William directed at her. 'Let's go in, shall we? I'm quite famished.'

What with the surly butler, Mrs Mountjoy and Bunny's jealousy, dinner promised to be a trial.

CHAPTER 4

Flora clicked the bedroom door shut behind her and leaned against it with a sigh. 'I'm exhausted.'

'No wonder. It's been an emotional day for you.' Bunny removed his tie with a whoosh of silk. 'The Vaughns have certainly gone out of their way to make us welcome. You must have been an exemplary governess.' Bunny perched on the edge of one of the wing chairs, bent and untied his shoelaces.

'I liked it, and Eddy was a lovely pupil.' Flora leaned her hip against the arm of his chair. 'The family were always kind, although the two older girls, Lady Amelia and Lady Emerald, didn't have much time for me, but Lady Jocasta was my real friend, until I became Eddy's governess. Then our lives took different directions and we grew apart.'

'No evidence of that this evening, you were chatting away like sisters.'

'When she wasn't flirting with you, that is.' Flora gently cuffed him on the head.

'Hah! What about Uncle William?' His sing-song tone indicated a certain resentment. 'He seemed keen to sit beside you before and during dinner. Should I be jealous?' He kicked off his shoes and tucked them beneath his chair.

'Don't be ridiculous, William Osborne is in his forties!' Flora gave a dismissive snort. 'He's a nice man though and he treated me like the fourth niece, although Jo was always his favourite. He gave me a copy of Christina Rossetti's, *Goblin Market* one Christmas.'

'I don't think I know it, but then I admit I'm not au fait with female poets'

'It's a poem about sisters because he knew I always wanted one of my own. Lady Vaughn was very disapproving for some reason, said it was unsuitable because of its hidden symbolism, whatever that means.' Flora shrugged. 'I treasured it because it wasn't a box of marzipans or set of handkerchiefs.'

'He apparently has hidden depths your Mr Osborne. I wonder why a man with so many attractions, not to mention affluence, has never married?' Bunny shrugged out of his waistcoat, and draped it across a chair.

'Why do you wish to know? Flora threw him a teasing glance over one shoulder. 'Is it because as an old married man you want everyone to follow the same joyous path? Or do you wish them to share your misery?' She retrieved the waistcoat and hooked it onto a hanger then placed it in the wardrobe.

'The former of course, it has worked out marvelously for me, though I'm still tempted to call him out over the attention he paid you this evening.'

'I believe that had more to do with his efforts to avoid Caroline Mountjoy.' She crossed the room to where he stood by the fireplace. 'Bunny? Was it my imagination, or did everyone seem on edge this evening?'

'A little, although again, I suspect the presence of that Mountjoy woman was responsible for that. Besides, they would hardly discuss details of your father's fatal accident over the lobster.'

'I didn't expect them to. No, it was more than that. I was conscious of everyone staring at me when they thought I wasn't looking.'

'I noticed that myself, but which struck me as more a protective concern. It's only been a day since the accident, so they would want to make sure you are bearing up. Perhaps you're ultra-sensitive to certain nuances at the moment, my love. It's understandable.'

'Maybe.' She fiddled with the trim on her sleeve. 'Lady Vaughn reminded me how little I had seen of Father this past year. I was so bound up with our new life together in Richmond, I didn't consider that he might be missing me.'

'He knew you would be back when you were ready.'

'That's what Lady Vaughn said, and that's the trouble. When I went to America for those months, he was always in my heart. A firm, immoveable presence, whether we were together or not. Now he's gone.' She stopped Bunny's protest with an upheld hand. 'No, I'm being neither morbid nor fanciful. I don't feel him any more – here.' She thumped her bodice with a fist, the mild pain vying with the inner ache that wouldn't go away. 'He'll always be in my head, but he's not in my heart anymore. He's left me.'

Bunny crossed the room in brisk strides and gathered her into his arms, her cheek pressed against his chest where his shirt stood open, the fine hairs soft against her skin. He didn't speak, both aware that words were not only superfluous but inadequate.

'Do you wish I hadn't taken you away from here?' Bunny asked after a long, thoughtful moment.

'No, of course not. My home is in Richmond now, with you.' *And your mother.*

'Have you been into your father's room yet?'

Flora shook her head, dislodging him. 'I can't face it. I know I'll have to go through his things eventually, but I need more time.'

'Of course. I understand.' He planted a kiss on her forehead, then eased back gently and finished unbuttoning his shirt. 'I hope that geyser in the bathroom is as efficient as it looks. I'd like a quick bath before bed.' He flung a flannel robe round his shoulders and made for the door.

'The water heater might splutter a bit when you first switch it on. Just bang it with your fist just above the spout,' Flora called after him.

Left alone, Flora undressed quickly, availing herself of the hot water a thoughtful maid had left in a pitcher on the dresser. She slipped beneath the covers and lay listening to the nocturnal noises

66

of the house, while she recalled that William Osborne was the one person who had called her father by his Christian name.

While she tried to work out if that was significant or not, the soft bed worked its magic on her weary muscles and she was asleep before Bunny returned from his bath.

Flora woke with a start and gasped for air. Bunny leaned over her, whispering gently. 'It's all right, sweetheart, there's nothing there.'

She forced herself to consciousness through a dense fog of sleep and menacing shadows, to find Bunny sat with his arms wrapped round her shoulders. 'Were you dreaming about your mother again?'

Flora nodded, her eyes narrowed against the bright sunlight that flooded through the window, surprised to see it was morning already. She brought a hand to her forehead that came away moist, waiting for her breathing to slow before attempting to talk again. 'It was so vivid this time. Just like when I used to live here.' She counted back in her head and realized it was more than a year since it had last happened.

'Was it the same as before?' Bunny released her and slid from beneath the bedclothes. He grabbed his dressing gown from the bottom of the bed and hauled it on. 'Or can't you remember?'

'I always remember.' She wrapped her arms round her tented legs, her chin propped on her knees.

'Go through it again. Perhaps you'll recall something different this time.'

'It's always the same dream. I'm in a room with whitewashed walls. The door is wide open and a shaft of sunlight has drawn a fan shape on the grey flagstone floor. I'm small. I know, because the furniture and doors are high above my head. The floor is shiny, as if it's just been washed and there's a rag rug of many different colours. A fireplace with a black-leaded grate and a kettle on a stand above it stands at the far end.'

'Keep going, I'm getting a good picture of the scene. What else?' Bunny knotted the silken cord and sat beside her again on top of the covers.

'A woman is there, and she's humming as she moves about the room. I cannot see her face, only her long skirt with her shoes peeking out below it, though I know she's my mother. I'm happy as I tug at the loops on the rug.' A shadow passed across the images and Flora shivered. 'Then someone else is there. A man. Again, I cannot see his face, but he lifts me into his arms and his voice rumbles against my head.'

'Your father?' Bunny scratched his head, yawning.

'I don't think so. I must know him though, because I curl my arms round his neck and he laughs.'

'Then what happens, Flora?' Bunny asked gently.

'Mother shouts something, screams in fact, and

68

I'm back on the rug again and frightened because of the noise. I start to cry.'

'Can you make out what they are saying?' Bunny massaged her shoulder gently.

'No, it's just loud voices, which upset me. They're arguing.' She squeezed her eyes shut, forcing herself to think. 'I crawl on my hands and knees to where Mother lies on the floor. There's blood seeping into the rug, but I don't know where it comes from. All I know is my mother is hurt.'

'Where's the man?'

'He's not there anymore. I'm scared and alone and Mother isn't moving.' She shrugged. 'Then I wake up. 'I've always been sure it's a scene from my childhood. I simply don't know when it happened or what it means.'

'Then where did it happen?' He gave the room a quick glance. 'Not here, if you saw a door to the outside. The basement kitchens in this house perhaps?'

'No, as I said it was a small room.' Flora propped her chin on her knees again. 'Much smaller than the main kitchen. I don't recognize it.'

'And you're certain the man wasn't your father?'

She shook her head. 'No, and I cannot imagine Father having hurt anyone in his life, let alone my mother. Anyway, I would have known if it was him, sensed him somehow and felt safe. I didn't feel that way in the dream, but then I wasn't scared either until I saw the blood.'

'You were too young to remember your parents together. Perhaps their relationship was, well, volatile?'

'That's possible, I suppose, though not something I want to imagine.' She fiddled with the broderie anglaise trim on her nightdress, unwilling to admit that the same thing had occurred to her. *Did her parents fight? Was that what had happened that day?*

'I'm sorry,' Bunny broke into her thoughts. 'I was playing Devil's advocate. I wouldn't dream of casting your father in a poor light.'

'I'm sorry too.' Her anger dissolved and she leaned against him. 'Suppose Father's refusal to talk about my mother was because something dreadful happened to her? Something he wanted to protect me from?'

'It's possible.' He tucked a stray lock of her hair behind her ear. 'However you pursue this or not, whatever you find will make no difference to you and me.'

She caught his hand in mid-air and brought it to her lips. 'Thank you, that means a lot.' A shiver went through her. Bunny might say he could face anything, but words were easy. What if the truth was truly awful and pulled them apart?

She threw back the cover and scrambled off the bed. 'There's no point my sitting here all morning trying to make sense of it. Not without more information.' Pushing the shadows to the back of her mind to deal with another time, she made for the door. 'I'm going to have a bath.'

'Hey, I was up first!' Bunny made a grab for her. Flora giggled and swiftly sidestepped him into the hall, turned and gave a wave before she closed the door on his protests.

CHAPTER 5

Despite Flora having won the race for the bathroom, she took longer to dress than Bunny. 'Don't wait for me,' Flora said when he announced he was hungry – again. 'I'll see you in the dining room in a few moments.'

'Are you sure?' he asked but was halfway to the door before she answered.

'Of course, and anyway, you make me nervous pacing like that.'

Needing no further encouragement, Bunny padded downstairs, leaving Flora to finish dressing.

The second black gown she had packed was a less elaborate style than the multi-layered creation of the previous day. Although the colour was no more flattering, the smooth lines skimmed her slender figure and made her look less sallow and middle-aged.

Her heart was still heavy, the slightest reminder of Riordan's presence in their rooms bringing tears close, but the mirror at least showed her eyes were clearer and no longer red-rimmed. She had also regained her colour and a little of her former vitality.

Downstairs, she hesitated outside the dining room door and ran her hands down the smooth material of the skirt before she reached for the doorknob. A passing maid Flora did not recognize bobbed a curtsey, so Flora was smiling when she pushed open the door, surprised to see the only occupants apart from Bunny were Lady Vaughn and Jocasta.

'Good morning, Flora,' Lady Vaughn said. 'Did you sleep well?'

'I did, thank you.' Flora removed all doubt from her voice, unwilling to explain her recurring dream or the hollow feeling when she thought of her father's room, empty for the first time she could remember.

Jocasta greeted her by way of a sideways grin and a nod at Bunny, whose head was bent to a plate of sausages and fried eggs, already half demolished. 'I suspect you don't feed him, Flora. The poor man is obviously famished.'

'Indeed I do,' Flora said on her way to the side-board. 'Though he does like a hearty breakfast.'

'You don't have to talk about me as if I wasn't here,' Bunny said between mouthfuls. 'I get enough of that at home with Flora and my mother.'

He had meant it light-heartedly, though Flora winced at recollections of her mother-in-law's continued disapproval despite Bunny's oft repeated assurances that Beatrice Harrington saw no woman outside the royal family as being good enough for her only son.

As she helped herself to scrambled eggs and

tomatoes from the bain-maries set out on the sideboard, Flora experienced a pang of guilt at having left Beatrice the previous morning in a combination of fury and hysterics at being abandoned, although apart from the entire hotel staff being at her beck and call, a half dozen of Beatrice's friends had invaded the hotel lounge on a mission to comfort her.

Bunny had insisted Flora's need was greater than his mother's and had not given in when Beatrice had feigned an attack of the vapours.

'What are you grinning at?' Bunny's mischievous smile warmed her as he poked the perfect yolk of a fried egg into a yellow puddle on his plate.

'Your mother actually.' She ran her hand across his shoulders as she passed his chair. 'I was thinking, maybe you could write her a short note to say we have arrived safely and hope she is well?'

His eyes widened in surprise, though if he experienced the urge to delve deeper he resisted. 'That's a kind thought. I'll do exactly that.' He rose and fetched more sausages from the sideboard. 'They're good!' he responded to Flora's sideways look.

'I like a man with a good appetite.' Lady Vaughn reached for the silver toast rack, her smile reserved for Bunny alone.

'Where is everyone this morning? Were we late risers?' Flora took in the untouched place settings at the other end of the table.

'Not at all.' Lady Vaughn poured coffee for herself, then held up the pot in enquiry. 'George is out on estate business and has taken Eddy with him. The fresh air will do the boy good as he's looking decidedly peaky lately.'

Flora held out her cup to be filled, choosing not to mention that she agreed, in case it sounded like a criticism. She may not be Eddy's governess anymore, but ingrained habits such as being alert to signs of fever or his mood were hard to undo.

'Uncle William is in Gloucester on personal business.' Jocasta nibbled delicately at her toast. 'He'll most likely be back for luncheon, I expect. That leaves just us four this morning.'

'I expect you're eager to begin arrangements for the funeral, Flora dear.' Lady Vaughn applied an almost invisible scrape of butter to her toast. 'If there's anything I can do to help, you mustn't hesitate to ask. I recommend Bartlett's in the Promenade for the floral tributes. They enjoy an excellent reputation.'

'Thank you, that's most helpful.' Flora relaxed in the atmosphere of the dining room enhanced by the gentle chink of china and a pervading smell of hot bacon grease and aromatic coffee.

Marrying Bunny had definitely altered her position in the Vaughn's social list recently, and despite the solemnity of this visit, she found she enjoyed the difference.

'I've been thinking about where my father should be buried,' Flora began. 'I would have liked to bury him with my mother, but I don't know where that is.'

'I cannot help you there, I'm afraid, my dear. George and I were abroad when – when Lily died.' Lady Vaughn flicked a sideways glance at her, and away again, too quickly for Flora to read the emotion behind it. 'We didn't return until the end of that summer, and by then it was all over.'

'What was all over?' Flora's gaze met Bunny's and held.

'Um – why the funeral of course.' Lady Vaughn crumbled a bread roll on her plate, her eyes cast down.

Jocasta opened her mouth as if about to say something, then quickly shut it again.

Flora took a deep breath, knowing if she didn't broach the subject just then she would never do so. 'I apologize if I'm venturing into awkward territory, Lady Vaughn, however I know very little about my mother. Father would never talk about her, so I hoped you might fill in some of the gaps.'

'Pass the sugar, would you, Jocasta?' Bunny asked, his voice over-bright.

'Pardon?' Jocasta jumped, startled, made a grab for the glass pot, and fumbled it. Sparkling cubes of sugar tumbled onto the tablecloth. 'Oh, sorry. I'm so clumsy.'

'This might not be the best time to discuss this particular subject, Flora,' Lady Vaughn whispered, nodding toward her daughter and Bunny who were busy gathering up the sugar.

Flora nodded, but disappointment must have shown in her face, for when Bunny looked up, he

76

crumpled his napkin and discarded it on the table beside the uneaten sausages. 'Perhaps this might be an opportune time for you to make good on your promise to show me the grounds, Jo?'

'I promised?' Jocasta frowned. 'That doesn't sound like me. I may have suggested a ride, but—'

'Even better.' He removed the slice of toast spread with cherry conserve from Jocasta's fingers, dropping it onto her plate, where it landed with a faint plop.

'I hadn't finished that!' Jocasta protested.

Ignoring her indignant scowl, Bunny tucked a hand beneath her elbow and guided her from the room. As he pulled the door shut, he winked at Flora over his shoulder.

'Those two seem to be getting along remarkably well,' Lady Vaughn said when they were alone.

'Yes, they do, don't they? Lady Vaughn, I—'

'Oh, my dear,' she interrupted. 'I hope we are friends now and you feel able to call me Lady Venetia.' Colour flamed in her cheeks beneath her face powder. 'Lady Vaughn is so formal, don't you think?'

Flora could not discern much difference, but thanked her with a gracious smile.

'As for your mother. I was very fond of Lily. She was a wonderful lady's maid. No one dresses my hair the way she did, even now.'

Flora sipped her coffee, which proved difficult through gritted teeth. Her mother's skills at coiffure were hardly paramount just then.

'Lily was always happy here,' Lady Venetia went on. 'At least until that unfortunate business.'

'What unfortunate business?' Flora's rapidly lowered cup clicked sharply against the saucer.

Lady Venetia closed her eyes and sighed. 'Oh dear, I didn't imagine you were unaware.'

'Unaware of what?' Flora said carefully, while at the same time a memory returned; of herself beside the table that stood in the hall, but at a time when it only reached to her shoulder. The stomach clenching fear of being discovered listening to voices through a gap in the door of the servant's hall. Their faces had long ago faded, though the tone in which 'Poor Lily' was spoken of remained.

Flora knew no one would have satisfied a child's curiosity had she asked the inevitable question, so she had kept the puzzling discovery to herself. Maybe now she would finally learn what they had meant, aware her heart thumped uncomfortably against her corset.

'I'm not unfamiliar with the proclivities of men and women,' Lady Venetia began slowly. 'Nor do I expect sainthood among my servants, though I have to admit shock when Lily fell into that trap which awaits pretty young girls with romantic hearts.' Her slim hand slid across the tablecloth and grasped Flora's. 'You see, Lily became pregnant when she was just seventeen.'

'I knew she married quite young?' Flora said through a suddenly dry mouth. Is that what all

78

the secrecy was about? A lapse in moral behaviour? Although shocking, it didn't seem dramatic enough somehow to explain all the secrecy since. 'This child, was it—?'

'You of course, my dear.' Her grey eyes filled with sympathy. 'Lily came to me in floods of tears when she discovered her condition. I was torn as to what I should do about it.'

The words, *'throw her on the streets'* and *'send her to the workhouse'* sprang into Flora's head, though as far as she knew, neither fate had befallen her mother.

'Then a few days later,' Lady Venetia continued, 'she came to me again and explained that she had decided to marry Riordan. That everything was settled so there was no need for her to leave after all. She could no longer be my maid of course, but she remained at the Abbey after her marriage.'

Flora fidgeted, confused as to why Lady Vaughn referred to it as 'an unfortunate business' if her parents had married before she was born. Or was she trivializing the situation and a hasty marriage was not easily forgotten? The world was about to enter a new age with a new king, but a quarter of a century ago, the Vaughns had lived in a time when Queen Victoria set a much stricter standard.

'Then it all worked out well for them?'

'It did,' Lady Vaughn said. 'It turned out well for them in the end.'

'Until my mother died,' Flora said, reminding her the story didn't end there. 'I have no idea if she was ill or met with an accident. No one talked about her when I was a child. It was almost as if she never existed.' She coughed, self-conscious. 'I'm sorry. I didn't mean to be sharp'

'I understand perfectly, my dear.' Her hand fluttered to her throat. 'However, as I said, George and I were in the South of France at the time, so we knew nothing about the circumstances. Everything was over by the time we returned.'

Flora found this hard to believe, but then why would Lady Venetia deliberately lie? 'Would anyone else in the house have been here at that time? Perhaps they might be able to tell me more about her?'

'Well, there's our housekeeper, Hetty Farmer, who's been with us for years, and Nanny.' Lady Vaughn scrutinized the ceiling, then waved her hand. 'Oh dear no, Nanny died last year.'

'I'm sorry to hear that. She was such a favourite with everyone,' Flora said. 'With your permission, I would like to talk to Hetty. She might remember my mother.' Hetty might also know what the 'Poor Lily' comments meant too, which didn't seem to tally with the facts she had a precipitous wedding.

'Of course, my dear, if you think it would help.' Lady Venetia relaxed back in her chair, her newly full cup held lightly in fingers that didn't shake.

'Thank you, Lady Vaug—, I mean, Lady Venetia.' Flora gained the impression that having shifted her attention to someone else, Lady Vaughn had pushed the shadow of Lily Maguire back into the past, where she resided more comfortably. But Flora hadn't given up hope of finding out what had happened to her mother, and her father, and she knew if rumour and gossip existed about either of her parents, she would more than likely find it below stairs.

CHAPTER 6

Flora pushed through the green baize door into the kitchens, a route she had taken so many times in her former life as governess. She only had the door open a few inches before the butler appeared from nowhere and blocked her path.

'May I help you, Mrs Harrington?' His tone was almost an accusation.

'I don't think so, er— Scrivens, is it? I was hoping to talk to Hetty. Is that not convenient?' She was no longer a servant, and what better time to challenge the man who had taken her father's place?

'Not at all, Mrs Harrington.' Scrivens' tone implied the opposite. 'However, mornings, as I'm sure you are aware, are extremely busy. Mrs Farmer won't have time for socializing.'

'I see.' Flora inhaled slowly, summoning patience. 'Then when would you suggest?'

'Perhaps after luncheon has been cleared away, Mrs Farmer takes her afternoon tea then.' He pretended to consider for a moment. 'Three o'clock might be more suitable.'

'Thank you.' Flora smiled sweetly and moved

past him before she succumbed to an urge to slap him. *Pompous man.* And when did anyone call Hetty, Mrs Farmer? Heart-searing emotion rose yet again at the thought of her father, who would never have been so abrasive to a guest in the house.

Flora was so intent on leaving his presence without a backward look, she found herself on the front drive with no recollection of what to do next and with a whole morning stretching in front of her with no purpose.

The stillness of the summer morning pulled her back through time, when summer was a time of picnics in the field stubble on sunny afternoons, and fishing for sticklebacks in the stream used primarily as an excuse to cool hot feet in the shallow, running water.

With no duties to claim her time, she wandered the pathways, picking out the areas of shadow to avoid the hot sun burning her skin. She strolled beneath a hornbeam arch that ran down one side of the long stone building that was once a Benedictine monastery, long enough ago for no one to understand quite what that meant. The abbey had kept its name, although had been subjected to Henry VIII's systematic dissolution in the mid-sixteenth century. The chapter house and refectory hall formed the main part of the house, set one in front of the other at different levels. The two high, uniformly square buildings with gabled roofs, thick stone walls and cavernous ceilings, one a floor higher. The original buildings were most likely purchased from the church by some enterprising soul, possibly as the result of a financial incentive given to Thomas Cromwell.

Lord Vaughn had informed Flora once that his family had not inherited the Abbey, but had purchased its jumble of run-down buildings some-time during the early Eighteenth Century.

His great grandfather had split the rectangular refectory into three floors, the lower rooms panelled, and a matching wide oak staircase that dominated the entrance hall installed.

The cloisters had all been demolished long ago – the only evidence it ever existed, a line of stone foundations along the edge of the kitchen garden, set too wide apart for the child Flora to use as stepping stones. The sight of the even row or round stones tempted her to use them in this way again, but conscious that falling into a ditch wearing deep mourning would be more shaming than then it had as a child, so she resisted the impulse.

The dormitory had been converted to the kitchens, dairy and storerooms, all required to furnish a wealthy gentleman's home, and bounded with early Victorian red-brick walls.

Flora entered the kitchen garden through a wooden gate, the latch slightly crooked just as she had always remembered it. She paused for a while on a wooden bench set against the far wall with a view of the vegetable plots; uniform square patches bordered by three rows of bricks with cobbled pathways in between.

She had always loved this space, where the maids chatted together and flirted with the gardener's boys, the entry used by the tradesmen and callers, who passed through at all times of the day. A noisy, busy place in sharp contrast to the serene grounds, but remote and empty rose gardens that were Lady Venetia's pride.

'Don't change much, does it?' a voice she knew, but had not heard for a while spoke from behind her.

'Not at all, Mr Bracenose,' Flora turned to where the estate manager regarded her from the same gate she had used a few moments before. 'And I'm very glad it hasn't.'

Bracenose was one of those men she had always considered old, even as a child. But close up she realized he must be in his early fifties. His mop of wayward brown hair almost matched his brown suit, teamed with a mustard waistcoat that was his version of livery.

Flora could never recall him wearing anything else except at the estate Christmas party. She always wondered if he had a new one delivered every couple of years, or it was indeed the same one. Not that she had ever had the courage to ask.

When he removed his felt hat, she noticed his hairline receded more than it had a year ago, and his jowls were softer too.

'How are you, Miss Flora?' He seemed to have trouble meeting her eyes. 'Please accept my condolences for your father. He was a good man.'

'He was, and thank you.' Her voice remained calm though once again mention of Riordan Maguire caused a stinging sensation behind her eyes. She swallowed and nodded to the triangular canes of bamboo that marched alongside one wall, the raspberry canes and potatoes in neat rows. 'The garden looks nice.'

'Something else which doesn't change.' He nodded gently.

'Mr Bracenose?' she asked on impulse. 'Do you know where my father was going that day?'

'What day would that be?' then in answer to his own question, added, 'the day he died?'

'He didn't have many friends, his life was here. I wondered where he could have been going on horseback. That wasn't like him.'

He shifted his feet and stared off. 'I've no idea. Far as I know it wasn't until he was missed that anyone knew he had gone.' He signed then gestured towards the kitchen door. 'Best be off. I-I have to make inroads into the accounts. Good weather has been keeping me away from my office.'

'Of course. I didn't mean to keep you.'

He inclined his head, replaced his hat and loped off along the herringbone path, leaving Flora to return through the gate and back onto the front drive, her circular route complete. The honey-coloured Cotswold stone walls of the front façade had softened over the years with creeping vines on one end of the gable that curled over the edges of the roof and the upper windows; a purple wisteria cradled the stone front porch, its base as thick as the trunk of a tree, it climbed the corner of the front wall and drooped over the stone porch, where lately carriages and the odd motor car pulled up to disgorge visitors.

The stepped façade was punched through with a row of symmetrical casement windows on two main levels, with smaller dormers in the roof line.

Flora shielded her eyes with a hand and counted the row of windows until she located her former bedroom, the one she had shared the previous night with Bunny.

As if thoughts of him summoned his presence, the coach house gates opened and Bunny appeared with Jocasta. He looked every inch the country gentleman in buff trousers, a well-fitted tweed hacking jacket and high leather boots.

A rush of pride filled Flora's chest at how handsome he was, his head bent to listen to something Jocasta said. Early morning rides that took an hour without ever leaving the estate had been the fabric of Bunny's life up until his own father's death when Bunny was a schoolboy.

Ambrose Harrington had left his wife and son in comparatively straitened circumstances, though far from impoverished. Presented with a need to earn his living, Bunny had thrown himself into the commercial world with enthusiasm. Did he miss that privileged environment, where the most pressing problem of the day was how to spend the time?

'Hello, Flora?' Jocasta spotted her and strode towards her, her riding crop held loosely in both hands and her face was flushed and healthy looking after her ride. 'What are you doing out here, looking so lost?'

'Is everything all right, Flora?' Bunny peered at her, concerned. 'You seem on edge.'

'Scrivens chased me out of the servant's quarters, even Bracenose seemed nervous to see me.' Flora released a nervous laugh.

'Scrivens chased you?' Bunny's eyebrows rose.

'Ah no, not literally. That's just me feeling victimized. He told me to come back this afternoon when it would be more convenient.'

'Cheek!' Jocasta pouted. 'A week ago he was simply the footman. That man takes his new position far too seriously. I'll have a word with him.'

'No, please, Jo, there's no need.' Flora pleaded. 'Anyway, he was right. Hetty wouldn't have had time for me straight after breakfast. I've been enjoying the sunshine, and wishing I hadn't left it so long to return. I forgot how much the Abbey meant to me until now.' She split a look between them. 'You weren't very long. I didn't expect you back so soon.'

'I've an appointment in Cheltenham this morning with my seamstress,' Jocasta explained. 'I also want to see Papa before I go.'

'Your mother said he and Eddy were in the lower field somewhere,' Flora said. 'Didn't you see them on your ride?'

'They came back to the house a little while ago,' Jocasta said. 'Apparently, Eddy became sullen and complained about being tired.'

'Shall I go up and see him?' Flora took a step in the direction of the house, but Bunny blocked her way.

'I know you only want to help,' he said gently. 'But you forget, Eddy isn't that little boy you once had to watch over.'

'Sorry. Force of habit. I have looked after him since he was ten, remember?'

'Bunny's quite right, Flora,' Jocasta said. 'Eddy is spoiled enough, and although you did a sterling job with him, I applaud Papa for sending him to boarding school. He's grown up a lot in the last year, although he can still be irritating. Like an ear of wheat trapped inside your dress.'

Flora didn't think he had changed much at all, apart from his physical height. She could still see the sensitive child who needed reassuring about monsters under the bed.

'I was about to take a walk over to the stables to have a talk with Tom Murray,' Flora said. 'He's still head groom here isn't he?'

'He is.' Jocasta nodded.

'Shall I come with you?' Bunny tucked his riding crop beneath one arm and removed his gloves.

'I don't want to intimidate him. If he does know anything, I want him to feel comfortable talking about it.' *Not like Bracenose did just now.* 'I'd like to ask about the horse Father rode that day as well. I have no idea whether or not that's important but it's somewhere to start.'

'Start?' Jocasta frowned. 'What is it you are trying to find out? It was an accident, wasn't it?'

'Flora simply needs to sort out the details in her head in order to come to terms with what happened.' Bunny wrapped a protective arm round Flora and hugged her to him, indicating she had been indiscreet. 'She's still shocked about the whole thing, aren't you, my love?'

'I'm sorry, I don't mean to imply criticism of anyone.' Flora resolved to be more discreet in future, or she would offend everyone who had thus far been so kind to her.

All she wanted to do was find out the truth about her father's death, though perhaps she was going about it the wrong way. But what other way was there but to ask questions? She couldn't put her worry into words, but something didn't sit right about this accident everyone had accepted so readily.

'What is it you aren't sure of, Flora?' Jocasta asked, evidently sensing her unease.

'Nothing specific,' Flora said before Bunny could answer for her. 'Just that Father was an insular man with few friends, and Cleeve Abbey was his life. He rarely left the estate, and had no private affairs that I knew of. What would send him off on horseback alone? I need to know where he went the day he—' she broke off, unable to summon the word that consigned him to oblivion.

90

'Nobody knows, or at least they haven't come forward to tell us.' Jocasta thought for a moment. 'Some of the inside staff did mention that he had seemed preoccupied lately.'

'Father was always preoccupied.' Flora sighed. 'His main fault was that he thought about things too much.' Something she had inherited perhaps? Should she just forget about it and let him go? After all there was nothing she could do which would bring him back?

'I wonder if it had something to do with that young girl who disappeared.' Jocasta tapped her crop against the palm of her hand.

'What young girl? Flora asked, suddenly alert.

'She worked in the kitchens, I think. Or was it the laundry?' Jocasta shrugged. 'Anyway, her name was um-Betty.' She waggled her fingers as an aid to her memory. 'No Betsy, Betsy Mason. She disappeared after the annual summer fête held at the Abbey.' She took in Flora's frown and laughed. 'Or perhaps I should have said left. I doubt there was anything mysterious about it. Most people thought she had run off with someone; a man most likely.'

Jocasta appeared to be taking the incident very lightly, the girl could be lying dead somewhere for all they knew.

'Have the police been informed of her disappearance?'

'I believe a constable called Jones questioned the staff after the fete, but I doubt he got very far.

There was a search as well, but what with all the fuss about Maguire-Oh,' she checked herself. 'Not that I mean it was unnecessary of course. But it was quite chaotic for a while. I'm afraid most people forgot about poor Betsy.'

Jocasta tossed her head, dislodging a strand of hair from the snood that held her bun in place.

A spark of interest ignited in Flora's head. Her father wouldn't have simply let a kitchen maid walk out of the Abbey without asking a few pertinent questions. Staff welfare was important to him. Why hadn't this girl Betsy been mentioned before?

Flora bit her tongue at the way Jo has so callously dismissed her father and asked instead, 'Did everyone in the district attend the fête?'

'Oh, you know how Papa loves to play Lord Bountiful. He throws the grounds open to the hoi polloi several times a year.'

'Sorry about all these questions, Jo.' Flora's voice became brittle. 'I need to clarify things for my own peace of mind.'

'Of course you do.' Jocasta patted Flora's hand. 'Maguire was an integral part of the Abbey and we'll all miss him.' She pouted in what she probably imagined was a sympathetic expression. 'And if it helps, then you must ask Tom anything you like, though I doubt he knows much more than the rest of us. He's doing well these days. Very different from that skinny boy with red hair who used to blush every time I spoke to him. He's quite an attractive man now.'

Flora's returning smile was perfunctory. Fond as she was of Jocasta, the fact that she referred to her father still as 'Maguire' even after he was gone illustrated the differences in their worlds. Or maybe Bunny was right and she was overly sensitive when that was what everyone at the Abbey had always called him.

The crunch of wheels on gravel brought their attention to where four beautifully matched horses and a black closed carriage rolled to a stop beside the front door. A uniformed footman jumped down before the wheels had stopped turning and flung open the door.

'Oh dear, that's Caroline Mountjoy's carriage.' Jocasta sighed. 'I expect she's hoping to run into William.'

'Shouldn't someone warn him?' Bunny's mouth twitched, evidently entertained by the idea of William being pursued by a wealthy widow.

'I don't think so,' Jocasta said through a mischievous smile. 'Uncle William ought to be used to predatory females by now. Let him take his chances.'

'Wicked girl.' Bunny nudged her in the casual, easy way of lifelong friends, which made Flora unsure whether to feel pleased or jealous.

The front door swung open and Scrivens appeared on the top step, his white gloved hands clasped in front of him.

The lady unhurriedly alighted her carriage and paused to give the façade of the ancient building a slow, appraising glance before she climbed the steps, brushing past Scrivens without an acknowledgement.

'I have an ambition to be just like Mrs Mountjoy.' Jocasta sighed when she had disappeared inside. 'She's buried two rich husbands, is still beautiful and now she does exactly as she pleases.'

'Is your Jeremy aware of this ambition of yours?' Flora asked.

'Don't be silly.' Jocasta pouted, her eyes glinting with mischief. 'I wouldn't wish any harm to come to my darling Jeremy. Though life can be a dangerous thing, you know.'

Flora stared at the ground, and Bunny gave a self-conscious cough.

'Would you both like to come with me into Cheltenham?' Jocasta split a look between them. 'We can take one of the new trams which run from Cleeve Hill right into the centre of town. But don't tell Mama, she doesn't approve of public transport. She says it's for the workers.'

Flora didn't comment, though she quite enjoyed travelling on trams. Beatrice also regarded them beneath her and insisted Flora take the carriage, even for the shortest journey. Flora had a plan to ask Bunny to teach her to drive his motor car, but had decided to wait until she was certain he wouldn't dismiss the idea out of hand. She didn't want to start a family rebellion.

'I wouldn't mind taking a proper look around the town,' Bunny said. 'But I think Flora has other plans.'

'I think you should go.' Flora said with enthusiasm. 'Jocasta could show you the pump rooms, which are quite impressive. Not to mention the park and lake, which are lovely.'

Bunny deserved a little entertainment and he hadn't seen the town properly before. He would never complain, but Flora's preoccupation with the reasons for her father's death must be hard for him. Her time was best spent here, trying to make some sense of everything that had happened. The answer might be simple, in which case need not trouble Bunny at all.

'What an excellent idea.' Jocasta bounced on her toes as if eager to be off. 'You can treat me to a cup of tea at the café on Pittville Lawn with dragons on the roof. I'll just go and change.' She set off toward the house, calling over her shoulder. 'I'll see you back here then in about fifteen minutes.'

'I thought she wanted to speak to Lord Vaughn first?' Bunny said, watching her go.

'That's Jocasta for you, a butterfly mind which flits from one thing to another. She means well, and she's a good friend.' Flora adjusted his immaculate collar.

Bunny stood passive and allowed her attentions. 'I suppose it would be one way to pass the morning while you interrogate the staff.'

'I don't intend to interrogate anyone,' Flora said carefully, aware he was only teasing. 'Though as least if you're in town, you'll be out of the way of that lady's clutches. And I don't mean Jo's.'

'No worries on that score, my love.' Bunny planted a swift kiss on Flora's cheek. 'I'm a married man and not nearly wealthy enough to attract the likes of Mrs Caroline Mountjoy.'

CHAPTER 7

Flora crossed the drive to a set of high arched wooden doors that opened into a three-sided range of stone barns round a cobbled courtyard, the neat arrangement constructed early in the previous century by a Vaughn ancestor. Apart from four equine noses poking over half stable doors, there didn't appear to be anyone about. In search of some life apart from the four-legged variety, Flora entered the building on her left, where the sickly sweet smell of hot horseflesh, dry feed, hoof oil and manure made her wrinkle her nose. A door stood open to one side, which gave a view of rows of hooks which bore bridles and saddle racks. Bales of hay had been neatly stacked in the loft above, while the floor where Flora stood was remarkably clean, devoid of any stray bits of hay or streaks of mud. Rakes and pitchforks hung on hooks in a line on the back wall; all signs that Tom had inherited his father's penchant for order.

Before his retirement to one of the estate cottages, the senior Murray had spent his entire life caring for the Vaughn horses; the coach house and stable blocks treated like his private temple. Flora guessed he most likely kept an eye on things even now.

Avoiding the shallow gutter that carried water to the drains, she came to an open stall where a man of about thirty stood in shirtsleeves beside a piebald pony and applied oil to the animal's hoofs. The pony raised his muzzle and whickered softly as Flora approached.

The groom straightened and swung round, his enquiring frown turning to delighted surprise at the sight of her. 'Miss Maguire. Uh, I mean Mrs Harrington. I heard you was here.' He dropped the oily brush into an earthenware pot on a bench and wiped his hands on a cloth draped across one shoulder. 'I'm that sorry about Mr Maguire. We was all shocked when he was found.'

'Thank you, Tom,' Flora said through the lump in her throat. 'Lady Vaughn invited us to stay until after the funeral but it feels strange being here without my father.'

'Strange for all of us, Mrs Harrington.' Tom had apparently lost his penchant for blushing, but he still swiped that stray lock of hair from his forehead in a self-conscious gesture. 'He treated everyone fairly did Mr Maguire. Don't seem right he had ta go.'

'We've known each other long enough for you to call me Flora.' She reached a hand to stroke the pony's velvet muzzle. 'Perhaps he didn't have to. Go that is.'

Tom's eyes narrowed into wariness, then softened

immediately. 'Don't know what you mean by that. It was an accident, no more.'

'Maybe. Would you mind telling me about the day my father died?'

'I don't know much, though I do know it weren't Diabolus's fault, whatever they say.'

'The Devil?' Flora did a rapid translation. 'Is that the horse my father rode? Is he as troublesome as he sounds?'

'Well, he's not the quietest of the bunch. Master bought him last year and he's taken a while to settle. One thing I do know is he didn't trample Mr Maguire. Not deliberate anyway.'

'How can you be sure?' Flora straightened. No one had mentioned that her father had been trampled. Lady Vaughn had said it was a fall.

'Well – I s'pose I can't.' His lower lip trembled and he swiped a hand beneath his nose. 'Not for certain, like. But he never bites or kicks when he's shoed, even when the lads come at him from the rear.'

'Did Diabolus have any injuries when he returned that day?' Flora asked. 'He may have stumbled or run into some wire or fence which might have been why he unseated my father.' She was reaching and knew it, however at this point she didn't know what direction she should take. Nothing made much sense.

'Nay. Not a mark on him. He wasn't sweating or nervy either. He just walked into the stable with his rein trailing. All quiet like. To be honest, Miss

Flora,' he picked up a curry comb from a wooden bench, then set it down again, avoiding her eye, 'I was surprised he asked for a horse at all. He's never done that before. In fact it was only because all the other horses were out that day, I agreed. Left to me I wouldn't have given him Diabolus at all.'

'Do you mean my father shouldn't have taken him?' Flora's voice hitched at the thought he had been given an unsuitable animal.

'I didn't say that.' Tom huffed a sigh, frustrated at her questions. 'It wouldn't have been my first choice is what I meant. Besides, Mr Maguire was insistent. Said he had something important to do, and ordered me to saddle him.'

'What was it he had to do that was so vital?'

'He didn't tell me.' He poked the toe of his boot against an uneven slab on the floor and wiped one hand across his brow.

Flora sighed inwardly. If only her father hadn't been such a private man.

'Just how dangerous is this horse?'

'He's in the third stall on the right. Look for yourself.' The words 'if you don't believe me' hung in the air between them.

He didn't seem worried at her seeing the horse at all, as if anything Flora saw would exonerate the horse. With little hope of learning anything new, she followed Tom along the row to the stall where a reddish brown horse munched on hay. His black mane, tail, edges of his ears, and upper legs categorized him as a bay.

Though the head swung toward her as she approached, the animal continued nibbling at the hay net, black liquid eyes studying her with mild interest.

'He doesn't look very troublesome.' Flora reached a hand to the muscled neck. The slightly oily flesh rippled beneath her fingers, but the horse remained passive.

A shaft of sunlight through the stable door gave the black mane a halo of blue. He was a beautiful animal.

'I thought Mr Maguire could handle him.' A note of apology crept into Tom's voice. 'I watched them top the rise and he looked good in the saddle.'

'I'm sure he did.' Her father had been an upright, well-built man, and still handsome at forty-three. 'I'm not trying to apportion blame, Tom. Nor am I suggesting my father was given an animal he lacked the skill to handle. He was evidently happy to ride Diabolus, or he wouldn't have taken him. I'm trying to find out what happened after he left here. Have you no idea where he went?'

He shook his head, repositioning the same sandy lock of hair. 'He was in a hurry, and didn't stop around for a chat like he normally did. When this boy here came back on his own.' He slapped the animal's neck firmly, but Diabolous didn't flinch. 'I alerted Lord Vaughn straight away. Master organized the estate workers in a search, though it was getting dark by the time they found him in Bailey Wood.'

Flora frowned. Bailey Wood wasn't on the Cheltenham road, nor in the direction of the village.

'It was unusual for him to ride. He always used the dog cart if he needed to go into town.'

'He didn't go into town though did he?' Flora murmured, mostly to herself.

'Look, Miss Flora.' Tom swiped his sleeve under his nose. 'It don't matter how many ways you ask. I don't know where he was going. He wasn't likely to explain himself to me in any case.' He turned away and began to scoop feed into a bucket with a wooden ladle. 'It was an accident, plain and simple. Diabolus must have trod in a rabbit hole or something and Mr Maguire was thrown. It was unlucky his hitting his head like that, but these things happen. Now if you don't mind, I have work to do.' He heaved the bucket onto his bent arm and strode down between the stalls.

'Yes,' Flora mused to his retreating back. 'These things happen.' At the last moment before he reached the door something struck her and she called him back. 'Tom? Do you happen to know a girl called Betsy Mason?'

Was it her imagination, or did he freeze for a second before he turned toward her?

His mouth twitched into a knowing smile. 'All the lads know Betsy. She's a real looker and knows it. She came to work in the kitchens about six months ago. I don't think she took to it, mind.'

'I hear she's missing.'

Tom lowered the bucket to the floor, an action which Flora interpreted as a play for time. 'Not missing, so much as took off. The fête was a month ago and she left the day after.'

'You know where she is then?'

He shook his head. 'Nay, why should I? Her uncle thinks she went off with some man. Not that he cares, sees it as good riddance.'

'Who is her uncle?

'Mr Griggs, the landlord of The Red Kite in Clayton village. Betsy came to lodge with him to help with the housework and look after him and his boy Peter. Not that Betsy was much good at laundry and such. More trouble than she was worth, Griggs said. Mind you, he ignored her mostly as his son hasn't been well.'

'Where does Mr Griggs think she went?'

'Don't think he knows or cares.' He snorted in derision. 'Betsy will be all right, she's a canny girl that one.' He heaved a long sigh and retrieved the bucket. 'Now if you don't mind, Miss Flora, I have to get the animals fed.'

'Of course, yes. I'm sorry if I'm keeping you from your work.' Flora let him go, sensing he couldn't get away from her fast enough.

Despite Lady Vaughn's repeated assurances, William did not put in an appearance for luncheon; a meal to which an increasingly annoyed Caroline Mountjoy had invited herself. When he failed to appear by the end of the main course, she had refused an exceptionally good *Charlotte Russe* and had taken herself home in a huff.

Bunny and Jocasta returned from their outing in good spirits, though Bunny's mood shifted to concern when he greeted Flora.

'How are you feeling? Not too lonely, I hope?'

'I'm fine, you don't have to keep asking me how I am. And don't feel guilty about enjoying yourself. Whatever I am going through will happen anyway.' She made an effort not to look sad, and pushed aside the questions her talk with Tom had stirred, determined not to spoil their luncheon.

Lord and Lady Vaughn left for an appointment in Cheltenham straight after the meal, so Jocasta instructed Scrivens to serve coffee on the sunlit terrace.

Flora smiled to herself at Scriven's sullen look as he set the miniscule cup in front of her, ignoring the fact he had slopped dark liquid into the saucer.

Bunny frowned and raised his hand, but Flora gestured it wasn't necessary. The man gained nothing by his hostility towards her, nor did she lose anything by it.

Shielding her eyes with a hand, Flora followed the fanned tail and white underwings of a red kite in the cerulean blue sky, as it soared and dipped above them and darted off over the Cotswold Hills.

That lone bird in an empty sky struck her as infinitely sad, reminding her that her father was gone. Pestering the staff for the details would change nothing, so perhaps she should accept what had happened with more grace and less suspicion, or she risked making herself appear ridiculous, even hysterical.

'You're miles away, Flora,' Bunny said, making her jump. 'You missed almost our entire conversation just now.'

'Sorry, just thinking.' *And glad to be here in the place father loved.* She glanced at Jocasta, who regarded her with her head on one side. 'We were just saying Eddy was quiet at luncheon, which wasn't like him.'

'I noticed that.' Flora brought her thoughts back to the present. 'He didn't eat much either, is he still below par?'

'I expect the wretch is malingering.' Jocasta relaxed against the cushions in a white-painted peacock chair and nibbled a Florentine biscuit. 'One minute he's all pale and shaky and the next he's flushed and energetic. I suspect he's trying to get out of accompanying Father to the county show. He's more interested in machines than livestock.'

Bunny leaned a hip against the boundary wall, cup and saucer in hand. 'I'll try not to discuss motorcycles with him, to avoid making things worse. I don't wish to bring down the wrath of Lord Vaughn.'

'Never mind my little brother,' Jocasta licked chocolate off her fingertips. 'Cleeve Abbey will be his one day, so it jolly well serves him right if he has to put some effort into learning how the estate is managed. Now Flora, what did you and Mother talk about at breakfast after we left? Your husband's tactic of dragging me away so you might talk in private wasn't exactly subtle.'

'Believe me that *was* subtle for Bunny.' Flora threw him an indulgent kiss, rewarded by his miming one back. 'I suspect Lady Venetia found my mother a difficult subject to broach.'

'In what way difficult?' Jocasta studied first Bunny's face and then Flora's. 'What did she say?'

'Apparently, Lily discovered she was pregnant with me although still unmarried. The situation caused your mother some unsettling moments.'

'I can imagine.' Jocasta poured more coffee for herself before settling back in her chair. 'Mama was always terrified of doing the wrong thing. The lady of the house was required to be a moral compass for one's staff in those days, even more so than now. Appearances counted so much more then, and if your staff strayed it was considered your fault.'

Flora's hand stilled, a biscuit halfway to her mouth. Was it her imagination, or was Jocasta unsurprised at what she had just said about Lily's pregnancy? She usually homed in on anything mildly outrageous with enthusiasm, and yet in this case reacted with disinterest. *Or had she already known?*

'Lady Venetia said my mother redeemed herself however by marrying the father of her child,' Flora said in an attempt to keep the conversation going.

'Did Mama actually say that, about Lily I mean?'
Jocasta poured more coffee into her cup with more than normal concentration.

'That's exactly what she said. Why?'

'Nothing, I just thought—' Jocasta glanced up at the clock on the tower above the stables, her eyes widening in shock. 'Goodness is that the time? I'm late meeting Amanda Liscombe.' Her cup clattered onto the table, spilling coffee onto the surface. 'She wants me to accompany her to some craft fair at Sudeley Castle. Must go.' She hurried inside without a backward look.

'Are you all right, Flora?' Bunny crossed the terrace and took the chair Jocasta had vacated.

'Was it my imagination, or was that performance entirely for my benefit?' She nodded towards the French door that had slammed behind Jocasta.

'What performance?' Bunny's brows puckered in confusion.

'Never mind.' Flora drained her cup slowly, her thoughts racing. 'Am I making an unnecessary fuss about Father's accident? Should I simply stop asking questions and just get on with mourning him?'

'You want my honest opinion?' Bunny returned his coffee cup to the table. 'I worry that you see shadows where there aren't any. I know this is utterly wretched for you, but only once you accept the circumstances of his passing will you be able to reconcile his loss.'

'I certainly cannot blame that beautiful horse.'

She summoned a reassuring smile. 'You're right, I should accept whatever the official verdict of the inquest and not try to make more of it.'

'I think that would be best.' Bunny scraped his chair closer. 'Will you continue to try and find out the truth of what happened to your mother?'

Flora hesitated, aware even her husband's patience had limits. 'I would like to put that ghost to rest if I can. But maybe there isn't anything to uncover about her death either. In which case, I'll have to face the fact both my parents are an enigma.' Smiling up at him, she held out her cup for a refill.

Bunny made no comment as he upended the coffee pot over her cup, but the sideways glance he gave her indicated he didn't believe her on either count, but he was prepared to let it rest for the time being.

Flora was happy to leave it that way temporarily, as something Jocasta said had sent her thoughts off in another direction. And then there was also Eddy. Was he simply tired and being overworked by Lord Vaughn, or was there something else wrong?

CHAPTER 8

At exactly three thirty-four, Flora eased open the door of the butler's pantry, a well-ordered room next to the door leading down to the cellar that contained the racks of bottles he had dusted meticulously every day. A floor-to-ceiling wooden dresser took up one wall, filled with books of tradesmen's ledgers dating back twenty years. The hooks where the household keys hung on identical wooden slips on the wall beside the door were labelled by hand in his careful cursive script. She inhaled on a tiny sob, forcing images of her father in his favourite workspace away.

'Good afternoon, Mrs Harrington.' Scrivens appeared silently behind her, his brow raised in sardonic enquiry as if she trespassed on his territory.

'I always liked this room,' Flora refused to let him intimidate her. 'So much of my father is still here.'

'Indeed,' he skirted the cramped space and took the chair behind the desk, leaving her to stand. Her lips twitched at his lack of manners, confirming her impression he wouldn't last long in his post. A head butler needed impeccable manners or how could he pass them on to the staff. She wondered how long it would take Lord Vaughn to come to the same conclusion.

'Is this a convenient time to call on Hetty, Mr Scrivens?' she asked, not bothering to hide her contempt.

'Of course, Miss Flora,' he replied as if the question were unnecessary. 'She's taking her tea at the moment. However, I'm sure she'll be delighted to see you.' He inclined his head with all the reverence of a crown prince dismissing an underling.

He did not look up as she left, her rapid, angry footsteps sounded along the flagstone floor. She inhaled a breath and gave the kitchen doorknob a sharp turn. The double height room with its vaulted ceiling was painted the same sage green Flora remembered, an eyebrow window above head height ran the width of the room, flooding it with daylight. The walls on one side were taken up by wooden dressers, the shallow shelves crammed with china tureens, copper jelly moulds and rows of shiny saucepans in varying sizes, from the palm of one hand to a soup tureen big enough to serve thirty people.

The massive fireplace with its roasting spit frame stood at one end, while at the other sat a black-leaded range for less ambitious cooking, its chunky metal doors and stained hotplates scrubbed to a shine every night before the kitchen maids were allowed to retire to bed.

The smell of baking, herbs and carbolic soap instantly propelled Flora back to her childhood. Days when the pine table that took up the entire length of the room reached her chin; the pattern of scars and scratches on its uneven surface a map of the meals produced over the years. How many biscuits and scones had she helped make on that same table?

Suspended in quiet between luncheon and afternoon tea, the kitchen stood cavernous and eerily silent, interrupted only by a clashing of pots and girlish giggles from the scullery next door, accompanied by a loud male shout from outside.

Hetty sat reading a newspaper in a wheel back chair beside the range, her salt-and pepper hair fastened in a tight bun on the back of her head. Her black skirt fell to an inch above swollen ankles and puffy feet, a delicate floral-patterned cup and saucer and tiny teapot sat on the table in front of her.

Flora took in the mutton-leg sleeves of the woman's black dress that was otherwise shapeless; though without an apron now she was not working. She might have been in mourning too, had not Flora known this was how Hetty always dressed.

'Hetty?' Flora paused beside her chair. The woman raised her head slowly from the newspaper, her eyes sharpened though her face did not so much as flicker in either recognition or welcome.

111

'It's Flora. Flora Maguire that was. Did Scrivens not mention I was coming?'

Hetty seemed uncertain of her, as if Flora were a stranger and not the girl who had practically grown up in this kitchen. Perhaps since her marriage Flora had changed more than she realized.

'Flora is it?' A crease appeared between the old woman's eyes as she considered this information. 'I was only saying to Mr Maguire the other day that I hadn't see you for a while.'

'That's right, quite a while.' Hetty must be at least seventy, so perhaps a month was similar to a year in her mind.

'Mr Maguire died, Hetty. Flora said gently, the words still painful to say.

'You don't have to remind me,' Hetty brought a work-reddened hand to her chest, the knuckles swollen and arthritic. 'A riding accident weren't it?' Her thin lips puckered. 'Though Mr Maguire's the last person I imagined would lose his life that way. Lord Vaughn maybe or even Lady Jo, they're always off about the place jumping fences. But Mr Maguire.' She broke off and shook her head. 'Now that did surprise me.'

'It surprised me too, Hetty. I don't suppose you knew where he was going that day?'

'Going, dear?' Hetty went back to her newspaper. 'He didn't tell me. Why should he?' She repeated the words with the same inflection Tom had. 'It were his day off. His time was his own.' Her eyes widened in a way which said one should never encroach on a person's privacy. 'That's why you're here isn't it? Cos he's dead?'

Flora winced. 'Yes, that's right. Do you happen to know if Father was worried about something in the days before he died?' The second the words were out Flora knew them to be futile. Riordan Maguire never confided his feelings to anyone. The chances of him sharing personal problems with Hetty were remote.

'No dear, Mr Maguire wasn't a brooder. He just got on with things.'

'That's what I thought.' Flora exhaled on a sigh. 'There's something else I wanted to ask, if you wouldn't mind?'

'What's that, dear?' Hetty lifted the newspaper higher, though her eyes moved too rapidly for normal reading. Flora had to fight an urge to snatch it away and demand she pay attention. Aware she should not take her frustration out on Hetty, she took a deep breath and forced a smile onto her face.

'Do you remember my mother, Lily? Lady Vaughn's maid?'

The woman's wrinkled hands stilled for a second, then she directed a smile past Flora's shoulder as if she were looking into another time. 'Course I do, dear. Lovely girl was Lily, and pretty as an angel.' Her eyes dipped to the page again. 'She's not here no more.'

'I know.' Flora closed her eyes, summoning patience. 'She died when I was a child. Don't you

113

remember?' Flora frowned. Had Hetty become more forgetful since the last time Flora spoke with her? In the past it was the odd misplaced word or an inability to recall names, but she seemed more vague now, almost disengaged.

'I remember everything, my girl,' Hetty snapped, as if to answer Flora's internal question. 'I've been here at the Abbey since God were a lad.'

Flora smiled at Hetty's stock response to anyone who dared question the running of her kitchen. She had heard it so often as a child, she had half believed it.

The clack of the door latch announced the arrival of a slender woman who looked to be in her late twenties whom Flora had not seen before. She must have come to work at the Abbey within the past year or so.

Her toffee-brown eyes were set in an oval face above a chin too pointed to be pretty, though she carried herself with confidence. A small white scar cut across her top lip that slightly fattened her nose, but at the same time was somehow attractive.

With a polite sketched curtsey to Flora and an indulgent smile at Hetty, the woman went straight to a bench table by the door where she began transferring eggs from the basket she brought with her into a white bowl.

'I'm not one to gossip,' Hetty said without acknowledging the newcomer. 'Though to my mind Lily should have stayed at home with her husband, not gone where she shouldn't have. Messing with things that didn't concern her. Not when she had a child to care for. Lovely little girl with pretty chestnut hair she had. Much like yours, dear.'

'That *was* me, Hetty.' Flora suppressed the impatient edge that crept into her voice. 'I'm grown up now.'

'You, love? No, that can't be right.' Hetty's eyes dulled. 'Lily's little one is no more than five or thereabouts.'

Flora sighed, unsure how to get the conversation on track again. A movement to her left showed the woman at the bench had stopped what she was doing, her hands stilled on the bowl and the way she stared at the wall ahead indicated she was listening.

'Hetty.' Flora's tone grew more frustrated by the second. 'What did you mean about Lily going where she shouldn't?'

'Ohh, can't tell you that, dear. Never went there m'self. Not a respectable place are those houses in Barnard's Row.'

'The cottages near Knapp Road?' Flora recalled the area was a notorious slum, due for condemnation in the not too distant future. Why would Lily have gone there? 'Is that where my parents lived when they were first married?'

'If you don't mind my saying, Miss.' The other occupant of the room turned from the bench, her hips braced against the edge and her hands clasped in front of her. 'Hetty's memory isn't what it once was. She confuses what happened last week with something from twenty years ago. She's been getting worse these last few months.'

'I *had* noticed.' Flora sighed. 'Odd that Mr Scrivens didn't think to mention it,' she added archly. *Nor Lady Vaughn either.* 'I suppose I didn't want to admit her memory might be fading. She's the only link I have to my mother, you see.' She indicated Hetty, who studied her paper with apparently no interest in their conversation. 'I hope I haven't upset her.'

'Don't worry, she'll have forgotten all about it five minutes after you leave.' She closed the space between them. 'It's Flora isn't it? Mr Maguire's daughter?' At Flora's nod she continued, 'Lady Vaughn said you were coming. I'm Amy, Amy Coombe.' Her hand drifted to her mouth as if she knew Flora was looking at the small imperfection, although at that moment that was not in fact true. 'I'm so sorry about Mr Maguire, he was a lovely man to work for.'

'Thank you, and it's nice to meet you, Amy.' Fresh grief rushed into Flora's chest. When would the pain lessen?

'I'm the assistant housekeeper,' she continued. 'I only came to work here a few months ago, which is why we haven't met before.'

'Maguire accused me of making those men sick, you know,' Hetty's sudden announcement brought Flora attention back to her. 'I told him, no one

116

ever suffered from my cooking, not in all the years I've been here.'

'Sick? Who got sick?' Flora split a look between the old woman and Amy.

'Some of the workers fell ill after the summer fête,' Amy gave an apologetic shrug. 'Mr Maguire thought it might have been food poisoning.'

'And my father accused Hetty of causing it?' Flora frowned, disbelieving. 'It doesn't sound like something he would say.'

'It wasn't.' Amy dragged a stool across the floor, and straddled it. 'Mr Maguire asked if the meat served at the fête was fresh, that's all. He questioned the butcher as well. It wasn't as harsh as it sounded, though Hetty took it to heart. She's complained about it at least twice a day since.' She hunched her narrow shoulders in a deprecating shrug.

Hetty had gone back to her newspaper, her unfocussed eyes scanning a page she still had not turned.

'What was my father's interest in these men?'

'They were all estate workers.'

'Did my father find out if it was food poisoning, or something else?' Flora asked.

Amy shook her head. 'If he did, he didn't tell me. I doubt it was serious, for they recovered fairly quickly. And before you ask. No, I don't know where Mr Maguire went the day he died. Hetty was having one of her restless days and I had to run the kitchens. I didn't even know he had gone.'

'I see,' Flora said slowly, though nothing had been made clearer.

'I have tea with Lily and her little girl every Tuesday,' Hetty interrupted them again. 'Fleur she calls her. Funny name, foreign I think, though it suits her.'

'I *am* that little girl, Hetty.' Flora had reconciled herself to the housekeeper's random train of the thought, unable to imagine what it must be like for Hetty to lose her grip on the past. Was the present equally as cloudy? 'That was the one thing I do know about my mother. She gave me the name Fleur when I was born. My Scottish grandfather felt it was unsuitable for a butler's daughter, he said he would call me Flora. Somehow it stuck and no one calls me anything else.' She carried on talking, her voice softer now as she concluded Hetty wouldn't remember what she had said, but it hardly mattered.

'They haven't found the girl, have they?' Hetty said, apropos of nothing.

'What girl, Hetty?' Flora responded out of habit, though she did not expect a sensible answer any more. 'Do you mean Lily?'

'Flighty bit that one.' Hetty snorted. 'All the men round here buzz round her like flies to sugar. Not just the young ones either. Not surprised she went off.'

'Who went off?' A shadow crossed Flora's heart as the words sank in. Was that what had happened to her mother? She had simply met someone else and ran away with him? It would explain the hurt in her father's eyes whenever her name was mentioned. It would also explain why she didn't have a grave. Flora's heart sank. Bunny was right when he intimated she might not like what she discovered. Why hadn't she listened to him?

Frustratingly, Hetty had reverted to silence, her attention back on the newspaper though she had made no attempt to turn a page the entire time Flora had been talking.

'I don't think she meant your mother,' Amy whispered.

Apart from Flora's recurring dream, she had a sepia-tinted photograph on her father's dresser of a fair haired, light-eyed woman with a gentle smile. A soft-voiced lady whom Flora had built up in her head as the love of her father's life, a perfect, beautiful being taken too soon, who left a broken-hearted man behind her. A man who could not even bear to hear her name. In the space of a single day that image had been shattered. She had learned her mother had got herself pregnant and had to get married, and that the whispers she had heard as a child were most likely because Lily Maguire was considered 'flighty' by the rest of the staff.

'I didn't know my mother. Maybe Hetty's memories aren't inaccurate. Lily could well have been a flirt everyone gossiped about in corners.' Flora rose from the wooden kitchen chair so fast, it toppled over onto the floor with a crash. 'I'm-I'm

119

sorry. I had better go.' She bolted through the rear door into the kitchen garden; a well-trodden route she took by instinct, where the harsh afternoon sunlight seared her eyes.

Amy's plaintive call for her to wait followed her, but she didn't stop as she ran along the tiled pathway to the end wall where a bench stood against the brickwork next to the gate that led into the stables.

She slumped against the wooden gate, uncaring that the rough wood threatened to snag her dress, her breath coming in halting gasps that tore through her lungs. How typical that Hetty's damaged memory recalled the one fact about her mother Flora didn't want to hear. Flighty! That's what she called her. Did everyone at Cleeve Abbey have the same opinion? She could hear them now. *'That governess who thinks she's something special is the daughter of that baggage who ran off. Poor Mr Maguire raised her all by himself. A saint he was.'*

Tears blurred her vision as she stumbled through the arched gate, which slammed shut behind her. She leaned against the brick wall, letting the wind tug her hair from its pins and stole her choked breath.

The ordered symmetry of the kitchen garden with its bean canes, herb beds and neat pathways had given way to the raw beauty of Cleeve Hill where wild gorse, drystone walls and hedgerows criss-crossed the undulating hills like a patchwork.

The air smelled sweet and green with a promise of rain. A pigeon's rhythmic coo came from the tree, while the sound of a hand mower rattled from somewhere beyond the wall.

She had once played on the hill, the rooftops of the town spread before her like a child's toy. As disturbing emotions crowded her head, she longed to let her feet take her down the incline once again, where a fall was only a stumble away and exhilaration replaced any fear she might hurt herself.

Her gut clenched at the thought she had not only lost her father, but the image she had carried all these years of her mother was now tainted. Had Hetty's memory been intact, would she have allowed her thoughts free rein after keeping them to herself for so long? Perhaps not, but Hetty's wandering mind took no one else's feelings into account.

As much as it hurt to know the truth, at least she wasn't being protected in ignorance any more. Flora at least knew what her mother was really like. She never did subscribe to the saying that ignorance was bliss.

Absorbed in her own misery, Flora didn't register voices until she heard angry words from the other side of the kitchen wall. The first voice she didn't recognize, though the second was the strident tone of Bracenose, Lord Vaughn's estate manager.

His voice was deep, more a low rumble, so she couldn't make out the actual words. However, whatever the first man had said seemed to infuriate

Bracenose, whose response, though indistinct, was gruff and threatening.

The second man laughed, apparently not intimidated by the burly estate manager. Seconds later, the gate flew open and hit the wall, revealing a red-faced Bracenose.

Flora had left it too late to pretend she had not been listening, so the look he gave her made it clear he was aware she had been eavesdropping. He narrowed his eyes and seemed about to say something, but at the last second changed his mind. Instead, he gave her a curt, grudging nod before he continued round the side of the house.

Flora waited, wondering who would have the nerve to challenge a man who had run the estate for years, but when no second figure appeared, she approached the gate and peered through, but the stable yard stood empty.

CHAPTER 9

The clock on the stable tower struck four just as Flora re-entered the house. She paused at the entrance hall mirror and rearranged her loosened hairpins, wiping away all remaining traces of tears.

In the sitting room Bunny sat sprawled on the sofa with a newspaper, one leg crossed over the other and an ankle swinging gently. He looked so relaxed Flora couldn't help but smile, for he might have lived at Cleeve Abbey all his life.

'There you are, Flora.' He looked up, caught sight of her face, and instantly his smile withered. 'My goodness, what *is* the matter?'

He crumpled the paper onto the sofa beside him and rose, drawing her into the room with a hand beneath her elbow.

'Do I look a dreadful mess?' She brought a shaking hand to her hair.

'Impossible. You're angelic as always, though anyone who knows you as I do can see you're upset.' He pushed the ruined newspaper aside to make room for her on the sofa before resuming his seat.

'Remind me in future to listen to you more.' She summoned a bright smile as she sat, but doubted it was convincing.

'I take it your interview with the housekeeper did not go well?' He angled his upper body towards her in a familiar listening pose.

'Hetty does remember my mother, but according to her assistant, Amy, she confuses recent memories with past ones.' Flora fumbled in a pocket for her handkerchief. 'She said Mother was a flighty thing who always had men flocking round her.' Her lips trembled and her nose ran, so she blew noisily into her handkerchief. 'Not that I should be surprised. After all, she started me without the benefit of a wedding ring.'

'I think you need a cup of tea.' Bunny patted her knee, then advanced on the trolley where a large teapot sat on a stand over a flame.

'Where is everyone?' Flora gave the room a swift glance.

'Lord Vaughn is in the office with William, they returned from Cheltenham a half hour ago. Eddy went to lie down. Poor chap's still not feeling quite the thing.' Bunny handed her a cup and saucer from which a wisp of steam arose. 'As for the ladies, I have no idea.'

She took a sip of the hot, smoky-tasting tea, which made her feel instantly calmer.

'Maybe you shouldn't pay too much attention to servants' gossip,' Bunny went on gently. 'In my experience, pretty girls often attract a certain amount of jealousy from others. I saw those photographs your father kept of Lily, and speaking as an expert, she was indeed a lovely woman.'

'I know, and thank you for such a generous view of her character.' Flora sniffed, cradling the cup in both hands. 'Hetty also said Mother spent a lot of time in a place called Barnard's Row. She *"went where she shouldn't"* were her exact words.'

'Where's Barnard's Row?' Bunny resumed his seat, the delicate china dwarfed in his hands. 'Could your parents have lived there at one time?'

'It's a notorious slum area in town. I doubt they lived there. Father couldn't have functioned as Lord Vaughn's butler had they not lived on the estate.'

'Perhaps there was a gap in his employment? Did they marry before he became butler here?'

'No.' Flora shook her head. 'They met here.'

'I see.' Bunny moved closer and wrapped an arm round her shoulders. 'Look, you said yourself Hetty's memory isn't what it used to be. She may have got it wrong.'

'It all fits, Bunny.' Flora wiped her nose. 'How do you feel about being married to the daughter of a loose woman?'

'Not like you to be self-pitying, Flora.' Bunny ran a finger gently down her cheek. He hugged her to him, his lips against her hair. 'What your mother did, or did not do doesn't matter a jot to me. I married you, not a ghost from the past. Besides, if she could see you now, she would be proud of you.'

'Would she?' Flora blinked tears from her lashes and rested her head on his shoulder, groaning as another thought jumped into her head. 'Your mother! Should she ever find out that mine was little more than—' she released a shuddering sob. 'Oh, Bunny I cannot bear it.'

He wrapped both arms tightly round her, murmuring endearments into her hair she was too distressed to appreciate.

Flora's own experience of gossip below stairs and rivalries that festered there returned. Perhaps what Lady Vaughn referred to as *'that unfortunate business'* was an isolated slip of Lily's, but one everyone remembered. It didn't take much to sully a young girl's reputation.

At that moment the door clicked open. Instinctively, Flora pulled away from him, a hand brought up to her hair where it had come away from the pins at the back.

'Sorry, did I interrupt?' Jocasta said in a way that displayed no regret whatsoever. She flounced over to the trolley and poured herself a cup of tea. 'I would have thought the honeymoon well and truly over by now. It's been a year hasn't it?' Balancing a slice of Madeira cake on the saucer, she crossed the room and perched on the sofa arm at Bunny's elbow.

'Sixteen months.' Flora sniffed and wiped her damp cheeks.

'Well, it's nice to see anyway.' She stirred her tea with tiny clicks of a silver spoon. 'What have you two been doing this afternoon?' She accompanied her question with a sly look.

'Flora has been interrogating the servants.'

'He's teasing,' Flora narrowed her eyes at him, which he countered by miming a kiss. 'Although I wish someone had warned me about Hetty.'

'Dear me yes.' Jocasta spoke through a mouthful of cake. 'Didn't Mama tell you? No of course she didn't,' she answered her own question. 'The poor woman is fine most of the time, Hetty I mean, not Mama. At times the old dear can be quite dotty. I take it today was a bad day?'

'It was, and speaking of your mama,' Flora said, 'I expected her to be here. I know how she loves her teatime rituals.'

'She had a migraine so went to lie down. She'll be better by dinner time I expect.'

'What a shame, migraines can be very distressing.' Bunny handed Flora her refreshed tea. 'My mother gets them sometimes.'

'No she doesn't,' Flora murmured. Bunny slanted a look at her and she smiled. He smiled back, nodding in silent acknowledgement that Beatrice Harrington regarded the word headache as too ordinary, so insisted she suffered from migraines.

'I ran into Tom when I took back the dog cart,' Jocasta said. 'The craft fair was positively dire in case you're interested,' she continued without waiting for an answer. 'He said you met Diabolus. He's quite magnificent isn't he?'

'He is indeed, although I most likely upset Tom

by implying the horse may have been to blame for Father's accident. Then made it worse by questioning whether or not he should have let Father take him.'

'He'll get over it.' Jocasta waved a careless hand. 'Besides, Diabolus is a pussy cat if you know how to handle him. Papa would never keep a bad-tempered animal on the premises. However, one can never tell what will spook a horse. Comes with the territory.' She swiped another piece of cake from the plate. 'Did Tom say anything of interest?'

'He didn't say much at all. Nor did he have an idea of where Father went that day, or why.'

'Perhaps your father used the wood as a shortcut on his way to somewhere else?' Bunny suggested. 'What lies beyond Bailey Wood?'

Jocasta scrutinized the ceiling for a moment. 'Mr McCallum's House is out that way, although I can think of no reason why Maguire would want to call on him.'

'Who is this Mr McCallum?' Bunny asked.

'Ah.' Jocasta wiggled her backside on the sofa arm closer to Bunny. 'Now there's a subject worth discussing. He was the object of Caroline Mountjoy's attentions before my Uncle William arrived and turned her head.'

'I think I remember him, vaguely.' Flora delved into her memory, unearthing an image of her escorting Eddy up the grand staircase to bed while a tall, dark man was shown into the sitting room.

128

'He bought the old brewery out at Battledown from the previous owner's heirs,' Jocasta continued. 'They were so glad to get rid of it, they threw the old man's crumbling pile in for free.' She hunched her shoulders in delight. 'He doesn't live there though, it's too dilapidated. He stays at the lodge, I think. Anyway, Mr McCallum is in his late thirties, incredibly handsome and has more money than God. Oops.' She cast a fearful glance at each of them in turn. 'Sorry, I'm not slighting anyone's religious convictions here am I?'

Flora couldn't help a smile erupting despite her bleak spirit. Jocasta could always be relied upon to lift her mood, reminding her of nights they huddled beneath the cover of her monumental bed in the ladies' wing and gossiped into the small hours.

'It was a few weeks before we went to America for Amelia's wedding.' Jocasta licked cake crumbs from her fingers. 'Don't remind Mother whatever you do. She made the mistake of inviting Mr McCallum here for dinner soon after he moved in. Amelia developed an immediate crush on him and threatened to call off her engagement. Mother was furious.'

Flora nodded slowly as a memory surfaced. 'He had the look of King Leopold of the Belgians as a young man. All forward brushed hair, sardonic brows and dark whiskers. Not that I know much about him.' She chose not to mention Lady Amelia's outburst that she couldn't possibly go to America now she had met the man she really loved was the talk of the servant's hall for weeks.

'Neither did anyone else, at first.' Jocasta crossed to the trolley and poured herself more tea. 'He didn't spend much time here until the last year or so. Since then it came out he's a divorcee.' She drew out the last word with relish. 'He's rich and very eligible. Jeremy almost didn't want me to stay for the rest of the summer without him until I promised faithfully not to spend any time with Graham McCallum. Isn't that sweet?' Jocasta pressed a finger to the crumbs on her plate and brought it to her mouth.

'Was his liaison with Mrs Mountjoy common knowledge, or simply rumour?' Flora asked.

'No rumour.' Jocasta peered over the rim of her teacup. 'For months, she was seen all over Cheltenham in his company.' She dropped the remains of her second piece of cake onto her saucer. 'Village gossip had them almost married off at one point. Then, for no apparent reason, they simply stopped spending time together.'

'Um—' Bunny interrupted them. 'If you ladies are going to discuss the landed gentry's love affairs, I'll think I'll just, um—' He backed toward the door, a finger pointed at some vague space beyond it.

'Well. He certainly lost interest fast, didn't he?' Jocasta exclaimed as the door closed behind him. 'No stamina for the important things, men.'

'I think he finds female gossip embarrassing,'

Flora said. 'However, I would love to know what ended the liaison between Mr McCallum and Mrs Mountjoy.'

'As it happens I've no idea,' Jocasta replied, thus rendering Bunny's swift departure entirely unnecessary. 'When Uncle William turned up all tanned and healthy from Durban a few weeks ago, she switched her attentions to him.'

'How did Mr McCallum take this transfer of Caroline's affections?'

'I never found out, and as far as I know it was never mentioned. Graham and Uncle William get on very well as far as I know, so they aren't love rivals. And you saw for yourself William has no time for her. Anyway—' she broke off with an airy wave of her hand. 'I shouldn't repeat village gossip.'

'Of course you should.' Flora knew Jocasta needed only the slightest encouragement, confirmed when she threw a conspiratorial glance at the door and leaned closer.

'Well, rumour says Graham conducted a liaison with someone else for some time. That Mrs Mountjoy found out about it and was furious. There was apparently some dreadful scene at The Queens Hotel.'

'I gather their alliance has ended too?'

'Hmm.' Jocasta paused to swallow a mouthful of tea. 'I've no idea. I don't believe in idle gossip.'

Flora almost choked on her last mouthful of tea. 'I don't suppose there were any witnesses to this alleged scene between Mr McCallum and Mrs Mountjoy?' Flora asked after a brief fit of coughing.

'Come to think of it, no.' She tilted her head on one side. 'Never mind Mrs M, did the staff have any useful information for you?'

'I only spoke to Hetty, who isn't exactly reliable, and Amy, who's only been here a short while. Perhaps I should simply accept Father's death was an accident which no one could have prevented.' She chose not to mention the more upsetting aspects of her interview.

'Papa will be so relieved.' Jocasta's features softened. 'He felt responsible for Maguire, you know. After all, it was his horse, even if the accident didn't take place on our land.'

'There was something else Hetty said which got me thinking,' Flora began. 'She mentioned that some people became ill after the fête. Father made some enquiries as to what had caused it.'

'The workmen you mean?' Jocasta nodded, thoughtful. 'Papa said they must have drunk too much of the free beer on offer.' She shrugged, the subject obviously of no interest to her.

'Might it have been food poisoning?

Jocasta frowned, the remains of her cake halfway to her mouth. 'I don't think I heard that. Maybe. I cannot say.'

'Did those men see a doctor?'

'I believe so.' Jocasta chewed her cake thoughtfully. 'He diagnosed some sort of neuritis. I'm not sure what that is, but apparently it damages the nerves and causes temporary paralysis. They lost weight rapidly and complained of being unable to get out of bed – though as I said, Papa was convinced they were malingering at first.' She took a sip of her tea, adding as an afterthought. 'Until one of them died.'

'What?' Flora straightened. This was the first she had heard of any death. Neither Hetty nor Amy had mentioned it. 'Hardly malingering then.'

'No, I suppose not.' Jocasta agreed, though with so little inflection she may have been talking about a lost sheep rather than a person. 'He was older than the others. Dr Fairbrother said his constitution wasn't strong enough to fight off the infection.'

'That's awful.' Flora said, though this explained why her father was so concerned. A man died, so naturally her father would have tried to discover why.

'Is there any more tea in that pot, Jo?' Flora asked, pushing the subject to the back of her mind.

'Have you seen my cufflinks, Flora?' Bunny called through the communicating door between their bedroom and the sitting room.

Flora slung a loose cotton gown over her chemise, not bothering to fasten it. The combination of her glowing skin after her bath and the warmth of the summer evening made her want to enjoy the freedom of being unrestrained, thus she put off dressing for dinner until she had to.

She sighed at his mildly accusatory tone and

unrolled a pair of silk stockings and laid them on the bed beside her combination drawers and corset cover. 'You're always misplacing your things,' she called back. 'How did you manage to keep track of your belongings at Marlborough?'

She withdrew an oyster-coloured corset from the cover, the pale pink of the sateen resembled a disembodied torso beside the other items. Heavily boned, it was more formal that the one she wore during the day, and designed to create a fashionable 'S' bend. Flora's girlish figure could hardly be described as voluptuous, but the garment accentuated her tiny waist.

'I didn't.' Bunny's voice was accompanied by the sound of drawers and cupboards being flung open at random. 'They disappeared with monotonous regularity. Oh, what's this?'

'What's what?' Flora replied, only vaguely interested.

'Newspaper cuttings.' Bunny said over the rustle of paper. 'From one of the Manchester papers. They were stuffed at the back of the bureau drawer. Don't know how we missed them earlier.'

At Bunny's urging, Flora had summoned the courage to begin the task of sorting through her father's belongings. His bedroom still proved too upsetting as yet, but she had compromised by agreeing to tackle the contents of his bureau. Riordan Maguire had stored what appeared to be every receipt, note and postcard that had passed through his hands during the previous ten years; all neatly tied with pieces of what looked like second-hand string.

'I didn't see any newspaper clippings.' Flora looked up from the neatly arranged undergarments. 'I don't think Father knew anyone in Manchester. What are they about? Court circulars or advertisements for silver polish?' She winced, aware it was too soon to make jokes at her father's expense, and yet for a moment she had forgotten he wouldn't be coming back.

'Neither,' Bunny said. 'They're about some incident at a brewery.' He appeared at the open door, a shoulder against the door frame as he scanned the pages in his hand. 'It's quite interesting actually.' His look swept her state of undress and slowly, he lowered his spectacles further down his nose and peered at her over them.

The hairs on her arms prickled as he stood watching her, but she pretended not to notice. After his insistence she stop looking for shadows, his own interest had been piqued without her having to do a thing. 'You were saying?' she prompted, self-conscious at the same time a ripple of excitement crept into her belly beneath his steady stare.

'Um, ah where was I?' He jiggled an arm of his glasses with his free hand and went back to the page. 'A Royal Commission was set up at the Westminster Palace Hotel in London to investigate the cause,' he read aloud, then gave a low whistle. 'One hundred and fifteen people died as a result of contaminated beer.'

'That's dreadful!' Flora's hands stilled on the soft fabric of a silk camisole. 'Even so, what an odd thing for Father to be interested in, unless—' She quickly skirted the bed, took one of the pages from him and began to read as a phrase she had heard lately emerged from the back of her mind.

The discovery that poison lurks in one of the most popular of the nation's beverages has been a rude shock to the inhabitants of Salford and its neighbourhood.

For about 4 months, the medical men of Salford have been called upon to deal with a considerable number of cases in which the complaint has been weakness and pains in the limbs, like 'pins and needles' in the hands and feet, general numbness and rheumatism all over. In more advanced cases patients declared themselves paralysed and quite unable to get about. Both men and women have sought medical advice and in all cases they were beer drinkers.

The Manchester Brewers Association analysed the beer and traces of arsenic were present, thought to be from sulphur used to treat the hops to prevent blight. Further investigation revealed arsenic in sugar used for brewing.

She reached the end of the article and stared at it unseeing. Contaminated beer. Is that what had caused the men at the summer fair to get sick? It would explain it in part, though not the question of why more people weren't affected. Lord Vaughn's fêtes usually attracted over a hundred people from the outlying villages.

'More of your father's things to dispose of, I suppose.' Bunny plucked the page from her fingers and headed for a box in the corner of the room designated for items set out for burning later.

'No, don't destroy them.' Flora took the pile from his fingers. 'They might mean something.' Her thoughts drifted, while snippets of conversations circled in her head.

'Like what?' He rifled through a drawer at the bottom of the wardrobe, apparently still on a quest for the errant cufflinks. 'That article is dated December the year before last. It's hardly news.'

'This one is a summary of the incident printed in a London paper, but this,' she held up a second cutting, 'is the original report. Father must have sent off to Manchester for a copy. The *Salford Reporter* isn't available in Gloucestershire.' Flora compared the two reports. One was much creased and yellowed, while the other relatively new.

'The significance of which is?' Bunny straightened, and splayed his hand through his hair as he gave the bedroom a swift glance. 'Where *are* those blasted cufflinks?'

'I don't know but Father must have kept them for a reason. And don't swear.' Flora slid the pages into the drawer of her nightstand with the intention of studying them more thoroughly later. 'There's a pair of cufflinks on the mantle in the

137

sitting room. Behind the clock. You must have left them there and forgotten.'

'Thanks.' He disappeared into the next room, but reappeared almost immediately. 'Found them!'

'I'll wager you didn't even look there,' she murmured as she shrugged out of the cotton gown, and let it fall to the floor. She wrapped the corset round her midriff over the chemise and hooked the metal catches at the front into place. Perhaps Father noted similarities between the Manchester incident and what happened here at the fête, but before he could ask the right questions, he died. *Or someone killed him.* The instant the thought jumped into her head she shook it away. If she voiced such a thing aloud, Bunny would assume she was deranged by grief and treat her accordingly. Or was it her grief which drove her to look desperately for reasons and answers that might not exist?

Flora stood in front of the cheval mirror, both hands braced on either side of her waist. 'I'm afraid I need your help to dress,' she said, her head turned toward him in anticipation of a ritual she looked forward to each morning.

Beatrice had dropped heavy hints that it was about time Flora engaged a lady's maid, but thus far she had resisted. Despite the inconvenience, she was unwilling to allow a stranger into their bedroom, which she saw as her and Bunny's private domain.

'Don't apologize.' Bunny aimed a lascivious grin

at her reflection in the mirror. 'I quite enjoy being your personal abigail.' He wound the laces round his hands, then gave them a strong, slow pull that emptied Flora's lungs of air. 'I wonder if Lord Vaughn performs this service for Lady Venetia.' He leaned closer, a smile in his voice, his warm breath caressing her ear.

'I very much doubt it.' The silk slid with a gentle whoosh as he adjusted the ladder of ribbons with deft fingers. She closed her eyes, her neck arched in invitation.

Although married a year, she was still shy about certain aspects of their intimate life, and initiating his touch was one of them.

On this occasion, Bunny obliged and his lips traced a spine-tingling line from her hairline to her collarbone.

'About that newspaper report,' he whispered suddenly into the hollow where her neck met her collarbone, his fingers stilled against her back. 'I heard that some estate workers became ill after the summer fête. Rumour says it was either food poisoning or an abundance of free beer. I only mention it because perhaps your father thought there was more to it, thus the newspaper clippings.'

'I was thinking the same thing myself.' She tipped her head back and to one side to receive his kiss on her neck. 'Might the beer have been contaminated? Like in Manchester?'

'The coincidence occurred to me, but here as well? That doesn't seem likely.'

139

'What about deliberate poisoning?'

'Why would anyone want to poison a field full of people?' Bunny snorted. 'Seems a bit far-fetched. Hold still, I'm almost finished.'

She released a gasp as his last pull on the ribbons drove her up on her toes. She pursed her lips and exhaled in a slow, silent whistle.

'It could have been accidental.'

'I suppose so.' Then a thought struck her, and she stiffened. *Father had fallen from his horse not far from the house of a man who owned a brewery.*

'Sorry, was that too tight?' Bunny asked. 'You flinched.'

'No, it's fine.' Flora took an exploratory breath. The corset creaked but barely moved. She wouldn't be able to eat much at dinner. 'You're good at this.'

'I'm getting lots of practice. Turn around,' he instructed.

Flora obeyed, her arms raised as he crossed the loose ends round her waist and tied them into a slip knot at the front.

'It's worth a discreet question or two in the right places, don't you think?' she asked, coyly tilting her head, aware the boned corset pushed up her breasts.

'Depends what you mean about the right places.' His eyes drifted downwards as he tied the knot with a final sharp pull. He took a step closer, ran his hands along either side of her cinched waist and across the exposed skin of her back, pulling her into his arms.

Her eyes fluttered closed as sparks lit her nerve endings, spread through her limbs and into her lower belly. She nuzzled the open neckline of his shirt, where she luxuriously inhaled the herbaceous fragrance of his *Eau Impériale* cologne he had applied after his second shave of the day.

'I have to finish dressing,' she murmured, though there was no conviction behind it.

'We have at least half an hour.' He removed his glasses and laid them absently on the nightstand at his side. 'All we'll miss is the sherry.'

She made a half-hearted effort to dart away, but he stepped sideways, caught her in mid run, and swivelled her towards him. Her squeal of laughter dissolved into a soft moan when his arms tightened round her, while he pressed small kisses along her neck and up to her ear.

She braced her hands flat against his chest, then slid her arms upwards, her fingers laced behind his neck. 'I wish you had thought of this before I put the corset on.'

'What would be the fun in that?' he murmured, as gently but firmly he eased her backwards onto the soft mattress.

Before her senses took over and she responded to his demanding kiss, Flora resolved to find out more about the beer served at Lord Vaughn's fête.

Later.

CHAPTER 10

'Everyone must already be in the dining room,' Flora said, when the only evidence of recent occupation of the sitting room was the numerous dents in the sofa cushions and an open, discarded magazine.

'The dinner gong went a while ago.' Bunny slid an arm round her waist and guided her along the deserted corridor. 'If anyone asks,' he lowered his voice outside the door, 'which I doubt, we'll blame our lateness on the inefficiency of the water geyser.'

'Bunny.' Flora halted him with a hand on his sleeve. 'You don't think it was, well wrong to do what we— I mean, with my father lying in the mortuary, we—'

Her conflicted emotions during their lovemaking had confused her. When sated desire had turned to quiet sobs, Bunny had silently held her without offering trite platitudes until her composure returned.

'No-I-don't.' He put emphasis on each word and tucked a loose strand of hair behind her ear. 'You have no reason to feel guilty. If anything, we affirmed that life goes on by our love. Your father would want you to grasp every moment of happiness, especially now he isn't here to care for you.'

'Thank you.' Flora fought back welling tears. 'I knew all that in my heart, but I needed you to tell me.' She slipped her hand into his as they entered the dining room, passing Scrivens on his way out, who gave them both a hard, insolent stare.

Confused by his hostility, Flora turned to watch him, his shoulders set as he strode back along the corridor.

'Ah, there you two are.' Lord Vaughn cut through Flora's garbled apology and ushered them inside. A table designed to seat thirty people sat in the centre of the vast room. Multi-branched candelabra had been set at intervals down its length, interspersed with bowls of fruit, nuts and flowers in a rainbow of colour across the snow-white cloth.

'I want you to meet our guest this evening,' Lord Vaughn said as she and Bunny took their seats. 'Mr Graham McCallum, this is Flora Harrington and her husband Ptolemy, otherwise known as Bunny.'

The newcomer rose from his place between Lady Venetia and Jocasta. He wore his dark wavy hair brushed forward from the crown onto his forehead and cheeks, falling short of his neatly trimmed side whiskers. A strong brow, narrow straight nose, and slightly upturned brown eyes fringed with thick lashes completed a face which would draw all female eyes in any company. No wonder he had stood out from the normal train of visitors to the house that day, even though Flora had only caught a glimpse of him from the staircase.

'Please accept my condolences, Mrs Harrington,' he said once Lord Vaughn had completed the introductions. His rich, deep voice had a hint of a Scots burr. 'I had a deep and admiring regard for your father.'

'Thank you, that's very kind.' He made no effort to release her hand, so she had to tug hard to release it from his grip. His sentiment pleased her though surprised her at the same time. Her father had not mentioned Mr McCallum in his letters, so the fact they were acquainted surprised her. She doubted theirs could have been a friendship, but mutual respect perhaps?

'I can see why Lady Amelia's head was turned,' Bunny murmured as he held out her chair.

'I thought you disapproved of gossip,' Flora whispered back, rewarded when his eyes flashed behind his spectacles.

'We were just discussing the coronation of the king.' Lady Venetia projected her voice across the room for Flora's benefit, while at the same time signalling the footman to serve the fish course.

'I don't know much more than I read in the papers,' Flora said. 'Other than the ceremony had to be postponed so he could have an operation.'

'They did it on a table in the music room,' Eddy said through a yawn.

'Spare us the details, Ed.' William winked at his nephew, evidently much at his ease since there

144

was no sign of Mrs Mountjoy. 'Suffice it to say he survived and is on the mend. He'll be back to his decadent ways in no time.'

'It was a poor show as it turned out,' Lady Venetia said. 'Most of the foreign dignitaries who went home when the king fell ill didn't return for the ceremony. They sent their ambassadors to Westminster Abbey instead.'

'No tragedy to my mind.' Lord Vaughn gave a disdainful snort. 'Kept the proceedings short and made it an entirely British occasion.'

'Mary Penniman is still livid every time the subject is mentioned,' Lady Venetia said with a trace of glee. 'She rented an apartment overlooking the route and they wouldn't refund the rental. An exorbitant amount she paid too, and to see absolutely nothing. She's threatening to sue.'

'I should imagine quite a few people found themselves in that position,' Mr McCallum said.

'The ceremony was a fiasco by all accounts.' Lord Vaughn spoke between mouthfuls of salmon. 'Archbishop Temple put the crown on the king's head back to front. Once down on his knees the poor old fool couldn't get up again. The king and several bishops had to haul him to his feet. Darned old fool.'

'The bishop, or the king, Papa?' Jocasta's eyes went wide and innocent. Flora brought her water glass to her lips to hide a smile as the same thought occurred to her.

'The bishop of course,' her father huffed.

'In case you hadn't guessed, Mr McCallum,' Jocasta said, toying with a sapphire pendant at her throat, 'we weren't exalted enough to have been invited to attend the coronation, thus we've reverted to carping and criticism.'

'Jocasta, really.' Lady Venetia sniffed, though her mouth twitched.

'Don't misunderstand me, Mama. I adore the Royal family,' Jocasta said sweetly. 'I'm only sorry poor Bertie has been made to wait so long to become king.'

'Despite his reputation with the ladies, I believe Edward the seventh will make a better sovereign than either of his parents believed he would.' Mr McCallum relaxed back in his chair, his benign gaze resting on each of the ladies in turn. A round of 'Hear, hears' went round the table and crystal clinked musically together.

'The traditional St Edward's Crown was too heavy for him,' Eddy said, evidently determined to educate everyone. 'They used the State Imperial one instead. Did you know Cromwell sold the original regalia after the civil wars? Flora taught me that.'

Flora smiled, embarrassed at this unexpected praise, and turned her attention to the subtly dill flavoured cold salmon. Having missed the first course, she discovered she was ravenously hungry.

'Thank you, Eddy.' Lord Vaughn laid an affectionate but restraining hand on his shoulder. 'I shall expect top marks in your history exams next term.'

Eddy blushed furiously as a ripple of polite laughter went round the table.

'You taught young Edward then, did you, Mrs Harrington?' Mr McCallum asked.

Flora looked up to find his steady gaze on her.

'Oh didn't I say?' Lady Venetia said loudly. 'Flora used to be Eddy's governess. She grew up here at Cleeve Abbey.'

Saved from answering, Flora continued her meal, though was aware of their guest's scrutiny throughout the rest of the course.

The conversation took another tack and Flora recalled what Jocasta had said about Mr McCallum as a businessman with an atavistic attitude towards women, which struck her as being in stark contrast to the handsome man with the kind smile. He wore his affluence with discreet style, the only evidence a diamond pin in his tie. With his overt good looks and the way he commanded not only Lady Vaughn's attention but Jocasta's, Flora understood how Lady Amelia and Caroline Mountjoy had both succumbed to his charm.

That the lady was conspicuous by her absence indicated her exclusion from the party had been deliberate in order to avoid tension between Caroline's old flame and the one she planned to ensnare. But that there was no animosity between McCallum and William appeared accurate, as the two men had plenty to say to each other, punctuated by frequent laughter and an easy banter.

'I believe you now own the brewery at Battledown, Mr McCallum?' Flora asked when the entrée was served, instigating the conversation she had played in her head since she had arrived at dinner and found Mr McCallum in attendance.

'Indeed, yes.' He sprinkled salt liberally on his vegetables. 'The place took some work to get up and running again. The previous owners had allowed it to become abysmally run down.'

'I gather you've made the business profitable now?' Flora summoned her blandest smile, while she tried to work out how to bring up the subject of contaminated beer.

He helped himself to a portion of potatoes from the plate the footman held out. 'I now supply a majority of the public houses in Gloucestershire.'

'I'm so glad your business didn't suffer from the rumours at all.' Flora sensed Bunny had gone very still, and broke off his conversation with William.

'Rumours?' McCallum's eyes sharpened and his water glass halted mid-way to his mouth.

'About those men who became ill after the fête?'

'Your father had already asked me that.' He slewed a sideways glance at her.

'I assumed he must have done,' Flora lied, pushing peas round her plate with her fork. 'We found some clippings about an incident in Manchester last year where sugars—'

'—had been contaminated from sulphur used to treat the hops against blight thus creating arsenical acid. I'm aware of the incident.' He cut her off with

148

a raised hand and passed the tiny silver tray with the salt and pepper pots along the table. 'Maguire showed them to me. In fact, at first I wondered if he didn't have a point.'

'You did?' Why this information should have surprised her she wasn't sure. 'Did you take the matter further?'

'I would have done, had Dr Fairbrother not refuted everything I said. His opinion was those men were all heavy drinkers and spent their lives in The Red Kite,therefore neuritis was the most likely diagnosis.'

'Was this before or after my father spoke to you about the Manchester incident?'

McCallum thought for a moment. 'After, I believe. I got the impression he didn't agree with the doctor either, but the men had recovered by then so the cause of their illness was of little interest.'

'Did you check your brewing processes, Mr McCallum?' Ignoring Bunny's hard stare she asked. 'I mean, in case your barley was contaminated by accident?'

'Of course I did.' McCallum frowned. 'Naturally I couldn't have misinformation about my brewery going about.' He dabbed his mouth with his napkin, leaned toward Flora and patted her hand that lay on the table. 'I apologize if you feel I'm being disrespectful to the dead. However at the time, even though I harboured the same doubts myself, I resented Maguire's implication I used tainted sugar in my brewery.'

'That Manchester incident was quite a scandal at the time,' Lord Vaughn joined the conversation. 'Nasty business all round.'

'Did you see the articles as well, my lord?' Flora asked, surprised he had been listening.

'Maguire mentioned something of the sort.' Lord Vaughn took a slow sip from his wineglass before continuing. 'He was worried the same thing had happened here, but there was no evidence to indicate that.'

'I see.' Flora dipped her head to her plate.

'The logic doesn't make sense anyway.' William was openly dismissive. 'There were at least eighty men at the fête, and only six of them fell ill.'

'One of whom died,' Flora reminded him.

'An elderly man with a heart condition, which the doctor will confirm should you be inclined to ask him,' McCallum said. Opposite her Bunny visibly flinched at his tone, while several pairs of eyes snapped up. As if he realized his remark was inappropriate, McCallum coughed and adjusted his tie. 'I apologize if I sound curt, but wouldn't want anyone to think I was responsible for a death.'

'Fairbrother's a doddering idiot.' Lord Vaughn sniffed. 'I doubt he could recognize a mass poisoning had the entire town succumbed.'

'Might we change the subject?' Lady Venetia interrupted. 'I really don't think this is a suitable conversation for the dinner table.'

'Not that I'm in a position to contradict anyone,'

her husband continued as if she hadn't spoken. 'I have no idea what causes neuritis. Perhaps we should invite that new female doctor to dinner. I would enjoy hearing her opinion on the matter. I heard she's quite an intelligent woman with strong opinions.' He waved his hand in a signal to the hovering nearby footman to replenish his wine glass.

'Oh, George, don't be ridiculous,' Lady Venetia scorned. 'A woman cannot possibly be a real medical professional. That's a man's province.'

'Is there really a lady doctor in the town?' Flora asked, intrigued. Without even knowing the woman Flora couldn't help silently admiring the courage and tenacity it must have taken her to succeed in such a sphere. She wondered how she might contrive the chance to meet her.

'There is indeed, my dear.' Lord Vaughn ignored his wife. 'Her name is Dr Grace Billings, and she has set up a surgery at her home in Pittville. Not that the good citizens of Cheltenham have taken her to their hearts, as yet. Though I've heard she's excellent with lady patients who require discretion.'

'That's because she's only allowed to treat women and children,' Jocasta said scathingly.

'In my opinion her husband should insist she devote her time to domestic duties rather than staring at bodies and risk catching diseases.' Lady Venetia's hand drifted to the high neckline of her dress. 'Especially as she is a mother of a small son.'

'What *do* you mean, Mama?' Jocasta demanded. 'Why shouldn't women be capable of studying any subject men do and with as much success?'

'It's not simply the books, dear.' Her fingers fiddled with a lace trim, obviously uncomfortable with the conversation. 'I cannot help feeling that a woman who aspires to medicine cannot maintain her natural modesty. She would have to look upon men's bodies in a way which should be reserved for their wives.'

'Incidentally,' Jocasta asked as if taking a sudden interest, 'how does arsenic get into beer by accident, Mr McCallum?'

Lady Venetia slumped back in her chair with a long-suffering sigh.

'Contaminated barley malt, or glucose and invert sugar used in the brewing process,' McCallum said. 'It's not unheard of.'

'Didn't anyone notice what was going on?' Lady Vaughn finally abandoned her sensibilities in favour of lively dinner time debate.

'In Manchester, many of the sufferers were inmates of the workhouse, some of them children,' McCallum addressed her as if they were alone in the room, making her flush. 'Thus condemned as being alcoholics. Not until people began to die in large numbers did the authorities think to explore further.'

'Did no one consider them special cases?' Flora experienced renewed anger for the victims. It horrified her that as indigents, they were assumed to be vice-ridden as a matter of course. 'I wasn't aware children drank alcohol.'

'Children often drink beer in slum areas of towns like Manchester, Mrs Harrington,' McCallum said gently. 'In some areas it's safer than the water.'

'Does that answer your question, Flora?' Lady Venetia asked, an edge to her voice.

'I'm sorry,' Flora stammered as heat rose into her face. 'I didn't mean to interrogate you, Mr McCallum.'

'Don't apologize. The incident here at Cleeve Abbey was upsetting.' He patted Flora's hand. 'And admirable of Maguire to take such an interest when neither the doctor nor the police gave the matter more than cursory attention.'

As if to confirm the subject at an end, the empty entrée dishes were removed by the footmen, who replaced them with portions of lavender-flavoured ice cream.

Flora smiled at the dish appeared before her, complete with the piped icing rose, beside which sat a tiny angelica leaf. Knowing it was her favourite, Hetty had always saved her some after dinner parties as a child and often made the treat on her birthdays. Had this particular memory broken through the fog in the housekeeper's head, or was it a coincidence? As she savoured the delicate, creamy mixture on her tongue, Flora liked to think the latter.

'I confess I too have an interest in motor cars, Mr Harrington.' Mr McCallum's voice cut across

Flora's thoughts. 'I believe you have plans to enter into the manufacturing side?'

'In a small way for the present,' Bunny replied. 'However, I hope to open a factory of my own one day.'

'Is that so?' Mr McCallum's brows rose. 'I would like to discuss that with you at some time. I have my eye on one of the new Daimlers.'

'I own a ninety-eight Panhard model myself, though I would love to have a look at the more recent models.' Bunny's voice was tinged with envy.

'Would you care to visit the *Trusty Motor Works* in Cheltenham tomorrow?' William asked. 'They have a four cylinder model on display.'

'I would enjoy that immensely.' Bunny's boyish grin disappeared and he turned a frown on Flora. 'Unless you have other plans for tomorrow?'

'None that include you,' Flora said, laughing. 'You go. I know how much you like engines.'

'We'll make a morning of it and perhaps take luncheon at the Queen's Hotel? They serve an excellent slow-roasted lamb shank.' William rubbed his hands together. 'What about you, McCallum?'

'It sounds splendid, and I do enjoy the food at The Queens, but I shall have to decline. Business commands my attention, you understand.' He turned his devastating smile on his hostess. 'Although I have to say I've dined like a king myself tonight. The salmon was exquisite, Lady Vaughn. My compliments to your cook.'

'I quite envy you young gentlemen your outing,'

Lord Vaughn spoke with a hint of regret. 'More interesting than my morning will be, I suspect. I have to attend a meeting of the committee responsible for the organization of the next Earthstopper's Feast. I've supported the hunt for years, so I'm expected to put in an appearance.'

'What exactly is an earthstopper?' McCallum asked. His question brought all eyes towards him. Some astonished and others perplexed.

'They're the terrier men on a foxhunt,' Jocasta answered, her brows raised in surprise. 'The night before the hunt, they go out with lanterns and stop up the fox earths and badger setts along the route.'

'Stops the foxes going to ground during the hunt.' Eddy stirred his spoon around a bowl of ice cream he had barely touched, replacing it in the dish with a clatter. 'Makes 'em easier to catch.' He yawned again, drawing his father's critical stare, and said something Flora didn't catch. Eddy straightened in his chair and made an effort to appear alert.

McCallum pushed his empty dessert dish away from him with some force. 'Isn't a dozen men on horses and a pack of hounds enough ammunition against one defenceless fox without cutting off their escape route?'

Lady Venetia dropped her gaze to the table, while Lord Vaughn's face flushed bright red. Flora's respect for Mr McCallum went up a notch. Having been raised in the country, the hunt was an accepted, if disagreeable part of her life, though privately she had never been comfortable with the destruction of small furry animals in the guise of sport.

'I take it you disapprove, Mr McCallum?' Jocasta propped her chin in her hand and gave him a flirtatious look.

'I've simply never been a follower of the hounds,' he replied.

Aware any attempt to steer the conversation back to her father or the brewery would not only be rude, but pointless, thus Flora relaxed and enjoyed her ice cream, while conversation turned to the Paris to Innsbruck motor race the previous June; their enthusiasm enhanced by the fact the event had been won by Selwyn Edge, an Englishman.

'I wish I had been there.' Eddy propped his chin onto one elbow. 'Must have been a fine sight.' His voice slurred a little, bringing Flora's attention to the fact his face was pale and yet a flush covered his cheeks and he appeared to have difficulty staying awake.

Lady Venetia murmured something to him and nudged his elbow off the table. Eddy jumped back in alarm, blinking rapidly.

Flora caught Jocasta's eye. 'Is Eddy unwell?'

'He's been up since six this morning.' Jocasta sipped from her wineglass. 'Probably just tired. He's not over his cold yet. I expect Mama will send him to bed when dinner's over.'

Belatedly, Flora recalled her former charge's welfare was no longer her responsibility. In fact she had overstepped her status in all respects lately. Both Lord Vaughn and Mr McCallum had answered her questions with more than reasonable explanations, so why did she still feel uneasy? Mr McCallum had entertained the contamination theory too, which had been refuted by the doctor. With all questions answered, what else was there to discover?

Lady Venetia rose to her feet, effectively bringing a halt to the conversation. 'Ladies,' she said, though apart from herself, only Jocasta and Flora qualified. 'I think it's time for us to withdraw to the sitting room.' She gestured to the footman, who sprang forward and pulled back her chair.

'Why would Mr McCallum choose to live in the Cotswolds, when he clearly has neither knowledge of, nor interest in country pursuits?' Flora asked Bunny as they scraped back their chairs.

'An aversion to blood sports is not a crime.' Bunny shrugged. 'I admire the fact he has the courage of his convictions, and Flora,' he halted her with a hand on her shoulder as they were about to part in different directions, 'perhaps you should stop looking for reasons to dislike Mr McCallum?'

Flora bridled, irritated he could read her so well. '*You* only like him because he's showed an interest in motor cars,' she teased. 'I don't suppose *he* cares what I think.'

Her conviction that a mystery hung over her father's death seemed remote and fanciful now.

Her guilt exacerbated by the fact she had repaid the Vaughns' hospitality by questioning a perfectly agreeable guest like a barrister. Had she invented reasons to dislike Mr McCallum? And if so, why? Because he was attractive to women and owned a brewery?

When Flora reached the bottom of the staircase she nodded to Lady Venetia, who stood with her arm round Eddy. He nodded a few times in response to what she was saying, then with a glancing kiss to her proffered cheek, he slowly climbed the stairs.

Flora watched them with affection, resolving not to search for shadows any more. Maybe she could reconcile herself to the truth about her mother as well, although surely someone on the estate must know what had happened to her? People simply didn't disappear without someone knowing anything – did they?

CHAPTER 11

Bunny's clothes smelled faintly of cigars and brandy when he joined Flora in their bedroom; not an unpleasant combination.

'I thought the evening was less fraught than the other night, didn't you?' Flora pulled the pins from her hair and let the heavy tresses cascade down her back. 'I'm beginning to feel more like a guest here. When we first arrived, I feared our presence was only tolerated because my father died on the Vaughns' property.'

'I don't get that impression at all.' Bunny's right shoe hit the floor with a thump. 'The family are very fond of you. There's only one person who has attempted to remind you of your former status, and she wasn't present tonight.'

'Mrs Mountjoy.' Flora smiled at her reflection. 'Did you notice how relaxed William was this evening? He doesn't like her much does he?'

'As a confirmed bachelor, I'm sure he's trained himself to spot a husband-hunter at a thousand paces.' Bunny propped his left ankle on his right knee and tugged off his other shoe.

'I've been thinking.' Flora removed her dressing

gown and let it fall on the chair behind her. 'Why did Father keep those clippings if Mr McCallum had convinced him the fête beer wasn't poisoned?'

'I thought we had abandoned the subject of poison.' Bunny dropped the shoe to the floor. 'Maybe Riordan forgot he had them, or he intended to discard them, but before he could do so, he met with the accident.'

'Possibly. I just feel he kept them for a reason.' She plumped up the pillows against the backboard on her side of the bed. 'The beer could have been poisoned deliberately couldn't it? Arsenic isn't difficult to obtain. Lots of people use it to rid their homes of rats.'

'Even so, it hardly seems credible McCallum would poison his own beer.'

'Maybe it wasn't him. It could have been a malicious prank or a deliberate intent to harm someone at the fête?' She eased between the covers. 'Is it possible that person knew Father had found out and to silence him they—'

'Dark secrets that roam the Abbey?' He waggled his fingers in the air, grinning. 'Now you've entered the realms of fantasy.'

'How do we know what goes on? I don't live here anymore. Perhaps something happened since I left which Father never mentioned to me. Maybe he died before he could unearth anything substantial.'

'We're here to bury your father, not solve a crime that might not even exist.' He removed his shirt which joined his trousers on a chair in an untidy pile.

Flora tried not to visualize the creases that would form in the material overnight, but resisted the urge to get up and put them away in the wardrobe. 'If Father thought—'

'You don't know what he thought,' Bunny interrupted gently. 'All the evidence points to neuritis from heavy drinking. Perhaps it's no more complicated than that.'

'A young girl went missing the same day.'

'Missing or left?' Bunny perched on the side of the bed. 'I heard she had run off with some young man.'

'No one knows who and she left without a word. The police are still making enquiries.'

'Why do you think the two things are connected?'

'I'm not sure they are, but Father would have heard about it. I cannot see him just ignoring a missing girl. And you might think I'm being unreasonable, that people die in riding accidents all the time. But I knew my father, he didn't ride.'

'Unless the inquest says otherwise, there's not much you can do.' Bunny leaned across the space between them and traced her jawline with a finger, his expression softening. 'You know, this reminds me of when you went poking about on the *SS Minneapolis* looking for clues when the Captain thought Parnell had died from a fall. You wouldn't let your feelings about that go then either.'

'His name was van Elder, and I was right then wasn't I?' Flora leaned into his touch, pleased to be able to remind him her instincts weren't always skewed by emotion.

'Indeed you were, and you didn't give up until the man was caught.'

'Exactly, so suppose for a moment that I'm right about this.' She wrapped her arms round her hunched knees. 'If, and I'm saying if, Father died because he was investigating a poisoning, don't I owe it to him to seek justice for his sake?'

'I understand your need to blame someone for Riordan's death, Flora. Really I do. However, people get very nervous when someone asks questions. They get defensive whether they are guilty or not and I don't want you to put yourself in harm's way.' The mattress dipped as he climbed into bed beside her. 'You're a married woman now with a home of your own.

'Not my home,' Flora said sulkily. 'It's more yours and your mother's.' She was being self-pitying but couldn't stop herself. Her father was the one thing that tethered her to the world. She had no other relatives and hadn't been married long enough to feel entirely at home with Bunny, much as she loved him. 'I'm an inconvenient addition without the power to make changes.'

'Inconvenient?' Bunny halted in the act of removing his spectacles. 'Why would you think that? Are you unhappy in Richmond?'

'I didn't mean it like that.' Or maybe she did,

162

and this was an appropriate moment to allow her real feelings to surface. 'Richmond is beautiful, and I enjoy living there.' It was true, she adored the neat Georgian house on the Thames, where their walks by the river on summer evenings had become one of her greatest pleasures.

'Then my mother is the source of your unhappiness?' His eyes clouded, making her wish she had not mentioned the subject at all.

'I'm not unhappy as your wife. It's all I ever imagined. Perhaps it's because your mother and I have some adjustments to make.'

'What sort of adjustments?' He folded his glasses and slid them onto the table beside the bed. She eased closer, and taking his cue, Bunny twisted the fingers of his free hand into her loose hair, tugging gently.

She leaned into his touch, glad she did not have to see the hurt in his eyes she was about to cause. 'I would like to be more of a wife and less a guest in her house.'

'My house too, my name is on the deeds, remember. In what way do you mean?'

She sighed, playing for time so as not to sound too critical. 'This might sound trivial, but your mother treats me as if I wasn't there most of the time. My opinion is not sought on any subject, from the meals we eat to which flowers she puts in the rooms. She hired two new kitchen maids last month without telling me. They just showed up in my room one morning when I was dressing.'

Bunny made no attempt to either comment or interrupt, which gave her free rein to bring up another complaint. 'Your mother has got into the habit of announcing bedtime whilst simultaneously switching off the gas lights. I've been left in the dark with an open book in my lap more than once.'

'I don't recall her doing that in my company.'

'Well of course she doesn't, she saves that for when you are out. I—' Afraid she had said too much, she bit back the rest of her mental list, especially the baby issue. Beatrice Harrington stood permanent guard for symptoms of pregnancy, a constant irritant to Flora but something Bunny would never understand. He would be delighted whenever that happened although had never intimated he was in any particular hurry. Beatrice, however went to great lengths to make Flora think the matter was entirely her responsibility – and therefore her failure. Her mother-in-law didn't seem to take into account that Flora had not conceived after a year of marriage and had begun to worry.

'I'm sure Mother doesn't mean to be inconsiderate,' Bunny said. 'Perhaps she feels she saves you the trouble when it comes to housekeeping issues.' She shot him a warning glance, at which he added, 'No, you're right. She ought to consult you.'

'Will you speak to her?' Flora pleaded. 'In a diplomatic, sensitive way of course.'

'When do I use any other manner of communication?' He tightened his arm round her. 'I promise

I'll give the matter some serious thought and have a strategy sorted out by the time we return home.'

'Thank you for understanding. Even if you do think I'm an overly fussy wife.'

Unless Bunny planned to build a brick wall through the centre of the house, a workable solution to her problem escaped her. Beatrice Harrington was a mistress of manipulation and achieved her own way with whatever weapons she could muster. Queen Victoria could have taken lessons.

'I'm looking forward to seeing the motor works tomorrow,' Bunny went on, the subject of his mother shelved. 'Will you be able to amuse yourself while I'm gone?'

'Oh, I expect so. I have a funeral to arrange, remember?'

'Would you rather I stayed to help? I can easily re-organize my outing.'

'No, of course not. You go. But I do appreciate the offer.'

'Goodness is that the time?' Bunny squinted at his bedside clock. 'Better get some kip or I'll be yawning tomorrow and William will think I'm bored.' He planted a kiss on her cheek, licked his thumb and forefinger and snuffed out the candle on his side of the bed.

Flora's thoughts were already miles away, thinking of what she would do with her day. She had the funeral to organize, having refused Lady Venetia's repeated offers to help. She needed to get on with it, but couldn't bring herself to discuss coffins and graves while she still had this mystery hanging over it all.

Then there was still the subject of Lily Maguire to settle completely, one which she intended to broach with Lady Venetia. She also wanted to visit the place her father was found in Bailey Wood. She might even pay a call on Dr Fairbrother. 'The doddering idiot' Lord Vaughn had referred to may have missed an important detail. She would have to find out where his consulting rooms were first, and borrow the gig to make the call. Should she mention her plans to Bunny or simply go off on her own?

Flora stared at Bunny's turned back for a moment, then tugged the coverlet over her bare shoulder and snuggled lower. No, it would be best to keep her plans to herself. The expression, 'it's easier to seek forgiveness than permission' ran through her head.

She might not have been a wife for long but knew never to start a disagreement at bedtime. Forced to sleep like bookends on a shelf while clinging to the edge of a mattress with their backs rigid, was rarely conducive to a restful night.

After breakfast the next morning, Flora saw Bunny off in William's elegant carriage, then went in search of Tom Murray. She discovered him in the kitchen garden, pitchfork in hand and his shirt-sleeves rolled to his elbows revealing muscular, bronzed arms. He didn't see her approach and continued chatting amiably to a maid who threw him repeated shy glances whilst she unclipped washing from a line.

Flora hovered by the back door, admiring of the way Tom's masculine form contrasted with the girls' delicate paleness, the pair framed by a row of white sheets that billowed like sails. Behind them rows of vegetable frames bursting with summer produce lent colour to a gentle, pastoral scene bathed in the glow of a summer morning that would have made a lovely painting.

The maid spotted Flora and bent to scoop a laundry basket from the ground. She sketched a polite curtsey, then nodded at Tom before making her way back along the path to the rear door.

'I'm sorry to interrupt,' Flora said to his turned back. 'May I have a word, Tom?'

Her prepared smile froze on her face as he turned around. A purple bruise covered a badly swollen left eye. 'Goodness, Tom, whatever happened?

He brought a hand up to his face as if he had forgotten about it, and ducked his head away. 'Nothing much, Miss. Horse kicked me.'

Had Diabolous caused this? On closer inspection, Flora noted the skin wasn't broken, so doubted any hoof had caused it, more likely a fist.

Tom wouldn't meet her eye, and embarrassed, Flora cast a glance over the garden. 'This might sound a strange question, Tom, but are you familiar with the exact spot where my father was found?' She wasn't sure why, but the need to see the place where he died mattered to her.

'I was in the search party.' He frowned at the memory, then a slight grimace showed the movement hurt him. 'I know the place.'

'Would you take me there?' She tried not to stare, but that eye looked painful. Whoever had inflicted it was evidently not averse to take on Tom, who was hardly frail.

'What, *now*, Miss?' At her pleading look he sighed. 'I cannot leave my work for long, but we could take the gig.'

'I would appreciate that, thank you. I won't keep you.' She was pressing her advantage as a guest and knew it, but Tom was the obliging sort and Lord Vaughn no tyrant.

'It's nay bother.' He held open the gate to allow her onto the drive first. 'The cart's in the end stable. I'll get it tacked up and we can go.'

The sound of wheels on gravel brought Flora's attention to a figure on a bicycle who entered through the Abbey gates. As it came closer it transformed into a constable who rode straight for them.

'Not him again,' Tom mumbled, his steps slowing to allow the cyclist to reach him. 'Good morning, Constable Jones.'

In no apparent hurry, the policeman dismounted, leaned his bicycle against the stable wall before striding towards them. A short, barrel-chested man, his uniform jacket strained against a slight pot belly, his buttons and collar flashes were highly polished.

'I needs a quick word with you if you don't mind, Tom?' He planted both feet apart in front of him and adjusted his chin strap. 'Morning, Miss.' He touched the peak of his helmet in salute to Flora, though he didn't ask who she was.

Content to remain anonymous, she nodded in response.

'What if I do?' Tom asked, suddenly belligerent. 'I can't tell you any more than I did the last time you were here.'

'Even so, I have to make my report for the sergeant.' He withdrew a small notebook from his top pocket, flicked it open. His head still down, he asked, 'That eye looks painful.' He took a pencil stub from behind his ear and licked it. 'Like to tell me how you got it?'

'Not particularly.' Tom removed a hand from the pitchfork and swiped it between his nose.

'I see.' His eyes flicked to Tom's face then back to his notebook. 'Has anyone reported seeing young Betsy Mason in the last few days?'

'Not since the fête, which is what I've been telling you all along.' Tom swung the pitchfork from one hand to the other, an act some might have seen as a veiled threat, though the sturdy policeman didn't flinch.

'I have to check if the situation has changed since then.'

'Funny how I'm the only one you keep asking

though, isn't it? Why don't you question Bracenose, or the footmen? They're as likely to know anything as me.' His eyes narrowed at the officer and his jaw worked as he spoke.

'Now, now, Tom, no need to take on. I'll get to them in due time. Has Miss Mason contacted you since she left?'

'If she left, then why all the questions? Or are you going to tell me you've found a body or something?'

'Now why would you go and say a thing like that, Tom?' Constable Jones tipped back his helmet and regarded him steadily. 'Are we likely to?'

'I've no idea.' Tom's grip on the pitchfork turned his knuckles white and alarm entered his eyes. He relaxed again as he seemed to remember Flora was there. 'Sorry, Miss, but I don't know what else to say.

Flora grew increasingly uneasy, unnerved by Tom's uncharacteristic hostility. Or maybe he just didn't like policemen? She debated whether she should discreetly withdraw, but curiosity won over and she stood her ground.

Constable Jones gave Tom a final hard look before scribbling something in his notebook. 'What about this Scrivens chap? He was at the fête that day? Has he been acting strangely of late? Sneaking off to places or acting nervous at all?'

'No more'n usual, as far as I know. The man's no friend of mine so I keep out of his way.'

'And the other chap, Bracenose? Was he paying more attention to the lass when she was here?'

'Bracenose? What road you going down there, Constable?' Tom snorted. 'You going to ask what Lord Vaughn thought of her too?'

'No call for attitude, young man. I'm only doin' me job.' His gaze swivelled to Flora. 'And who might you be, Miss?'

Flora assumed he had taken her for one of the staff. Perhaps she still looked like one.

'Mrs Harrington. I'm a guest of Lady Vaughn's, and I have never been acquainted with Miss Mason.'

'Ah, pardon me I'm sure.' His pencil swung from Tom to her. 'I'nt you the daughter of Maguire who was head butler here? I heard she married a Harrington?' His eyes clouded as memory returned. 'Please accept my condolences about Mr Maguire. He was a good man. T'were a nasty business his accident.'

'Thank you.' She looked away, surprised the effect a kind word from a stranger made.

'Ah well, if there's nothing more, I'll be off then.' He returned the notebook to his pocket and backed away. 'I trust you'll inform the constabulary if you do hear anything, Tom?'

Tom's jaw jutted forward and he looked about to say something he might regret. Flora cut across him.

'Shouldn't it be the other way around, Constable? Isn't your job to find the young lady and return her to her family?'

171

Constable Jones didn't answer, merely saluted her again and retrieved his bicycle.

'I'll go and fetch the cart.' Tom started for the stable before the policeman and his bicycle were halfway to the gates.

'*Has* there been any news about Betsy Mason?' Flora hurried to keep pace as he strode into the stable.

'You think I was having Jones on then?' Tom's laugh reflected the return of his easy manner. 'I'll repeat what I told him. No one's heard from Betsy since she left the fête.'

'I see,' Flora bit her lip. The fact he said 'left' and not 'was taken' struck her as an interesting distinction. 'Was she with anyone that afternoon?'

He shrugged. 'Might have been. Can't rightly remember. The field was full that day.'

Her gaze strayed again to his discoloured eye as he held open the door to the carriage house.

'Were you and Betsy courting?' Flora didn't know where the thought came from. Maybe it was the way his eyes took on a faraway look when he said her name.

'Courting?' Tom's lips twitched into a slow smile 'Let me explain 'bout Betsy.' He rested the pitchfork handle against his shoulder, both hands crossed over the top. 'Have you ever been close to an otter, Miss Flora?'

She shook her head, wondering where the conversation was going.

'That first time all you can hear are her whistles

and chirrups as she stays out of sight because you're a threat to the holt. If you're patient and wait, quiet like, she'll creep out to take a look at you. She'll watch you for a while, and may even purr a little, but then she's off again in a rustle of undergrowth and a tiny splash.

'Then one day, she's crouched on the riverbank and gets so close, you can even make out the pink scars on her nose pad from where the boar grasps her with his teeth when they mate. Minutes pass as you stare at her and she stares back as you take each other in. Then before you know, she's gone again. You can't help but smile then cos you know if you wait long enough, she'll be back.' He hooked the pitchfork onto a rack on the wall and continued on to where the gig sat on the tiled floor.

Flora smiled, impressed with his analogy. Was Betsy aware of how he felt about her but didn't dare ask?

'Aye, well.' He ducked his head away. 'That's what it was like with Betsy. She's one o' those rare creatures who needs time and patience to get to know. That uncle of hers treated her more like a maid than a member of his family.' He brushed dust off the gig seat as he talked. 'Not his fault I suppose, he's been a miserable soul since his wife died last year. He never did have much time for Betsy. Even less now his lad can't do the heavy work in the pub.'

He gave a low sigh that deflated him. 'And now she's gone.' He scooped his jacket from the top of the low door and nodded to where the horses stood in the row of stalls behind them. 'Excuse me, Miss Flora, while I get the gig sorted.'

Flora took the hint and returned to the drive to wait, mulling over what Tom had said. His annoyance at the policeman's questions seemed out of kilter, or was it simply frustration at their ineffectual methods? Either that, or Tom's anger was borne of jealousy because he knew who the man was Betsy had run off with? Whatever the truth of it, she was certain that if anyone had hurt Betsy, it wasn't Tom Murray. He would have died first.

CHAPTER 12

'Miss Flora?' Tom held the rein loosely in his hands, his right foot braced against the angled baseboard. 'Is it true Mr Harrington has one of those horseless carriages?'

'Yes, Tom, he does,' she said, disappointed. She had hoped he was about to reveal something of interest. They were ten minutes out of Cleeve Abbey and these were the first words he had spoken in a silence broken only by birdsong and the scurrying of small furry creatures in the hedges. 'He wants to open a manufacturing business, but for the present he works with a man who makes motorcycles.'

Flora's black gown clung to her back as the hot summer sun bore down on her. She should have brought a parasol but hadn't wanted to keep Tom waiting in case he changed his mind and found more pressing jobs to do.

'Those mechanical bicycle machines?' His brows rose. 'Aren't they even more dangerous than motor cars?'

'Everything is a risk in the wrong hands.' She repeated what Bunny told her when they had the same debate. 'Building one motor car can take a long time and Mr Harrington has to have each component for the engine made specially. Besides, they'll be very expensive when they are available. I should imagine most people will need horses for a good while yet, if that's what worries you.'

'Not especially. Motor cars cannot travel through thickets and over bushes the way horses can. Though mebbe I should learn to drive one. To be ready like.'

Flora turned to study his profile, bemused but impressed at the same time. 'I think that would be a good idea, Tom.'

Without warning, he pulled the cart into a layby, and jumped down onto the grass. 'Bailey Wood is up there, Miss.' He hooked a thumb in the direction of a thick group of trees, attached the rein to a post-and-rail fence, then reached to help Flora down. 'We'll have to walk the rest of the way.'

'How far is it?' Flora glanced down at her heavy black skirt, then up at the closely packed trees ahead.

He shrugged, a gesture that was beginning to annoy her. 'You were the one who wanted to come, Miss.'

'I did indeed.' Flora sighed. 'Lead the way then.'

The route was hard going as Flora weaved her way between the closely packed tree trunks, a thick layer of decaying leaves covered the soft ground underfoot that gave off a damp loam smell.

Twisted roots poked through the surface of the dark earth, and threatened to trip her up, while low branches brushed her face, and grabbed at her sleeves. Shafts of light punched through the canopy above them, growing less frequent the further in she went.

'How did Father manage to ride through this?' Flora kept her attention on her feet.

'He couldn't have, not on horseback,' Tom said, forging ahead like a goat on the uneven ground. 'A path runs over higher ground beyond the tree-line. I couldn't bring the gig round that way, so through the trees is the most direct route. You did say you wanted to know where he was found.' The ground was dotted with rocks, some small enough to be pushed aside with a foot, while others were two or three feet high, the gaps in between dotted with tiny pink sowbread flowers.

Tom reached back a hand to assist her up an incline to where a pathway ran, too narrow for a cart, although the number of hoof prints showed the route was well used. She paused to unhook the hem of her skirt from a low branch, then stepped awkwardly on a piece of uneven ground which sent pain into her ankle. She gritted her teeth, not daring to complain.

'Mr Maguire was found here, Miss Flora.' Tom nodded to an outcrop of larger boulders. 'He were unlucky. The rocky bit peters out a bit further down. Had he fallen there he would have probably got away with bruises. He landed on one of those rocks.' He coughed into his fist and backed discreetly away, leaving her alone with her thoughts.

Flora waited for the pain to rush into her chest, and fresh tears well in her eyes, but nothing happened.

She stood in a pretty spot where thin shafts of sunlight formed an impressive lightshow in a place where people rode, walked and sat with their families and maybe even their lovers. There was nothing there; no sense that a death had occurred in that spot, no indentation in the ground, no signs of a mortal struggle, or even a blood-stained stone.

'I wish I knew why he came here?' She raised both arms and let them fall again. 'This is a difficult route for an experienced rider, let alone someone who never rode. The path is narrow with too many twists and turns, not to mention all the low hung branches. And look at all these rocks.'

Tom kicked at the ground with a toe of his boot, hands in his pockets. 'Mr Maguire was a strange one.' At her hard stare he added, 'a good man, and fair. But he were a loner. You know that more than anyone. He never spoke to no one less he needed to.'

Flora exhaled, resigned. 'Yes, that's exactly what he was like.'

'Are you all right, Miss Flora?' Tom asked gently.

'I'm fine, Tom. Thank you.' All she could hope for her father now, was that his last moments were neither fear nor pain filled. If only she had made more of an effort to see him since her marriage. A sob rose in her chest for all the things she couldn't change, while a breeze disturbed the canopy of trees above her, carrying with it the fragrance of wet earth, grass and wildflowers. 'We can go back now.'

With a silent nod, Tom slipped his hand beneath her elbow and helped her down the slope which seemed steeper than the upward trek a few moments before. 'What's that, Tom?' She pointed to a square, grey building she glimpsed through the trees. Squat and low, it looked as if it had grown out of the hillside.

'That's Mr McCallum's house.'

'It's closer than I thought.' The track emerged from the wood and ran in an uneven line toward the house through a gentle sweep of a wild meadow.

'I'd better get back, Miss Flora.' Tom's apologetic voice interrupted her thoughts.

'Yes of course.' She followed him back to where the horse stood nibbling the grass verge in the sunshine. As they set off back the way they had come, the clop of hooves and an occasional call of a skylark were the only sounds.

'You know what you asked me the other day, Miss Flora?' Tom broke the companionable silence. 'About where Mr Maguire might have been off to the day he died?' He stared straight ahead, swaying gently with the movement of the cart. He looked as if he had forgotten what he was going to say, but she resisted the urge to prompt him, and waited. 'Well,' he said after a moment, 'Mr Maguire asked Bracenose about those men who became ill after the fête.' His inflection on the estate manager's name conveyed dislike. 'Not that I was listening, not on purpose. They were outside the stable door and I was inside cleaning tack.'

'I didn't think you were, Tom. Go on.'

'Mr Maguire talked as if he thought the beer had made them ill.'

Flora nodded. 'Do you know why he thought that?'

'No idea, but Bracenose took umbrage. He said Mr Maguire had no right to question him, like he had accused him of something.'

This came as no surprise. The estate manager had been at Cleeve Abbey for longer than her father had, and assumed this gave him special privileges. He had the reputation of being a surly, bad-tempered man rumoured to be less honest than she should be, but Flora had always found him polite and gentle. Bracenose must have known Lily, perhaps he could tell her what she needed to know? Why didn't she think of it before?

'He was in a bad mood for days,' Tom went on. 'He didn't join the search for Mr Maguire either.' His brisk nod indicated he had done his duty and what she chose to do with the information was her business.

'I see, thank you, Tom.' The question of the contaminated beer had already been solved. Or had it? There could also be any number of explanations for Bracenose's failure to join the search. Lord Vaughn could have sent him on a different errand elsewhere.

Thus preoccupied, it took a moment for Flora to register that Tom had guided the cart into a left fork on a track that ran between the fields. 'Why are we on this path, Tom? We used the main road on the way here.'

'It's a shortcut back to the Abbey. It brings us in at the rear of the stables instead of the front drive.'

They passed through a set of slightly crooked white gateposts in need of a coat of paint, beyond which straggly hedgerows changed to manicured privet and neatly trimmed grass verges. 'Is this part of the estate?' Flora frowned, not recognizing it.

'The main house is over there.' The track disappeared round a small rise, and evidently eager to get back to his work, Tom flicked the reins so the horse picked up its pace. A small gate appeared on Flora's left, beyond which a small white house stood encircled by hedges; its red tiles and roofline reminiscent of the Abbey, but in miniature. A diamond of bottle glass was set into a wooden front door beneath a stone porch between a pair of wooden pillars. A grey gabled roof with twin bay windows flanked a small tiled porch over the front door.

As the gig came level with the fence, Flora's stomach gave a lurch and she gasped. 'Stop!'

Tom reacted immediately and brought the gig to an abrupt halt. The horse pawed the ground and mouthed its bit in protest.

'Whatever's wrong, Miss Flora?' Tom couldn't keep the annoyance from his tone. 'The Abbey's just round that corner. We're nearly there.' He pointed ahead with his whip.

'I know this place. The diamond shaped pane in the front door stirred a memory. 'I've been here before.'

'Probably. It's part of the estate. You're likely to have been here.'

'No, not recently. A long time ago.' She climbed down from the gig onto the road. 'Could we stop here for a moment?'

'As you wish.' His sigh implied he would never understand females, as wordlessly, he secured the rein to the hook beside the brake handle.

Flora pushed open the waist-high wooden gate and stepped onto a paved pathway set with green, red and beige tiles. 'Who lives here, Tom?' she asked over her shoulder.

'No one on the estate.' Tom now lingered at the gate. 'Lord Vaughn rents it to a solicitor from Southam and his sister.'

'The house looks empty.' Flora approached the solid front door which resisted her touch. 'It's locked!' she said, disappointed.

'I don't think we should be in here, Miss Flora.' Tom threw a nervous glance behind him.

Ignoring him, Flora cupped her hands against the leaded glass and peered inside. An open fireplace faced the window in a neat parlour, empty but for a vase of dried flowers, flanked by two armchairs. Various pieces of dark oak furniture had been arranged round the room, with oil lamps and figurines set at intervals. After the jolt of recognition that had brought her there, this room wasn't at all familiar.

Tom's hunched shoulders conveyed his reluctance as he followed her down the path. 'I really should get back to work.'

'Give me a minute.' Flora squinted into the next window along and froze. Her stomach felt as if a hand had gripped her innards and twisted.

She straightened and took a step backwards. It was all there. The black-leaded range, the scrubbed pine table, even the rag rug on the floor she remembered from her dream. A door at the other side, though closed, she knew led to the rear garden. The china set on the tiny dresser was unfamiliar, as were the pots on the stove – but the room was the same. She had sat on that rug, rolled marbles on that grey flagstone floor. She could even recall the two-foot long crack in the largest slab of stone that sat in front of the leaded range.

'Are you all right, Miss Flora?' Tom's voice held impatience, as if he had asked the same question several times, and she had not heeded him.

A roaring filled her ears and she could feel again the scratch of her mother's skirt against her hands. The terror she had felt as a small child flooded back and she squeezed her eyes shut. 'This is where it happened.'

'Beg pardon?' Tom asked, a frown in his voice. 'Where what happened?'

She brushed past him and retraced her steps to the road, her hands shaking as she climbed back onto the gig. 'I-I have to get back to the Abbey.'

'That's what I've been saying this ten minutes since, Miss,' Tom murmured from behind her.

From the end of the deserted hallway came the low tone of a man's voice, followed by a nervous-sounding female one. Flora turned a corner and almost walked straight into the butler, Scrivens, who had backed Amy into a corner, trapping her by the servants' door. His dirty blond hair was in need of a comb, his close set eyes narrowed in anger.

'I never want to hear you mention that again.' He prodded her shoulder with the finger with each word.

'I would never gossip, sir. I only repeated what—' Amy broke off, her eyes widening as she caught sight of Flora over the man's shoulder.

Scrivens straightened, took a step back and drew himself up to his full height. His eyes when they met Flora's held a challenge but neither embarrassment nor remorse.

Flora stared him down, determined not to let him intimidate her. Long seconds passed and then he gave a slow dip of his head in a bow that was more insolent than polite, and murmured, 'Mrs Harrington,' before he pushed through the door and disappeared into the servants' quarters.

The door flapped gently behind him on oiled hinges as Flora took in the girl's flushed cheeks. 'What was that all about, Amy? He looked as if he was about to strike you.'

'It was nothing, Miss Flora, honestly.' Amy dropped her gaze, her teeth chewing her bottom lip as she hoisted the pile of linens higher in her arms. 'Just a difference of opinion is all. He doesn't like his orders being questioned.'

'It looked more than that. He sounded as if he were threatening you.'

'Not exactly.' Amy hesitated, as if debating whether or not to explain.

'You can trust me, I won't tell anyone,' Flora urged.

'He went somewhere on his day off last week and didn't come back 'til next day. He overheard me asking one of the maids where he went, just casual like, I didn't mean anything by it.'

The one thing her father never allowed in the servants' hall was bullying. It seemed his spirit had been forgotten already and if she could do something about it, she would. 'I would be happy to mention this to Lord Vaughn if you wish? I know he wouldn't allow it, he's a kind man and would be discreet—'

'Oh, no, Miss.' A flash of fear entered Amy's brown eyes. 'That would only make things worse. Mr Scrivens runs the servants' hall now. We all have to get used to his ways.' Her eyes darted in the direction the butler had taken, then back to Flora.

'Are you sure?' Frustration sharpened her tone. The man shouldn't be allowed to get away with treating the staff like that.

'I am. Miss. And it's kind of you, but well you'll be gone soon and I shall still be here. With Scrivens.'

'Yes, I see.' Reminded again of her father's absence, she chose not to linger on that thought, so quickly pushed on. 'Actually, I'm looking for Lady Vaughn. Do you happen to know where she is?'

'Her ladyship has gone into Cheltenham.' Amy looked about to push through the green baize door, then changed her mind and hurried at Flora's side as she strode the long hallway. 'Miss Flora.' Amy overtook her and halted in front of her, shifting the linens in her arms higher. 'Could you spare me a moment?'

'Could we do it other time, Amy, if you don't mind?' Her head still full of the white-painted lodge house which had stirred her most disturbing memories. The building was tucked behind high hedges and on a narrow back road she had rarely used, but how had she never realized it was there when she had lived at Cleeve Abbey for most of her life?

'Of course, Miss. Another time.' Amy sketched a curtsey and stepped aside to allow her to pass. She sighed and muttered to herself before turning back the way she had come.

Her air of dejection halted Flora outside the sitting room door. She was about to call Amy back when Jocasta called to her from inside the room.

'Is that you, Flora? I would know that purposeful stride anywhere.'

'Yes, it's me.' Flora stepped into the room and looked back over her shoulder, but Amy had gone.

'I'm playing lady of the house during Mama's absence.' Jocasta stood before a console table with ornamental gilt legs, a basket of assorted flowers beside her she was using to fill a heavy-bottomed porcelain vase decorated with Chinese symbols.

She held up a long-stemmed pink rose. 'Not that I'm making a very good job of this particular task.' She dropped a second flower back into the basket with a grimace and thrust a forefinger into her mouth. 'Beastly things keep attacking me,' she said round it. 'How's your morning been—' she broke off and frowned as she caught sight of Flora's face. 'What's wrong? You look as if you've encountered something awful.'

'Not exactly.' Flora paused, unable to summon words that wouldn't sound like an accusation. 'Jocasta, do you recall if my parents lived in an estate cottage before we moved into the attic apartment?'

'A cottage?' Jocasta stuffed flowers into the vase haphazardly, her eyes studiously averted. 'We have several, I believe. Which one would that be specifically?'

'It's more like a lodge.' Flora watched her mangle another rose into a mess of scattered petals, suspecting Jocasta knew exactly which one she meant. 'This one sparked a particular memory.' She plucked a magenta gerbera from the table and brought it to her nose. Despite the glaring pink colour and velvety petals, the bloom had little smell. 'I've seen it before.'

'There must be lots of cottages on the estate I know nothing about. We used to play in those meadows behind the stables, don't you remember?' Jocasta's voice took on a high-pitched, excited quality. 'Most likely you saw it then.'

The flower stem broke with a tiny snap, leaving Flora's fingers slick with water. She hadn't mentioned the cottage was behind the stables.

'It's almost time for luncheon.' Jocasta laid the scissors in her hand onto the hemp covering that protected the table. 'The men are in town and Mama won't be back in time to eat with us, so how about I ask Scrivens to serve ours on the terrace?' Abandoning the flowers, she skirted the table. 'We'll talk then. I promise.' Was it Flora's imagination or was there a deeper inflection to her words?

'That sounds lovely, thank you.' Flora would have to be patient a little longer.

The open-sided glass canopy attached to the terrace had been designed to reflect light, with its filigree ironwork, white-painted trellises and the matching chairs and tables scattered around the paved area. Manicured flowerbeds in the parterre below a set of shallow steps provided an expanse of soft green broken by white blooms. The only colour variation was Lady Venetia's rose garden beyond the hedge, where red, apricot, yellow and pink appeared in riotous contrast.

Flora debated whether or not she should mention to Jocasta the incident with Amy and the butler despite her promise, or respect the girl's wish to treat it as nothing. She pushed the thought away, conscious she couldn't solve everyone's problems, not with so many of her own to contend with.

Their luncheon was a cold collation of meats and delicately arranged salads and fruit perfect for the hot weather. Bees buzzed in the nearby flowers and occasionally flew close to the girls' faces, drawn by the sugar on the table.

Flora batted a particularly persistent drone away with her fan, having almost convinced herself Jocasta had forgotten her oblique promise to talk about the lodge. She was therefore surprised when she brought the subject up without prompting.

'Papa rented that cottage, lodge, or whatever it is, to some legal man who wanted to live out of town.' Jocasta concentrated on pouring iced water into two glasses. 'It had not been lived in for years, and the shrubbery was up to the roof until six months ago, which may explain why you've never noticed it before.'

'Possibly.'

Flora pushed her food round her plate with a fork, not fooled by Jocasta's causal tone. For someone who didn't know which cottage she meant, Jocasta certainly had plenty of details at her command.

'It's part of a memory I cannot place.'

'Maybe you once visited someone there when you were younger and the image has persisted?' Jocasta swirled her glass, ending the ice cubes into a tinkling frenzy.

'You don't believe that any more than I do.' Flora's patience snapped. She took a deep breath. 'The more I think about it, the more I am certain that I lived in that cottage when I was very small. It was there that someone, a man, hurt my mother in the kitchen. I remember every detail of that room, but I can't recall the man's face.' She stopped and looked away. 'Well, maybe not every detail. However, that scene features in disturbing dreams I have had throughout my childhood.'

'I never knew you had nightmares?' Jocasta's glass hit the table with a click. 'Why have you never mentioned them to me?'

'I don't know.' Flora shrugged. 'They were part of my life for as long as I can remember, so didn't strike me as worth mentioning. They're not so frequent now, in fact I hadn't had one for a while. Until my first night under this roof two days ago.'

'You mean, being here at Cleeve Abbey has brought them back?'

'It seems so.' She shrugged. 'Bunny thinks they will persist until I find out what happened to my mother eighteen years ago.' She hoped that to invoke her husband's name might make Jocasta more open as the two of them seemed to like one another.

'I don't know what to say, Flora.' Jocasta's

features twisted in what appeared to be an internal wrestle with her conscience. Her eyes closed briefly and she sighed. 'Look, I don't know as much as you think I do, but once, I heard Papa refer to the white lodge as "Lily's house". When I asked him about it, he said it was in the past. Over and done with. You know how people are with children. They expect a child's memories to be as short as their own.'

'They aren't.' Flora's breath hitched. Had Jocasta deliberately kept this from her? Or did she regard it as unimportant and not worth mentioning?

'No, and those dreams of yours are proof.' Jocasta plucked Flora's hand from her lap and massaged it gently, the facets of her diamond engagement ring winking as they caught the sunlight. 'I was very young at the time. Mama and Papa had returned from a trip, and I had missed them so much, I sneaked away from Nanny and hid behind a sofa in their room. I planned to jump out and surprise them, but they began arguing with my grandmother, which is why the episode stuck in my mind.'

Flora waited as Jocasta paused to take a sip of water. Her nerves tingling at the thought that, finally, she was about to hear something important.

'Grandmamma was perfectly calm and she didn't raise her voice once, but Papa did.' She lowered the glass and stared into it. 'He was shouting things like, "How could you leave Maguire to cope with the situation on his own? Is the child all right?"'

Is the child all right? A sudden breeze stirred the treetops and Flora shivered, though the sky remained clear.

'I'm sorry if you think I hid things from you, but at the time I didn't understand their significance.' Jocasta leaned closer, her expression sympathetic. 'Do you remember your mother at all?'

'Not very well. I know what she looked like from photographs Father gave me. I can even recall her voice, but I didn't know what sort of person she was.' She recalled her favourite picture was of Lily reclined on a lawn with her feet crossed at the ankles, smiling up at the camera from beneath a wide straw hat. The thought of that photograph now made her strangely uncomfortable, as if her memory of her mother, however small, had been tainted.

'You should speak to Mama, but she might not be willing to discuss it.'

'Why? I thought your mother liked mine.'

'I know, but – look.' Jocasta's pretty features twisted in anguish but did nothing to spoil her looks. 'When Mama married Papa, she was very conscious that her family were involved in trade, when Papa was from a long line of landowners. Very lucrative trade, but still trade. Papa didn't care a fig as theirs was a love match, but my grandparents did. Mama had a difficult time those first years trying to live up to them.'

'I understand, and in fact sympathize.' The

spectre of Beatrice Harrington loomed. 'But what has this to do with my mother?'

'Nothing, everything?' Jocasta hunched her shoulders. 'I don't know, I'm simply warning you it might not be easy. Mama may have pushed this incident you talk about, whatever it was, into the recesses of her mind. She does that a lot. If talking about your mother is abhorrent to her, she'll never tell you anything.'

'You could be right, though perhaps having something more solid would make her open up more. You make it sound hopeless.' Flora closed her fan and slapped it into her lap.

'Not necessarily. I'll see what I can do with Papa, though he's been distracted lately.' A frown appeared between her brows. 'Whenever I speak to him he looks straight through me as if he hasn't heard, so I make no promises.'

'I appreciate your help, whatever form it takes.' Flora slid her hand over Jocasta's on the table between them and squeezed. 'I'm grateful to have someone on my side other than Bunny.' Despite Jocasta's occasional reticence, Flora felt she wasn't keeping things from her deliberately. Jocasta appeared as confused about what had happened to Lily Maguire as she was.

'Nonsense, we're friends aren't we? Now, tell me more about this dream you keep having.'

CHAPTER 13

Flora declined Jocasta's invitation to visit friends in Clayton village that afternoon, with the excuse she had a lot to think about. She stood on the front drive and watched Jocasta expertly negotiate the gig with one hand on the reins, the other raised in a cheery wave.

Smiling at the girl's irrepressible nature, Flora turned back to the house, just in time to see Mr McCallum emerge from the wicket gate at the entrance to the stable block.

'Good afternoon, Mr McCallum,' Flora greeted him.

'I'm delighted to see you're still talking to me, Mrs Harrington.' His boots crunched on gravel as he strode towards her. His tweed cap and riding jacket made him look every inch the country gentleman. 'I thought perhaps you still held my brewery responsible for the epidemic after the fête.'

'Please call me Flora, and I do apologize for interrogating you the other night. It was unforgiveable of me, but I'm still reeling from my father's death.' She paused beside the fountain and waited for him to join her. She adopted her most congenial smile and the tone to go with it, hoping she sounded convincing, because something told her there was still a great deal to discover about the handsome Mr McCallum and his brewery. The newspaper clippings about another brewery her father kept weren't some odd coincidence.

'To lose someone is never easy.' His voice softened as he neared her. 'Especially when their demise is sudden and unexpected.' He raised a foot to the stone border of the fountain in the middle of the drive, his riding crop gently tapping his palm. 'He was a determined man, your father.'

'Determined is a good description of him. I mean, of how he used to be.' She rubbed at the tight feeling in her midriff that always intruded, still unable to believe she would never see him again. 'What brings you back at the Abbey so soon, Mr McCallum?'

'I was out for a ride on Cleeve Common and my horse cast a shoe.' He aimed his crop over his shoulder at the stables behind him. 'Lord Vaughn mentioned the farrier would be here all day, so I took advantage of his open invitation to use his services.'

'Must have been a hard ride to cause that?' Flora recalled the rocky path in the wood that was difficult to negotiate on foot, let alone horseback. She fell into step beside him as he strolled the drive towards the road.

'Not by me,' his attractive laugh rang out. 'Mrs

Mountjoy borrowed the animal last, though I doubt she pays much attention to such details. The shoe hung on by one nail and couldn't be left.' He caught Flora's bemused glance and laughed. 'Ah, I see gossip about myself and the lady has reached you?' Flora's cheeks heated and he laughed again. 'I confess I was flattered by her attentions when I first came to live here. She too was new to the area, and introduced me into her circle. However, she sought a more permanent arrangement between us, which I did not.'

'You and Mrs Mountjoy are still on speaking terms?' If what Jocasta had said about the end of their liaison having been less than amicable, his easy generosity came as a surprise.

'Of course.' His eyes met hers in surprised candour. 'We're civilized people after all. Besides, I've learned not to take offence at the chatter of local gossips. My name has been linked with more than one female since I arrived, whether accurate or not.'

At the sound of wheels on gravel, his hand shot out and grasped her arm. He hauled her onto the grass verge, just as a tradesman's horse and cart swept past them, sending a spray of tiny stones over her shoes.

'Goodness, that was close.' She inhaled a shocked breath.

He frowned at the receding cart as it continued on toward the house. 'Most likely he didn't see us as he came round the bend.'

Sudden warmth spread into Flora's face as she realized he hadn't released her arm. She eased away from him and continued walking, but if he noticed her embarrassment he gave no sign. 'Do you prefer the bachelor life, Mr McCallum?'

'Um-I'm a widower, actually.' His frown deepened and he poked the toe of one boot fiercely at a clump of roughened grass. 'When my wife died I needed a fresh start and decided to leave the north behind.'

'I'm very sorry.' Until he was safely married again, Flora suspected he would forever have to fend off the attentions of women like Caroline Mountjoy.

'I respected your father, Mrs Harrington.' He clasped his hands behind his back, head bent. 'I was sorry to hear what happened to him.'

She was about to ask him to call her Flora, but changed her mind in case it might cross an invisible barrier. Instead she decided to pursue the subject Mr McCallum had raised. 'I'm still trying to discover the exact circumstances of the accident, but few people appear to know much.' She ducked her head beneath a low branch. 'To your knowledge, did my father often go out alone on horseback?' Flora turned toward him, a hand raised to her eyes against the sun's glare.

'I couldn't say.' He took the left-hand path that would bring them back to the house and Flora fell into step beside him. 'Did you know that the man who died after the fête once worked for Lord

Vaughn's grandfather? He trained your father when he first came here.'

'Mr Hendry?' Flora recalled a craggy face and the stooped walk of an old man she saw occasionally in the village. 'I didn't realize that. Poor man.'

'I believe it was because of Henry your father was so keen to unearth the reason for the men's illness.'

'I don't suppose you happen to know where my father went on the day he died?' Flora clasped her hands behind her back, her skirt rustling as she walked. It was too hot to wear black but she saw it as a sort of penance. A small one to endure to acknowledge his life.

'I sense you suspect there was more to his death than you have been told?' He halted and turned toward her, one brow raised.

'That's the point. I don't know. I went to Bailey Wood this morning, to take a look at where he died. It's quite near where you live I'm told.' His eyes narrowed and fearing she had insulted him, added, 'I'm sorry, I don't mean to imply anything. My husband is of the opinion I'm searching for shadows where there aren't any.'

'Perhaps you should listen to him, although it's quite normal to try and apportion blame when someone dies.' He extended his elbow and she slid her arm through his and set off again along the path that circled the wide front drive. 'If it puts your mind at rest,' he said gently, 'as far as I'm aware, Maguire didn't come anywhere near my house. In fact I wasn't even there. I dined at the Abbey that night, as did Caroline Mountjoy. We knew nothing about the accident until the following morning.'

'I see,' and again I apologize for asking so many questions. I'm doing it with everyone I meet at the moment and I'm sure they are becoming annoyed with me. After all, everybody keeps telling me what a terrible accident it was, so why can't I just accept it?'

'We all look for reasons when we have lost someone. There's no logic to it.'

'No, there isn't. Thank you for your understanding.' He certainly said all the right things, though something about his story struck her as a little too perfect, with no hesitation or having to think about his actions that night.

She glanced sideways and caught his eye and groaned inwardly. What was wrong with her? When had she stopped trusting people? He had been perfectly civil and not baulked once at her prying. If Bunny were here he would be nudging her by now to be more discreet.

'If you're still concerned, Flora,' Mr McCallum said after a moment. 'You could always ask Dr Fairbrother. I'm sure he could answer any questions you may have.'

'I had considered doing just that, but I'm not sure how to approach him.'

'Directly, would be my advice.' He slanted a

sideways look at her, a gleam in in his eye. 'What are your plans for this afternoon?'

Flora shrugged. 'Bunny's in Cheltenham with Mr Osborne and not due back for a while. I suppose I'm stranded here.'

'Then if you'll permit, I would be more than happy to escort you into town to see the good doctor. His consulting rooms are at the Sandford Road Hospital. That's where—'

'The town mortuary is,' Flora finished for him. In some strange way, should the doctor tell her nothing new, being physically close to her father somehow appealed. 'We have no carriage at our disposal and your horse is with the farrier.'

'Then we'll take the tram.'

'The tram?' Flora blinked, surprised. 'You know I had forgotten about those. The service had not been implemented when I lived here.' Dare she travel on a public tram with a virtual stranger, alone?

'Come now.' His eyes took on a teasing glint. 'Are you worried about your reputation? Or is it the tram which makes you hesitate? I assure you they are quite safe.'

'We do have them in Richmond,' she replied, though reluctant to admit she had never actually ridden on one. Beatrice Harrington regarded them as conveyances for the lower orders and always insisted Flora took their carriage. 'What about your luncheon appointment?'

'That was with my lawyer. He sent a note round first thing cancelling. So I'm at your disposal.'

'Wouldn't you need to change?' She indicated his riding clothes.

'One thing I have learned since living in the country, my dear Flora, is that riding attire is accepted everywhere.'

Flora hesitated, but his invitation became more attractive by the second and as he had covered all her reasons for not going into town, perhaps now was as good a time as any to confront the doctor.

'The tram stop is a mere three minutes' walk from here,' he went on when she didn't respond, 'We could be in Cheltenham and back before tea time.'

'I'll fetch my parasol.'

Flora stared at the vehicle as it whirred to a gentle halt beside them, an elongated box curved at the front and decorated with a gold trim. Set below the number seven picked out in gold, sat a round lamp that resembled a single eye.

'Where would you like to sit?' Mr McCallum asked as he helped her up the first two metal steps onto the platform.

A man in a military-style uniformed jacket with a double row of brass buttons set in a long 'v' from shoulder to hip greeted them from the open platform; his kepi style bearing the word 'Motorman' in brass letters above the peak.

Mr McCallum purchased their tickets from another man with the word 'Conductor' picked out in the same brass script on his cap, tucked them into his waistcoat pocket, his head inclined to indicate she lead the way.

'I've never seen a single storey tram before,' Flora said as they moved to the rear of the carriage. 'The ones I've seen in town have two stories.' She chose one of the upholstered seats at the rear beside a window. The seat wasn't very comfortable, the upholstery thin and the back very upright, making her hope the journey wouldn't take too long.

'Ah, only single cars are allowed on the Cleeve Hill run as it's so steep. They discovered that after an accident on the trial run. The car overturned and two engineers were killed.'

'And you didn't think to mention that before you invited me?' She gaped, horrified.

He waved her off. 'Past history. Since the single storey rule it's proved extremely safe. In fact it's so popular, the company plans to expand into Leckhampton on the other side of town next year.'

'How does it work without horses? Do they use petrol like motor cars?'

'These are electric cars imported from America by the Cheltenham and Cleeve Tramway. Did you notice that long metal handle at the front? Electricity flows through that from those overhead wires,' he said, sliding onto the bench seat beside her.

'I hope it's as safe as you say.' She peered through the window on her right to were the wires ran overhead. She had only recently got used to the idea of electric lights Bunny has installed in the house. 'It's not very full,' she said, mainly to hide her nervousness. Only three other passengers occupied the bench seats, none of them women.

'Not at this time of day. You wait until the shops and businesses close and the workers set off home to the outlying villages. You'll be lucky to find standing room only then.'

A sharp, ting-tang' sounded and Flora jumped, grabbed the rail on the back of the seat in front, her breath held as the tram car began moved off. As she acknowledged that their progress would be more a sedate trundle than careening down the hill at breakneck speed, she relaxed and enjoyed the ride. The height of the car enabled her to see over the hedges and into garden walls as they passed through the pretty high street of Prestbury village through places she wouldn't normally see as the tram stopped at intervals to allow passengers on and off.

'You seem to have settled in Gloucestershire quite well, Mr McCallum.' She met his steady gaze, roving his features as she decided he really was a most attractive man; a conclusion which sent heat into her face. What was she doing, exchanging flirtatious looks with a man other than Bunny?

'You lived at the Abbey for quite a while, I believe, Flora?' he said, drawing her attention from the window.

'Most of my life,' Flora replied.

'The family must think very highly of you, I

doubt many former servants are treated so well.'
She shot him a hard look and he added, 'Not that
you were a servant – as such.'

'Quite.' She pulled her mouth into a smile which
she knew didn't reach her eyes and turned back
to the window, unsure whether or not he had
intended to insult her. Or perhaps she was being
too sensitive?

'I was raised with their daughters,' Flora said
after a moment. 'It wasn't until I was older that I
became Eddy's governess.'

'The Vaughn's eldest daughter married well, I
heard. An American wasn't it?'

Flora turned her head a fraction to study his
face, curious as to where the question came from?
Her years as a governess had taught her caution
where discussing her employers was concerned.
However his face held none of the keen interest
in her answer, so he must simply be keeping the
conversation going.

'Lady Amelia, and yes she lives there now. I
accompanied them to New York for the wedding.'

'My goodness, a privilege indeed. How did you
like America?'

'New York is a fascinating city with such wide
streets and some amazing houses. They call their
holiday mansions "cottages" when they are as large
as Buckingham Palace.' She debated whether to
mention that she met Bunny on the voyage home,
but perhaps that was too much information on a
second meeting.

Near the outskirts of town, the road flattened out between terraces of elegant white stone villas with neat front gardens set behind wrought-iron railings.

Flora returned the enthusiastic waves of pedestrians as they passed, while small girls in pinafores smiled and pointed at the tram from the side of the road, demonstrating it was still a relatively new innovation to the town.

The driver took the wide curve that took them past the gates to Pittville Park with its ornamental arch built to celebrate the late Queen's jubilee. The roads grew busier, as carts and carriages and walkers crossed the metal lines of the tramcar. Flora winced as a horse-drawn vehicle spilled through the gate onto the road in front of them and veered alarmingly into their path but was steered expertly away before disastrous contact was made. The tram slowed as it passed through the main High Street and out again, finally coasting to a stop on Sandford Road, where Flora released a held breath that they had arrived safely.

'That was quite an experience, Mr McCallum, and much quicker than travelling by horse and cart,' Flora said as he helped her down the steps. 'I'm amazed at how reckless some carriages are, but despite all that, I did enjoy the ride.' She harboured a slight satisfaction at the look on Beatrice's face when she reached home and recounted her adventure.

'I'm glad.' He indicated a solid honey-coloured

building with pillared portico over a short flight of steps, with two square wings on either side. 'The General Hospital and Dispensary is along there. I believe the good doctor would—' he broke off, glanced past her shoulder and froze. Flora turned to where Bunny emerged from a carriage and four that had halted on the road alongside them.

CHAPTER 14

'Goodness, where did you come from?' Flora summoned an uneasy smile that hovered between pleasure and embarrassment. 'I imagined you would be on your way back to Cleeve Abbey by now.'

'We were, actually.' Flora caught the hard line of his mouth as he returned Mr McCallum's handshake. 'Osborne insisted I see the new transport system.' He indicated where William sat on the seat behind him. 'You can imagine my surprise when I spotted my wife being assisted out of a tram when I thought you were at Cleeve Abbey.' The firm set of his jaw meant she had some apologizing to do, but it would have to wait.

'Mr McCallum was kind enough to take pity on me while you and William went off to look at motor cars.' Flora squeezed his arm as a warning not to sound quite so abrasive, but if he noticed it he gave no sign.

William watched from the carriage, his upper body angled forward through the open door, an amused smirk tugging at his mouth.

'Most kind of you, McCallum.' Bunny's manner

teetered on the edge of politeness. He gave the road a swift, enquiring glance. 'I didn't realize there were any spas or teashops along this road.'

'Actually, we were on our way to the hospital.' McCallum met Bunny's gaze with amusement. 'Flora expressed a wish to discuss her father's case with Dr Fairbrother.'

'Case, Flora?' Bunny inflected criticism into two words. 'I thought we had agreed to await the inquest?' He pointedly removed Flora's hand from McCallum's arm and tucked it beneath his own. 'Thank you, McCallum, I shall take charge of my wife now.'

'What's all this?' William alighted the carriage, an enquiring look on his face.

'It's nothing.' Flora said. 'The inquest will be held at the mortuary, I'm told, and well—'

'Oh quite.' William flushed and stared at each of them in turn. 'Though I expect they have a separate room for the proceedings. It won't be in the actual – um . . .'

'I realize that,' Flora reassured him.

William coughed into a fist. 'Well then, what say I find a local hostelry and take some refreshment while I wait for you both? Care to join me, McCallum?' He rubbed his hands together, his cheerful demeanour going some way to diffuse the fact Mr McCallum and Bunny had reverted to a staring match.

'Oh no, please don't wait for us.' Her face flamed at being the subject of Bunny's overt jealousy. 'I have no idea how long we shall be. We can take the tramcar back. Thank you, Mr McCallum. You've been the perfect gentleman.'

'It's been a pleasure, Flora. I hope we will meet again soon.' He tipped his cap and followed William back to the carriage. 'I'd like to take you up on that, Osborne. Where shall we go?'

'I thought the Queen's,' William replied, closing the door on the two of them.

Flora watched the carriage move off with a set jaw, furious at Bunny for having behaved so badly. Though at the same time she rather liked the fact he was so possessive. He had never demonstrated such feelings before. Perhaps now he would understand what it was like for her when pretty women blushed and flirted with him in her presence. Unsure which emotion was uppermost in her head, she kept her mouth firmly shut.

'Why didn't you tell me you wanted to come to the hospital?' Bunny performed an about-turn and changed sides, which put him on the outer side of the road. 'I would have accompanied you.' Even when he was annoyed with her, Bunny always put her welfare first.

'Because I hadn't made up my mind it would be today.' She grasped his arm tighter as they approached the wrought-iron gates. 'You gave me the impression you saw it as a fruitless exercise. And Mr McCallum offered.' Flora peered up at him from beneath her hat brim. 'Do I have Mr McCallum to thank for your change of heart?'

'I haven't changed my heart – I mean my mind. I can only hope that whatever the doctor has to say will finally put your mind at rest. Anyway, it's too late to reason with you now. We're here.'

They climbed a short flight of steps set between Doric pillars three storeys high, where a uniformed porter admitted them into a double-height entrance hall that smelled of carbolic soap, disinfectant and decayed flowers.

Bunny explained his request to a man seated behind an oversized oak desk, and they were directed to the end of a cavernous corridor with a barrel ceiling; the antiseptic smell worsening with each step.

A middle-aged nurse with an uncompromising expression and ferret-sharp eyes glared at them from a much smaller desk set before another set of double doors. Her expression unchanged when Bunny repeated his request.

'I'll enquire as to whether the doctor is available to see you,' she said, her tone implying she harboured grave doubts as to the possibility. 'Wait here.' She sniffed and disappeared through the double doors.

A sign above their heads read 'Mortuary' in black letters on a white board. Flora's knees buckled, and she might have fallen had not Bunny's arm been clamped hard round her waist.

'Are you sure about this?' he asked.

'Very sure. I simply hate the smell of disinfectant.'

She approached a row of wheel back chairs against a wall painted a shiny bilious green, and sat.

Nurses in frilled caps and starched white aprons tied at the back into large bows marched past them.

'I take it this jaunt wasn't an arrangement you made with McCallum at dinner the other night?' Bunny angled his head toward her, one brow raised.

'Of course not.' Her teasing laugh fell flat when he did not return her smile. 'He was merely being, well—'

'Flirtatious, devious, manipulative, enigmatic? Do feel free to stop me when I reach the correct word.'

'Hush. He's none of those things, and you were very abrupt with him just now.'

'Is this the same Mr McCallum whom you thought may have poisoned an entire garden fête with his beer?'

'If you recall, I entertained other possibilities as well as that one. And if I'm not mistaken, you left that dinner the other night with a rather positive impression of McCallum yourself,' She broke off as a porter in beige overalls approached pushing a trolley.

'I concede that, he did come across as the perfect guest. Although,' he said in the tone of someone who had more to add. 'William happened to let slip an interesting snippet about your escort over luncheon.'

Flora held her breath as the porter got closer,

a squeaky wheel on the trolley protesting with each turn as she tried not to imagine what lay beneath the sheet. 'Oh, what was that?' He drew level and when she saw the contraption was empty, she closed her eyes and exhaled, relieved.

'That Mr McCallum reputedly,' Bunny drew the words out slowly, 'conducted an affair with that girl who went missing.'

Flora jerked her head round and stared at him. 'Betsy Mason?'

'The very same.'

The door swung open and crashed against the wall, halting their conversation. The same nurse as before beckoned to them with an upraised finger. 'Dr Fairbrother will see you now.'

Her feet slapped against the rubber floor as she led them into a room lined with bookshelves crammed with leather-bound ancient tomes, their spines cracked and faded from long handling. A massive oak desk, its surface almost invisible beneath piles of papers, occupied the centre of the floor, with barely space between it and the shelves. The far wall contained two glass-fronted cabinets filed with medical instruments which Flora tried not to examine too closely.

Bunny held out a wheel back chair, identical to the ones in the hallway, and bade her sit. He was in the process of taking the other when the door opened to admit a slightly plump man with sparse silver hair combed straight back over his head, not thick enough to conceal his pink scalp.

'My name's Dr Fairbrother.' He acknowledged them both with individual nods before taking the scuffed leather chair on the far side of the desk. 'How may I be of assistance? Though I might warn you at the outset,' he balanced a pair of gold rimmed pince nez on his snub nose, 'I only treat couples who have been unsuccessful in conceiving for at least two years.'

'I assure you we haven't—'

'That isn't why were are here—'

Bunny and Flora responded together.

At these vehement denials, Dr Fairbrother gave a start, his round eyes blinking behind the thick lenses. He folded his hands on the desk and nodded gently while Bunny explained the purpose of their visit and Flora's relationship to Riordan Maguire.

'Ah yes, of course.' He cleared his through when Bunny had finished. 'Allow me to offer my condolences, Mrs Harrington. I wish more could have been done.' He removed the pince nez, and placed them on top of a pile of papers, then folded both hands together. 'What do you wish to know?'

'We—' they began simultaneously, broke off and exchanged a pained look.

'I wish to know how my father died,' Flora began again. 'I was told he fell from his horse and hit his head.'

'That's precisely my conclusion.' He leaned back in his chair, his bemused smile indicating there was nothing else to say.

'I need more than that,' Flora persisted. 'I-we wish to know the nature of his injuries.'

'Mrs Harrington,' Dr Fairbrother addressed her as if she were a small child, 'I'm aware the deceased was your parent, and in my experience, relatives often feel the need to seek explanations other than the obvious for an unexpected death. However, to describe Mr Maguire's actual injuries in detail would be too distressing for a young female. In all conscience I cannot do it.'

'My gender aside, sir,' Flora said through gritted teeth, her patience growing thin, 'I wish to know what actually killed him?'

'I'm not sure what it is you wish me to say.' The doctor blinked behind lenses that magnified his gooseberry-coloured eyes to alarming proportions.

'If I knew what I wanted you to say, I wouldn't be here.' Flora gripped her closed parasol to stop the tremble in her hand.

'Flora.' Bunny placed a warning hand on her forearm.

'I'm sorry, I didn't mean to be rude.' Flora exhaled slowly through pursed lips. 'I'm not very comfortable in hospitals.' She pasted on a smile. 'Dr Fairbrother, what I have been told amounts to little more than hearsay and rumour. I would be reassured to hear specific details from a professional gentleman of your obvious standing.'

He puffed up his unimpressive chest at this blatant flattery. 'Quite understandable, my dear. Suffice it to say, Riordan Maguire fell or was thrown from his mount and sustained injuries from the fall itself and from the horse, which possibly in its panic to get away, trampled him.'

'What sort of injuries were they?' Flora persisted. 'Impact, crush or force?'

He blinked in surprise, his gaze going straight to Bunny as if he sought help. 'Er, well, there was evidence of impact injury to his ribs.'

'What about his head?' Her hands clenched in her lap so hard, they began to cramp. Although it pained her to hear about her father's injuries and imagining the fear and pain of his last moments, she needed to know everything or she would never come to terms with his death.

'His skull contacted with a rock which caused catastrophic injuries.'

'Did you attend the scene, Doctor? And see the actual place where he fell?' Flora leaned forward in her chair. 'You see, I'm confused as to why anyone would take a horse through that particular area. The ground is rocky and steep in places and the trees are close together. Not easy terrain for a horse.' *Or a rider with a painful hip.*

'You are correct about the wood, and I admit I was also surprised he didn't use the clearer track farther up the incline.'

'Why were you surprised?' Bunny asked.

'Well, I examined him quite soon after he was found, but could find no reason why his horse would throw him in such a secluded area away from the road.'

'That thought occurred to me too.' Flora recalled the short but arduous trek Tom had taken her through the thick woodland.

'Some horses shy if a bird flies out of a tree,' Bunny said. 'Was there anything else you didn't expect, Doctor?'

'Something I did expect actually. Blood. There was very little on the ground and I couldn't see any rocks with bloodstains on. I looked for one to help me gauge the level of impact but couldn't find any.'

'Did it rain that evening?' Bunny asked. 'Between him being reported missing and finding him perhaps?'

'Not a drop for a couple of weeks. The ground was quite dry, almost parched.'

'Why do you think there was no sign of any blood?' Flora worried a thumbnail with her teeth, trying not to imagine her father lying on the ground, bleeding. 'Not even on the rocks where he fell?'

'I have no idea, but it was almost dark by then, so a bloodstain might have been there but I missed it.'

'Could a stray hoof have caused the head injury as opposed to a rock?' Bunny asked.

'Quite possibly.' Dr Fairbrother blew a breath between his pursed lips as if agitated by their questions. 'Though there were no hoof marks on his skull. Or it might have been a fallen tree trunk that caused it.'

'If that was the case, wouldn't traces of bark be left in the wound? Or indeed rock, if that had been the cause?' Flora was rapidly losing patience. The doctor appeared content to accept whatever explanation was presented, as if he were uninterested in the real cause. Or didn't wish to voice too strong an opinion in case it was challenged later.

'Er— well, I didn't actually – er—' He propped his elbows on his desk and steepled his fingers against his lips like a headmaster about to deliver a lecture. 'If it's any consolation, Mrs Harrington, in my opinion, his death came quickly. One of his ribs fractured and punctured his heart. I doubt he suffered much, if at all.'

Flora swallowed, not liking his use of the word 'much'. 'That's some comfort, Dr Fairbrother.' *Though not much.* Flora's throat burned with emotion, but she recovered quickly, unwilling to display female sensibilities in front of this man. Not when it would prove him right.

'I'll give my full report at the inquest,' he split a slow look between them. 'I gather you'll both be present?'

'We shall.' Flora eased forward in her chair. 'One other thing, Dr Fairbrother, did my father ask you about the men who became sick after the summer fête?'

'He did indeed.' The doctor straightened, suddenly wary. 'He had some strange notion about them having been poisoned. He even tried to show me some old newspaper articles which he appeared to regard as relevant.'

'You didn't agree, I take it?'

'I diagnosed their symptoms as peripheral neuritis, nothing more. A not uncommon ailment among the working classes.'

'Did you actually read the report my father showed you?' Flora demanded, ignoring Bunny's firm squeeze of her forearm. The more the man talked, the less she thought of his abilities.

He shifted in his seat. 'I-uh gave it some cursory attention and found the report inconclusive.'

'Why?' Bunny asked.

'The amount of arsenic found in the Manchester beer did not exceed four parts per million. That's hardly enough to constitute poisoning. It could have come from the water used in brewing.'

'Maybe that was the case in Manchester, but there might have been more on this occasion. Did you test the beer served at the fête?' Flora asked, determined not to let the man dismiss her the way he had her father.

He released a long sigh. 'By the time Maguire came to me, the remainder had been thrown away. Besides, the men recovered, so whatever the cause is not a matter for alarm now.'

'Mr Hendry didn't recover,' Flora said. 'He died.'

'My dear,' Dr Fairbrother extended both hands and smiled, 'the man had chronic bronchitis and was over eighty.'

Flora opened her mouth and closed it again. This was getting them nowhere.

'Is that all?' The doctor slapped both palms on

the desk and stood, indicating the interview was at an end.

'May we see the body?' Bunny asked suddenly.

Flora turned her head and stared at him as pride surged through her. He was taking her misgivings seriously after all.

'That's most irregular, Mr Harrington.' Dr Fairbrother blinked. 'Relatives normally view the bodies at the chapel of rest. This is a medical establishment and not conducive to, well—' He picked up the pince nez and polished the lenses with a scrap of cloth.

'Even so,' Bunny said, louder this time. 'If I saw his injuries for myself, I could reassure my wife that no doubt exists. And with her mind at rest, she won't bother you again.'

Flora's heart leapt, aware the conversation had taken a turn which had surprised Bunny and now, wanting answers for himself, he had taken on a task he knew she would find too distressing. A demand she thought had been made on impulse, while the reality was far less palatable. Silently she thanked him for stepping to act for her.

'Er, yes I see. Mr Harrington.' Dr Fairbrother started down at his desk for a moment as if coming to a decision. 'I shall comply on this occasion, provided of course that your wife remains here.'

Bunny followed the doctor through the same door the doctor had arrived from. At the last second before it closed behind him, he turned back and gave her a reassuring look.

She mouthed a silent thank you, to which he nodded again.

A moment later, the sour-faced nurse returned. 'The Doctor has requested that I offer you tea,' she said, with barely concealed resentment; the task evidently too menial for her capabilities.

'Thank you, but no,' Flora said.

'Very well.' The woman sniffed as if having offered such a kindness did not deserve rejection, and withdrew.

Left alone again, Flora paced the floor, trying not to imagine what Bunny was looking at. Despite her resolve, lurid images crept into her mind and she tugged at the fringe of her parasol until the stitches gave way.

After what seemed an eternity, Bunny returned alone.

Flora opened her mouth to ask him a question, but before she had uttered a word, he gripped her arm and guided her along the hallway, his pace forcing her into a brisk stride toward the main doors.

'He was right not to let you come into the morgue,' Bunny said, his face grim. 'It's no place for you, or for any woman.'

The sun's hard glare after the gloomy building as they stepped outside made Flora shield her eyes with a hand. 'I'll debate the role of women within the medical profession with you another time. Now if you'll tell me what you saw in there.'

He exhaled a long breath before he answered. 'I

believe the good doctor missed something.' He slowed to a leisurely stroll as they sauntered to the Sandford Road tram stop.

'That's hardly surprising. Did you see how thick those lenses were and that pronounced squint? I doubt he would recognize either of us from twenty feet,' Flora said, partly to delay what he was about to tell her.

Despite her quest for the truth, now it came to it she asked herself if she really wanted to know. However he died, her father wasn't coming back.

'I'm sorry I made you do this,' she said on impulse, aware she had forced his hand where this visit was concerned. Bunny had only accompanied her to prevent Mr McCallum doing so. 'I really appreciate that you didn't simply take a brief look so you could say everything was as expected.'

'I forgive you.' He took her hand in his. 'If you'll forgive me for treating your instincts as emotional imaginings.'

'Of course, always.'

'Only I'm now convinced your father was murdered.'

CHAPTER 15

Despite the heat of the afternoon, a chill entered Flora's veins and spread through her limbs like ice water. The busy street tilted around her and she hardly noticed the arrival of the tram, submitting without a murmur when Bunny ushered her onto the platform and into a seat on the tramcar. She waited until the conductor rang the bell and the carriage set off before she could trust herself to speak.

'Tell me what you saw, Bunny,' she forced the words though a dry throat.

'I shouldn't have blurted it out like that, I'm so sorry. You turned so pale just now I thought you were about to faint.' His hand crept into her lap and grasped hers.

'I know I've been pushing everyone to give me answers, but deep down I wanted to be proved wrong, that this really was a random accident. Now I have to face the fact someone deliberately hurt my father, possibly someone he knew, dealt with every day of his life. Someone who professed to be his friend.'

The word 'murdered' repeated in her head as

the tram's familiar whine accompanied its steady progress through town.

'Are you sure you are ready to hear the details?' Bunny said.

'Not really, but I must.' She gripped his hand hard and gestured for him to continue.

'Everything Dr Fairbrother said was true.' He bent toward her so the other passengers scattered on the row of seats on either side of them could not hear. 'An open head injury and impact damage to his chest. Three days of lying in a cold room enabled the bruises to come out, so the hoof prints showed up more clearly.'

Flora squeezed her eyes shut against sudden dizziness. Never had she imagined they would discussing her own father in such a cold, dispassionate way. It felt like a betrayal.

'Some of the hoof prints were smaller than others.' Bunny drew his finger in circles on the pad at the base of her thumb. 'The difference was small but plain to see. The larger ones looked careless, the others were sharper, more even.'

'And that means what?' She was sure she knew, but needed him to say it aloud.

'That he was trampled. Deliberately.'

'I thought horses wouldn't stamp on a body on the ground if they could help it,' Flora's voice rose slightly with the burn of tears in her throat.

'Not as a rule, although I've known a badly disciplined horse can be aggressive enough to hurt a man. An ill-treated one might also behave that way.'

223

'Diabolus isn't aggressive and he's been well schooled.'

'Flora, two horses made those marks. One to get away and the other—' He laced his fingers with hers and squeezed.

Someone was with Father when he died, and who had probably killed him.

'Did you put that to Dr Fairbrother?'

'I tried, but he stands by his professional opinion, that Mr Maguire's horse caused the injuries.'

'How can he say that?' Several curious looks turned her way and she lowered her voice to a whisper. 'If the hoof prints were different sizes?'

'He thinks it's open to interpretation. He's a stubborn man, I'm afraid.'

'If I become ill while we are here, do not summon that man to examine me,' she snapped, then inhaled slowly as blood coursed through her thighs into her stomach, turning the sudden chill into an uncomfortable heat. 'In fact, if I so much as cut my finger, I forbid you to call him.' She could feel her hysteria rising.

'Understood.' A hint of a smile tugged at his mouth which faded when he examined her face. 'I'm so sorry to bring this to you, but you aren't a coward, Flora. I know you wanted the truth above all.'

'And now I have it. Serves me right for being so stubborn because there's nothing I can do to bring him back.' *Father was murdered. Someone deliberately trampled him – it was the only explanation that made sense.* She scrambled for a handkerchief and dabbed at her wet eyes. 'He's been taken from me, Bunny. He shouldn't be dead, it wasn't his time.'

'What do you want to do now?' He tucked a strand of hair behind her ear.

'I'm not sure what we can do.' She leaned her head against him, dislodging her straw hat. 'Dr Fairbrother will simply give his blinkered opinion at the inquest and the whole matter will be forgotten.' She slanted a sideways look up at him. 'Could we get another medical opinion?'

'Possibly, but not before the inquest.' She started to protest and he pressed a finger to her lips. 'Coroner's verdicts can be overturned with new evidence.'

That was some sort of consolation, though not much.

They had reached the Prestbury Road and its uniform terrace of tall, square houses with iron-work balconies. The neat gardens with their multi-coloured flowers in boxes and beds blurred into a kaleidoscope of colour as tears continued to spill onto her cheeks.

Whoever killed Riordan Maguire would pay for what they did. She would make sure of that.

Flora barely spoke during the two-hundred-yard walk back to the Abbey from the tram stop, where the entire town lay out below them like toy bricks scattered on a blanket. When the gates came into view, memory returned and she clamped a hand on Bunny's arm and jerked him backwards. 'The cottage!'

'What cottage?' He peered at her over his spectacles.

'I had completely forgotten. I found the cottage from my dream. It's right here, on the estate.'

'Are you sure?' He frowned, then his face instantly cleared. 'I'm sorry, of course you are. Is it close by?'

'Yes, and no.' Flora increased her stride along the drive back to the house so he had to hurry to keep up with her. 'It's on the far side of the stables down a rarely used lane. Well, rarely used by me anyway. Tom said it was a shortcut when he drove us back from Bailey Wood. I'd take you there now, but we ought to get back and change for dinner.'

'I would like to see it, especially if you think you once lived there when you were small.'

'I can't be sure.' Flora gave this some thought as they climbed the front steps and pushed open the main door. 'I was certain when I saw it that it had once been home, but I cannot find anything else out about it. Jocasta wasn't much help. I know something happened there which affected me enough to recur in my dreams for all these years.'

'You would think someone here at the Abbey must know what happened.' Bunny retrieved a letter from the hall table as they passed, their climb up to the second floor accompanied by the sonorous clang of the dressing bell in the hall below.

'Someone must. I just have to find out who.' Flora's mouth watered at the thought of dinner and she hoped she could last another hour without her stomach grumbling.

Before entering the bedroom, Flora paused in her father's sitting room and rested a hand on the backrest of the right hand wing chair set before the tiny iron fireplace. Her father's chair. A clear memory returned of the thousands of times he had sat with his head tilted back against the upholstery. He had always been such a gentle man, self-contained and firm, but without a malicious bone in him. Who would want to murder him? And why?

'We'll find out what happened, Flora,' Bunny said, guessing her thoughts, his eyes sad but determined. He stood at the open bedroom door and shrugged out of his jacket.

'I hate to think someone on the estate might be responsible. I lived here all my life. Suppose it's someone I know?' Flora took a deep breath and removed her hand from the chair, then went to join him. 'No matter how unsavoury, we have to find out the truth.' She turned her back to him so he could undo the row of buttons on her dress.

'The alternative is that we ignore those newspaper clippings and write off the second set of hoof prints. Neither of which I can see you agreeing to.'

He replaced his glasses, tore open the letter he had collected in the hallway and gave the pages a brief scan and frowned.

She came to stand behind him, her hands on his shoulders. 'Is your mother well?' she asked, recognizing her mother-in-law's bold script on the discarded envelope.

He sighed. 'I think so, although she has listed several complaints here about the hotel. It seems the food is cold by the time it reaches her room.'

'Then why doesn't she eat in the dining room?' Flora rolled her eyes as she turned to select a gown from the wardrobe. More black, but she could endure it when she remembered she wore it in respect for Riordan.

'And mix with the hoi polloy?' He slanted a look up, one sartorial eyebrow raised. 'At least she makes no mention of moving to another hotel.' He read on in silence for a few heartbeats. 'The kitchens will have to be rebuilt, though there was no structural damage to the house itself. She says the soot and charred stench has permeated almost every room, which I rather think is her excuse to have the house redecorated from the attics downwards.'

'Considering you arranged all the work before we left, I feel that's a bit harsh.' Flora's cheeks burned with righteous indignation as she changed out of her petticoat. She always made an effort not to exhibit resentment that Beatrice's comfort was always Bunny's first thought, reminding herself she would be an old woman herself one day, and if Bunny treated her with half as much care, she would be fortunate.

'You know Mother. Nothing is too trivial not to make a drama out of.' He dragged a chair up to the bureau beneath the dormer window and sat. 'I'll reply to this before we go down to dinner.'

Flora was about to add she hoped Beatrice's plans did not include their bedroom, but in the face of Bunny's pensive frown she changed her mind. She dropped a kiss behind his right ear and set to combing out her hair. The thick tresses often resisted her efforts to curl and fix to her head without sliding down her back again. Life would certainly be easier with a lady's maid to help.

With nothing more to do to her ensemble, she picked up a magazine and settled in the twin of the wing chairs beside the fireplace. She couldn't concentrate and discarded the magazine after a few pages, then repeated the action with a brochure for current events scheduled for the Winter Gardens.

'The White Viennese Band is due to play on the thirteenth,' Flora read aloud. 'And there's to be a Municipal entertainment to include a cinematograph show of the coronation procession in Montpellier Gardens at the end of the month. I forgot how lively this town is. Comes of living so close to London, one forgets other places have their own cultural pursuits.'

Bunny's response was a distracted mumble, but he did not lift his head from the desk.

Flora sighed, tossed the magazine aside and came to stand behind his chair, admiring his neat, uniform writing that covered two pages of the thick notepaper. She caressed his shoulder and trailed the other hand through the soft hair at his nape. 'I can't concentrate on anything. And you need a haircut.'

'I know,' he murmured, a smile in his voice. 'About the haircut. Perhaps I'll go into town tomorrow.' He reached back and covered her hand on his shoulder with his own. 'Why don't you go down? I'll finish this and join you in a few moments.'

'All right, but you might mention to your mother that I'm not over fond of the colour soil brown.' She escaped the room before he could respond.

'Her ladyship has a guest to dinner this evening, Mrs Harrington,' Scrivens said, his gaze fixed on a point over her shoulder. 'Lady Vaughn, Mr Osborne and Mrs Mountjoy are in the sitting room taking pre-dinner drinks with Lady Jocasta.'

'Thank you, Scrivens.' Flora refused to meet his eye as she let herself into the sitting room. Though curious as to the identity of this guest she chose not to ask the butler in case her enquiry was met with contrived ignorance, or worse a blank stare. She was never fond of bullies, and this one always smirked when he looked at her. Maybe he thought it beneath him to treat the daughter of a butler as his superior? Well he would have to accept it, as she refused to be intimidated.

'Good evening, everyone,' Flora proceeded to greet each of the company in turn, her brow rising at the sight of Caroline Mountjoy who sat immodestly close to William on a sofa large enough for four people.

William stood when she entered and his greeting delivered, he eased away from Caroline when he sat down again, but she closed the space between them and stroked his forearm with one hand.

Flora suspected it would only take him five minutes to find a reason to extricate himself.

'I do hope you've had a productive day,' Caroline addressed Flora.

'I have, thank you.' Her bland response was in stark contrast to the fact her day had consisted of interrogating a doctor and discovering her father was murdered. Then the thought struck her that there might be a murderer in the house, maybe this room.

'How are you, Flora?' William asked. 'This must be a difficult time for you.'

'It is, but everyone has been very kind.' Though tempted, she wasn't prepared to let Mrs Mountjoy know what she had been doing.

Caroline shifted closer to William, as if reminding him she was there. 'While you've been enjoying the delights of the town, Venetia has been working on your behalf. Go on, Venetia, dear, do tell her.'

'Er, well I wasn't going to mention it until later.' Lady Venetia flushed a deep red. 'But as you've broached the subject, Caroline.' She cleared her throat and began. 'Flora dear, you remember Mr Cripps, our minister? Well, he's agreed to hold the service of committal for Maguire and has reserved a place for him in the graveyard. Right near the rea wall, where he'll have a view of the hill he loved so much.'

Flora was about to remind her that Maguire would never have a view of anything, ever again, but she checked herself. There was no need to be uncharitable.

'That's, um, thoughtful of you, Lady Venetia.' A footman paused in front of Flora with a tray and she automatically accepted a glass of sherry, though she didn't want one. Silently she chastised herself for procrastinating, torn between annoyance that Lady Venetia had pre-empted her, and gratitude that she evidently thought Flora was too upset to make the arrangements herself. How would she react if Flora told her she had delayed arranging the funeral because she wanted to find out who had killed her father first?

'I thought, well, as it isn't possible to have him laid to rest beside your mother, the place where he spent his life would be the next best thing?' Lady Venetia's triumphant smile dissolved at Flora's lack of reaction. 'Did I do wrong, my dear?'

'Of course you didn't.' Caroline's shrill laugh made Flora wince. 'It was very kind of you, Venetia. Wasn't it, Flora?'

'Er yes, most considerate.' Flora fidgeted on her chair, annoyed with herself at her procrastination, which was because she could not face never seeing her father again. Organizing his burial was too stark, too finale. She wasn't ready.

'Perhaps you could submit a list of hymns and

a few bible verses for Mr Cripps to peruse in the meantime?' Lady Venetia suggested.

'An Anglican service, Mama?' Jocasta pushed away from her artfully arranged pose beside the French doors that stood open onto the garden. 'Wasn't Maguire a Presbyterian?' She swept a glass of sherry from the tray the footman had left on the sideboard before he withdrew, then took the vacant space next to Flora.

'Oh dear, that didn't occur to me.' Lady Venetia stared round the room stricken.

'He was, yes,' Flora said gently. 'Please don't concern yourself, Lady Venetia. Father would hardly expect a service conducted according to the *Westminster Directory of Public Worship*. St Jude's will be more than acceptable. I'll call at the vicarage tomorrow and talk to Mr Cripps.'

'Another drink anyone?' William slapped his thighs, rose and headed for the sideboard. Left abandoned on the sofa, Caroline pouted.

'Not for me, thank you,' Flora held up her untouched glass, then murmured to Jocasta, 'two minutes.'

'Beg pardon?' Jocasta asked, sotto voice.

'I gave William five minutes to find a reason to remove himself from Mrs Mountjoy. It seems I underestimated him.'

Jocasta's subsequent fit of suppressed giggles was observed by Caroline with an expression that bordered on hostility. Or was it for Flora's benefit alone? She couldn't tell.

Bunny paused in the door frame, a, 'what-have-you-done-now?' look in his eyes as he took his seat beside Flora, who gestured she would explain later.

Then her father's wry smile jumped into her mind in appreciation of a good joke and her composure returned.

William replenished his sherry glass, then held up the decanter in enquiry to the rest of the room. When no one accepted he returned it to the tray.

'I'm curious, Flora. Do explain about this Westminster Service you mentioned.' Ignoring Caroline's entreaty to return to his seat beside her, he took a chair and dragged it next to the sofa Flora and Bunny occupied.

'I was being irreverent actually,' Flora murmured. 'But since you ask. My father's family were Covenanters.'

'What's a Covenanter?' Jocasta asked, eliciting a sigh from Caroline.

'I suppose they were the early Puritans, though I could be wrong about that.' Flora became aware she was the centre of attention. 'It began in the 1630s with the Kirk declaring God was the head of the Kirk and not the King, which was the cause of all sorts of conflict during the Civil Wars. The guide says there should be no kneeling, prayers or eulogies in either church or graveside at funerals.'

'Actually, that sounds just like Riordan,' William said. 'He hated anything that smacked of false flattery.'

'You're right, he did indeed.' Flora met his warm smile and returned it. 'He hated all that public opining of the departed and tearful displays of affection. I might even suggest to Reverend Cripps we dispense with all that.'

'Not even a rousing, "Guide me O Thy Great Redeemer"?' Caroline's mock-astonished smile and burst of harsh laughter jarred, made worse by the fact no one joined in. 'Sounds positively dismal. And surely we aren't going to discuss funerals over the sherry?' She held out her glass to William for a refill.

'I think we just did.' William rose again to comply with Caroline's request. 'And wasn't it you who raised the subject in the first place? Mrs Mountjoy?' He raised the glass to Flora before handing it back to an openly sulky Caroline.

To Flora's relief, the conversation quickly changed from funerals to horse racing which they hoped might return to the town.

'There used to be races practically on our doorstep in the early eighteen hundreds, but it died out with local protests on gambling.' Lady Venetia relaxed, as if she was more comfortable on familiar ground. 'Now that Baring Bingham has bought Prestbury Park, we may have organized racing again. We had two days of steeplechasing this last April which was very successful. A regular hunt and jump racing will bring an altogether different society back to the town.'

'Jocasta,' Lady Venetia gave an exasperated sigh

as the round notes of the dinner gong intruded, 'go and see where your father and Eddy have got to.' She gestured to everyone to leave the room. 'Do go in, I'm sure George will be along in a moment.'

'Are you really going to organize a Covenanter funeral?' Bunny whispered as they strolled arm in arm along the hall to the dining room.

'Elements of it would be nice, though I wouldn't have thought of it without Caroline's high-handedness.' Flora sighed.

Bunny pulled her gently aside as Caroline swept by on William's arm, her eyes narrowed at Flora as she passed.

'And another thing, that woman doesn't like me,' Flora said when she had moved out of earshot.

'Now you *are* imagining things.' Bunny took her hand and sniffed the air appreciatively. 'I wonder what's for dinner. Whatever it is smells delicious and I'm starving.'

'You're always starving,' she sighed as he slipped his arm round her waist and guided her along the hallway.

CHAPTER 16

After breakfast the next morning, Flora and Bunny walked the mile into South Cleeve to the small parish church. With the Abbey behind them, they paused on the hill to admire the view which stretched across gentle fields all the way to the purple outline of the Malvern Hills in the distance.

'Lord Vaughn seemed preoccupied at dinner last evening,' Flora observed as Bunny helped her negotiate an uneven pathway that ran beside the road.

'He spent all day in Gloucester at a livestock sale with Eddy. They were both very tired when they got home, had a late supper and went straight to bed.'

'I hope he isn't going to make poor Eddy work every day of his summer holiday,' Flora said. 'The boy should be out and about having some fun. He won't be refreshed and ready for the new term at this rate, no wonder he's looking quite peaky.'

'Lady Venetia did mention calling in Dr Fairbrother to take a look at him.' He guided her onto the grass verge to allow a horse and cart to pass by. 'Lord Vaughn declared it unnecessary fussing and vetoed it. Eddy saw him a week or so ago apparently when his fatigue was put down to growing pains.'

'I suppose Dr Fairbrother couldn't get that wrong,' Flora conceded as they negotiated the slight incline down to the church.

'I've always liked this quaint little building,' Flora said, pausing as Bunny bent slightly to open the lychgate set in the low drystone wall. The cross shaped building with its oolitic limestone walls appeared to have grown out of the ground, or maybe it had simply sunk into its plot over the years.

'An unpretentious church, my mother would call it, unlike the gothic Victorian piles intended to intimidate everyone with the temerity to walk through the doors.'

'Father told me once that this churchyard was so crowded with graves during the last century, they pushed the earth almost up to the windows.'

Bunny grimaced. 'I thought your father wasn't a member of this congregation?'

'He wasn't, but he was interested in architecture.' Flora led the way along a meandering path to the arched front door of the vicarage at the rear of the church. 'I would have liked to bury him somewhere like Saint Mark's on Cleeve Hill, which has more Baptist and Wesleyan influences.'

'What made you agree to this one?'

'Apart from Lady Venetia's interference, you

mean?' She rolled her eyes. 'Well, partly because St Marks is only ten years old and has no churchyard.'

'I thought all village churches did?'

'Not those built after eighteen fifty-three. There's been a church on this spot in some form or another since the late seven hundreds.'

'What a mine of fascinating information you are, my Flora.'

'I pick the most interesting bits out of history books to spout at dinner parties.' She twirled her parasol over her shoulder. 'Makes me look cleverer than I really am.' She nodded to where a row of ancient lopsided grey headstones dotted the space around the building like broken teeth. 'Most of the old graves here have been relocated and a new graveyard established in the field next door.'

She stepped beneath the low wooden porch, one hand raised to the door knocker until she realized she was alone. She lowered her hand and turned back to where Bunny halted on the path behind her, his head tilted to one side while a smile tugged at his mouth.

'Aren't you coming with me?'

He nodded. 'I was just reminiscing about the last time we were here.'

'Our wedding?' She swung the parasol onto her other shoulder and strolled back to join him.

'It was on a day exactly like this too.'

Flora nodded. The sun shone down on the little church exactly as it had then, the only sounds a whisper of insects in the grass and occasional birdsong. As if everything had stilled in anticipation. She had felt like a princess when she had stepped down from the Vaughns' carriage on her father's arm.

'What do you remember the most?' Bunny tilted her chin with a finger, turned her face back towards him and tucked a stray curl behind her ear.

'I think it was the moment when I paused in the porch so my bridesmaid could arrange the train of my dress. Someone must have said I was there and you turned a casual shoulder in my direction. Then you just froze and stared at me. And kept staring as I walked towards you.'

'A shaft of sunlight came through the door behind you as you bent slightly towards your friend as if you were giving a blessing. You looked all ethereal and made of light. Like an angel.'

'How long did it take you to realize I wasn't one?'

He chuckled. 'When Eddy's pet frog escaped during the reception and made Lady Jocasta scream.'

'Oh yes, I went into full governess mode, didn't I?' Heat flooded her face at the memory. 'I even tried to send him to his room until Lady Vaughn stepped in.'

'Eddy never did find that frog though. I like to think the poor thing made its escape and is busy spawning hundreds of other little frogs now.'

'Never mind that. We were talking about the service. What did you think when you saw me?'

'That I couldn't believe I didn't imagine you. I half expected you to disappear in a puff of smoke before you reached me. Then my groomsman nudged me in the ribs to remind me I should move to the altar, and I realized you were not only real, but on your way to marry me. You smiled at me just once, then lifted your chin toward the vicar as if giving him permission to begin.'

'I didn't know what it really meant to live with those vows. I had heard them before of course, and always wondered if I would get them word-perfect when the time came, but beyond that— I was so naïve in thinking it was straightforward.'

'The ceremony, or marriage?'

'Marriage of course.'

'Are you disappointed?'

'Never.' She adjusted his tie, which didn't need adjusting but gave her an excuse to touch him. 'Marriage is more complicated than I believed, but more wonderful too. Living with you has made me more resilient.'

'Are you talking about my mother?'

'Of course not.' She turned a look of mute surprise on him, but when his lips twitched, hers did too. 'Well, sometimes. But if she's the worst test our marriage is put to, I'm confident we'll survive.'

'Good, I was getting worried after the fire fiasco. I doubt Sarah Bernhardt could have made more of a drama out of it than Mother.'

'Without you,' Flora went on, determined not to be side-tracked by jokes about Beatrice, 'Father's death would have been insurmountable. I expect there will be more grief, more testing of our bond, but I'm not afraid because I have you. I'm not alone.' She turned her head to where the slightly crooked church door sat beneath its stone archway, feeling more complete and at ease since hearing of her father's death.

'I promise to be your best friend, the holder of your dreams, your keeper of secrets and the first voice you hear when you wake, and the last before you sleep.' He bent and brushed his lips across her forehead.

'You know,' she stepped closer, pressing the length of her body against his and stared up into his eyes, 'I think I like those vows better than the original ones.'

'I do too. Perhaps we could come back to this spot once a year and repeat them?' He cupped her cheek with one hand. 'Just so we never forget.'

'That's a nice idea.' She turned her lips into his palm as a stab of pain bunched beneath her ribs. 'Although the next time we come here, it will be to bury my father.'

He nodded slowly, ran a finger along her jaw and tapped the end of her nose. 'And I will be right here by your side. Are you ready?'

The middle-aged housekeeper who answered Bunny's knock showed them into a low-ceilinged sitting room that looked like something out of Charles Dickens with its abundance of burgundy red and forest green fabrics. Every surface sported a fine layer of dust, with books, open and closed, piled in precarious towers on every surface, including a blackened stone fireplace.

'By the look of things, I doubt the housekeeper is allowed in here.' The finger Flora ran along the surface of the desk came away dirty.

Bunny ducked his head close to her ear and whispered, 'Remember – no bagpipes at the graveside.'

Flora bit her bottom lip to prevent a smile. 'Why not, he loved them if played properly.'

'Too mournful,' Bunny said, just as the clack of the door latch announced the arrival of a spare man in a navy blue suit and clerical collar. He stumbled over the rug as he approached them, his right hand held out in welcome, promptly knocking over a pile of books.

Flora bent to help retrieve them but the man rushed forward and took them out of her hands. 'Don't worry about those, my dear.' He placed them on top of another pile and, having dusted a chair with a handkerchief dragged from a pocket, motioned Flora into it.

Reverend Cripps was not an attractive man – in his mid-fifties with a long face, permanently moist myopic eyes, and thinning hair that showed a pink scalp. The elbows of his flannel jacket bore badly sewn-on leather patches, and his trousers, when he turned to sit, were shiny at the rear. If he wasn't such a cliché, Flora might have felt sorry for him, as he fit perfectly into the life he had chosen for himself.

'Allow me to offer my sincerest condolences,

Mrs Harrington.' He gave Bunny's hand a brief shake before he motioned for him to sit, then turned back to Flora. 'Your dear father will be greatly missed. He took such an interest in the community, especially in the days before his death.'

'Thank you.' Flora shifted in her chair and stared at her hands, aware Riordan Maguire had had little time for the social-climbing reverend and only ever set foot in his church for Christmas Eve Mass.

'Do excuse the mess.' He belatedly realized the chair he had offered Bunny held a pile of magazines and rushed forward to remove them. 'My housekeeper is growing old and doesn't appear to see the dust anymore.' He flapped the handkerchief at an upright chair, stirring dust motes into a shaft of sunlight. 'I wouldn't dream of discharging her, she's been with me for years.'

Over a pot of weak tea and a plate of iced fancies, most of which were consumed by the reverend, Flora chose a list of prayers and hymns including 'Abide With Me' and 'Amazing Grace', neither of which were likely to offend Riordan Maguire's Covenanter heart.

'I was sorry not to include your father in my congregation, Mrs Harrington,' Rev Cripps viewed her over his glasses.

'Er, no.' Flora felt five years old again. 'His work often required him to remain at the Abbey. However he always attended Christmas and Easter

Services. Perhaps he'll arrive at the Heavenly gates with a silver cloth in his hand?'

'I beg your pardon?'

'I think what my wife means,' Bunny interrupted. 'Is that shepherds traditionally carry a hank of yarn with them to Heaven to explain why they were unable to attend services. Perhaps Riordan Maguire will offer a similar explanation.'

'Oh, I see.' His otherwise humourless face split into a wide smile. 'Therefore I'm certain the Lord will make allowances.'

'Such confidence,' Flora muttered. 'Well, I think that's about everything.' She gathered her gloves and parasol in a prelude to leaving.

'Before we go,' Bunny said, gesturing Flora back into her chair, 'I wonder, Reverend if you would expand on something you said when we arrived?'

Flora turned to look at him, but he held up a finger to indicate she would understand in due course.

'Do refresh my memory. What did I say?' He blinked, bemused.

'About Mr Maguire's efforts on behalf of the community prior to his death.'

'I meant the incident at the fête, of course.' He turned a well-worn spectacle case over in his hands.

'Which incident was this?' Flora forgot about leaving, and waited for him to continue.

'That young girl who went missing. Maguire was one of the last persons to talk to her at the fête.' At Flora's start he rushed on. 'I don't mean to imply there was anything untoward about that. No, he was comforting her after her altercation with Mr McCallum.'

'I'm sorry, Reverend, but you are confusing us,' Bunny halted him. 'What altercation?'

He hesitated. 'Perhaps I shouldn't have mentioned it, especially now all the fuss has died down.'

'We'll treat whatever you say in confidence,' Flora said, wishing he would just get on with it.

'The situation between Betsy and Mr McCallum.' He looked at each of them as if broaching a well-known, but taboo subject. 'I believe your father tried to counsel the girl, but she did have a some-what spirited nature and refused to listen.'

'Did have?' Flora's eyes widened.

'*Has*, she *has* a spirited nature, of course. I didn't mean anything by that.' His cheeks turned blotchy red. 'Mrs Mountjoy asked Mr Maguire to speak to the girl. She felt Mr McCallum's generous nature had been misunderstood. As Betsy worked at the Abbey, Mrs Mountjoy thought your father was best placed to persuade her to stop pestering him.'

'Did she indeed?' Flora murmured, bemused by the idea of Mrs Mountjoy on a quest to protect Mr McCallum's reputation.

'And you say Mr Maguire acceded to this request?' Bunny asked.

'I cannot say for sure, although the day of the fête was when everything seemed to come to a head. Mr Maguire and myself were near one of

246

the tents when we heard what sounded like an argument which got quite heated. Then Betsy came running out, quite distressed.'

'Betsy and Mr McCallum were in this tent? Alone?' This from Bunny.

'Why yes, didn't I say that?' He spectacle case clicked as he opened and closed it.

'No, you didn't. Where did she go once she ran out of the tent?'

He shrugged. 'Across the fields, away from the Abbey.'

'Did Mr McCallum go after her?' Flora asked.

'Not that I saw. I believe he remained at the fête.' He turned to Flora. 'Your father said he would handle it and went after her.' He broke off and tapped the knuckle of his index finger against his top lip as if regretting what he had said.

'What happened then?' Flora prompted him.

'I was called away at that moment to judge the cake baking competition. But I saw Mr Maguire a while later with Mr McCallum. I assumed Mr Maguire took him to task about upsetting Betsy as they both appeared quite agitated.'

'I don't suppose you happened to hear what they were saying?' Bunny asked, the implication that Rev Cripps had an unhealthy interest in everyone's actions was obvious to Flora, but hopefully not to the vicar.

He shook his head. 'I was too far away, but it was evident by their hand gestures they were both quite angry. Then Mr McCallum stalked away and your father went to supervise the teas being organized by the Abbey staff.'

'What about Betsy? Where did she go after her argument with Mr McCallum?'

'I assumed she had gone home. It was only the next day that I learned she had left the village.'

'Mr Cripps, you said yourself Betsy was distressed.' Flora kept her voice calm but found her impatience with this man difficult to hide. 'She ran off, presumably in only the clothes she stood up in, and no one has seen her since. You do know the police are looking for her?'

'Apparently so. I believe they questioned both Mr McCallum and your father, amongst others of course.'

'Surely they didn't think my father had anything to do with Betsy's disappearance? He would only have spoken to her—'

'Please don't misunderstand me.' He raised a hand, halting. 'I doubt that very much. Besides, he spent the rest of the afternoon at the fête, as everyone will tell you.'

'What do *you* think happened to Betsy Mason?' Bunny asked. His hand closed on Flora's in her lap, as if he sensed her growing anger.

'I don't indulge in local gossip or speculation, Mr Harrington. In my position, one needs to place oneself above such things, naturally.

'Naturally,' Flora murmured, though her sarcasm passed him by.

'I did mention to Mrs Mountjoy that I believed

the uh-liaison to be over, but she didn't seem at all interested.' He blinked, evidently confused. 'I thought that quite strange, after the fuss she had made. The only reason I mentioned this at all was because you've been asking questions, I—'

'Who said I was asking questions, Mr Cripps?' Flora asked.

'Why Mrs Mountjoy did, when I saw her yesterday.'

'Mrs Mountjoy seems to insinuate herself into most situations, apparently,' Flora said through pursed lips. 'Though my interest was never in Betsy Mason.' *Maybe it should be?*

'She's a good woman and has the interests of the community at heart.'

Flora gave him a weak smile as she tugged on her gloves, experiencing a sudden urge to leave the dusty vicarage as soon as possible. 'Good day to you, Mr Cripps.'

CHAPTER 17

'That was unexpected,' Bunny said as they retraced their steps around the side of the church. 'Maybe Reverend Cripps hasn't heard the gossip about Mrs Mountjoy and McCallum.'

'I don't believe that for a moment. More likely he saw it as respectable.'

'I gather you don't think much of our venerable reverend?'

She tightened her grip on Bunny's arm as they left the neat churchyard behind them and strolled the grass verge beneath a row of trees that lined the road, going from shadow to sunlight and back into shadow again.

'He's typical of his class and generation. He's the type who aligns himself with the highest-ranking member of his congregation, content to slander anyone lower on the social scale. Like poor Betsy. I didn't hear him criticize Mr McCallum.'

'You could be right.'

'I know I am. I attended his Sunday school as a child, although as a butler's daughter he saw no advantage in cultivating my good opinion.' Flora slowed her steps as they negotiated the incline at the top of the High Street. 'Oh dear, that sounds bitter doesn't it?'

'A little.' Bunny massaged her arm with his other hand. 'I don't like to think of anyone being unkind to you. Didn't your father have a word with him?'

'I didn't carry my complaints to him. Besides, the hierarchy of a servants' hall dictates what sort of life you have. The maid's children get bullied by the housekeeper's. The groom's children are lorded over by the estate manager's and so on. I fared better than some.' Her thoughts went back to what Reverend Cripps had said about the fête. 'If Caroline Mountjoy had turned her attentions to William,' Flora began, 'why the keen interest in what McCallum and Betsy were doing? Unless it was simply to cause trouble for him after being rejected.'

'Who knows? A woman scorned and all that.'

She halted and dragged him back a pace. 'Is my judgement flawed in some way? Because as soon as I think I begin to understand our Mr McCallum, something else comes to light which throws his entire character open to speculation again. He's like a ghost slipping through cracks.' She set off again, her feet picking out the smoother areas of the uneven road.

'He's not the only one.' Bunny interjected. 'That Scrivens gives me the creeps the way he appears out of nowhere. Then there is the estate manager, who would rather circuit the entire grounds rather than acknowledge anyone.'

251

'Mr Bracenose?' Flora frowned. 'He's always been quite nice to me. Surly maybe and abrupt but that could be his manner.'

'More like shifty I would say. Tom Murray has his secrets too, I mean how did he get that shiner?'

'Ah you noticed that? He says he walked into something but it looks more like a fight to me.'

'And to me. Over Betsy do you think?'

'It wouldn't surprise me. Betsy could still be lying out there.' Flora recalled the tightly packed trees in Bailey Wood, where little light penetrated. The damp and musty atmosphere would turn into thick mist at night when the temperature dropped. She shivered just thinking about it.

'I doubt it. From what I've heard, the search for your father was quite comprehensive. Had Betsy still been in the area she would have been found. Maybe on this occasion gossip is accurate and she simply left.'

Flora had no response. This was so different from hunting down clues on board the Minneapolis. There she had no emotion invested in the guilt or innocence of strangers. Cleeve Abbey was her home, the people in it integral to her life; even the ones she barely knew were friends of those she loved.

In the village high street, they rounded a corner of a building whose cob walls jutted into the road. A sign swung above their heads which bore a pale-bellied bird with a fantail which declared it was The Red Kite public house.

'S'cuse me, Miss,' a man murmured, head down as he skirted round them, applying a broom to the dirt road.

'Mr Griggs?' Flora said, recognizing him. 'It's Flora. Don't you remember me?'

He raised his head, his eyes dark and hostile and his lips pressed into a firm line. In seconds his eyes lit with recognition and he tugged at his cap. 'Beg pardon, Miss Flora. Didn't recognize you for a moment.' He crossed swollen, arthritic knuckles over the broom handle. 'I 'eard about Mr Maguire,' he said in a bald, bland statement with no emotion attached.

Andrew Griggs couldn't have been above forty, but a life of hard work and personal tragedy meant his years didn't sit well on him. Fine lines radiated from his piercing blue eyes, while deeper ones carved grooves between his nose and mouth. He held himself like a man with a heavy burden, stooped and defeated.

'Thank you. In fact I'm Mrs Harrington now. This is my husband, Mr Harrington.' She indicated Bunny, who thrust out his hand. 'I heard about your niece, Betsy. You must be very worried.'

Griggs hesitated, wiped a hand on his trousers and shook Bunny's. 'Betsy!' He snorted and swiped a sleeve beneath his nose, the broom held loosely in his other hand. 'Nothing but trouble that girl, from the day she came to live 'ere. Always chasing the men she was, though they didn't exactly make it difficult for her.'

'I heard she was, *is*, a very pretty girl. She commanded a lot of attention,' Flora said, implying the situation may not have been entirely Betsy's fault.

'Couldn't get a decent day's work out of her.' Griggs' top lip curled, unimpressed. 'Always going off at all hours. Wasn't as if I could manage without the help, either. What with my Peter showing the signs of the consumption that took off his mother.'

'Again, I'm very sorry to hear that.' Flora recalled a tow-headed boy who played on the village green. He had been about eleven when she last saw him but thought at the time he looked younger. 'What does the doctor say?'

'Doctor?' Griggs snorted, the broom swaying precariously in his hand. 'Haven't got money fer doctors. I get a tonic from the pharmacy in Montpellier Street when I can afford it. Reginald Meeks makes it up for me. Peter seems to perk up for a while after taking it. Anyway, not much can be done if it is the consumption.'

He didn't add that he had lost his wife to the illness, though from pragmatism or a deep-seated bitterness that he was about to lose a child too was unclear.

'Mr Griggs,' Bunny gave the façade of The Red Kite a sweeping glance, 'I take it you're the land-lord here?' Rewarded with a curt nod, he went on, 'Did you hear about the beer at the fête being contaminated?'

'Heard about it!' Griggs turned his head and

spat on the ground, his eyes bright with resentment. 'I don't like to cast aspersions on good men, Miss, but your pa did me no favours on that score.'

'What do you mean, Griggs?' Bunny took a step forward, shielding Flora.

She tightened her hold on his arm, reassuring him she was in no danger.

'Maguire asked some pretty damning questions about the beer I serve here.' Griggs waved a hand at the public room behind him. 'Practically accused me of buying home brew, which everyone knows is illegal.' A bead of spittle settled on his bottom lip, which curled into a grimace. 'As if I would do something that stupid. I get all me beer from McCallum's.'

'I'm sure my father didn't mean to accuse you,' Flora said. 'He wasn't that kind of man.'

'Nay, well mebbe not.' His mouth twitched as if he realized he had gone too far. 'Someone must have heard him though, because when those men got sick after the fête, they went to the White Hart for their ale.'

'Is that still the case?' Bunny asked. 'Are villagers still boycotting the pub?'

'Well, no. Mr McCallum proved there was nothing wrong with his beer after your father stirred things up. Had his place inspected and everything. He told the parish council meeting that all my beer came from his brewery and had been passed as fit.'

'Then the matter was settled, Mr Griggs,' Flora

said stiffly. 'I'm sure my father wouldn't have let anyone blame you after the truth was revealed.'

'Aye, well.' Griggs hefted the broom in both hands again. 'All I know is I lost money. And with Betsy running off like that, and everyone thinking she was no better than she should be, well, I can do without the aggravation.'

'Are you certain Betsy ran off?' Flora asked. Perhaps he knew more than they did at the Abbey. 'Did she have a particular gentleman friend?'

Griggs shook his head. 'Could have been any one of them scruffy youths who hung about her. Betsy wasn't one to relish her own company, if you see what I mean.'

Griggs didn't appear at all concerned about his niece, or care whether or not she was safe. Most of Griggs' complaints appeared to be the creations of a discontented man. Not that he did not have good reason to feel sorry for himself. However, there was something about self-pity that repelled people, and Flora wasn't immune.

Griggs ducked his head. 'My condolences anyway for Mr Maguire, but I have to get on. There's only me to do all the work now and I'm due to open in half an hour.'

'Of course,' Flora said, relieved. 'Don't let us keep you.'

The cool, dark interior of the taproom was in stark contrast to the relentless, blinding sun that reflected off the white painted walls as Flora and Bunny set off again towards the Abbey.

256

Every step was an effort and before long Flora was breathless. Her black calico blouse was the thinnest she could find but it clung to her damp skin. 'Slow down a little, Bunny, this heat is giving me a headache.

'Not far to go now.' Bunny grasped her hand and pulled her up the incline, past the green where a group of children played ball near the fountain. They passed the local store where trestle tables lined up outside bore boxes of fresh vegetables and plump red strawberries and aromas of nutmeg and thyme wafted through the open door.

Bunny worked his charm on a shopkeeper and purchased a bag of ripe strawberries, leaving the woman blushing at his effusive praise about her immaculate establishment.

'Did you notice,' Flora asked, gripping the brown paper bag as they set off again, 'Griggs was scathing about Betsy's male admirers, but he didn't mention Mr McCallum, who hardly fits the "scruffy youth" category.' Flora peered up at him. 'What are you thinking?'

'That Reverend Gibbs seemed inclined to absolve McCallum of wrongdoing in respect of Betsy. Perhaps he is more sinned against than sinning.' Bunny bit his lip in a gesture which told Flora he was about to alter his opinion, but didn't know where to begin. 'I should have mentioned this before, but from what both William and Lord Vaughn said over billiards last night, McCallum wasn't actually involved with Betsy.'

'You told me yesterday that he was.' Flora dragged one foot in front of the other, kicking up puffs of road dust with each step.

'I may have jumped the gun there.' Bunny winced. 'It appears McCallum is the target of women, he doesn't chase them. Lord Vaughn said your father was convinced Betsy had set her cap at him, but there was no actual relationship. I suspect that wasn't a break-up of a love affair the vicar saw at the fête, but a rejection.'

Flora dug a hand into the bag of strawberries. 'That's the conclusion I came to, especially after what McCallum told me about his wife.' She spoke through a mouthful of the sweet, red flesh that dribbled juice down her chin.

'Then it looks like your new beau was the innocent party.' Bunny's voice held reluctance. 'Not only did he sort out the misunderstanding over the beer, he didn't seduce Betsy either.'

'You sound disappointed. And he isn't my beau.' She wiped her face on a handkerchief but her chin still felt sticky.

'There's nothing so attractive as a grieving widower who eschews female company. Women see him as a challenge,' Bunny said. 'Perhaps Caroline had no more luck than Betsy, and was jealous of her, so she asked the vicar to intervene.'

'Even though as you say, there was no relationship between them?'

'Perhaps Mrs Mountjoy believed there was and set out to ruin it. We know she was genuinely

258

interested in Mr McCallum before she turned her attentions to William.'

'Hmm, I suppose so.' The beginnings of a heat headache began to pummel her temples and a trickle of sweat pooled around the waistband of her bombazine skirt. Hetty's famous lemonade would have been very welcome just then.

'Or,' Bunny mused, 'Caroline decided to stir up local feeling against McCallum out of spite. A woman scorned and all that.'

'You are trotting out all the clichés today aren't you?' Flora laughed. 'Jocasta told me Caroline had shifted her attentions to William when he arrived from South Africa. There was no suggestion of any rejection on either side. Even if she had, would she go to the length of poisoning McCallum's beer simply to soothe her own hurt pride?'

'You've met the woman. She's not exactly shy and retiring is she?'

'No, but that does seem excessive. If she was responsible, she hurt more people than Graham McCallum.'

'Not everyone has your social conscience, Flora.' Bunny extended a hand to assist her over a stile. 'They see only their own ambitions, disregarding inconvenient things like consequences.' He circled her waist with both hands and lifted her onto the dirt path.

'Our devising scenarios is all very well,' Flora waved off a bumblebee that flew close to her face with the bag of strawberries, 'but we have no real evidence. More importantly, how does my father feature in all this, to the extent someone would want him dead? I wonder if the fact Caroline got Bracenose to do her fetching and carrying has any bearing.' Flora followed the flight of a blue butterfly as it floated between gorse flowers on the grass verge.

She was about to set off again when she realized Bunny wasn't at her side. She turned back to where he had halted several paces behind her and stared about in confusion.

'Why are we walking this way?' He raised both hands in bewilderment. 'It's no more than a cart track through a field.'

'I thought you would like to see the cottage. If I remember correctly, it's this side of the stables and on the other side of this bend.'

The white-painted building with its neat red-tiled roof looked as empty as when Flora had first seen it; the windows like vacant eyes behind which nothing moved. The lawn needed mowing and a gardener would have shaken his head over the weeds that had sprung up between rows of marigolds and nasturtiums.

'It's quite pretty, like a picture on a box of Peak Freans shortbread biscuits.' Bunny stood at the waist-high gate and tilted his head on one side, then the other. 'I wouldn't have thought it was the sort of place which would give anyone nightmares.'

'Haven't you read Hansel and Gretel?' Flora smiled up at him from beneath the rim of her straw hat, her attention caught by a movement to her right. What looked like a female figure disappeared behind a tree at the rear of the garden. A flash of a yellow skirt and a hat trailing a white ribbon disappeared into the next field behind the cottage, too far away to make out a face, or even the woman's hair colour. She stared at the spot for several seconds, but the figure did not appear.

Her gaze returned to the cottage, while images like sepia photographs with blurred edges marched through her head. The rug on the kitchen floor, the crack in the flagstone, the ponderous black cooking range, all overlaid by the sight and smell of blood; everything that made her dreams so disturbing. Her breathing quickened and she became aware Bunny stood behind her, his hands on her shoulders.

'Take a few slow, deep breaths, Flora,' he said in a low whisper. 'A week ago you didn't know about this place. It's just a house. Bricks, mortar and wood. It cannot hurt you now. Think of it as a puzzle you have to find the pieces to.'

'It isn't the house. It's what happened here which haunts me. I wish I knew exactly what it was.' She shielded her eyes with one hand and scanned the line of trees to the right. In the distance she saw the woman again but was too far away to make out her age or features, just the long yellow skirt as she moved from tree to tree away from them.

She didn't recognize her, but then she hadn't been to the Abbey for a year, so there could be any number of new people in the area. Amy for instance or even Mrs Mountjoy, though the figure didn't look like either of them. Was she merely taking a walk in the lanes, or deliberately trying to be seen? Perhaps she didn't even know Flora and Bunny were there?

'Flora, are you listening?' Bunny's raised voice brought her attention back to him. 'I said maybe there's a spare key at the Abbey somewhere. Perhaps you could ask—'

'The tenants are away, I don't want to intrude without their permission.' Blood rushed through her veins in a flash of heat at the thought of venturing over the threshold. She pulled Bunny through the gate by his sleeve. 'Let's get back. I could do with a cool drink, it's so hot today.'

'I was thinking about the landlord at the Red Kite,' Bunny said suddenly. 'Fate appears to have handed him a difficult hand, but even so, he seemed more worried about his reputation than the possibility people had been made ill from his beer.'

'It wasn't his, he bought it from Battledown Brewery,' Flora reminded him.

'I still think he should have been more concerned.

'Losing customers for something that wasn't his fault could have been a reason to seek revenge. He's also Betsy's uncle and at his own admission he wasn't exactly enamoured of her behaviour. Is it possible he lost his temper and hurt her?'

'You think her battered body lies behind the

barrels in his cellar?' Bunny waggled his fingers in mock menace in front of her face.

'Ugh!' She batted his hand away as a gruesome image jumped into her head. 'No, I don't. In fact no one believes she isn't alive, well and living with a man. Perhaps my imagination is too vivid and I automatically link the word "disappeared" with "done to death"?'

'There is that, Miss Amateur Sleuth. Which brings us back to your father. What's the connection?'

'Other than his nosing around might have angered someone, I don't know.' Flora sighed as the stables of Cleeve Abbey came into view. 'We appear to have reached an impasse.'

CHAPTER 18

'Death by Misadventure, which is what we expected.' Bunny braced open the door of the mortuary and ushered Flora onto the short flight of steps at the entrance into the morning sunshine.

'I shouldn't have stood up in front of all those people, should I?' Flora sighed. 'I suppose I ought to be grateful the court officer didn't throw me out.' In an effort to force Dr Fairbrother to acknowledge Riordan Maguire couldn't have been alone at the time of his death given the two sets of hoof prints, she had interrupted his testimony, and thus embarrassed herself.

'Well, I thought you were wonderfully brave.' Jocasta clicked open her parasol and twirled it onto her shoulder. 'Don't you, Uncle William?'

'I thought the coroner was going to have a seizure.' A smile tugged at William's mouth.

'He didn't listen though did he?' Flora descended the steps on Bunny's arm. 'Just insisted "any pertinent evidence should have been presented before now".' She mimicked the man's superior tone, even down to his slight lisp.

'Court officials, especially coroners, don't like strong-minded ladies correcting them in public,' Bunny said.

'You're so much the solicitor sometimes.' Flora nudged him playfully. 'Everything measured and formal with no margin for deeper emotions.'

'I understand your frustration, my love, but emotions have no place in a court of law. That's not to say I don't care. I've had to learn to temper them with common sense to obtain the desired result.'

'You even talk like a solicitor,' Flora mumbled to herself, though without malice. It wasn't Bunny's fault he saw things differently. Not that her impulsive behaviour had made any difference. 'Perhaps I was being over-optimistic to think something might have come to light at the last moment.'

'Like what?' William held open the carriage door for them. 'That someone would come rushing in, yelling, "I saw it all, m'lud, and he was done to death by that man over there"?'

'Uncle William!' Jocasta chided. 'Despite not wishing to sound like my mother, this is hardly the time for jokes.'

'I'm sorry. I don't mean to be insensitive.' Though William's grin showed no sign of apology. 'I hate the way this whole business has dragged your spirits, Flora. I miss that sweet, funny girl who smiled so easily.'

'I appreciate you both trying to make this easier for me.' She hugged Bunny's arm with both hands and turned a smile on William. 'I don't even mind your jokes, not really. Father wouldn't have either.

William flushed, looking more like an embarrassed schoolboy than a man in his early forties.

'I thought I would melt in that room.' Jocasta dabbed her face with a handkerchief. 'You must be very uncomfortable in that black gown, Flora, it looks heavy.'

Only half listening, Flora glanced over her friend's shoulder to where a familiar face snagged her attention. Mrs Mountjoy leaned out of her carriage window, a hand on the sill as she spoke to a man on the roadside of the carriage; a middle-aged man in a brown tweed suit who nodded occasionally but added little to the conversation.

Flora narrowed her eyes to bring them into focus and gasped. 'Isn't that Bracenose talking to Mrs Mountjoy? What are they doing here?'

'So it is.' Jocasta followed her gaze. 'I don't recall seeing either of them at the inquest.'

'Neither did I,' Flora mused, thoughtful as she watched the conversation escalate with arm gestures and jutted chins on both sides.

'Mind you,' Jocasta added, 'she's always asking Papa if Bracenose can perform some errand or another for her. I'm surprised Papa doesn't ask her to contribute to his wages.' She tugged at Flora's arm. 'Come on, William and Bunny are waiting.'

'I'm coming.' Flora glanced back but her view was blocked by a brewer's dray that passed by on the road just as Graham McCallum stepped into her path.

'Mrs Harrington.' He removed his hat and sketched a polite bow. 'Allow me to offer my condolences. I know you were hoping for a different outcome of the inquest.'

Flora flinched, assuming he meant her unfortunate outburst, though his expression remained sympathetic.

'Ah, I fear I might be held responsible for that.' Bunny joined them. 'McCallum knows more about horses than I do, thus I asked in what circumstances might a horse trample someone on the ground.'

'Really?' Flora kept her expression neutral, though she wished Bunny had told her he had discussed his theory with Mr McCallum.

'Very much in alignment with yours, I imagine,' McCallum replied. 'A sudden sound could have frightened the animal. It stumbled and an inexperienced rider might have dropped the rein. Without guidance the horse would bolt. Not that I could say for certain it happened at all without examining those marks. It might be possible to match them to a specific horse.'

'Other than Diabolous? We are talking about a different horse, Mr McCallum,' Bunny added.

'Well of course.' He held both hands out in a gesture of surrender. 'However the Coroner has delivered his verdict. All the speculation about how many horses and which it was will make no difference now.'

'No, of course not,' Flora said perfunctorily. The fact that there were more horses in Cheltenham than trees, made the task virtually impossible in any case. 'Thank you anyway, Mr McCallum, for appearing as a witness at the inquest, I mean. It cannot have been easy for you being candid about the nature of your confrontation with my father.'

'I told the simple truth, and Maguire had every right to ask me about a possible contamination at my brewery. Especially when you take the Manchester incident into consideration. However, I did take his questions personally, thus my reaction may have been overly harsh.'

'That's kind of you to say so, but I'm sure my father wouldn't have blamed you.' Mrs Mountjoy's carriage rumbled past them, though Flora's quick glance revealed no sign of Bracenose. 'I hope we haven't made you miss your lift.'

'I beg your pardon?' A frown appeared between his brows which struck Flora as quite genuine. Unlike his smile, which didn't reach his eyes.

'Mrs Mountjoy has just left.' Flora nodded to where the carriage turned a corner. 'I assume you came to the inquest together?'

'Um-no, we did not. I had no idea she planned to attend.' He gave a curt inclination of his head, and replaced his hat. 'Good day to you, and my condolences again.'

'Why did you ask him that?' Bunny asked, as he helped Flora up the step into the carriage. 'You know he and Mrs Mountjoy no longer spend time together.'

'Just testing, I suppose.' She watched McCallum walk away. 'They're friendly enough for her to borrow his horses, so it occurred to me they might be pretending not to like each other.'

'Which would imply her attentions to William are an act,' Bunny lowered his voice as William stood mere feet away. 'Which I don't think is likely.'

'I suppose you're right. And as Mr McCallum said, the Coroner has given a verdict with no room for ambiguity. Perhaps I should give up.' The second the words had left her she regretted them. How could she let Riordan Maguire down. If the situation was reversed he would never have merely shrugged his shoulders and moved on.

'Did I hear you say Mrs Mountjoy borrowed a horse from Mr McCallum?' Jocasta took the seat beside Flora, who slid into the far corner to make room.

'That's what he told me the other day.' Flora adjusted her skirts. 'Why?'

'I could swear I heard her say at dinner the other night that she never rode?'

Before Flora could give this statement some thought, Jocasta was speaking again.

'It was a poor show for Mama and Papa not to attend the inquest. I think they should have been there.'

'It's not important.' Flora chewed her bottom lip in an effort not to show she was hurt. She had always imagined she and her father were more to Lord and Lady Vaughn than employees. Jocasta's reminders of their absence today though told her that they weren't and only made her feel worse. 'After all, there was no real reason for them to come. They've been very kind to me through this awful experience.'

She propped her elbow on the window frame, the knuckles of one hand pressed lightly against her lips, as the carriage waited to pull into traffic. Her attention caught by the figure of Dr Fairbrother on the hospital steps in what looked to be a heated altercation with a young man.

The stranger looked to be in his mid-twenties with black hair brushed back from an attractive, even-featured face. From that distance she couldn't see the colour of his eyes but guessed they too would be dark. He stood with one foot on a higher step, a hand on his hip in a leisurely stance, revealing the scarlet lining of a biscuit-coloured suit. In contrast, Dr Fairbrother jutted his chin, his hands clenched at his fists. As she watched, the younger man threw his head back in a laugh, which appeared to incense Dr Fairbrother, who abruptly turned and strode toward a hansom parked on the road, his cheeks flushed a furious red.

'Who's that young man with Dr Fairbrother?' Flora asked no one in particular.

'That's Reginald Meeks, the pharmacist,' William replied from the seat beside her. 'Nice young man and very knowledgeable. Fairbrother calls him a "damned pill grinder", if you'll pardon the expression. They're renowned for their differences of opinion.'

Flora's last view of Mr Meeks was him shaking his head slowly at Dr Fairbrother's retreating back, a wide smile on his face.

Despite his protests of reluctance to leave her alone after the inquest, Flora had insisted that Bunny enjoy some male company this afternoon and he had ventured out with William to a local hostelry to try their pies. Flora had come into the dining room, joining Lady Venetia and Jocasta for luncheon.

'Where are Eddy and Lord Vaughn?' she asked, as she took a seat.

'Yes, where is Eddy, Mama?' Jocasta gave the room a sweeping glance as if her brother might be hiding somewhere. 'Not like him to miss a meal.'

'I assume he's off on the estate somewhere with your father.' Lady Venetia picked at a dry bread roll. 'They normally have a picnic luncheon sent out to wherever they plan to be.'

'Papa is in Gloucester,' Jocasta said. 'He told us at breakfast, don't you remember?'

'Oh yes.' Lady Venetia waved a distracted hand. 'Then I assume he's taken Eddy with him. In which case I don't expect them back before tea.'

Neither Lord Vaughn or Lady Venetia had thus far not made any reference to the inquest apart from a vague. 'As we thought then,' when Bunny conveyed the verdict, let alone offered anything by way of an excuse for their non-attendance. Or perhaps she was expecting too much. Lady Venetia had told them earlier they must stay at the Abbey for as long as they wished.

She filled a water glass and passed it to Flora. 'Incidentally, my dear, have you finalized all the arrangements for the funeral, or is there something I can do to help?'

Flora hesitated. Seeing Reginald Meeks outside the coroner's office earlier had crystallized an idea she had toyed with all the way home. A talk with the young man who had so angered Dr Fairbrother might reveal something interesting. 'Actually, I need to make a final visit to the undertakers this afternoon. I should go and see the florists as well.'

'You're welcome to take the gig,' Lady Vaughn said. 'I doubt anyone needs it.' Flora was about to decline, but was reluctant to get into an altercation about the unsuitability of her travelling by tram, so she merely smiled her thanks.

'Mama,' Jocasta shot Flora a 'don't interrupt me' look before continuing, 'what do you know about the cottage on the west side of the estate? The one behind the stables? Flora was out that way yesterday and recognized it.'

Flora inclined her head in a silent reminder that they had agreed to tackle her parents separately.

'I was going to ask Papa,' Jocasta added as if she read Flora's thoughts. 'But he's been so occupied with Eddy and the estate he kept fobbing me off.'

'I don't think I know which one you mean, dear. We have so many.' Lady Venetia's hand drifted to her neck where she fiddled with a chain of her necklace. 'More salad, Flora?'

'It's a white-painted cottage with a red roof and a darling little porch.' Jocasta took the dish from her mother and passed it to Flora. 'Isn't that how you described it?'

'Yes, that's right.' Flora took a spoonful of lettuce and tomato she didn't want. 'Tom brought me back that way from Bailey Wood the other day.'

'I know nothing about it, I'm afraid.' Lady Venetia's growing flush said otherwise. She had opted for clear soup for luncheon and strong coffee which indicated she was watching her weight.

'I think you do, Mama,' Jocasta persisted. 'I'm certain Papa mentioned once that Maguire and his wife lived there when Flora was a small child.'

'My darling, that was all so long ago.' Lady Vaughn performed a mildly passable imitation of Hetty, blinking myopically, a finger held to her cheek. 'I cannot be expected to recall everyone who has occupied the estate cottages during the last twenty years.'

'Were you aware Flora has a recurring dream about that house? Quite a disturbing one actually, which began during her childhood. If you know something, I do think you ought to tell her.'

Jocasta was evidently not going to let the subject go, for which Flora was grateful, although her gratitude vied with her reluctance to upset her hostess.

273

'My dear Flora, you've never mentioned such a thing to me.' Lady Venetia covered Flora's hand with her own, then withdrew it quickly. 'But then children have fertile imaginations. Lady Emerald had a similar problem when she was about ten that involved a rabbit, of all things, she—'

'Mama!' Jocasta slapped the table, making Flora jump. 'I would have thought you could have done better than revert to defective memory.'

'I don't know what you mean, Jocasta. Really I don't.' Lady Venetia's mouth twitched and her hand went back to her neck.

Jocasta opened her mouth again, about to ask her next question with some force but Flora gave a tiny shake of her head, forestalling her. Lady Venetia's obvious distress didn't seem worth the trouble, no matter how much Flora wanted the truth, leaving Jocasta to take her temper out on a slice of ham instead.

A tense silence ensued for the rest of the meal, broken only by the click of cutlery on china and an occasional clearing of throats.

'We shan't be in for tea, Jocasta.' Lady Vaughn stirred her coffee with a tiny silver spoon as delicate as her fingers. 'Your father and I have tickets for a choral recital at the Winter Gardens being performed as part of the coronation celebrations.'

'I hope you enjoy it, Mama,' Jocasta's voice was brittle.

'I doubt it. Look at that sky, not a cloud to be seen.' She laid down her spoon and stared through the window with a deep sigh. 'The building is like a greenhouse and gets insufferably hot during the summer. The last time we went there I almost fainted.'

'Why don't you take a blanket and sit on the grass in Imperial Square. One can hear every note just as well from there.'

'Jocasta, really!' Lady Venetia's chair screeched as it scraped across the floorboards. 'I don't know what poor Jeremy will do with you when you're married. You have no social sense at all. Blanket on the grass indeed.' She swept from the room, leaving an air of affront behind her.

'I think you upset her,' Flora said as the door closed with an ominous click.

'Don't be fooled, she couldn't care less about blankets. She's angry about my mentioning the cottage, although I doubt the truth is half as bad as our speculation.'

Flora had thought so too, but chose not to say so.

'Mama takes everything too seriously.' Jocasta drifted to the sideboard and poured herself more coffee. 'When I was small, Grandmamma liked to remind Mama that Grandpapa was a member of the New Club in the Promenade.' At Flora's perplexed frown, she went on, 'Mama's father being in trade meant he was blackballed, and Mama has never forgotten it.'

'That sounds very harsh, Jocasta. Not the black-balling, I knew the club had a rule about only

275

allowing "visitors of approved rank in society", but that your Grandmamma mentioned the fact.'

'Hmm, she could be something of a snob.' Jocasta delivered this understatement with a shrug. 'I only mentioned it to show you how socially aware Mama has always been.'

'And you are telling me this for what reason?' Flora asked, suspicious of her falsely casual tone.

Jocasta took a sip from her cup on her way back to the table. 'I heard Mama and Papa talking last night. And I say that as if it were a coincidence, but truth be told, I had to creep about for ages before I heard anything interesting.'

'You are incorrigible, Jocasta.' Flora jiggled her water glass, setting the ice chips tinkling. 'And what *did* you hear?'

'I'm not sure. However your mother was mentioned. And well, you know when people are talking about something they have known about for ages so they don't actually say the words, they just speak in a sort of clipped code?'

'That sounds as if whatever was said made no sense,' Flora said, disappointed.

''Fraid so, but I'll tell you anyway. Papa said, "You know we shall have to face it sometime," then a, "we've not spoken of it for years. Why should things change now?" from Mama.' She waved an airy hand in Flora's general direction. 'All very frustrating actually. I wanted to rush in and tell them to stop being so enigmatic and spit it out.'

'But you didn't, and nor did they?'

'No,' Jocasta sighed. 'I still don't know what they were talking about.'

'Yet you said they mentioned my mother?'

'Hmph,' Jocasta said on a mouthful of petit four, swallowing. 'I did, didn't I? Now what was it? Oh yes, Papa said, "Lily didn't want anyone to know what she was doing, which is why she told no one."'

'What was she doing?' Flora frowned.

'Sorry, no idea.' Jocasta hunched her shoulders, then caught sight of Flora's face, adding. 'Oh dear, have I made things worse?'

'More frustrating, certainly.' Flora crumpled her napkin and discarded it onto the table. It appeared she would have to do more investigations on her own if she was going to find out what had really happened to her mother. She toyed with the idea of asking Lord Vaughn, known for his pragmatic nature, certainly more so than his wife. Flora rejected that notion immediately. If he wouldn't spare time for Jocasta, she stood no chance at all. And what if he merely reiterated Hetty's garbled story about Lily's dubious past, but in more devastating detail? That would only remind them of mistakes best left forgotten. Only Flora didn't want to forget.

CHAPTER 19

Flora eased open the stable door and peered inside, greeted by the smell of fresh hay and the sweet tang of manure. A horse whinnied, and a hoof made harsh contact with the clay-tiled floor.

'May I help you, Miss Flora?' Tom loomed in front of her, sending her back a pace.

'You made me jump, Tom.' Flora pressed a hand to her bodice, aware she was blushing. 'Your eye looks a lot better.'

A greenish yellow bruise was all that remained of his injury. 'Thank you, Miss.' He ducked his head, dislodging a hank of hair that slipped over the offending eye.

'Lady Venetia said I could borrow the gig this afternoon,' Flora went on, breaking eye contact. 'Would you mind organizing that for me?'

'Sorry, Miss.' His shoulders slumped. 'Mr Bracenose took it out yesterday and must have hit a rock or something. The axle is broken and I won't be able to repair it until tomorrow.'

'Oh, well, don't worry. I can always get the tram, though don't mention that to Lady Venetia, she won't approve.' She turned to leave, then thought of something and paused. 'By the way, Tom, has that Constable Jones been back again?'

'Jones?' Tom's eyebrows rose in a poor attempt to intimate he didn't know what she was talking about. 'Not since you saw him the last time.'

'I hoped he had some news, that's all. You must be worried that nothing has been heard from Betsy since she left.'

'I suppose so, Miss Flora, but she'll be back when she wants.' Quickly he added, 'I mean, I expect she will.'

Flora turned away again just as a loud thump came from somewhere over her head. She halted and scrutinized the ceiling, then tilted her head in enquiry at Tom.

'My dog.' Tom shrugged, then reached past her and grasped the door which led to the groom's rooms, preventing her opening it any further. 'She's just a pup, so is still a handful.'

'I didn't know you had a dog, Tom.'

'Aye, Miss.' He swallowed, and flicked a glance at the ceiling. 'A black and white collie. I shut her in my rooms when I'm working. She gets a bit fretful.'

'Seems a shame to keep her locked upstairs. I'm sure Lord Vaughn wouldn't mind another dog on the grounds.'

'She's a daft little thing, and not well trained yet so not to be trusted, but a good lass. I'd better go up and see to her presently or she'll start to howl.'

He backed up a few steps and waited, most probably hoping Flora would take the hint and leave.

'Oh, Tom,' Flora called him back again, trying not to smile at his nervous jump and the way he arranged his face into innocence. 'Have you seen Master Eddy this morning?'

'He's usually around here somewhere at this time.' He paused with his hand on the wooden handrail, frowning. 'Come to think of it, Miss Flora, not since yesterday.'

'I've seen so little of him since I arrived. He and Lord Vaughn seem to be busy on the estate lately. I expect I'll catch up with him before we leave.'

'I'll be sure to keep a look out and if I see him, I'll let him know.' His attention drifted back to the stairs.

'Thank you, Tom.' She returned to the drive, idly wondering why Tom thought it necessary to keep his dog confined. The estate had plenty of working animals who slept in the outhouses, but ran free during the day. Had her focus not been elsewhere, she might have thought there was more to his story than he was willing to reveal, but by the time she had reached the tram stop, Tom and his dog were forgotten.

The Montpellier Pharmacy occupied a corner in a shopping district on the edge of the town, close to where the original spa stood that had made the area fashionable during Regency times. Tall, right-angled windows topped with stained glass in patterns of purple grapes and lush green leaves gave it a majestic appearance, whilst apothecary jars in various sizes filled with coloured liquids crowded the window.

'Not everyone can read, Flora,' he had told her at the time. 'Those are symbols to show the pharmacist is well-trained and therefore educated enough to mix his own medicines.'

As a child, Flora's childish imagination had conjured them into magical solutions that could cure every ailment, and she had been disappointed when her father had explained the enchanting bottles were purely decorative and held nothing more than coloured water.

A tightness formed in her chest and she forced the memory down as she pushed open a glazed door set in the corner of the building which rattled in its frame, setting off a loud jangling of a bell.

A solid wooden counter ran the width of the shop, behind which a floor-to-ceiling wooden dresser took up the entire back wall. From just below hip-height, rows of shelves containing square jars filled with powders of various colours rose to the high ceiling. From tiny rocks to fine white sand, each jar was labelled with both English and Latin names. Beneath the shelves were rows of rectangular wooden drawers with metal label holders attached, stacked five deep and containing more entrancing chemicals, herbs and concoctions used in the dispensing of medicines.

Flora inhaled a combination of antiseptic, carbolic

and lavender from a basket of handmade soaps on the counter that evoked long-ago memories.

The same young man she had seen outside the coroner's office appeared from the rear. He wore a leather apron tied round his waist, his shirtsleeves rolled up to his elbows and held in place by thin black bands of elastic.

'Mr Meeks?' Flora began. 'You don't know me, but I'm—'

'Mrs Flora Harrington,' he finished for her. 'I saw you at the inquest this morning.'

Flora took the hand he thrust toward her, his grip strong and warm without being intimidating. 'If you don't mind my saying so, I admired your interrupting Dr Fairbrother's testimony. I've often wished I had the courage to do the same thing myself.'

'Oh yes, that.' Flora's face flamed and she withdrew her hand. 'I shouldn't have spoken out. My husband wasn't impressed, and he's a solicitor.'

'Nonsense. Inaction on any front promotes apathy, when it's obvious changes need to be made.'

'Did you disagree with what Dr Fairbrother said?'

'I often disagree with that pompous quack.' His frown didn't match the light of amusement in his almost black eyes. 'Not about your father's accident, mind you, I didn't have an opinion on that one way or another. However, I felt his diagnosis of neuritis for Lord Vaughn's workers was off the mark.'

'Actually, that's what I came to ask you, Mr Meeks.

I believe my father had a theory too. I have no proof, but something occurred at the summer fête which might relate to why he died.'

'Like what?' Reginald Meeks' expression transformed from levity to seriousness in an instant. 'I was at the fête, but didn't notice anything untoward. Do tell me more.'

'Are you sure this is convenient?' Flora gave the shop a sweeping glance, but there appeared to be no other customers. 'I mean you're at work.'

'One of the advantages of being one's own master, Mrs Harrington, is one can take a break whenever it suits.' He gestured for Flora to follow him to the rear of the shop, where a marble-topped counter held a pestle and mortar for grinding powders beside a set of gleaming gold scales for weighing babies. 'I need to remain in plain sight of the shop in case a customer comes in.' He beckoned her to where a hinged partition created a modicum of privacy.

Flora placed her bag on the counter. 'Now, what were you saying about neuritis?'

'That I didn't think it was correct.' He folded surprisingly muscular arms across his chest. 'Peripheral neuritis is normally associated with heavy drinkers. Lord Vaughn would never have allowed that in his workers and to my knowledge discharged more than one man who frequently got drunk at work in the last year. He always said drink and plough shears did not make a good combination.'

'And so they don't,' Flora murmured. 'Did anyone exhibit symptoms who didn't attend the fête? For instance, anyone who drinks at the Red Kite?'

'I know what you're thinking, Mrs Harrington. Despite what the rumours said, Mr Griggs doesn't sell contaminated beer. If he had, more people would have become sick.'

'What do *you* think made the men ill, Mr Meeks?'

He hesitated, his lips pursed. 'I'm not a doctor, so please don't quote me. I thought their symptoms were more closely related to some sort of heavy metal poisoning.'

'Arsenic, for instance?'

He smiled and nodded. 'I see you've read the report of the Manchester brewery incident? Your father showed that to me. Quite astute of him to think the two were related.'

'Mr McCallum refutes that his beer could have been poisoned.'

'Indeed.' He uncrossed his arms and ran the knuckles of one hand along his jaw. 'Interesting. I heard he had the whole place shut down for several days and inspected.'

'Which means any poison must have been deliberately added to the beer at the fête, and only the fête.' Flora studied his expression, but he showed no surprise, only interest.

'Your father didn't mention that. Is it the conclusion you've come to?'

'Perhaps it's safer to say I'm toying with the idea.

May I ask what you were arguing about with Dr Fairbrother after the inquest?'

'Ah, you noticed that did you?' He ran a hand through his thick black hair, leaving it tousled. 'I challenged him as to why he hadn't mentioned Mr Maguire's suspicions. And mine come to that.'

'What did he say?'

'Only that it wasn't relevant to Maguire's death. He even accused me of scaremongering.'

'Is that why you came to the inquest?'

Reginald nodded. 'I hoped I might be called as a witness, but Dr Fairbrother must have told the coroner it wasn't necessary.'

'What did you think?'

'Honestly?' He raised a mobile brow, but didn't appear to expect a response. 'Neuritis affects the nerve endings and shows up in different rates and severity in each individual. Sometimes the paralysis comes first, or for some, tiredness is the only symptom. Then comes muscle weakness, weight loss, tremors. Those things don't occur simultaneously in six different patients.'

'And these symptoms are similar to arsenic poisoning?'

He nodded. 'When I made the same observation to Dr Fairbrother, he called me an "unqualified pill grinder".' His boyish grin showed no malice at this insult, which made Flora admire his self-confidence even more.

'Mr Griggs told me you've given him medicine for his son, Peter.'

He bit the corner of his bottom lip. His head tilted. 'Ah, now that's not quite true. The tonic I gave him is no substitute for a doctor's care, which Griggs cannot afford.'

'Is Peter not improving?'

'He's no worse, I know that. Griggs is convinced Peter displays signs of early consumption. What I give him is an antipyrine and syrup mixture, which won't cure a disease like that in any case, only ease the symptoms. Peter has no paralysis as yet, only fatigue that comes and goes. And no,' he held up a hand when Flora was about to speak, 'I doubt Peter drank beer at the fête. I'm aware some fourteen-year-old boys do with the approval of their families, but Griggs frowned on it. He knows how easily drink can become a dangerous habit, he sees it every day at The Red Kite.'

'When I spoke to Mr Griggs, I got the impression he had felt nothing more could be done for Peter.' As if he was reconciled to losing him and had washed his hands of Betsy.

'Try and see it from his point of view.' Reginald's eyes softened with sympathy. 'Griggs watched his wife die slowly, which must have been hard for any man. Now he faces the prospect of watching his only child go the same way. It's a cruel life, Mrs Harrington. Don't mistake his disappointment for disinterest. He's heartbroken.'

'You put it very succinctly, Mr Meeks.' Flora liked this man, who seemed to see life's trials clearly and had a firm grip on where he stood in the world. He reminded her of Bunny in some ways. 'Do you think Peter has consumption?'

'That's where my experience falls short. All I have to guide me is his father's description of his symptoms. Griggs says that Peter seems quite well at times, a bit pale and scrawny, but he's always been like that. He had rheumatic fever as a child. Then he has days when he cannot drag himself out of bed.'

'Mr Meeks,' Flora began carefully. 'Would you let me see the poison book?' Despite his open, friendly attitude, she was still a stranger and he was within his rights to refuse.

Instead, he laughed. 'Your father had the same thought, but I'll tell you what I told him.' He withdrew a leather-bound volume from beneath the counter, and set it in front of her. 'As you'll see, it's full of familiar names who bought arsenic for various uses – including McCallum's butler, Amy Coombe and Mrs Mountjoy. In fact Reverend Cripps's housekeeper's name is there too.'

'I see what you mean. It doesn't help much, does it? We cannot regard everyone who buys arsenic as culpable or the whole town would be under suspicion.' Her gaze swept down the page again. 'I cannot see any larger than normal amounts purchased either. Nor more frequent ones.'

'You don't need to buy arsenic in its pure form.' He slid the book back across the counter. 'Soaking fly paper in water results in an effective suspension. Some women use it to whiten their skin.'

'I would never attempt that myself. I would be too worried about how much I absorbed.' Flora had an ambiguous attitude towards cosmetics, her insecurities about her looks vying with her wish not to appear fast.

'Another thing, is—'

The jangle of the shop bell interrupted whatever Reginald Meeks was about to say next, and he turned as a middle-aged man in a homburg hat wandered in.

'Excuse me a moment,' Reginald left her side and advanced on the new arrival, hands extended in welcome.

Flora waited as the two men embarked on a discussion of the qualities of various brands of hair pomade. Finally, the man made a choice and, accompanied by the pharmacist's enthusiastic praise as to his choice of the perfect product, the pharmacist wrapped the purchase in brown paper and showed him to the door.

'I was about to say,' Reginald said on his way back across the polished floor. 'Arsenic reacts differently in certain people. A small dose can make one person quite ill, while another will remain unaffected. However, if ingested over time, it accumulates in the system and breaks down the organs.'

'Will it always kill?'

'If taken for long enough, definitely.'

'I wasn't aware of that.' Flora gasped as the truth hit her like a cold wave. The symptoms Reginald had described for Peter exactly matched those Eddy displayed. Tiredness, pallid complexion, lack of appetite. Eddy was built like a railing but was always hungry. He never missed food voluntarily. How could she have been so blind? She had been so focused on the sick workers and who might be responsible, she had allowed the situation with Eddy's health to pass her by.

While debating what to do, she barely registered the jangle of the shop bell and the rattle of the door frame that announced the arrival of another customer.

'I ought to go,' Flora said, apologetic and eager to be off at the same time. 'I'm interrupting your work.'

'Not at all,' Reginald assured her. 'This has proved most enlightening.' He glanced past Flora's shoulder to where his smile wilted at the edges. 'Good afternoon, Mrs Mountjoy.'

Flora swung round, her surprised gaze meeting Caroline's serene one.

'How nice to see you, Flora.' Caroline lifted her free hand as if preparing to bestow a gesture on a minion. Her sharp eyes slid over the poison book beneath Flora's hand and then back to Reginald. 'I see you've discovered the excellent Mr Meeks.' She cast him a flirtatious look that would have discomposed most young men. Reginald, however, returned her look coldly. *Not an admirer then?*

'What brings you here, Flora?' Caroline asked. 'When there's a perfectly adequate apothecary in Bishop's Cleeve?'

Flora searched for a credible response, but decided she didn't need one. She wasn't required to explain her actions to Caroline Mountjoy. 'Completing a few personal errands. What brings you here?' *Buying arsenic perhaps?*

'Your Beecham's Pills, Mrs Harrington.' Reginald emerged at almost a run from behind the counter, and pressed a brown-paper-wrapped parcel into Flora's hands. 'I do hope your husband's sore throat gets better soon.'

'Yes, er thank you.' Flora kept her eyes averted. Had she met his eye just then she would have burst into laughter.

'Sore throats in summer are quite rare, but I suppose not unheard of.' Mrs Mountjoy didn't respond to Flora's question and sashayed towards her, trailing a hand through the basket of soaps on the counter. 'I'm glad to have run into you, Flora dear. I wanted to invite you to tea at my home tomorrow.'

'Thank you, Mrs Mountjoy, although I'm not sure what my husband's plans are. I'll let you know when I've spoken to him.'

'Oh no, I don't want any men around.' Her gazed flicked over Flora with ill-concealed scepticism. 'No, my dear, just you and me. Besides, if Mr Harrington isn't well, he ought to remain in bed and keep warm. Do say you'll come.'

Flora placed the unwanted package in her bag.

She had to get back to the Abbey and tell them about Eddy. Then halted as she recalled his parents weren't at home. William and Jocasta might be, as well as Bunny. But if Eddy was really sick, he would need more than her concern. He would need medical attention.

'Tea, Flora,' Caroline tapped her arm, making her jump. 'I said is three thirty convenient?'

'I, uh, I'm sorry, I must go.' Flora moved past her. 'Good afternoon, Mrs Mountjoy.'

The pharmacist strode across the floor and hauled open the door with a scrape of warped wood and a harsh jangle of the bell. 'You're a brave woman to snub her,' he whispered as he bowed her onto the pavement. 'Her tentacles reach a long way.'

'She doesn't intimidate me,' Flora murmured, then louder. 'If you would put the Beecham's on Lord Vaughn's account, I'll settle with him later.

CHAPTER 20

O ut on the street again, Flora debated what to do first; go for the tram, or waste another ten minutes walking to Dr Fairbrother's office? A quick glance at the Rotunda clock behind her told her it was after three, but before she could make up her mind, she saw Caroline Mountjoy emerge from Mr Meeks' shop.

Unwilling to attract the woman's attention for a second time that day, Flora ducked into the doorway of the butcher's shop next door. Through the plate glass window a well-rounded man in a striped apron scrubbed at tiles that bore traces of blood and scraps of raw meat. He looked up when he saw her in his doorway, a look of enquiry on his round face. Flora fretted on the pavement in the afternoon sun. Her dress stuck to her skin and her hair felt damp on the back of her neck. She aimed a polite smile in the butcher's direction before checking the road again; relieved to see Mrs Mountjoy's carriage was no longer beside the kerb.

She rapidly retraced her steps to the pharmacy, which was empty. Mr Meeks stood behind the counter, his head bent as he counted white pills into a bottle, the harsh clatter of the bell as she entered bringing his head up.

'Back again, Mrs Harrington?' He rested both forearms on the counter and grinned at her. 'You're quite safe. Mrs Mountjoy is most likely halfway home by now.'

'I'm not at all concerned about Mrs Mountjoy,' Flora snorted. 'I've a favour to ask which you may think presumptuous, but please listen until I have finished.'

'That sounds serious.' Unruffled by her curt tone, his smile persisted as he returned the bottle to its place and folded his arms over the bib of his leather apron. 'Fire away.'

'I think Eddy is displaying the symptoms of arsenic poisoning.'

'Are you sure?' His smile faded and he dropped his arms to his sides. 'No, of course you are or you wouldn't—' He pushed a hand through his immaculate hair, leaving it standing up on one side. 'What can I do?'

Flora released a relieved breath that she didn't have to waste time persuading him.

'I have to take someone with me to the Abbey who knows something about arsenic poisoning.'

'What about Dr Fairbrother? He'll be in his surgery at this time.' He flicked a look at the clock on the wall then back at her.

'I thought of him first, but changed my mind. I'm sorry if that sounds unreasonable, but he's already got things wrong once. At least I'm pretty sure he has. I don't want him to dismiss me as hysterical and convince Lord and Lady Vaughn I don't know what I'm talking about. I need someone with more authority, and thought of you. Would you come back to the Abbey with me?'

'Of course, but I'm not a doctor. Why would Lord Vaughn listen to me?' He considered a moment. 'However, there is someone we could ask, but I'm not sure how Lord Vaughn would view a woman doctor.'

'You mean Dr Billings?' Flora brightened. 'I've heard of her. Do you think she would help?' She hesitated, dismayed. 'But, I don't know where to find her.'

'I do.' Reginald tugged his apron over his head and slung it on a hook behind the door to the rear of the shop.

'Mr Meeks, I didn't mean you to go to all this trouble. If you could give me some directions I'm sure I could find her myself.'

'Nonsense. Give me a moment to close the shop and we'll go together. Her surgery is in Pittville Parade, which is too far to walk, so we'll take the tram. He rummaged in a drawer, picked out a jar and placed it on the counter. 'We'll take this, it's magnesium sulphate, which might help if his heart rate has become thready.' He pulled out another bottle that joined the first. 'Sodium bicarbonate might be useful too.'

He went to a hook on the wall and shrugged into his jacket, slipping a jar into each of the larger pockets. Collecting his bowler hat, he guided her back to the door where he flicked the 'Open' sign to 'Closed' and ushered her onto the street. 'Some medics make their patients chew charcoal biscuits, but in my view they do little but taste awful,' he added, locking the door behind him.

'I do appreciate this,' Flora said as they hurried towards the tram stop.

'Not at all.' He nodded to where a tram whined to a halt. 'You've made my day considerably more interesting. Not that I would wish anything bad to happen to Viscount Trent, of course. Now tell me, exactly what these symptoms are?'

He paid the fare for both of them and when they had taken their seats, Flora described Eddy's recent behaviour. His lethargy and lack of appetite, as well as his pale complexion which should have been tanned and healthy at this time of year.

'Do you think I'm right?' she said when she had finished.

He nodded slowly. 'Certainly sounds like heavy metal poisoning. How do you think it happened?'

'I'm not sure, but the only answer is that somehow, Eddy got hold of some of the beer at the fête.'

'That was nearly a month ago, he wouldn't still be suffering now. If there was arsenic in the beer, and I'm saying 'if', there was nothing proved, the estate workers who drank it succumbed immediately afterwards. They recovered fully within a couple of weeks. Symptoms wouldn't persist this long unless—'

'He kept drinking it,' Flora finished for him.

'Exactly.' He lifted one brow in admiration. 'If he ingested tiny amounts over a long period of time he would exhibit chronic, though milder symptoms.'

'I'm not certain how or when, but it's the only thing I can think of.'

'Interesting that you should suspect arsenic poisoning. Mr McCallum thought the same thing.'

'Mr McCallum did?' She hadn't expected that. 'When?'

'Dr Fairbrother told me, and with some degree of skepticism too. Said the man had got it all wrong and it was neuritis. He didn't like it when I said McCallum had a point either. The good doctor and I disagree on many things.'

Flora reverted to thoughtful silence, surprised that Mr McCallum would do such a thing if it was his own brewery which would likely be held responsible. While her thoughts raced she became aware they were stationary and fidgeted on her seat. 'What's holding us up?'

'Looks like an argument over right of way.' Reginald strained his neck to see ahead. 'The trams are so new to this town, no one is quite sure of the rules about positioning of other traffic on the roads. The authorities should address it before accidents happen. Ah, here we go. Don't fret, Mrs Harrington, we'll be there soon.'

'You were saying about Mr McCallum?' Flora asked when they got going again.

'Ah yes, well Mr McCallum asked my opinion. He wondered if it could be poisoning instead. I thought it odd at the time, I mean, if I had disagreed with the good doctor, it wouldn't have done McCallum any favours.'

'That's exactly what I think,' Flora bit her lip. 'Perhaps he simply wanted to make sure.'

'As it happens, I didn't contradict the neuritis diagnosis at the time. Not until your father came to me with his articles about the Manchester brewery.'

'Did what he said change your mind?'

'It did, actually, but the men had recovered by then, so it seemed pointless to take it further.'

'But you still thought it might have been arsenic which made them ill?'

'It was a possibility, yes. Though it never occurred to me Eddy Vaughn could have been affected or I would never have let the matter drop.'

'You weren't to know. I've been staying there and it's taken me a few days to notice what was going on. I knew Eddy looked peaky but I didn't consider that he might be genuinely ill. I was so focused on my father's – accident, I went along with what everyone else thought.'

'And what did everyone else think?'

'Summer colds, growing pains, laziness?' She shrugged, aware saying it aloud sounded feeble now.

'Sounds about right, especially if Dr Fairbrother saw him. You were once his governess, weren't you?' At her nod he smiled. 'That explains the maternal instinct. Must be difficult to turn that off simply because your life has changed.'

'It is, and thank you for understanding. Sometimes even my husband finds that difficult to accept.' She flushed at the thought she had been disloyal to Bunny, but Mr Meeks didn't seem to notice.

'That didn't take long, did it?' He nodded to where the Pittville Park Gates loomed in the front window of the tram. 'This is our stop, the surgery is in Pittville Parade, which is just along the terrace there and on our right.'

No. 3, was a tall narrow, white rendered house comprised of four storeys, in the style of the properties of the Georgian kings, though it had been built in the last fifty years. A small front garden sat behind black railings, a short flight of steps led to a black front door on the upper ground floor.

In response to Reginald's knock, a forbidding-looking woman in a grey dress answered the door. She looked to be in late middle-age with a slab face, empty, disinterested eyes and her hair scraped back from her forehead, making her skin look shiny. If this was Dr Billings, Flora didn't hold out much hope for a sympathetic hearing.

'Is Dr Billings available?' Mr Meeks asked.

Flora released a relieved breath, but her next words were no more encouraging.

'The doctor is not available. The surgery is closed. I suggest you come back in the morning.' She had the door halfway closed again when

Reginald braced his hand against it, forcing her backwards. 'A moment of her time wouldn't hurt, surely?'

'This is an emergency,' Flora pleaded. 'Couldn't you ask Dr Billings to at least speak to us?'

'Dr Billings has finished for the day,' the woman said, as if she had turned to more important matters. She gestured for Reginald to remove his hand, when a female voice spoke from behind her.

'Who is it, Agnes?'

'Some people, Doctor,' the woman gave Flora a head-to-toe stare. 'Not known to you,' she added as if that settled the matter.

'Really, Agnes, what have I told you about callers? I never turn away prospective patients.' She insinuated herself in front of the servant, sending her back into the hall. 'I'm sorry about that. I'm Dr Grace Billings, is there something you need?'

A woman of about thirty stood on the threshold, her dark hair gathered on top of her head in a loose bun. She was not a pretty in the conventional sense, being possessed of a broad forehead, a slightly protruding chin and a thin-lipped mouth set in a straight line. Her direct dark eyes were the most animated part about her, though with a slight cast to the left one that pinned Flora with an open, candid stare. She held a small boy of about three in her arms, his thumb stuck into his pink mouth, his legs wrapped round her waist.

'Allow me to introduce myself,' Reginald removed

299

his hat. 'I'm Reginald Meeks from the pharmacy in Montpellier.'

'I believe I've heard of you, Mr Meeks. Your reputation precedes you. And don't look so apologetic. I grew up in my father's chemist shop in Bristol, thus I appreciate the extensive knowledge required for your profession.'

'It's kind of you to say so.' He turned an attractive shade of pink. 'This,' he indicated Flora, 'is Mrs Harrington, who believes she has identified a case of arsenic poisoning.'

'Two cases,' Flora added. 'Which have gone unnoticed for some time and need your help.'

'Days or weeks?' the lady asked without preamble.

'A couple of weeks. Please, could you come?'

Without another word, Dr Billings pressed the child she held into the housekeeper's arms. 'Take Frederick for me, Agnes. I have to go.' Ignoring the boy's whining protests, she took a light coat from a hook on the wall and shrugged into it. The little boy snuffled in the housekeeper's arms and before closing the door behind her, his mother planted a kiss on his rounded cheek.

'I brought magnesium sulphate and sodium bicarbonate,' Reginald showed her the bottles in his pockets.

'Excellent.' The doctor held up the square leather bag she had retrieved from inside the door. 'I'm not sure of my supplies and from what you have both said, there's no time to lose. My gig is in the mews. It will take a few moments to hitch the horse, then we'll be off.'

'Allow me to help. I'm quite good with horses.' Reginald moved toward the side gate.

'His name is Jed. The groom, that is, not the horse,' Dr Billings aimed a wry smile in his direction as she called after him.

'It's very kind of you to come at such short notice,' Flora said, self-conscious to find herself alone with the doctor. 'Especially for someone you don't know.'

'Not kind, Mrs Harrington. It's my profession to heal the sick.' She busied herself with fastening the buttons of her green coat, her leather bag tucked neatly between her feet. 'Incidentally, where exactly are the patients?'

'Lord Vaughn's residence at Cleeve Abbey. One of the boys is his son.'

'I see.' Her hands stilled on the last button for a second, then as if she made up her mind, she retrieved the bag. 'I hope that won't cause any problems.'

'Why should it?' Flora replied, with confidence. 'Lord Vaughn is quite liberal-minded and one of the rare creatures who actually likes women and appreciates them as intelligent beings. He has three daughters who have played a part in that opinion.'

'Suddenly I feel slightly more at ease.' Dr Billings smiled, a gentle, knowing smile that told Flora that given the right circumstances, they could be friends.

'Have you always wanted to be a doctor?' Flora asked, fascinated. She had never met a woman who had attended a university before, which made her if not tongue-tied, then unsure where to begin as questions filled her head.

'As long as I can remember. It began in my father's chemist shop where I developed an early love for chemistry. My sister, Mary, is a doctor too.'

Flora was about to ask what it was like to heal but was interrupted by the arrival of Mr Meeks as he pulled the gig to an abrupt halt in front of them.

'I think you might be wrong, Doctor.' He grinned before jumping down to help the women up the step. 'The horse didn't mind being called Jed at all.'

Dr Billings laughed, a full throated sound that lifted the heavy atmosphere immediately. She handed Mr Meeks her bag with the aplomb of a duchess, with a curt, 'I'll drive.'

The two-mile journey to South Cleeve seemed to take far longer than usual, made more frustrating when the gig was passed by a tramcar on Cleeve Hill which upset the horse. Finally they reached the top of the hill and passed through the Abbey gates.

Flora's feet barely touched the ground as she hurtled up the front steps, and fumbled with the oversized door catch which stubbornly refused to turn.

'Allow me.' Reginald wrested it from her and gave the ancient iron ring a firm twist.

The massive oak slab that had greeted monks in grey habits centuries ago swung open with a creak as the three burst into the hall.

The ornamental mirror at the bottom of the staircase showed that Flora's straw hat had slipped to the back of her head, the end of the black ribbon tied round the crown had come undone, and the end lay across one shoulder. There was no sign of Scrivens as she led the way to the sitting room.

Bunny looked up as the three of them entered, crumpled his newspaper in his lap and rose. 'Flora, whatever is the matter? You're quite breathless, have you been running?'

'I have.' Flora took off her hat and removed her gloves, which she tossed on a chair, together with her bag that contained the Beecham's pills. 'Where's Eddy?'

'We don't know,' Jocasta said, sighing. 'The wretch hasn't been here all afternoon.' Her gaze slid over Dr Billings to Reginald. 'Mr Meeks, what are you doing here?'

'What's going on, Flora?' William eased forward on the sofa and set down his teacup and saucer on the table in front of him.

'This is Dr Grace Billings.' Flora conducted a brief introduction. 'There's no time to explain, it will take too long. We need to find Eddy.'

'You're the lady doctor?' Jocasta asked, open-mouthed. 'I didn't think you would look so, well – ordinary.'

'Jo,' William warned.

'I didn't mean it like that, it's just with all this talk about how unnatural it is for a woman to study medicine, I thought—'

'Please don't upset yourself, Lady Jocasta.' Dr Billings inclined her head. 'I shall accept that as a compliment. Some male members of the medical word regard me as the devil incarnate equipped with horns.' She looked round vaguely. 'Now, where is the patient?'

'He isn't here, apparently.' Flora's voice hitched in panic. 'When did any of you last see him?'

'Now I think about it, not since breakfast.' Jocasta eyed the bulky outline in Mr Meeks' pockets made by the medicine bottles. 'Papa returned from Gloucester at about two o'clock, but Eddy wasn't with him. Mama and Papa left for the matinee assuming he would be back for tea, but he hasn't turned up, and well, to tell you the truth, I'm getting a little worried.'

Flora groaned. She had forgotten Lord and Lady Vaughn were at the Winter Gardens that afternoon. 'We have to find him.'

Bunny advanced on Flora and waved the rest of them into silence. 'Flora what's this all about? Has something happened to Eddy?'

Flora opened her mouth to explain, but her breathing had quickened and not knowing where to begin, she hesitated.

'From what Mrs Harrington has told me,' Dr Billings took command of the conversation, 'They might be suffering from arsenical poisoning. He needs medical attention immediately.'

'Eddy is ill?' Jocasta's face turned from mild enquiry to horror.

'You said they,' William rose to his feet. 'Who else are we talking about?'

'Peter Griggs has the same symptoms,' Flora said, slightly calmer now. 'His father thinks he has consumption, but I – we, aren't so sure.' She looked at Reginald, including him in her statement.

'Mrs Harrington might well be right.' Dr Billings hefted the leather bag she had placed on an empty chair. 'Both boys could be suffering from poisoning. Now how do we find out where they are?'

A chorus of, 'surely nots', and 'are you sures'? followed.

'We don't have time to argue,' Flora silenced them. 'Jocasta, are Eddy and Peter particular friends?'

'They played together all the time when they were small, but.' Jocasta shrugged, and a flush crept up her neck. 'Papa feels Eddy needs to make friends of his own sort now he's at Marlborough, although I know they catch up in secret when Eddy comes back for holidays.'

'Perhaps they're together at The Red Kite?' Flora asked, insistent. 'Or is there somewhere else they usually go?'

'Slow down, Flora, you're panicking.' Bunny placed a firm hand on her arm. 'Firstly, tell us how you think the boys have come to be poisoned.'

'I can't slow down.' His calm reasoning made

her more agitated. 'We have to find Eddy. Dr Billings needs to see him as soon as possible to assess how badly he's been affected. For all we know it might be too late.'

'What?' Bunny and William said together.

'Mr Harrington,' Reginald interrupted, 'it's possible the boys got hold of some of the beer from the fête and have been sneaking off to drink it. If they have consumed small quantities over a long period of time, it explains why they are both still sick.'

'Eddy doesn't drink beer,' Jocasta protested. 'Father only lets him have the odd sherry before dinner.'

'He's fourteen, Jo.' William snorted then walked to the bell pull. 'Don't tell me you did everything you were told at that age. Heavens, girl, you don't do it now.' He took instant command of the situation. 'We'll try The Red Kite first and see if Griggs knows where either boy is. What's the quickest way to get there?'

'I have my gig outside,' Dr Billings, said calmly. 'It will hold two of us and both boys if we find them. No more, I'm afraid.'

'I'm tempted to summon the carriage but it will take too long to get that organized.' William massaged his forehead with one hand. 'Doctor, you and Bunny go in the gig. I'll follow on horseback as soon as I can get a mount saddled. I'll do it myself if necessary.'

Scrivens arrived from wherever he had been

hiding, his expression vacant to the point of boredom; William issued instructions as to what to tell Lord and Lady Vaughn when they returned.

'If you'll allow me, sir,' Reginald interrupted him, 'I could remain here to do that, and have somewhere made ready for when you return.'

'Good idea, Mr Meeks,' Flora announced. 'Because I'm coming too, so Bunny, you'll need a horse as well because I shall be in Dr Billings' gig.'

'What about me? He's my brother,' Jocasta protested.

William grabbed her arm and held her back. 'I think you should wait here with Mr Meeks.' He raised a brow at Reginald who acquiesced with a gesture of one hand. 'If your parents return before we find Eddy, they'll need a familiar face to reassure them. And let's face it, Jo, you're not good in a crisis.'

'I refute that!' Jocasta yelled, but William had already gone.

Flora mouthed a thank you to Reginald, pressed Jocasta's hand in sympathy before she ran out onto the drive and climbed onto Dr Billings' gig.

'William knows where we're going,' Flora said to Bunny, who nodded and ran towards the stables after William. 'I do hope we find them in time.'

'You're convinced the boys are together?' Dr Billings turned the gig in a tight circle and set off towards the gates.

'I cannot be sure, but it's likely, if Eddy has been sneaking off on his own.' She gripped the seat with both hands and hung on. 'I don't know what we'll do if not.'

'We'll face that when we get to it.' The doctor urged the horse faster. 'If no one has seen them all day, time might be of the essence.'

CHAPTER 21

'Where exactly is this public house?' Dr Billings asked, slowing the gig a little as the road levelled out and became a winding High Street with tightly packed houses on both sides.

'Just past the next corner, the pub juts into the road so you cannot miss it. There's a horse trough opposite where the men can tether their horses.'

Flora had only just spoken when the gig rounded the bend and the unmissable sight of The Red Kite came into view.

'Over there on the right,' Flora called as Dr Billings brought the gig to a halt.

Flora fretted, debating whether or not to go inside or wait for William and Bunny, while the doctor secured the reins to one of the metal rings designed for horses.

'What are you waiting there for?' Doctor Billings hauled her leather bag from the flatbed and cocked her chin in the direction of the pub. 'We won't find them out here.' Without waiting for an answer, she pushed open the door to the taproom and went inside before the door flapped shut behind her.

Recalling the hard looks Mr Griggs had levelled at her on her last visit, Flora reluctantly climbed down and followed.

The taproom had small square windows and a low-beamed ceiling which contributed to its gloomy yet cosy appearance. Dr Billings stood at the counter, waiting to speak to the landlord, and Flora came alongside her.

The bar had recently been opened, some chairs still turned upside down on the tables, the tiled floor shiny and wet from a recent wash evidenced by a strong odour of carbolic soap.

Mr Griggs sauntered slowly from the back room, his eyes narrowing when he saw the upright woman in his pub, followed by a deep frown when he spotted Flora.

'What are you ladies—' he began, but Dr Billings held up a hand to silence him.

'I have no patience with your male sensibilities. I'm here to ask the whereabouts of Edward Vaughn and your son.'

'My son? What do yer want with 'im?' Mr Griggs' face darkened.

'I don't have time to explain, but if you have any information, it would be much appreciated.' Dr Billings met his glare with one of challenge.

'Haven't seen Peter for hours.' Griggs' angry glare turned to puzzlement. 'He went off somewhere this morning.' He grabbed a wet glass off the counter in front of him and set to polishing it with a cloth. An odd thing to do in the circumstances,

Flora thought, but then he wasn't aware of the circumstances and Dr Billings seemed unwilling to tell him. So as not to worry him perhaps?

'Was he alone?' Flora asked, incensed when he answered her with a bored shrug.

'You must have some idea where he's gone?' She brought a fist down on the counter, sending the man's eyebrows into his hairline.

'I've a pub to run, can't be chasing after him all day.' Griggs sniffed. 'He looked a bit washed out earlier, so I told him to get some fresh air. He's prob'ly down by the stream fishin' fer stickle-backs. What's the lad done anyway?'

'He hasn't done anything, Mr Griggs.' Flora touched Dr Billings' arm gently. 'We're wasting time. No point worrying him until we know for sure'. She flicked a swift look at Griggs and away again. 'We'll have to make a search field by field.'

'I agree.' They retreated to the door when Griggs called them back. 'There's a shepherd's hut on the hill. The village nippers take picnics up there sometimes.' He stared at the glass he held and shrugged. 'Don't know what yer makin' all this fuss is about. He gets tired easily so never stays out long.'

'I know where the hut is. The boys used to go there a lot.' Flora ran back to the gig and climbed the step. 'We can go as far as the rise, but we'll have to work our way down the hillside on foot.'

The doctor nodded, flung her bag into the back

311

and took the reins, just as approaching hoof beats behind them announced the arrival of William and Bunny.

'Do you know where they are?' Bunny reined his bay mare in behind the gig. William rode the more spirited Diabolus, who crabbed sideway, mouthing the bit, but William seemed to have no trouble controlling him.

'We think Eddy's with Peter,' Flora called. 'It's about a quarter of a mile further on. A stile into the field beside a signpost marks the spot.'

William nodded, spurred Diabolus into a gallop, followed by Bunny's mount, a chestnut with a white flash on its chest. They had disappeared round a bend by the time Dr Billings had manoeuvred the gig back onto the road. Flora squeezed her eyes closed and sent up a silent prayer, something she didn't do very often.

By the time Dr Billings drew the gig to a halt on the brow of the hill, the summer dusk had spread fingers of pink and grey light over the hillside. The two horses had been secured to the gate beside the stile, though there was no sign of either William or Bunny.

'This way.' Flora bunched up her skirts and clambered over the stile. She turned back to offer the doctor a hand, but the woman needed no help and set out towards a squat, stone hut that lay below then, only the roof visible from the road. The long side was set into the earth of the incline, the three exposed sides made of packed stone open to the winds that swept across the soft fields towards the Malvern Hills in the distance; a view Flora had no time to appreciate as she made her way sideways down the steep incline, watching for uneven tufts that would turn an ankle or send her to the bottom.

A low wooden door gave entry to the hut from the narrow end that lay open, the shadowy figures of Bunny and William visible inside.

'Are they there?' Flora halted at the door. The interior was only large enough for two truckle beds set on either side, a tiny stove on the wall between them for colder nights in the field. The only light came from a tiny window, but Flora could just make out the figure of Eddy on one of the narrow beds. Peter sat on the floor, his head resting on the thin mattress at Eddy's feet. Two earthenware jugs lay between them, the air heavy with the hoppy smell of ale and peat.

Dr Billings shouldered past Bunny, eased William aside and crouched beside Eddy, whose collarless shirt was undone at the neck, his lips colourless and a sheen of sweat sat on his pale skin.

Flora stood, helpless and terrified, a fist shoved against her mouth as she fought tears and watched the doctor examine his eyes, press her fingers against the side of his neck and nod slowly.

'I can feel a faint but steady pulse,' she said over one shoulder.

'Drunk, do you think?' Bunny asked, wiping a handkerchief over Eddy's damp forehead.

'More than that.' Dr Billings bent one ear close to his mouth. 'His breathing is shallow and he's barely conscious. We must get them back to the Abbey immediately.' She split a look between the two men. 'Can you manage to carry them?'

Nodding, William hefted his nephew into his arms with a grunt and carried him outside.

Bunny lifted Peter, who was smaller and wirier, but still a cumbersome weight.

'Bring those jugs, too,' Dr Billings gestured to Flora. 'Any remaining beer will need to be analyzed.'

Made of rough clay the two earthenware jugs were painted in two tone brown, with chunky handles and cork stoppers. They looked heavy, but came up relatively light in Flora's hands, though her climb back up the incline proved more difficult with both hands full. Her foot slipped several times on the stiff tufts of grass and she almost dropped one of the jugs.

Bunny reached the top first with Dr Billings close behind who supervised laying Peter on a thin layer of folded blankets on the flatbed, with Eddy alongside when William reached the summit.

'They'll be all right won't they?' Flora's hand trembled as she adjusted Eddy's shirt where it gaped at the neck. *They have to be.*

'They are both quite feverish, but I doubt their organs are breaking down yet.' Dr Billings climbed back into the driving seat but avoided Flora's eye as she performed her skillful about-turn in the road. 'We'll see you back at the Abbey,' she called to William, as he and Bunny mounted their horses.

'They'll likely get there before us,' Flora said, though Dr Billings didn't comment.

Flora crouched in the back of the gig between the boys, one hand gripping the side as they bumped and careered down the hill. 'Eddy, can you hear me?' She laid a tentative hand on his shoulder, but his only response was a low moan.

'I doubt he's conscious,' Dr Billings shouted back to her, her eyes on the road and the reins held firmly in both hands.

'Peter hasn't stirred since we found him.' Flora bit her lip, her gaze moving from one boy to the next in search of some sign they knew what was going on. Their bodies jerked and swayed with the movement of the cart but otherwise they remained motionless.

'He's worse, I'm afraid.' Dr Billings shouted without turning her head. 'Either he ingested more of the arsenic than Eddy, or he was weaker to begin with.'

'Thank you for coming,' Flora said. 'I ought to tell you that Dr Fairbrother is Eddy's doctor, but he said Eddy was suffering from growing pains.'

'That doesn't surprise me.' Briefly she glanced over her shoulder. 'Fairbrother hasn't opened a medical book for years. His diagnostic abilities tend towards guesswork and hyperbole.'

After a short, but frantic downhill ride, the carriage turned in at the gates to Cleeve Abbey.

The stable doors stood open, indicating the men had indeed arrived first.

Dr Billings had barely halted the horse before Jocasta burst through the front door and came hurtling across the gravel, then went straight to the rear of the gig.

'Eddy! Eddy can you hear me?' She stroked his pale face with one hand but he didn't stir; her face twisted in anguish.

'Most probably not, I'm afraid,' Dr Billings replied, easing her away to allow Bunny and William to carry the boys into the house. Bunny took charge of Peter, his limbs swaying like a rag doll as they carried him up the front steps, his face unnaturally bloodless.

'Eddy looks awful.' Jocasta bounced on her heels beside them. 'Will he be all right? And poor Peter,' she added, though as an obvious afterthought.

'Give the doctor a chance, Jo.' Flora held her back with a firm grip on her shoulders as they followed Bunny and William inside. 'Are your parents back yet?'

'What? Oh yes. They returned about twenty minutes ago. Mama threw a fit of hysterics and Papa has been shouting at me as if this was all my fault.' Her voice rose, indignant, then she calmed again. 'Mr Meeks has been marvellous. He calmed them down and explained everything.'

'We'll go and join them while Doctor Billings examines the boys,' Flora attempted a reassuring tone, but her own mind was whirling. 'There isn't much she can say yet. I'm sure Eddy will be fine now we know what the problem is.' She wasn't so sure about Peter, but they would think about that when the doctor had seen him.

Flora stood with Jocasta in the hall as the small procession climbed the stairs. A flustered Lady Venetia made to follow, but Dr Billings turned on the bottom step and barred the way.

'If you'll allow me to conduct my examination, Lady Vaughn. I'll let you know what I conclude as soon as possible.'

'And who, exactly are you, ma'am?' Lady Venetia looked her up and down in disgust. 'I thought there was a doctor out looking for my son?'

'There was, and I am, Lady Venetia,' Dr Billings paused to answer. 'However, I would prefer not to stand here debating with you as to my credentials when your son needs my urgent attention.' She turned away abruptly, skirts swaying as she climbed the stairs.

'I'm coming too,' Reginald bounded up behind her.

Dr Billings halted, staring vaguely at the pharmacist for a few seconds.

'Two heads, Doctor.' Reginald grinned. 'You never know, even pill grinders know a thing or two about poisons.'

She smiled, which transformed her plain features into near handsomeness. 'I never believed otherwise, Mr Meeks. I would welcome your assistance.'

'George!' Lady Venetia's voice rose to a screech.

'Did you hear what that-that—' Words failed her and she huffed a breath. 'A woman doctor indeed! Where's Dr Fairbrother? He ought to be here.'

'Venetia, there's no time for this. Let the lady do her work.' Lord Vaughn eased past her and hurried up the stairs, calling to William as he went. 'Take them to the bachelor wing, it's the closest. I'll show you where.'

'She looks very capable' Jocasta's face held admiration.

'It was an emergency and—' Flora broke off, uncomfortable to be on the end of Lady Vaughn's horrified stare. 'Come into the sitting room, Lady Venetia. I'll explain everything.'

'I wish someone would.' Lady Venetia cast a longing look at the tail end of the procession as they disappeared round the corner of the staircase.

Lady Venetia didn't wish to hear Flora's explanations, nor Jocasta's open delight that they had a real female medic in the house. She remained stoically silent in a wingback chair and stared into the empty fireplace, the words, 'My poor boy' spoken every few moments, as if Eddy was doomed.

After a few moments, William and Bunny returned with Lord Vaughn, apparently banished from the sick room until Dr Billings had something to tell them. They took their dismissal in good part and Bunny sat with Flora and Jocasta on a sofa, while William poured fortified wine for them all.

Lord Vaughn paused just inside the door, his face vague as if he didn't know what he was doing

318

there. Flora thought he had aged ten years since breakfast. She bit her lip, blinking hard as tears threatened. Eddy was their only son and the Vaughns worshipped him.

'I read somewhere that arsenic poisoning cause ridges in the fingernails?' Bunny whispered. 'I haven't spotted that in Eddy.'

'Nor have I. But once that happens, it's often too late.' William handed Flora a glass. 'It's Madeira,' he said when she stared at it, confused.

Nodding, she took a sip. The liquid slid easily over her tongue, mildly sweet with a hint of orange. She took another, a whole mouthful this time and warmth flowed through her and the tension dissolved.

Jocasta released a sob and William pressed a glass into her hand. 'Don't worry, Jo. That Dr Billings looks as if she knows what she's doing.'

'I hope so,' Flora whispered. 'I was the one who brought her here.'

Reginald Meeks' appearance just then brought everyone to their feet.

'The Doctor is still with them,' he announced confidently. 'I have nothing new to add other than she thinks Flora was right. They have arsenical poisoning which accumulates in the system, however she doesn't think it has reached lethal levels.'

'I'm sure he'll be fine, Flora,' he whispered as she chewed at a thumbnail. 'They both will.' Bunny slid an arm round her, but his compassion only made her feel worse.

'I wish I had realized sooner. I could see he wasn't well, but everyone thought it was no more than fatigue or a summer cold.'

'The fête was three weeks ago,' Jocasta reminded her. 'If Eddy's been drinking the stuff regularly since then, *we* should have noticed the signs. We didn't, so don't blame yourself.'

'Eddy isn't your responsibility any more, Flora,' Bunny added. 'No one considered poison until we got here.'

'Father did.' Flora switched thumbs but gave up when it wasn't helping.

'I know,' Jocasta gripped Flora's forearm gently in a gesture meant to comfort. 'You did exactly what Maguire would have.'

Somehow, that didn't make her feel any better.

'Every morning since he returned from school,' Lord Vaughn said to no one in particular, 'I made him go with me on the estate to learn how it worked. When he said he was too tired I just told him to buck up and get on with it.' He pushed a hand into his thinning hair and held it there.

Flora sipped the Madeira, while Lady Venetia appeared too overwhelmed by her own anxiety to reassure him. It was left to Jocasta to soothe his guilt.

'We all thought he was just malingering, Papa. You know how lazy Ed can be.'

'I'm partly to blame,' William said from where he sat, his feet splayed and hands held loosely between his knees. 'I went up to his room a couple

320

of times to say goodnight and he wasn't there. I assumed he had sneaked out to collect birds' eggs or some other boyish prank. I put it down to youthful mischief, but now I realize he had sloped off with that Griggs boy, and—' He jumped out of his seat as Dr Billings entered the room, Bunny and Lord Vaughn following suit. Reginald Meeks was already standing, so he acknowledged her with a nod.

Lady Venetia's stage whisper filled the room. 'Whoever heard of a woman doctor? Does she know what she's doing?'

'I have.' Flora lifted her almost empty glass. 'Dr Elizabeth Garrett Anderson.'

'Thank you, Mrs Harrington,' Dr Billings took centre stage. 'A lady who qualified thirty years before I did, so perhaps I'm not such a novelty. And do sit, gentleman, you make me nervous crowded round me like that.'

'I've never heard anything like it.' Lady Venetia continued to sniff into a lace handkerchief while the gentlemen resumed their seats.

'Let her speak, Mama.' Jocasta replaced her empty glass on the sideboard, returning to lean against the arm of William's sofa, her arm draped across his shoulder.

Flora stayed where she was, her free hand gripped in her lap so hard, her fingernails made crescent-shaped dents in her palms.

'Well, what's the verdict?' Lord Vaughn demanded in an attempt to regain control, but his voice shook slightly. 'Will my son recover?' By force of habit, he offered her one of the full glasses that stood on the tray, which she accepted graciously.

'As I surmised when we found them, both boys are indeed suffering from chronic arsenical poisoning.'

'My Eddy isn't – damaged is he?' Lady Venetia clutched a hand to her chest, her eyes moist with unshed tears. 'We had a maid once who didn't wash after putting arsenic down for the rats. They said her organs had begun to break down, and—' she broke off, her face white.

Lord Vaughn lurched to the sofa where she sat and began kneading her shoulders.

'With good nursing, I'm confident they will recover completely.' Dr Billings took a long sip from her glass before continuing. 'The source of the poison has been isolated, though I understand there is no remaining beer on the premises?'

'I'll have a thorough search made and ensure there isn't,' Lord Vaughn said. 'Though as far as I am aware it was all removed on the day.'

'Even so, it would be wise to make certain, my lord.' Dr Billings inclined her head. 'I advise a light, nutritious diet for your son and liquids only for Peter for the time being. The most important thing now for both of them is rest. My colleagues in the medical profession might prescribe charcoal biscuits to help break down what remains of the poison, but in the past I've found these ineffective.' She exchanged a smile with Reginald which told

Flora they had come to an agreement about treatment. Or perhaps Dr Billings had guessed Lord Vaughn would seek a second opinion from Dr Fairbrother when she had gone.

'And Peter?' Flora asked. 'How is he?'

'His condition is considerably worse,' Dr Billings said. 'In his case, we can only wait and see if there is any residual damage.'

'Poor boy,' Jocasta murmured.

'Has anyone informed Mr Griggs he is here?' Flora asked.

'I'll do that.' Dr Billings set her still full glass on the table, which told Flora she had only accepted it to make a point. 'I'll call in at The Red Kite before I return to town. Peter isn't ready to travel yet, therefore would it be acceptable for him to stay here until he is stronger?'

'I-I suppose so,' Lady Venetia said vaguely, the notion evidently puzzling to her.

'And might I call on Viscount Trent tomorrow to see how he's going on?' Dr Billings added. 'Or would you prefer your regular doctor to attend to him?'

'I think that would be far more suitable,' Lady Venetia said.

'Absolutely not!' Lord Vaughn cut across her. 'Dr Billings, I would welcome your attendance on Eddy. We all owe you a great deal and it's only right you should see his illness through.'

'I think you owe your son's life to Mrs Harrington, my lord. If she hadn't brought attention to his health, he would have gone on ingesting the poison until nothing could have been done to reverse its effects.' Dr Billings gave a final inclination of her head, hefted the leather bag into her arms and headed for the door.

'I'll see you out,' Lord Vaughn said, displaying unusual hospitality.

'I must go and see my Eddy.' Lady Venetia jumped up with uncharacteristic agility and ran from the room. Flora had never seen her run before.

'Dr Billings,' Reginald Meeks waylaid her, 'might I cadge a lift with you back to town?'

'Of course. In fact, would you mind coming with me to see Mr Griggs? Perhaps we could also discuss the best methods of removing heavy metal poisons from the bloodstream?'

They left the room together deep in conversation.

'I didn't expect that.' Bunny said. 'A lady doctor in Lord Vaughn's sitting room.'

'Lady Venetia wasn't very happy about it,' Flora said, relieved it had all ended relatively well.

'I cannot begin to thank you, Flora,' Lord Vaughn returned from seeing the doctor out and crossed the room to stand beside her. 'I accepted Fairbrother's word without question, and as a result we might have lost Eddy.' He slumped onto a chair, his head down, while Jocasta went to him and wrapped her arms round his neck.

'I still feel responsible,' Lord Vaughn said, his voice dull. 'My father was not a strong man. He suffered bouts of weakness and fatigue during his life and died quite young. When I observed similar behaviour in Eddy, I didn't want to admit he might have inherited the same traits. So I ignored it.'

'Eddy isn't Grandpapa.' Jocasta propped her chin on top of his head, her features a more delicate, feminine version of his own, but startlingly similar. 'He'll be well again before you know it. You'll see.'

'Father identified arsenic poisoning in the workmen, but he never got the opportunity to explain. He put me on to it, and Mr Meeks explained how arsenic affects the body.'

'I'm not sure how Dr Fairbrother is going to view my engaging a female doctor. Mrs Billings has caused quite a stir in the town since her arrival. There's something else, Flora.' Lord Vaughn drew her onto the sofa. 'Fairbrother isn't always careless, just a little absent sometimes.'

'What do you mean?'

'Bunny mentioned what he saw when you visited the mortuary, and I got to thinking about your father's accident. I was going to mention it to you this evening, but all this happened and—'

'Mention what?' Flora prompted.

'I ran into him in town this morning. He said he had words with Mr Meeks after the inquest which made him think again about the case.'

'I think we witnessed that, didn't we, Flora?' Bunny said.

'He told me he had reviewed his notes on Maguire,

and, well, he's more inclined to accept he overlooked certain details about his death.'

'The hoof prints?' Bunny said.

'Exactly. He now thinks you were right, Bunny, and they were made by two different animals.'

'Well that's something, I suppose,' Bunny said.

Flora sat frozen. *Her father had been deliberately trampled.*

'But that would mean Maguire was murdered.' Jocasta slumped down beside Flora, her arm round her shoulders. 'I'm so sorry, Flora. We all thought it was an accident.'

'Would Dr Fairbrother be willing to confirm that to the coroner?' Flora asked, her throat tight.

'Believe me, my dear, the man is contrite. I obtained his promise to do so first thing in the morning.' Lord Vaughn's sympathetic look made her eyes well with tears.

'But, Papa, who on this earth would want to kill Maguire?' Jocasta demanded, voicing the question that kept repeating in Flora's head.

'Come in.' Eddy's response to Flora's knock at his bedroom door was barely audible.

He lay on his back and stared at the ceiling, a copy of Kipling's 'The Man Who Would Be King' open beneath his hand on the coverlet, though he made no attempt to read.

'How do you feel?' She perched on the side of his bed, her chest tight at how frail he looked.

He had a grey tinge to his skin and blue half-moons like bruises beneath his eyes.

'I've been rather stupid haven't I, Flora?'

'What were you thinking, young man?' she said in mock anger, stroking his sweat-soaked hair away from his forehead. 'Drinking at your age indeed?'

'The boys at school slip out of the dorm for a pint at the local sometimes. They invite me, but, to be honest, I don't like the taste much. I thought this would be a good way to, well, practise. Then the older boys wouldn't make fun of me because I retched each time I tried it.'

'Did it work?' Any frustration she might have felt at his irresponsible behavior drained away. Not that she could ever stay angry with him for long; a combination of his father's vulnerability and his sister's sense of mischief made him an attractive character.

'Sort of.' He screwed up his nose. 'I'm still not keen on the taste. I would much prefer a lemonade, but the other boys would call me a sissy if I ordered that in the pub.'

'Those other boys aren't worth listening to.' Her natural protectiveness rose that he had to make himself ill so as to ward off unkind bullying. 'When you're grown up, you won't need to apologize for not liking the taste of beer.'

'Just as well, because I definitely won't touch it again now. I'll probably stick to brandy instead.' Flora was about to make a comment when his eyes widened as he asked, 'What do you think of the lady doctor?'

'I like her, but more importantly what did you think of her?'

'She's very nice, like the school nurse but cleverer. And her hands aren't cold.'

Flora tweaked the collar of his pajama jacket and stroked his hair. If she ever had a child like this one she would be more than delighted. 'Dr Billings is coming back to see you tomorrow. Will that be all right with you?' Hopefully he hadn't developed an aversion to females in the professions like the previous generation.

'Of course. Why wouldn't it?'

'No reason at all.' Flora smiled. There was hope for Eddy in politics yet. He was still pale, but obviously on the mend and up to talking, so she decided she needed to ask him something. 'Eddy, I was wondering, how did you get hold of that beer in the first place?'

'Peter and me were behind one of the tents with some leftover cake we snaffled from the food tent. Mrs Mountjoy walked by with Mr Bracenose and told him he was to get rid of whatever was left.' He slid a sideways look at her as if anticipating a rebuke.

'Cake eh?' She ruffled his hair. 'Don't worry, I shan't demand you confess everything. What was that about Mrs Mountjoy?'

'She bought the beer for the fête. Bracenose to collect it from Battledown Brewery in one of our carts.' He broke off with a cough that threatened to turn into a full blown fit.

Flora handed him a glass of water, waiting while he took a sip. Did Caroline want Vaughn staff and vehicle used to keep her part quiet? An odd thing to do if she was playing the charitable neighbor.

The coughing subsided and Eddy swiped a hand across his mouth as he handed back the glass. 'Thanks. Bracenose has a soft spot for Mrs M as they're always whispering in corners. Don't know why she doesn't get an estate manager of her own instead of using ours all the time.'

'Why do you suppose she wanted the beer thrown away?' Flora mused, more to herself than posing a question.

'Dunno.' He hunched his shoulders in a familiar, endearing gesture. 'She paid for the stuff, so maybe she regarded it as hers by rights. Or she didn't want the men to drink all night and be unable to work the next day.'

'Very public-spirited of her,' Flora mumbled under her breath. Though why would Caroline care what happened to the leftover beer? 'What did you do then?'

'When the workmen carted it away, we heard them say what a waste it was to destroy it, so why shouldn't they keep it for themselves, so when they weren't looking—'

'These men, did they happen to be the same ones who fell sick a little later?' Flora interrupted.

Those men must have drunk all that leftover beer at once, which was why they were so badly affected.

'How did you know?' Eddy turned his head on the pillow towards her.

'Never mind. I gather you and Peter grabbed the jugs when they weren't looking and hid them in the shepherd's hut.'

'You know everything.' Eddy gasped, his eyes wide. 'Do you know, if you did that in the seventeenth century, you'd have been hanged as a witch.'

'It's nice to know my history lessons weren't wasted. Now tell me the rest.'

'Well, we had no idea it the beer was making us sick. Though I should have known better than to drink anything that awful woman bought.'

'That's not a nice way to speak about Mrs Mountjoy, Eddy.' Flora fought a smile. 'Don't you like her?'

'No. Whenever she finds me with Uncle William, she always dismisses me like I'm a nuisance. As if I didn't know she's chasing after him. She must think I'm stupid.' He arranged his face in an expression of disgust as a flash of his old self shone through. 'She was quite rude to McCallum that night. I hope she feels guilty about everything now.'

'Which night was this, Eddy?'

'The same night Maguire was found. What with all the fuss after Diabolus came back on his own and everyone went rushing off to look for Maguire, I forgot about it. Then when I heard they had found him and he was – well you know.' He flushed and plucked at the coverlet with nervous fingers. 'It went completely out of my head.'

'Of course, I had forgotten Mr McCallum and Caroline Mountjoy were invited to dinner that night. What did you see, Eddy?'

'I don't think Ma and Pa invited *her*, she must have invited herself. She does that you know. Probably to catch Uncle William, but he took himself off to the study after dinner, so she went into the garden with Mr McCallum instead. They came in through the side gate, and walked straight past Peter and me, so we snuck up behind a bush and listened.' He brought a hand to his mouth, eyes wide as if he realized what he had said. 'You won't tell Pa will you? He hates that sort of thing.'

'I cannot possibly condone eavesdropping, Eddy.' Flora tried not to laugh, being guilty of the same thing herself more than once. 'But I can probably let it go on this occasion. Could you hear what they were talking about?'

'Only the odd word or two, nothing that made sense. Then Mrs Mountjoy went back inside, but Mr McCallum stayed in the garden and smoked a cigarette.'

'I see. No harm done then, now you must get some more rest.' She rose and tucked the cover round him, but he grasped her hand, halting her.

'That's not all. Scrivens arrived and started talking to Mr McCallum, who got very angry. He shook his fist at him and waved his arms about. Scrivens had his head down as if he was apologizing.'

'I don't suppose you could hear them?' Flora eased back onto the mattress again. She would have given a lot to know what that encounter was about.

'No, that's when Maguire found us. He sent Peter home and told me to go to bed. Which was a bit rich, because he stayed behind the bush and carried on listening.'

'My father was there?' Flora's intention to leave Eddy to sleep dissolved. Had whatever he heard between McCallum and Scrivens the reason he took Diabolous out that night?

'I didn't leave straight away,' Eddy said through a yawn. 'But Maguire had forgotten about me. He was too intent on what Scrivens and McCallum said, but it didn't make much sense anyway.'

'Try and remember, it might be important.' Her desire to hear what happened next vied with the fact Eddy was tiring. His voice had begun to slur and he yawned repeatedly

'Mr McCallum said . . .' Eddy screwed up his forehead in concentration. 'That Scrivens had fudged the job, so he couldn't be trusted. That now he would have to do it himself.' Eddy's face relaxed into a lazy smile. 'I'm pretty sure that's what he said.'

'What did Mr McCallum want done?'

'I don't know.' Eddy hunched his shoulders again. 'Maguire acted all strange then and spoke like Pa does when he's trying to keep his temper; all clipped words and no sentences. When I got up to my room, I saw Maguire through my window on his way to the stables. That must have been when he had Diabolus saddled, though I didn't actually see him leave.'

'What about Mrs Mountjoy and Mr McCallum?' Her words took on a sharp edge, evidenced by Eddy's widening eyes. 'Did you see them leave?'

'I-I don't know. She'd gone by then, I heard her carriage leave.' He stretched beneath the covers yawning. 'McCallum arrived on horseback, so I don't know what time he left. I'm sorry Flora, did I do wrong? Should I have told someone?'

'No, of course not. I didn't mean to upset you.' She forced calm into her voice as she tucked the covers around him, though her thoughts raced. If only she knew what had passed between them that night. 'I doubt it would have made any difference. Not for my father anyway.' Something she had heard scraped at the edge of her brain, but dissolved before she could grasp it.

Eddy's eyelids fluttered closed and Flora rose. 'You get some sleep now.' She removed the book from beneath his hand and placed it on the bedside cabinet, checked the window was on the latch and the curtains fully drawn; all the tasks she performed like clockwork when he was younger.

'I won't, and Flora,' he halted her at the door, 'what will you do now?'

'Firstly I intend to speak to Mrs Mountjoy.'

'Well don't drink anything. Dr Billings said there was something nasty in that beer. It wouldn't surprise me if she had put it there.' Eddy leaned up on one elbow and punched his pillow into submission before laying down again.

'Night, Eddy.' Flora pulled the door closed behind her and leaned against it. Caroline and Mr McCallum's liaison was supposed to have ended when she turned her sights on William. Why was she having secret conversations in gardens with Mr McCallum? And what had her father overheard that made him angry enough to ride off somewhere on horseback, only to end up dead?

CHAPTER 22

Flora and Bunny were the first down to breakfast the next morning. The French windows in the dining room stood open, flooding the room with early morning sun, while a welcome breeze puffed the voile curtains like sails.

'Did you get any sleep at all?' Bunny said as they set the plates of food selected from the bain-maries on the sideboard at their places and sat.

'Not really. I couldn't stop thinking about what Eddy told me. Did I disturb you?'

'Only a little, which isn't surprising. It looks like something was going on between the unholy trio which your father tried to prevent.'

'Not simply a failed love affair either, or why would Scrivens be involved?' Flora slit open an envelope she found beside her plate, from which a heavy violet scent wafted as she unfolded the page.

'What's that?' Bunny asked, a cup of coffee raised in one hand, a copy of the *Cheltenham Chronicle* in the other.

'Caroline Mountjoy has invited me to tea this

335

afternoon.' Flora studied the looped handwriting that covered the entire page. 'After all the panic of yesterday I had forgotten all about it. I virtually snubbed her when I saw her in town.'

'You aren't going to accept are you?' Bunny looked up from his paper. 'Not after what Eddy told you about secret conferences in the garden?'

'I'm not sure. She might be able to tell me more about the night my father died.'

'I thought she had already denied any knowledge.' Bunny snorted and snapped the paper. 'I doubt she'll be more forthcoming now. I suggest you decline. Your excuse being it's inappropriate because you are in mourning.' He discarded the newspaper and attacked his breakfast with enthusiasm, dismissing her.

'Why are you so adamant I shouldn't go? It's only afternoon tea.' Flora frowned. Bunny wasn't usually so autocratic.

'Dr Fairbrother plans to visit the coroner with his revised evidence this morning. I don't think it would be wise to stir things up until the police decide what steps to take.'

Flora picked at her scrambled eggs in silence, still confused by his attitude. It was Bunny who would confirm their murder theory, yet now he seemed happy to step away and let others take it further. 'We've no idea how long that will take and we can't stay here indefinitely. You know better than most that the wheels of authority turn slowly.'

'Not in the case of murder. Don't underestimate

Lord Vaughn's either, he fully intends to put his weight into opening a new investigation.' He covered her hand with his on the table. 'Look Flora. The last few days has been hard on you, what with finding out Riordan was murdered and Eddy almost dying. You've done enough, so perhaps you should leave it to others now?'

'If you're worried, why don't you come to Mrs Mountjoy's with me?'

'William and I have an appointment this afternoon.' Bunny added a slice of toast to his side plate.

'What sort of appointment?' Flora stared at the sheet of violet notepaper beside her plate. Why didn't he want her to go? What was he not telling her?

'Oh, it's nothing much, just a gentlemen's club thing.' He spread butter onto the toast and took a bite, not looking at her. 'However, should you be determined to go to Mrs Mountjoy's in order to find out what she knows, why not rearrange the outing for tomorrow? I'll be free to accompany you then.' He chewed on his toast and disappeared behind the newspaper again.

Flora sprinkled salt on her eggs, prevented from replying by the arrival of William, with a chattering Jocasta.

Still peeved with Bunny's continued secrecy about his afternoon plans, Flora left him with William, their heads close together at the breakfast table.

She emerged into the hall in time to see Hetty's rear end disappear through the baize door into the servants' quarters. Sighing, she swung round and almost collided with Amy.

'Good morning, Miss Flora.' Amy nodded toward the door that still flapped gently. 'Was that Hetty I saw in such a hurry?'

Flora sighed. 'Yes, she didn't seem inclined to stop and talk. I must have made her uncomfortable with those questions about my mother. Serve me right, I suppose.'

'One thing about Hetty's memory lapses is she never bears grudges. She will have forgotten what you talked about by now.'

'You're right, I didn't think of that.' Flora smiled

'Your mother wasn't flighty, by the way.' Amy lowered her voice. 'Far from it.'

Flora frowned. 'How would you know that?'

Amy cocked her chin at the rear hall in an almost furtive gesture. 'Let's talk outside.'

Intrigued, Flora followed her along a narrow corridor, through the glazed door at the end and onto a short flight of steps down to the kitchen garden.

Even this early in the day, the sun had backed the brick paths to stark white as Amy weaved through the herb beds, from which the scents of basil, and thyme rose. Flora broke off a piece of rosemary as they passed, rubbed it between her fingers and released the woody fragrance.

At the far wall, where a bench had been placed

beneath a plaited arch of hornbeam, Amy indicated Flora should sit. She obeyed in silence, hoping the air of conspiracy wasn't simply Amy's idea of making her day more interesting.

Amy eased onto the wooden slats beside her, her hands hooked over the seat on either side of her knees. Her knuckles stood out white against the dark wood and she stared straight ahead, as if she was summoning the nerve to begin.

Flora waited.

'I was twelve when Lily went missing,' Amy said finally.

'You knew my mother?' A rush of blood surged through Flora's thighs and into her belly, making her skin hot beneath the black material. Combined with the fact that would make Amy about thirty when her physique and diminutive height made her look far younger came as a shock. 'I don't understand. If your family worked at the Abbey when I lived here, I would have known.'

Amy shook her head. 'I lived in town then. I only came to work here a few months ago.'

'I see, but then how—'

'Lily had a friend,' Amy cut her off. 'A Miss Eliza Sawyer who ran the Frances Owen Memorial Home in Hewlett Road.'

'I don't think I know of it.'

'That's what it was called then, it's the Gloucester Diocesan Home for Little Girls now.'

'*That* name is more familiar. What did this home have to do with my mother?'

'Please.' Amy grasped the bench tighter as she rocked back and forwards. 'Let me finish. I've been trying to pluck up the courage to tell you for days, but the time never seemed right. Then after Hetty upsetting you so badly, I realized you didn't know much about your mother's life here.' Amy's growing unease reached her across the space on the bench.

'I'm sorry, please go on. I promise not to interrupt.' Her stomach churned with excitement that finally she was about to hear from someone who knew Lily Maguire. Really knew her and didn't rely on gossip or rumour.

'Lily Maguire,' Amy began, 'was a kind, loving person. She heard about Miss Sawyer and her work at the home and whenever she heard about families where the children were being mistreated, she wanted to help. She persuaded several families to let their youngsters be taken in. Those who couldn't afford to feed them.'

'I see.' Flora's breathing grew rapid, but in a pleasant, delighted way that helped obliterate the doubts which Hetty, and in some ways Lady Venetia, had created. Despite any faults she may have had, Lily was a good person, or she wouldn't have helped disadvantaged children.

'Your father didn't approve and they argued about it.'

'Why didn't he?' Forgetting her promise, Flora stared at her, then realized it was an unfair question. As Amy had said she was only twelve. How could she know?

'Not because he didn't see the good she was doing,' Amy answered her question nonetheless. 'I think it was because he worried about her going into the worst parts of town. Not everyone was willing to hand their children over to do-gooders. She came in for some abuse.'

'I see,' Flora said again. *Is that what Hetty meant about Lily going where she shouldn't?* 'Please, Amy, do go on.'

'It was like a proper family at the Home, not like one of those orphanages run as workhouses. There were only eight of us and we were looked after by a mother and a father, well they were Matron and Superintendent, but it was almost the same thing. We slept no more than three to a room and had our own cupboard for our things. We even had a cat and a dog to look after. As I said, like a real family.'

'It sounds lovely. I take it you went there?'

'Only because Miss Lily fought for me. I wasn't an orphan. I lived with my father and siblings, though it wasn't much of a home and Miss Lily wanted to help.' She slanted a sideways look at Flora. 'Are you all right? You've gone quite pale and you're shaking. I'm sorry if this is a shock, but I felt you should know.'

'I'm fine.' With an effort, Flora composed herself. 'No one has ever spoken about this side of my mother's life before. I want to hear all of it.'

'I don't know all of it.' Amy shrugged. 'All I can tell you is, one night Lily came to our house in

Barnards Row to plead with my father not to put me on the streets.'

'What?' Flora gasped. 'Your own father would have done that?'

'He would, and worse.' Amy's features hardened, but her eyes held no self-pity. 'My mother died a few months before of the cholera. Pa, myself and my six brothers and sisters lived in Arm and Sword Yard. Not the prettiest part of town, I can tell you. Anyway, Pa worked at the brewery. This was years before Mr McCallum bought it and created all those new jobs. In those days it had been run into the ground and no one's job was secure. Pa was laid off.' Amy's resigned shrug indicated she had come to terms with these details long ago. 'Mind you, even when he worked, his wages went on drink rather than the rent, so we hardly knew the difference.'

'How did my mother hear about you? Through this Miss Sawyer?'

Amy fidgeted on the seat, as if embarrassed to have revealed so much. 'Pa could only get farm work in the summer months, and that was patchy, so things got worse for us. One winter when there was no food in the house, the parish got involved. They were talking about sending us to the workhouse and splitting the family up into separate homes. Miss Sawyer and your mother came to see us. It was then Lily suggested us girls go to Frances Owen to give him a chance to get back on his feet. I would be trained to go into service and the younger girls would too when they were older. The boys would go to The Elms, which was a home for pauper children.'

'That all sounds horrible, though I imagine better than you had to endure with your father.' Flora pressed her hand to her bodice as pride welled, crushing the disappointment she had endured since her talk with Hetty. 'Why has no one told me about this? Why keep it hidden like some shameful secret? My mother was trying to help.'

'Do gooders don't always get the appreciation they deserve,' Amy said. 'I can't speak for the Vaughns, I wasn't here at the time, but it surprised me too when you said you knew so little about Lily. Perhaps Lady Venetia didn't want anyone from her household mixing with those sorts of people?'

'That's possible. Lady Jocasta did say her mother was very conscious of her social position in those days.'

'And because your father didn't want her talked about, the good things she did were ignored too.'

'That's very astute of you, Amy.' *And made perfect sense.* 'Sorry, I interrupted you when I promised I wouldn't. What was your father's reaction to these plans for you and your brothers and sisters?'

'Huh!' Her snort of derision was harsh and damning. 'He was eager enough for the boys, but as for me and my two sisters.' She broke off and stared at her feet. 'Let me put it this way. He said we would earn more on our backs than in a kitchen in some fancy house.'

'I'm so sorry.' Flora closed her eyes and exhaled, unable to imagine what could have become of Amy in such a life.

'He threw Lily out that first time, but she came back. Bless her.' Amy smiled then as if remembering. 'Dad was drunk, as usual, ranting like a madman and throwing things. Lily shoved me out the back door and told me to go to Miss Sawyer's.'

'Didn't she come with you?'

Amy shook her head. 'She said she'd be along, but couldn't leave Pa with the little 'uns when he was like that. I think she stayed to try and convince him to let her bring them too, so I hung about in the alley waiting for her. There was snow on the ground that night and it got colder and darker. I was shivering badly and could hardly feel my feet as I was wearing only a thin dress and no coat, so I gave up and went to Miss Sawyer's house. I thought maybe Lily had gone another way and got there before me, but she wasn't there. We waited all night, but she never came.'

'What happened to her?' Flora frowned, trying to reconcile the scene in the cottage with this Mr Coombe shouting at her. Some of the details fitted but not all. Did her mother take her to his house that night? Or did he come to the cottage behind the stables and attack her there?'

'I don't know.' Amy dropped her chin, her eyes squeezed shut. 'No one does. She never came back.'

'What about the police? Didn't they try to find her?' Flora shook her head as if dislodging the thought. 'I'm sorry, of course they did. What about her body?' The blood and the coppery smell came back to her as a firm and vivid memory. She hadn't imagined it. Her mother *had* been hurt, she was sure of it.

Amy shook her head. 'They didn't find one, but did everything they could. Pa would never admit to having done anything to her, even though most people on our street would have sworn Pa would have done murder for the price of a pint. I was the only person to have seen him with her that night, and I was too young for them to take my word.'

The police couldn't convict him without a – a body.' She turned a grim smile on Flora. 'He wasn't a popular man, my Pa.'

'Wasn't?' Flora sighed, dismayed. 'You mean he's dead?' Flora gasped, disappointed. Another link to Lily snatched away. Would she ever find out what happened to her mother?

'Yes. God rot him. And before you ask, my sisters were only four and five at the time. They wouldn't remember or understand even if you asked them.'

'And your brothers?'

'They were out thieving for Pa that night.'

'Did anyone think my mother might still be alive?'

'Of course!' Amy's eyes rounded. 'Your father did. But even he had to accept that Lily only had the clothes she stood up in. The dog cart she took to Pa's was found in the street the next morning. Your father and Miss Sawyer had posters put up in the district for a year after she disappeared. No one ever reported seeing her.'

'That's why no one knows where she's buried.' Flora blinked back tears.

'Because she was never found, some people said she must have run away, but Maguire refused to believe that.'

'What *did* your father say about what happened to my mother?'

'That they argued and he threw her out. When he sobered up and realized I had gone, he assumed she had taken me with her.'

'You never went back to your father's house?'

Amy shook her head. 'Miss Sawyer brought my sisters to the home soon afterwards. What with Pa under suspicion of murder, he was in no position to object. He was never charged, but the neighbours pretty much turned against him. My sisters are both in service now and the boys, well—' She hunched her shoulders philosophically. 'I heard they ended up back with Pa. They're most likely back to thieving and the drinking like him. Could be dead for all I know.'

'I'm sorry. Did you believe your father's story?'

Amy's eyes flashed. 'Of course not, but I couldn't prove anything.' She lowered her voice though there was no one about to hear them. 'I'll always be grateful to Lily for getting me into the Frances

Owen. I was only supposed to stay for three months, those were the rules, but when they saw how good I was with the younger ones, I was kept on for a year. Then they got me a room at a lodging house and work at a bakery in Prestbury. I didn't like it though, all that flour got to my chest and made me ill.'

'I don't blame you. Where did you go then?'

'Miss sawyer got me work at a housemaid at one of the houses on Pittville Lawn. I stayed for nearly eight years until my employer died. Then your father helped me get my position here. As Hetty's condition grew worse, he suggested to Lord Vaughn that I replace her as housekeeper when she retires.'

Flora clamped her lips shut, nodding. It was just like her father to step in and help someone like Amy. But then why had he objected so strongly to her mother involving herself with the less fortunate? The two premises seemed at odds to one another. Or had she missed some detail which would make sense? 'Do you like working here, Amy?'

'I've been fortunate to have two excellent employers and steady work. There are many who never have such opportunities.' She spoke like someone who had reconciled herself to her lot in life, but had been forced to abandon her own dreams in consequence. 'Her hand drifted to the small scar on her lip again. 'I've learned the skills which qualify me as a good housekeeper, despite my Pa always saying I was stupid. At twelve I never imagined I would read Dickens in my spare time and keep account books. Now I could get a position almost anywhere.'

'It's quite clear you are very far from stupid. And Amy,' Flora twisted on the seat to face her, 'when Hetty spoke about the girl who was a flighty piece, did—'

'She didn't mean Lily,' Amy interrupted. 'I tried to tell you at the time but you were so upset and went running off. That was Betsy Mason. She looks like your mother used to, which is probably why Hetty got them confused.' Amy rolled her eyes. 'Everyone here believes Betsy went off with one of her beaus, and will be back when she gets tired of him.'

'Constable Jones came here the other day asking if anyone had heard anything,' Flora said. 'I have never met her, but I do hope she's all right. You hear of awful things happening to friendless young girls.'

'Betsy's got her head screwed on.' Amy tsked. 'She's not the type to let anyone take advantage of her. Happened here once or twice, but she sorted them.'

'What do you mean?' Flora began to wish she had formed a closer alliance with the servants instead of trying to prize snippets from family. Servants knew everything and if you knew how to ask, were far more forthcoming. At the same time she acknowledged that as a governess, she was slightly removed from below stairs. That or she must have been asking the wrong questions all this time.

'Scrivens for one. He took a fancy to her. When she came to work in the kitchens, he would send her into the dairy or down the cellar to fetch things, then follow her down.' 'Surely you aren't shocked?' Amy said when Flora released a gasp and stared at her lap. 'You must have seen that sort of behavior yourself when you worked here?'

'Actually no. Not personally. My father would have been quick to put a stop to that sort of thing.'

'Oh, he did,' Amy smiled. 'I saw it myself more than once. He was very strict with the men, and threatened dismissal without references if they were caught pestering the maids. Against their will I mean.' She grinned and Flora grinned with her. 'Betsy gave Scrivens short shrift, I know that. He came back with a split lip once that I know of. It might be an odd thing to say, but if Mr Maguire was still here, someone like him would never have been promoted to Head Butler.'

'I agree with you there, and good for Betsy.' Flora recalled what she had told Bunny about the servants' unspoken rules, thought she was fortunate not to have encountered unwanted attentions herself. Maybe because her father had been there to protect her?

'Did she ever complain to my father about Scrivens?' Flora asked.

'I'm not sure, though Betsy wasn't the sort to need

intervention, she had her sights set higher than a footman, which was what Scrivens was then.'

'Really?' Graham McCallum's name sat on her tongue but she waited for Amy to confirm the gossip.

'Rumour says,' Amy broke off and bit her lip. 'No, I shouldn't sink to that level. I'm an assistant housekeeper not a scullery maid.'

'Go ahead, Amy, I won't tell a soul.' Flora felt a sudden kinship with this woman, who had made something of herself from a bad beginning.

'Well.' Amy cast a swift look round the garden, but apart from two gardeners at the far end of the vegetable beds, they were alone. 'Betsy was walking out with Mr McCallum up at the manor. They were spotted a couple of times in Bailey Wood, canoodling, or so the talk went.'

'That's not the first time Mr McCallum has been mentioned in relation to Betsy,' Flora mused. Which contradicted his own account of being a grief-stricken widower, not to mention the story he had told Bunny of his discouraging a besotted maid.

'That doesn't surprise me.' Amy snorted. 'They still talk about him in the servant's hall about the kerfuffle when Lady Amelia tried to cancel her engagement.'

Flora smiled, conjuring the memory. 'At the time it was treated as an unrequited infatuation on Lady Amelia's part.'

'That's not quite accurate.' Amy's smile widened,

making the white scar on her lip more pronounced. 'Hetty caught them in Lord Vaughn's study one night in what was referred to even today as "a compromising situation".' At Flora's start of surprise, Amy added, 'This was back when her memory was sharp. She's forgotten it now. Mrs Mountjoy set her cap at him too, but she got nowhere. Got her sights set on Master William now, though I doubt she'll get anywhere with him either. She's too eager that one, if you see what I mean. Puts men off.'

'I think you're right.' Flora decided not to pursue the subject, it appeared nothing was a secret at the Abbey. 'Thank you, Amy. You've answered some questions I have always puzzled over.' *Though not all.* 'And I'm glad my mother helped you get away from that life.'

'I'll always remember Lily, Miss Flora. She was lovely. Pretty as an angel and with a beautiful speaking voice. The way she stood up to my Pa was something else as well.'

Flora smiled through sudden tears, saddened that she did not have a similar memory to draw on. 'This Miss Sawyer, does she still have connections with the home?'

Amy nodded, dislodging her cap and revealing nut brown hair. Flora imagined she was much prettier when it wasn't confined by stiff white cotton. 'She's quite old now, so was given the post of Honorary Superintendent.' Amy released a sigh. 'There aren't many like Miss Sawyer and Lily in this world.'

'I agree.' Flora squeezed Amy's hand, conscious of the roughened skin on her palm and finger pads. 'Thank you, Amy, for letting me know my mother was a good person.' *Maybe I can now let her rest, wherever she is.*

The distant clang of the church bell brought Amy's head up. 'Goodness, is that the time? I'd better get back and make sure Hetty hasn't put sugar in the vegetables.' She hesitated after two steps and turned back. 'I'm sorry about your mother. Her not having a proper burial, I mean. But everyone did their best to get my Pa to tell them what he had done.' With a final shy nod, she took off at a run back to the house, reaching the door just as the bell stopped ringing.

Flora fumbled in a pocket for a handkerchief as Amy's story repeated in her head. She imagined what it must have been like for poor Amy, inadequately dressed for the cold weather and waiting all night for Lily to come. She crumpled the lace in her hand and dabbed her wet cheek, then froze as the details of her dream played in her head.

The cottage door had stood wide open and a shaft of warm sunlight spilled onto the flagstones. She wasn't six then but much younger. Too young to speak or understand what was happening. Too young to comfort her mother as she lay beside her on the floor. Someone had hurt Lily years before, when Flora was a small child. But who?

CHAPTER 23

Flora had no concept of how long she sat pondering what Amy had said, the only sounds an occasional fluting song of a blackbird and a low continuous buzz of a bee. When a scrape of leather on stone and a masculine cough alerted her to Bunny's presence, the sun had slipped behind a cloud and a cool wind brought goose bumps onto her arms.

Flora did not turn her head to look at him, but when he eased down next to her and slid an arm round across the back of the bench, she released a tiny sigh.

'How did you know I was here?' She leaned her head against his shoulder, the tweed of his jacket rough on her skin.

'It's a kitchen garden, and where I can always find you at home.' He pressed his chin into her hair. 'Is this a happy silence or a sad one?'

'Both.' She took a deep breath and eased upright. 'Amy told me a very interesting story. About my mother.' She told it the way Amy had, haltingly at first, and when she reached the part where Lily

Maguire had been searched for but never found, she was crying again.

'Goodness, that's quite a tale.' Bunny took the handkerchief from her hand and wiped her tears away. 'And this Amy person, she's reliable is she?'

'I don't have any reason not to believe her.' Flora sniffed into the handkerchief that had been reduced to a damp rag.

'How do you feel about your mother now?'

'I'm upset because I knew nothing about it, of course, but I'm very proud of her. She did a fine thing for Amy, and who knows how many others.'

'And so you should be.' His arm tightened round her and he tucked a strand of hair behind her ear with his free hand. 'Though the fact that she was never found is dreadful.'

'I understand now why Father was so reluctant to talk about her. Having failed to protect her from a character like Amy's father, he must have carried so much guilt with him all these years. He couldn't bear to bring those feelings to the surface again.'

'He must have put her in a box in his memory and locked it tight,' Bunny said, his chin against her hair. 'As a sort of defence mechanism I suppose.'

'Defence—' She pulled back and peered up at him through moist lashes. 'Have you been reading Sigmund Freud again?'

'Maybe a little.' He gave a self-conscious cough, and pushed his spectacles further up his nose with a middle finger. 'Perhaps he thought you would blame him for not saving her from whatever fate overtook her?'

'I would never have done that, but maybe he didn't dare take the risk?' She settled back against the bench with a sigh. 'If only I had known all this when Father was alive, we could have put Mother to rest between us. He died believing I wouldn't understand.'

'I'm sure he would have found an opportunity to reveal everything when the time was right. He didn't expect to die so young.'

'Amy's father is dead too, so we'll never know what happened to Mother after all this time. Or where she's buried.' Flora shivered.

Bunny made a noise of agreement and kissed the top of her head. 'Where she lies makes no difference to your mother. You're the one who needs to let her rest.'

'I'd still like to know what happened in that cottage.' She twisted to face him, her tears drying on her cheeks. 'I'm certain I was quite small when it happened. Perhaps it had something to do with the refuge? An angry father or brother who didn't approve of her interference. He might have confronted Mother in her own home?' That Mr Coombe might have killed her after all still niggled at her brain. And if so, had he buried her on the estate somewhere?

'It's possible you will never find out,' Bunny planted a kiss on her forehead. 'If your mother survived whatever happened in the cottage some years before, that incident might have been irrelevant to her disappearance.'

'Possibly. And I still don't know why someone would want my father dead. Maybe it's all connected?'

'We cannot let it colour our future.'

'Speaking of things we don't know,' she nestled her forehead into his neck and traced his jawline with a finger, 'are you going to tell me where you and William plan to go this afternoon?'

He removed her hand gently from his face and placed it in her lap. 'Nice try. I'll explain everything when we get back. Then, if you still insist on going to Mrs Mountjoy's tea party, we'll go together.'

Flora didn't mention she planned to ask Tom to bring the gig round to the front door later that afternoon. She would only be a couple of hours and would probably be back at the Abbey before Bunny was aware she had gone.

The horse pulled the gig at a brisk trot along the empty road in the afternoon sunshine as Flora followed the brief instructions outlined in Mrs Mountjoy's letter.

A hundred yards or so from the gap in the hedge that gave a view of Mr McCallum's house on the rise, a gatepost bore the legend *Beaumont Place*. Flora reined the horse to a leisurely walk, then a full stop on the verge beside the gate, surprised to find she was almost at the spot where Tom had brought her to see where her father died.

Bailey Wood separated Mrs Mountjoy's property

from Mr McCallum's. Was it possible her father had headed here on the night he died?

Beyond a pair of wrought-iron gates with slightly crumbling posts stood a gravel drive lined with rhododendron bushes which curved out of sight, obscuring the house. Flora secured the brake, climbed down onto the road and gripped one of the wrought-iron curlicues on the gate, which gave with a high-pitched squeak.

She suppressed a shiver, just as a figure stepped out from the shrubbery a few feet away.

'Mr Bracenose!' She stepped back a pace 'I didn't expect to see you here.' Was his presence a coincidence, or had he lurked in the bushes waiting for her?

'What're you doing here, Miss Flora?' The unsightly scar that cut across the top of his nose loomed unnervingly close as he regarded her with angry suspicion. Stories circulated when she was a child as to the cause of that scar, which varied from a kick from a horse to an attack with a pitchfork as a young man.

'I might ask you the same question.' She swallowed, relieved to find her voice did not shake. 'Isn't this Mrs Mountjoy's house?' She glanced past him, though the house wasn't visible from where they stood.

'You always were a nosy brat,' Bracenose's harsh laugh made the scar whiten, but his tone was more of resigned amusement than insult. He stood with his feet splayed and his hands tucked

357

into his pockets, both thumbs outward. 'Lord Vaughn knows I do work here on occasion. I've been out making checks on the fences.'

'I see. Well good day to you.' She made to push open the gate in the hope he might take the hint and leave, but instead, he grasped her upper arm and levelled his face close to hers. 'What are you doing here?'

'I-I beg your pardon?' She ducked in her chin and tried not to flinch at the smell of tobacco on his clothes.

'I don't want any careless talk about me with Mrs Mountjoy.' He cocked his head toward the house.

'I can assure you, you're the last subject we intend to discuss.' She eased her arm from his hold and ostentatiously brushed the fabric of her sleeve. 'Unless there's something you wish to say to me.'

The horse took a step forward, lowered its head and nibbled at his fingers. His belligerence dissolved, his eyes softening as he stroked the soft muzzle

'Is there something worrying you Mr Bracenose?' Flora couldn't be afraid of a man to whom animals gravitated. Even the estate dogs came running for petting and treats when he appeared. Maybe she could even forgive his 'nosy brat' comment if he was scared.

'You've been asking about those men who fell sick after the fête.' He licked his lips, as if he knew he ventured onto sticky ground. 'It wasn't my fault. I only did what she told me. Those barrels were sealed when I collected them and still sealed when I handed them over at the Abbey. If they were tampered with, it wasn't me. I'm blowed if I'm taking the blame for what happened to John Hendry.'

The horse dipped its head and ripped tufts of grass from the verge, chewing noisily. Flora glanced at the road behind her on which no traffic had passed since their conversation began.

'Why should anyone blame you?' Flora tried not to let her voice shake. Eddy had been right, Caroline *had* bought the beer for the fête. If she didn't put the arsenic in it herself, she surely knew who did.

'Maguire suspected there was something wrong with the beer.' He cocked a thumb in the direction of the fence. 'She's going to blame me, and get me into trouble. I know she is. And you're going to help her.'

'If you had nothing to do with it, of course I wouldn't get you into trouble,' Flora insisted.

'Hah! Who'll they believe? Mrs lah-di-dah, or an estate worker? I know how these things work.' He stepped closer, sending Flora back against the hedge, but his voice when it came was soft, almost ingratiating. 'Look, Miss Flora, I might have got this all wrong, but if you'll take my advice, turn that gig round and go back to the Abbey. That woman isn't right. She's got a mean streak in her.'

'Did she poison the beer?' Then a thought struck her and before she could stop herself, blurted.

'She got you to do it? Is that why you carry on working for her? Because she has a hold over you?

A shadow passed across his features, as if he was trying to work out which question to answer first. 'I didn't see her do it, but she was there when the pitchers were set out on the picnic tables. She said if I told anyone, she would say I did it. Tell them she saw me.'

'I heard Lord Vaughn's son almost died.' A flash of fear entered his eyes. 'I would never have let him be hurt. I've known the lad since he was a baby.'

'Then maybe you have no need to worry about what she says. After all, only a few people were affected, and they recovered. Except Mr Hendry of course, but he had a heart condition.'

'Ay, well. Nice of you to understand, Miss.' The colour left his face as he relaxed and bobbed his head in an embarrassed nod.

Flora moved toward the gate but he slapped a hand the size of a small shovel on her forearm. His face loomed close, the scar on his nose large in her vision.

'I'm sorry if I frightened you, but you need to be careful with that woman. I think she knows.'

'Knows? What does she know?' She glanced at the hedge that separated her from the house and back to his face again. The pressure of his hand hot through the fabric of her sleeve. 'If something is worrying you about Mrs Mountjoy, shouldn't you speak to her about it. I really don't know what this has to do with me, I—'

His grip tightened. 'I didn't mean to let it slip. I liked your mother. Lily, was a sweet girl and always respectful to me.'

Flora froze and stared at him. How had the conversation taken such a turn? 'What has Mrs Mountjoy have to do with my mother?' She glanced pointedly down at his hand hooked round her arm, then back up at his face. He flushed and removed it.

'Sorry, Miss Flora. I'm not doing a very good job at explaining.' He licked his lips and glanced back at the gate. 'Just do as I ask and go back to the Abbey.'

'Mr Bracenose? Do you know what happened to my mother?'

'Nay, Miss I don't.' He met her eager look with confusion. 'She was just gone one day without explanation. Anyway, you watch that Scrivens, he likes to goad people.'

'I'll bear that in mind, thank you.'

'I haven't finished, Miss.' He stepped closer, and she recoiled, the tobacco stench stronger than ever. 'Think on this. Scrivens boasted that he was going up in the world, very soon.'

'I know you're trying to be helpful, but none of this means anything to me unless . . .' *Did Caroline ask Scrivens to poison the beer for her and threaten to blame Bracenose instead? Or was there something else?*

The plea in the man's eyes told her he was telling the truth. Making up her mind, she tugged the rein of the gig clear of the fence post and began

361

to pull the horse round back the way she had come. If Caroline Mountjoy was devious enough to threaten the estate manager, and also had dealings with Scrivens, this was the last place Flora wanted to be.

'Flora, is that you out there?' A strident female voice called from beyond the rhododendron bushes.

Flora froze. A cold sensation ran through her veins despite the bright afternoon sunshine, and torn, she hesitated. Should she make an excuse and leave, or brave it out with Caroline? Why hadn't she listened to Bunny and waited until he could accompany her?

'Mr Bracenose,' she whispered, taking a gamble, 'would you do something for me?' At his nod she rushed on in a whisper. 'Go back to the Abbey and ask my husband to come for me? Tell him it's urgent. And hurry.' Her fear had transferred from the scared looking man in front of her to what awaited her on the other side of the shrubbery.

'I don't like leaving you here, Miss Flora.' His voice dropped to a whisper.

'There you are, Flora!' Caroline appeared on the other side of the wrought-iron gate, her fingers of one hand curled on the upright as she pushed one side open. Her penetrating eyes slid from Flora to the workman and back again. 'What have you been saying to my guest, Bracenose? She looks positively anxious.'

CHAPTER 24

'As you are here, Bracenose,' Caroline said over her shoulder as she propelled Flora across the gravel, 'would you take Mrs Harrington's gig to the stables?' Her fingernails dug into the flesh of Flora's upper arm. Fear gripped her, and her heart pounded. She debated whether to resist, but a deeper part of her said if she wanted the truth, she needed to hear what Caroline had to say. Forcing herself to relax, she turned to where the man hovered, the reins in his hand and mouthed, 'Go!'

His worried expression changed to one she hoped was of understanding, but before she could see if he had obeyed, she lost sight of him as Caroline swept her around a curve in the drive to the open front door.

If the danger was real, at least she would have sent back a message.

The house was newer than Cleeve Abbey by several hundred years, and more compact, with honey-coloured ashlar stonework that bore signs of decay round the windows and where it met the slate roof. Two deep bay windows sat on either side of a front door, giving it a symmetrical, slightly smug look. On any other day, Flora would have found the house delightful, but just then she wished she was anywhere else.

'My butler has the day off,' Caroline said in response to Flora's nervous glance at the empty hall into which she was almost dragged. 'What were you saying to Bracenose just now?' Caroline demanded.

'Um – I ran into him on the road. He thought I was lost, but I told him I was coming here.'

'I see.' Caroline closed the front door with a final click. Without releasing Flora's arm, she led her to the back of the house through a gloomy hallway devoid of decorations. No pictures graced the walls or even a mirror; simply an uncarpeted floor and paintwork that had begun to peel.

In contrast, the sitting room held all the trappings of a lady's private haven; an assortment of sage green sofas in different styles vied for dominance with upholstered chairs. Two sets of French windows lined one side of the room opposite a marble fireplace that had begun to yellow with age.

'It was kind of you to invite me.' Flora perched on a small sofa Caroline indicated. Her voice sounded normal but her stomach knotted.

'I'll ring for tea.' Caroline twisted the handle in the wall, confirming Flora's suspicion she was the only guest.

Her brief examination of the olive walls revealed

several mediocre pastel drawings of local beauty spots, and a square of lighter paint on the far wall, indicating where a painting had been recently removed. The curtains were patched in places, as if the house had not been refurbished in some time, and she detected an underlying tang of mildew.

Its slightly shabby appearance reminded her of what Jocasta said about Caroline Mountjoy and her two husbands. Perhaps they weren't as rich as the lady wished everyone to believe?

'I don't envy you being garbed in black bombazine in this weather,' Caroline said without a trace of real sympathy. 'Mourning is such a trial, don't you find? I had to endure it twice.' She broke off as a nervous-looking maid trundled a laden tea trolley into the room, caught the door frame with a corner, and then almost tipped the entire contraption on the edge of a rug.

Caroline gave a frustrated sigh, at which the maid abandoned the trolley, bobbed a hasty curtsey and retreated.

'At least the inquest on Maguire is over with.' Caroline poured tea and handed Flora a cup without asking how she took it. 'What was the verdict again? Misadventure?'

'As we expected, yes.' Flora took a surreptitious sniff of the tea, but the brew, though dark brown didn't smell of anything but tea. Did arsenic have a smell? She pretended to take a sip but did no more than wet her lips.

While returning the cup to its saucer, she caught sight of a copy of the *Cheltenham Examiner* that sat open on a side table. The inquest had made the late edition. Had Caroline checked the facts before asking, or was she reassuring herself there had been no surprises?

'Such an unpleasant necessity, don't you find?' Caroline paced the room, her skirt rustled as she walked.

'I've only attended one,' Flora said carefully.

'I hope you've dropped the idea there was something suspicious about your father's demise?' Caroline slowly stirred her tea.

'What made you think that?' Flora returned her steady look, though her heartbeat rose a notch.

'Someone must have told me, though I cannot recall who.' She gave an unconvincing shrug and regarded Flora over the rim of her cup. When she lowered it again, her lips were dry. 'I expect Bracenose was gossiping about me outside just now. The man's a positive menace.' Her features hardened. 'What did he say?'

'Mr Bracenose?' Flora held her breath, aware of an air of menace that permeated the room. The French ormolu clock on the mantelpiece, one of the better pieces, stood at a little after four. How long would it take Bracenose to reach the Abbey. Another five minutes? Ten?

'Did you hear what I said?' Caroline's voice broke into her frantic thoughts.

'Er, sorry, no.' Flora jumped slightly, sloshing tea into her saucer.

'I said, dissembling isn't your forte, my dear.' She placed her cup and saucer gently on the mantle. 'I'm sure you must have heard all the rumours since you arrived. About me and Mr McCallum.' She didn't pause long enough for Flora to respond and rushed on, 'I was genuinely in love with him, you know, but marriage was out of the question. The brewery was not a success and he doesn't even own the house he lives in. Such a dreadful shame, when I was prepared to do whatever he wanted of me.'

The hairs on Flora's neck prickled and she eyed the door. She would make an excuse as soon as possible and leave. Or forget the excuse and simply get out of there.

'Mrs Mountjoy,' Flora began, aware her voice sounded higher than normal, 'I appreciate you trusting me with a confidence, but this has nothing to do with me.'

'Has it not?' Caroline circled the sofa like a restless cat, then perched her hip on an arm of the sofa. 'I assumed otherwise since you've been asking all sorts of questions. I hope I haven't been left out, or I shall feel quite neglected.'

Flora returned her cup to the saucer with a sharp click, tired of feigning ignorance, which wasn't working anyway. 'All right,' Flora began. 'I'm curious as to why Mr McCallum would put arsenic into his own beer?'

Caroline's eyes widened with something like admiration. 'Well, I didn't expect you to be quite so forthcoming. I imagined we would have this protracted accusation and denial session before we reached the true purpose of the meeting. I quite like your directness.'

'That doesn't answer my question,' Flora moistened suddenly dry lips. 'You don't deny it, so why not explain his reasons?'

'Now you are being naïve, dear. It was for the insurance of course.' Caroline's condescending tone implied Flora was being slow. 'It was supposed to be a contained incident. He didn't want to start an epidemic, simply provide evidence of contamination to verify his claim. The brewery would recover eventually as one of the main employers in the town.'

Flora gasped. 'Mr McCallum is a fraudster?' she blurted before she could stop herself.

'An ugly word, but accurate I suppose.' Caroline pursed her lips as if the thought had only that moment occurred to her. 'Graham thought his scheme was infallible until Maguire paid a visit to the brewery. That man was far too intelligent to be a butler. He went sneaking round the warehouse and guessed immediately that it was empty and concluded the business was in trouble. How could Graham claim for contaminated goods he hadn't bought?'

'That's a good question. How could he?'

'The receipts of course. Faked naturally, but no

one would have suspected but for Maguire's meddling.'

'Was Mr Bracenose involved in this scheme of yours?'

'My, you have been busy.' Caroline fiddled with a jewelled necklace at her throat. 'I suppose he was useful at first. Quite enamoured of me actually, which is why I was able to manipulate him. That didn't last though, and now he's become – difficult. He's developed a conscience and wants to pour out his soul.'

'He didn't say anything to me, which is why I asked,' Flora lied, more as an attempt to keep her talking.

'You're not a good liar, my dear.' Caroline sighed. 'Not that it matters now.'

Flora wasn't sure what she meant by that, but chose not to ask. Caroline skirted the sofa and when her back was turned, Flora upended her teacup into a nearby vase.

'Why did Brasenose put the arsenic in the fête beer?' Flora asked. 'I assume he did so on your instructions, but what for?'

'Quite genius really in its simplicity. Graham was bound to be asked by the insurance assessors why he had destroyed the sugar.'

'Sugar he had never actually purchased?'

'See, you *do* understand?' Her ingratiating smile made Flora want to slap her. 'He would cite the incident at the fête as proof the sugar was contaminated with arsenic. Just like it was in that Manchester brewery a couple of years ago. The insurance would pay up and all our problems would be over.'

'We were careful about the amount of arsenic. I only put in enough to make people ill for a few days. No one actually died.' She broke off with a frown. 'Oh yes, one old man did, didn't he? Still, one cannot control everything. It worked out well overall.'

'But something went wrong? My father discovered what you were doing?' *Or why was Flora here?*

'Exactly. Those newspaper clippings Graham gave him fooled him at first, but not for long. Not when Maguire insisted on visiting the factory and saw the warehouse was empty. Then that fool doctor misdiagnosed those men as having neuritis.' She tutted, impatient. 'Graham couldn't insist the reason was arsenic, or it would have looked suspicious.' Caroline returned to the trolley and retrieved her cup. 'More tea?

Flora handed over her cup automatically, resolving to consult one of Bunny's books on human behaviour by Freud. Was it normal to discuss fraud, death and tea in the same sentence with no trace of conscience? Was the woman ruthless, or merely blind to her own actions?

'No sugar for me, thank you.'

'Oh, sorry. Too late, I'm afraid.' She handed Flora the newly filled cup.

Flora slid a look at the vase at her elbow, satisfied it could accommodate another cup without being noticed in case Caroline had planned a similar *prank* for her with any spare arsenic she had lying about.

'I had a special reason for inviting you here today,' Caroline began. 'One which I hope you'll find it in you to understand.'

'Why would you need *me* to understand anything?' Flora fidgeted. One moment the woman issued veiled threats and in the next breath exhibited a desire to be understood.

'I realize that after all your enquiries, yours and your husband's, that it's only a question of time before Graham's crime is discovered.'

'My husband's?' Flora frowned. Was that what Bunny was doing today? Delving into Mr McCallum's activities? If so, why hadn't he told her?

'That's what I said, and thus far I cannot be implicated. Don't look at me as if you know something I don't. And if you think Bracenose will tell you what he knows, forget it. He knows I'll make things far worse for him if he did that. No, what I need you to know that I never intended to hurt Eddy. He's a charming boy and Venetia is my friend.' She twisted her hands in front of her. 'I was desperate for funds and Graham was going to share the insurance money with me. However I swear to you, I had nothing to do with what happened to Maguire.'

'What *did* happen to him?' Flora braced herself for the details she had longed to know since hearing of her father's death, but now dreaded to hear. 'Why did he come here that night?'

'How do you know he came here?' Caroline's face paled beneath the two circles of rouge she had applied to her cheeks. 'Who told you?'

'That's not important. Just tell me.' She gripped the sofa arm, her fingernails sinking deep into the loosely stuffed upholstery.

Caroline's eyes fluttered closed, and when she opened them again, they were soft, almost pleading. 'I had just returned from dinner at the Abbey, when Maguire arrived in a furious temper claiming to know why Graham had poisoned the beer at the fête. He demanded Graham withdraw his insurance claim or he would expose him.'

Her father would never have walked away from something so blatant as intended fraud. She could visualize him now, stern and indignant but refusing to be silenced. She eased along the sofa, putting some space between them. 'But Mr McCallum wasn't prepared to do that?' If she put the blame squarely on McCallum, maybe Caroline would seem less panicked.

'We couldn't let that happen. Marriage wasn't possible, I know that now, but I couldn't bear for him to be imprisoned for something so trivial.'

'Hardly trivial. He still tried to break the law,' Flora said, though there was no emotion behind it. Her thoughts were still running inside her head. Why wasn't marriage possible for them? They might not be rich, but they could still make a comfortable life for themselves. Or maybe that was naïve, and comfortable wasn't acceptable in their world? People like Caroline and McCallum required much more. 'Caroline,' Flora asked gently. 'What happened to my father?'

'*I* happened to him.' A male voice brought Flora's head up to where Graham McCallum pushed away from the door frame. 'It's remarkably easy to make a spirited horse rear.' He strode into the room with the slow confidence of a man with nothing to fear.

'It was you!' Flora's cup rattled against the saucer as she returned it clumsily to the table. She leapt to her feet as anger surged through her. 'You killed my father!'

'Graham.' Caroline lurched towards him. 'I didn't tell her anything. She knew what we did with the beer, I—'

'Be quiet, Caro. You've said enough.' He brushed her aside, directing a smile at Flora that held no warmth. 'I didn't tell you to invite her here for a cosy female chat.'

Chastened, Caroline backed away, a fist pressed to her mouth. It wasn't only love that made her cling to the man, but fear too.

'Unfortunate, but necessary.' A flash of distaste crossed McCallum's face, though it was gone in an instant, replaced by triumph. 'I knew he would take the quickest route back to the Abbey, so I waited on the edge of the wood.' He strolled to the fireplace, both feet planted apart as if he owned the room. 'I even offered him money, more than he could have earned in a decade, but the short-sighted fool was completely unreasonable.'

'You didn't have to kill him!' Flora shouted. Her hands clenched as she fought the urge to rush at him and drag her fingernails down his face.

'What choice did he give me?' McCallum's upper lip curled as he reverted to the excuse all villains hid behind: blaming their victim for their own fate. 'I could see he wasn't comfortable on that horse. It took little effort to unseat him. He hit his head when he fell, so all it took was a little encouragement with my whip send my horse over him and the deed was done.'

'Then you moved him.' It all fitted with what she had heard about the scene in Bailey Wood. They didn't find any evidence of two horses in the earth because he didn't fall there.

A scream of fury built inside her at the thought her father had found himself at the mercy of this ruthless, cold man with no one to help him.

'I sent his horse off and dragged the body to uneven ground with a few rocks to make a fall look more credible. The coroner accepted it as an accident.' McCallum sighed and regarded Flora as if she were an annoying insect. 'But you simply couldn't leave well alone.'

'That was how your mount loosened a shoe?' Flora knew she pushed him but couldn't help herself. 'When I asked you what you were doing at the Abbey that day, you said it was because Caroline had borrowed the horse.'

'Me?' Caroline turned a venomous glare on McCallum. 'Why would you say that?' She backed away slightly, her face working as she processed what he had said. 'You intended to blame me, didn't you?' Her mouth opened as she gasped. 'If you were found out, you would let everyone believe *I* killed him?'

'Stop fussing, Caro.' McCallum sneered. 'No one can connect that horse to Maguire's death now.'

Flora was about to disabuse him but changed her mind. If the second set of hoof prints could be matched to McCallum's horse, he could still be prosecuted for murder. While he thought himself safe, perhaps there was still a chance she could get out of this house in one piece. Her logic deserted her and terror took over at the knowledge this was a man capable or fraud, deceit and had already killed one person. Did he intend to kill her too?

Where was Bunny?

'Had Maguire simply kept quiet instead of threatening to expose me, he could have ended his days as a pensioner in one of the Vaughn's cottages,' McCallum went on, evidently comfortable with the sound of his own voice. 'As it was, he almost ruined everything.' He paused in front of Flora, his chin jutted and his face inches from hers.

Flinching, she stepped back, the back of her legs coming up against the sofa. A sensation of being trapped flooded through her but he moved away again. She released a breath, though her heart thumped uncomfortably in her chest. This man definitely meant her harm.

A cold dread settled into her stomach, and she couldn't move. She eyed the door again and then the French windows, but the former was too far away to reach; the latter blocked by Caroline.

'I'm sure you feel a certain righteous indignation at what I did.' McCallum held his hands open, palms outwards. 'However, there's no proof apart from Bracenose's testimony, and he'll do what I tell him.' He confirmed what Caroline had said earlier, though from what she saw outside, given enough encouragement, Bracenose might be willing to testify against these to. Unfortunately the pair of them stood between her and her way out.

'What about Scrivens?' Flora wasn't sure what the butler's part had been, and couldn't imagine why he would have been arguing with her father. Unless it was something to do with Betsy Mason's disappearance.

'He's in too deep to risk talking, after all, he helped me move Maguire's body.'

Rage swept through Flora's veins, and her face felt hot as an unwelcome image of the two of them dragging her father deeper into the wood invaded her head. Tears threatened, but she blinked them away. That wasn't the way either to defeat a man like him. Maybe she could divide them instead. Play on Caroline's fear that she had unwittingly been involved in a situation beyond her control.

'I have a question,' Flora began, 'why involve Caroline in murder? You don't hang for being an accomplice to insurance fraud. Murder, on the other hand, is quite different.'

'Graham, is that true?' Caroline closed the space between them and grabbed at his sleeve. 'That I could hang?'

'Use your head, woman.' He roughly shrugged her off. 'She's trying to turn us against one another.' The smug sneer on his face contrasted with Caroline's bewilderment. 'Which is rich if you consider what I did for you.'

'For me?' Caroline frowned, genuinely confused. 'What have you done for me?'

'Scrivens would do anything for a few pounds, though as it turned out, he spent a night at the Petersham Hotel at my expense and he still managed to fail spectacularly.'

Flora's triumph that her ploy had worked instantly dissolved as Eddy's words came back like a distant echo. *That idiot Scrivens fudged the job, so get it done right this time.* It felt as if she had been punched in the stomach. Bile rose in her throat as the horrifying facts dropped into place. 'You sent Scrivens to set the fire in our basement?'

'What does she mean, Graham?' Caroline's panic had turned to fury. 'What fire?'

Ignoring her, McCallum picked an imaginary piece of fluff from his jacket. 'You've been very clever, my dear Flora.'

'There could have been eight people in that house.' Flora's anger returned. 'You risked killing us all because of insurance fraud? What are you, insane?' His presumed intimacy made her flesh crawl. More so because she had liked this man, even trusted him when he had spoken with such feeling about his dead wife. Or was that too all part of his deception?

'That, I admit, was a mistake,' McCallum went on. 'Scrivens had no experience with arson. He miscalculated.'

'It was an amateur attempt.' Fury made her reckless, though she knew that to goad him might make him more dangerous. 'I still don't understand. My father was about to have you arrested, so I can see why you prevented him, but why me? What have *I* done to you?'

McCallum turned his cruel smile on Caroline. 'Do you know, Caro, I actually think she has no idea.'

'No idea of what?' Flora demanded, irritated with his self-satisfaction and penchant to play games.

He chuckled, lending a sinister element to an already incomprehensible conversation. 'Isn't it obvious, my dear? Maguire wasn't your father, William Osborne is.'

CHAPTER 25

'What a ridiculous suggestion.' Furious at this slur on not only her mother but herself, Flora marched towards the door. 'You're lying. This is an attempt to justify your story.'

She made to shove past him when his hand closed on her upper arm in a vice-like grip and he brought his face close to hers. Her vision went out of focus as his face blurred and receded in front of her.

'Without you, Mrs Harrington, Caroline had a clear road to Osborne and his money. And by that I mean *we* had.' He shoved her roughly backwards, continued to the door and pulled it firmly closed. He strode to the trolley and poured himself a cup of tea as if they were all part of some pleasant social ritual. 'Bracenose let slip to Scrivens who you were.' He waved the pot vaguely in Caroline's direction but she shook her head. 'Scrivens told Caro here, and loyal dear that she is, she told me.'

'It's true, but you must believe me, Flora,' – a sheen of sweat formed on Caroline's upper lip and she twisted her hands together – 'I would never condone any harm coming to you.'

379

'But it isn't true!' Flora almost screamed. 'Riordan Maguire was my father. And you killed him!'

Ignoring her protests, McCallum strode slowly back to the wing chairs beside the fireplace, one ankle crossed at his knee in casual comfort.

'Did you know what he planned?' Flora demanded of Caroline, gesturing to McCallum,

'No! Never. I knew nothing about any fire.' Caroline wrung her hands like a Shakespearean heroine, her former bravado gone. 'It's not as if it would have worked anyway. William was never interested in me. I used every wile I could think of, but he hardly notices I am there.'

'Do shut up, Caro,' McCallum snapped. 'Maybe not right now, but in Osborne's grief at losing his daughter, you could have comforted him. He wouldn't be the first man who married from a sense of gratitude. You would have thanked me afterwards.' He peered at Flora from beneath lowered brows, like a tiger ready to pounce. 'You still might.'

'I am *not* his daughter!' A rush of blood surged through Flora's veins as the implication of Caroline's garbled excuses and McCallum's proud boast sank in. *It couldn't be true? Could it? But if not then why the fire, the quest for William's money? This contrived meeting?* She tossed her head and regarded McCallum steadily. 'Even if what you say is true, it makes no sense. Mr Osborne has never offered me anything.'

'That's not what he told me.' McCallum adjusted his jacket flap over his thigh, his foot swinging gently. 'Not directly of course. He wasn't likely to reveal a past indiscretion so freely. Who would? But when I suggested he invest in my business, he refused on the grounds he had already committed his capital to a trust fund for his family.'

'He probably meant his nieces and nephew.' Flora searched for holes in his story, still unwilling to believe he told the truth. His lies were all part of his scheme to unbalance her. Make her vulnerable so when he pounced she wasn't prepared.

'Hardly.' McCallum's eyes took on a calculating look. 'Lord Vaughn has provided well for those girls of his. He's already married two of them off to rich husbands and has a third lined up for the youngest. The boy will inherit the estate and the title. Oh, and Osborne didn't tell me about you, by the way. Maguire did.'

'My father knew?' Flora broke off, horrified. 'About, about Mr Osborne?'

There had never been so much as a whisper or a careless word to imply Riordan Maguire wasn't her real father. Or was that what the 'poor Lily Maguire' comments had been about? But her father had loved her, hadn't he? The father who had raised her. And she, Flora, had loved him. She still did.

'Did he know about your mother and William?' McCallum snorted. 'Of course he did. That night, when I met him near the wood, and told him I knew about you, he changed his tune. Said he would keep quiet about the insurance fraud if I swore never to go near you. He wasn't to know that I had already sent Scrivens to deal with you. Couldn't let some by-blow stand in the way of a lucrative Osborne fortune, now could I?'

'My father would *never* have agreed to such terms. He was an honourable man and wouldn't hide—' But then he had hidden one of the most vital truths about her all these years? What was she supposed to believe when everything she had ever known no longer made sense?

'You miscalculated.' A slow anger burned in her chest. 'If Scrivens had succeeded, and he no longer had me to protect, Father would have gone straight to the authorities.'

'And that,' McCallum pointed his free hand at her, 'is why I had to finish him off.'

Flora clenched her fists, willing him to stop talking so she could think, but his voice droned on.

'You can imagine how I felt when Lady Vaughn announced you were alive, well and on your way here with your husband.' His low, menacing laugh made Flora's insides knot until she could not keep still any longer.

'I'm not listening to this!' She swept her still full cup and saucer from the table and hurled it at McCallum's head.

He ducked, the china smashing on the slate hearth behind him. His own cup upended, and brown liquid splashed the front of his shirt. He made an impatient tutting sound as he dabbed at the stain. 'Flora, really, you've quite ruined this shirt.'

Caroline gave a moan of dismay and bent to the shards of china on the floor.

Aware she had only a split second to act, Flora lunged for the French doors, praying they weren't locked. The door handle gave beneath her hand, and she erupted into the sunlit garden, though with no clear idea of which direction to take. Was she at the back of the house or the side? Which way was the road?

The French door slammed against the wall. 'Get out of my way, woman!' McCallum was seconds behind her.

Flora plunged to the right, into a wall of dense, dark green shrubbery of towering rhododendron bushes. The thick foliage blocked out the bright sunlight, a maze of tightly packed bushes with wrist-thick trunks she had to manoeuvre through with no idea which direction she took. Branches grabbed at her skirt and tugged her hair from its pins as she pushed her way through the pungent earthy smell of the uneven ground beneath her feet.

McCallum's shout came from close by, sending Flora's heart into her throat as he called to Caroline to check the front.

Loud rustling and low curses followed. Too close. She fought the impulse to run and dropped into a low crouch. If she made as much noise moving through the bushes he would be on her in seconds. She hunkered lower, taking a sideways look through the leaves. She had stopped at the edge of a terrace that led down to a lawn which resembled more an overgrown meadow than a garden. Waist-high grass sprinkled with ragged poppies was surrounded by thick hawthorn and brambles as well as a wall of more untamed rhododendron bushes. She surveyed the disorder, oddly grateful that Caroline's failure to keep her garden in check afforded so many places to hide.

The terrace had weeds poking through the paving stones, the walls broken in places. A wooden hut that might have once been a summerhouse occupied one corner, which she rejected as too obvious a place to hide.

McCallum waded through the grass toward the hut and she hunched lower. He disappeared inside for mere seconds before he hurled the door back into place with a furious curse; the crack of wood echoing across the empty garden. He swivelled around in a sweep of the back of the house. 'Flora!' He drew out her name in a sing song voice that made her heart skip a beat. 'Don't be stupid, girl. You can't stay out here forever.'

Temptation to scream back at him that he was wrong clawed at her, but aware that was exactly what he wanted, she clamped her lips together. A bird called from somewhere and the buzz of insects added to the roaring in her ears. Her forehead stung where a branch had caught it above one eyebrow, the warm trickle that followed told her she was bleeding but she ignored it. Her ankle throbbed where she had twisted it on a rough piece of ground, but not enough to slow her down.

'There's no way you can get out, Flora.' McCallum's voice came again, this time from further away. 'This property might be neglected, but its fences are secure. You may as well give up.'

'Shut up, you murderer,' she whispered under her breath and peered through the leaves again. McCallum was nowhere in sight. Was he going back to the house or coming this way?

The line of bushes concealed a path that ran along the side of the house, at the end an impenetrable wall of brambles and overgrown nettles stood between her and the front drive. A glimpse of the railings through the tangle indicated she was headed in the right direction, but how to get through?

If she could avoid Caroline and find her way to the front of the house. If she could keep out of McCallum's way long enough. If Bracenose had not locked the gate when he left. She groaned inwardly – too many 'ifs'.

She eased through the thick shrubbery onto the path, but the only way open to her was through a glazed door that led back into the house. If she could stay undetected and reach the front door and onto the path, she might be able to reach the gates. If they were unlocked. Would they expect here to go back inside the house?

Her breathing came short and rapid, making her dizzy, but if she stayed there she would be seen. Shielding her eyes with a hand, she stared through the glass into what looked to be a snug, or maybe a housekeeper's room; its far door open onto the dingy hall she had passed through when she arrived.

Her teeth gritted, she tugged the handle downwards. The door opened with a low, creak and assuming McCallum wouldn't expect her to go back inside, she crept through the sparsely furnished room. It was about half the size of the sitting room and equally shabby. She stood behind the door for a moment, her ears pricked, listening for footsteps or voices, but heard nothing.

She peered round the jamb to where the hall ran from the back of the house to the front. The glazed front door with its stained glass flower pattern mocked her from the far end. Gathering her courage, she stepped into the hall and ran in that direction, feet pounding the thin carpet, the floorboards bouncing beneath her as the door grew larger in her vision.

She was almost there when a shadow loomed from a room on her left. McCallum's hand closed round her wrist and he hauled her roughly backwards, her arm behind her back and he slammed her into the wall, face first. Terror surged through her as the air was pushed from her lungs, her cheek jammed against the slightly damp plaster, his other hand gripping the back of her head. Her eyes flew open in fear, the feel of his warm breath on her neck making her skin crawl.

He must have done the same thing as she had and backtracked through the sitting room she had first run from.

'Did you really think I got you here to let you spoil everything?' he growled in her ear.

'Graham,' Caroline called from the far end of the hall, both hands pressed to her cheeks, her eyes wide and fearful. 'It's no use. What good would hurting her do now?'

'You'll do what I say, Caro. My plan might still work.' McCallum twisted Flora's arm as if to make a point.

She gripped her bottom lip between her teeth but refused to cry out, though the pain made her feel sick – as if her arm was being pulled from its socket.

'Heard of suicide through grief, have you?' He pushed her harder into the wall, sending her shoulder into a spasm. 'Let's see. I reveal the truth of your birth over tea with Caroline, the shock of which is so great, you know that when your respectable husband discovers you were nothing but a bastard, he'll insist on a divorce. With nothing left to look forward to, why wouldn't you end your life?'

He laughed again, the low, self-congratulatory laugh of a confident man. Or an insane one. 'Perhaps the spot you choose it also the same one your father's horse threw him? Is that enough shame and grief to send you temporarily mad? I think so and I'll certainly make the police believe you were deranged enough when you went rushing out of here. His hold on her arm relaxed slightly and she shifted a hair's breadth, easing the pressure on her ribs, but not enough so she could wriggle out of his grasp.

'Come on, Flora.' He yanked her by the hair away from the wall, twisting her a half turn towards the door. 'Let's go and find a suitably large rock, shall we?'

Anger and pain swept through her and, defiant, she lifted her left foot and putting as her full weight behind it, brought the narrow heel of her boot down hard on his instep.

He issued a furious yell of agony, followed by a colourful curse, his hold slackening enough for her to lever her arm from his grip and jab her other elbow into his throat. Before he could recover, she whirled around, straightened her hand and thrust two fingers into his eyes, congratulating herself she had not trimmed her fingernails that morning. He screamed, brought one hand to his face and staggered blindly towards her.

'Graham!' Caroline gasped and dashed towards him.

Aware he would be on her again in seconds, Flora shoved Caroline hard. She careered into him and together they staggered against the wall, sliding to the floor in a tangle of ruffled skirt and trouser legs. Flora ran for the front door, assuming from the thumps and curses from behind her, he had bundled her aside, but she didn't stop to look.

She fumbled with the catch for several heart-stopping seconds until it finally gave and she jerked it open, threw herself off the porch and lurched in the direction of the gates. They weren't visible from the front of the house, but with each footstep she prayed they had been left open. Her throat burned with the effort of pulling hot summer air into her lungs, spurred onwards by her pursuer's low growl of anger as he pounded after her.

How long had she been inside the house? Surely Bracenose had reached the Abbey by now? Perhaps Bunny hadn't returned from his mysterious appointment yet? Or had Bracenose deserted her and she was on her own?

Cursing the fact she was hampered by layers of petticoats and a corset, she vowed not to make it easy for him. Unless he was willing to strangle her on a public road, her feet and fingernails might buy her some time.

These thoughts raced through her head in a half second, while the rhythmic sound of hooves drew closer. From the corner of her eye, she sensed a hand reach out to grab her and swerved sharp right, just as a horse-drawn carriage took the curve into their path.

She only had time to register a pair of flared nostrils beneath rolling eyes as the bulk of a horse filled her vision. Instinctively, she threw herself sideways just as something hard caught her hip, sending her sprawling onto the gravel. She rolled right, just as she caught sight of the driver's mouth opening in a terrified yell as he hauled back on the reins.

The horses thundered past in a blur of shiny brown flanks, flailing hooves and wheels, followed by the driver's frantic 'Woah!' and a high-pitched feminine scream.

Flora's heart drummed in her chest, her breath coming in short, ragged gasps as she fought for control. She tried to move, but the grinding pain that radiated along her left leg changed her mind. She lifted her hands gingerly, one stretched out on the gravel and the other half twisted beneath her. A brief look told her a layer of fine gravel lodged in both palms beneath which blood oozed. Slowly, her limbs responded to her silent plea to work, causing a burning pain into her hands.

The sound of a carriage door being flung open followed by the crunch of footsteps on gravel drifted toward her. Shouts from far off penetrated her consciousness. Another scream, then a frantic call of her name, but she couldn't think or make sense of any of it.

'Oh, my God, we ran you down.' Bunny hauled her clumsily upright and gathered her into a suffocating hug, her face nestled in the gap between his shoulder and neck. 'Flora, are you all right? Can you speak? Where are you hurt?'

His *Floris* cologne filled her senses, but ridiculously, all his frantic pleas did was make her giggle.

'Not your fault.' She found her voice at last, though tears hovered close. Then memory returned and she grabbed his lapel, sending sharp pain through her injured hand. 'McCallum. He was right behind me. He was going to—'

'Don't worry about him, sweetheart,' Bunny whispered. 'He can't hurt you now. Can you stand?'

'I think so.' She put her weight on her left leg which sent fresh pain through her side. Lethargy overcame her, and she flopped back down again. 'Leave me here. I'll get up in a minute or two.'

'Silly girl, you can't stay here.' He ran a brisk hand down each of her legs in turn, then did the same to her arms. 'I couldn't have borne it if we had arrived too late,' he muttered as he carried out his examination.

'Well you didn't.' She giggled again, light-headed. 'And you're being rather forward, Mr Harrington.' Her lip quivered and tears threatened. 'I cannot tell you how good it is to see you.'

Bunny wrapped an arm round her waist, pulling her gently to her feet. 'Come on, let's get you into the carriage.'

The horses stamped and threw up their heads, their necks gently stroked by a young groom who murmured soothing words in an attempt to settle them.

Every muscle protested as Bunny guided her up the step into the driverless carriage. Favouring her sore hip, she manoeuvred into the corner seat by means of a series of hops and slides.

'Someone screamed.' Flora frowned, remembering. 'Caroline. Is she hurt?

'No.' Bunny's clipped tone and the fact he avoided her eye told her something awful had happened.

'I hope you brought the police?' She angled her head to see the length of the drive through the window. 'McCallum mustn't get away, he—' she broke off as the full weight of what she had discovered crashed in on her. 'He killed Father.'

'I know, darling.' Bunny reached through the carriage door and grasped her hand in both of his. 'William is here, and-uh McCallum didn't get away. He was so intent on catching you, he ran straight into us.' He gave an almost imperceptible nod past her shoulder.

Flora turned and followed his gaze to figures of William and the coach driver about ten feet away. On the ground between them lay Graham McCallum, his head twisted at an unnatural angle, his lips pulled back from his teeth in a grimace.

'Is he—' Flora's question was made irrelevant as William removed his jacket and placed it over the top half of the body. She waited for the shock of his death to hit her, but nothing happened. No sympathy or even triumph, simply mild surprise. After all McCallum had said, done and threatened, he had succumbed to a similar end as her father. Crushed beneath the hooves of a horse.

She slanted a glance sideways, to where Caroline stood unmoving by the open front door, her face stark white while large tears carved lines into a layer of face powder.

'She wore cosmetics,' Flora said idly, then grasped Bunny's sleeve in the fingers of one hand. 'I'm so sorry I didn't listen to you,' she gabbled. 'I had no idea he would be here, or I wouldn't have come.'

'It's not important now.' Bunny stepped back, his place taken by William.

'Are you all right, Flora?' His voice shook slightly, and he seemed different somehow. The same man she had always known but a shadow lurked behind the normally sparkling eyes and ready smile. Or was that her own mind twisting what McCallum had told her? He must have been lying. It couldn't be true about William and her mother.

She murmured something unintelligible, her head down as she rearranged her ruined skirt over her knees, ignoring the burning in her hands, though she senses a loaded look had passed between William and Bunny.

'I'm glad,' William said shakily. 'I'll uh-see you both back at the Abbey.'

'There's no reason why you shouldn't come back with us,' Bunny suggested, while Flora continued to stare at her hands, which were badly grazed with streaks of blood mixed with dirt and torn skin.

William made a sound as if about to say something, then seemed to change his mind. 'Uh, no, I'll stay here and wait for the police. Caroline is in a dreadful state.' Flora jerked her head towards

393

him and he rushed on, 'Not that I care after what she has done, but I want to make sure she says the right things to the police when they get here.' He cocked his chin at the pathetic figure on the porch who appeared to have aged a decade. 'She hasn't grasped that she'll has some explaining to do. She might even face charges.'

Bunny clambered into the carriage beside Flora, the slam of the door making her wince, and wrap her arms round herself.

'You'll have to speak to William at some stage,' Bunny said gently. He tugged a handkerchief from his top pocket, pulled her nearest hand toward him and gently wrapped it around the worst of the cuts. 'He would have talked to you before today, but I made him wait.'

'It's not true you know. About William.' She snatched her hand away and finished tying the cotton herself, though she made a rough job of it one-handed.

'I'm afraid it is,' he said, his voice almost a whisper.'

'It can't be. And if it is, then why didn't you *tell* me?' She avoided his eye, conscious she was being cruel, but couldn't help the raw anger that surged inside her mixed with humiliation that she had been lied to for so long. Her more rational inner voice told her it wasn't Bunny's fault, but he was closest, thus destined to bear the weight of her resentment. The other Flora, the one who had been terrified, threatened and had run for her life wanted nothing but to fall into his arms and feel safe again. Have him whisper his love to her, reassure her that nothing would change. That he wouldn't demand a divorce as McCallum had implied.

'Don't, Flora.' Bunny wrapped an arm round her stiff shoulders. 'I didn't want to keep it from you. William told me last night and asked that I wait until he could speak to you in private. Neither of us imagined you would find out like this.'

'He's lied to me all his life. And mine.' Flora ran her unbound hand along her skirt but stopped when the fabric caught on the cuts and made her wince. 'He always wanted me to call him Uncle William. Did you know that?'

'What else could he have done? Your fath— Riordan insisted you must not be told. William respected his wishes as Riordan was the one who raised you.'

'And that's another thing. Why?' Her breathing came fast and painfully as her emotions threatened to overwhelm her. 'Why did he raise me after my mother went missing? He had no responsibility for me. I wasn't his.'

'Because he loved you, of course. You were all he had left of Lily.'

'Did-did William use Mother and then leave her? Is that how it happened?'

'Not the way he tells the story.'

'The way he tells—' She turned away, unable to take everything in. 'This is too much all at once. I'm still coming to terms with the fact that

McCallum killed my father.' Bunny looked about to speak but let it go with a sigh. 'And yes,' she added. 'I'll still call him my father, because that's what he was.' She was grateful when he didn't contradict her, but simply nodded and remained silent.

With the horses now calmed, the driver turned the carriage in a full circle. Before they reached the curve in the drive, Flora stared through the rear window. Caroline was nowhere to be seen, though a footman stood beside the body on the ground.

William had mounted the front step to the house, his feet apart and hands in his pockets. He gazed at the retreating coach with a look of regret, mixed with abject misery.

CHAPTER 26

'McCallum was always so calm, so sure of himself,' Flora said. 'He even encouraged me to question Dr Fairbrother about my father's accident. Why would he do that when he might have incriminated himself?'

'He knew the doctor was stick to his conviction Riordan had died accidentally. Perhaps he hoped with your questions about poisoning he might change his mind about his insistence the farm workers had neuritis which posed a risk to his insurance claim.'

'Why didn't he get another doctor to look at the workmen? Someone more intuitive would have detected the arsenic. Reginald Meeks did.'

'When the original diagnoses exonerated the brewery? That would have been even more suspicious. He wasn't going to let it go though as he sent a sample of the mash to the Owens College Laboratory, the one who did the original tests in Manchester. They verified it contained arsenic most likely from contaminated sugars. McCallum sent the report to the insurance company because, in his words, he did so in an attempt to confirm the doctor's diagnosis. He knew all along it would do the opposite. McCallum claimed he had bought tons of the stuff which he would have to destroy. They were on the verge of paying his claim too, but that's unlikely now.'

'I think Caroline did invite me to tea quite innocently. Then she heard Bracenose telling me he thought he would be blamed for the fête incident. She changed her story.'

'In which case why was McCallum there?' Bunny dabbed her forehead with another handkerchief that came away bloodied. 'Don't give her any credit, they were in it together. You were lured there for a reason.'

'Is that why you didn't want me to go to her house today?' She winced as his finger encountered a sore spot.

Bunny nodded. 'William suspected Caroline and McCallum were up to something, so he suggested we do some investigation of our own. He saw Caroline and McCallum together on the night of your father's death when their liaison was supposed to have ended. Then when McCallum argued with Scrivens, he knew there was more to it.'

'Eddy saw that too. But I didn't know what it meant at the time. Scrivens set fire to our house.' Flora shuddered at the thought of how much worse it might have been had the blaze not been discovered.

'I know.'

She jerked around to look at him, the sudden

movement making her head spin. 'How do you know? I only discovered that this afternoon.'

'It's complicated. Anyway, let's not worry about that now. I'll explain later.'

'I'm still not clear as to why McCallum wanted *me* dead. I'm no threat to either him or Caroline.'

'Think about it, Flora. You're William's heir, so getting rid of you gave Caroline and McCallum a clear run to his money.'

'I'm not his heir. And even if I was, had Caroline become his wife, she would have been entitled anyway unless he changed his will.'

'She couldn't guarantee that. Caroline has looks and charm but even she doubted she could captivate a man like William enough to persuade him to disinherit you.'

'She was clearly in love with McCallum.' Flora recalled the woman's stricken face as she stared down at her lover's lifeless body. 'Did they also plan to get rid of William eventually?' A shiver than crept up her spine at the thought though its existence puzzled her. William was nothing more to her that Lady Venetia's brother and Eddy's Uncle. Then why did the idea of his loss to bother her?'

'I don't know, but I wouldn't discount it. Neither of them had any morals.'

'I'm furious with myself at having misjudged McCallum so badly.' She always had prided herself on being a good judge of character, but with his alluring eyes and attractive smile, he had completely fooled her. 'Leopold of the Belgians had a bad reputation where women were concerned too.'

'Hmm, what was that about Belgians?'

'Oh, nothing. McCallum's disgust at fox hunting during dinner the other night made me think he was a sensitive soul, yet when it came to disposing of a human being, his conscience had not troubled him at all.' Idly she wondered if he had ever been married, but pushed the thought away as being of no consequence now.

'Don't punish yourself, Flora. McCallum wasn't as clever as he thought. William and I paid a call to his brewery this afternoon. He had laid off half his workforce and sold some of his dray horses. It didn't take much for his foreman to let us into his office.'

'By the look on your face I assume you found something interesting.'

He nodded. 'Those newspaper clippings your father had, well McCallum had them too, and a lot more. He had a whole file of information about the Manchester incident. Did you know two years ago he lived there?'

'No, I didn't. He said he came from the north, but was no more specific than that.'

'He tried to pass himself off as a country gentleman but gave himself away when he didn't know what an earthstopper was. That's when William first suspected him. I did some checking with an investigator we sometimes use in my law firm.'

'You did all this without mentioning it to me?'

'I wasn't sure I would find anything, and didn't want to get your hopes up until I was sure. You had enough to deal with, what with losing Riordan, the inquest and then the funeral. All this stuff you were trying to unearth about your mother upset you even more until your talk with Amy. Then Eddy being poisoned and you the only one who noticed.' He lifted both hands palms upwards and let them fall again. 'I was trying to spare you, but as it turned out, you thought I wasn't taking your suspicions seriously and put yourself in danger.' He massaged his forehead with one hand. 'I cannot believe I handled everything so badly.'

'You didn't. I was the stubborn one and you were right, I was distressed over Father, and the questions about my mother. You were right to try and rein me in a little. I'll listen to you in future, I promise.'

'I believe you said that once before. When we were aboard the Minneapolis.'

'Um, possibly. And you were just a little jealous of McCallum too, weren't you?'

'Of course. But I wasn't going to reveal that.'

If only he knew how clearly his feelings were written on his face when he stepped out of the carriage on Sandford Road – he might as well have painted himself green. 'What did your investigator find out?'

'McCallum,' he began, unable to keep the triumph from his voice, 'was a Mancunian accounts clerk with a talent for massaging clients' books. He embezzled the company he worked for and used the proceeds to buy the brewery at a knock-down price. Unfortunately for him, bringing the place back to full production proved more expensive than he imagined, thus the insurance claim. Fairbrother wouldn't co-operate with the diagnosis, but when Riordan suggested poison, it played right into his hands.'

'So he was an ally, until Father discovered he was trying to get rid of me so he could have William's money. It all makes sense now. Horrible, evil sense.' She leaned back against the upholstery, swaying with the movement of the carriage as it traversed the country road. 'All those men at the brewery will lose their jobs now, won't they?' She thought of Amy Coombe's harsh childhood when the brewery failed before, and all the other Amy's and their mothers whose lives would now be blighted due to the actions of one man.

'If they don't find an affluent enough buyer who can bring the brewery back up to scratch again, it's more than likely.' Bunny ran tentative fingers along her wrist, as if suddenly shy. 'Bracenose was pacing the drive when we arrived and practically threw himself at the horses. We didn't stop to wait for a full explanation, but when he told us where you were, we turned around and came straight to Caroline's.'

'Then when I saw you thrown to the ground by the carriage, I thought I had killed you. I never want to experience such stomach-churning terror again.'

Flora summoned a weak smile, tempted to remind him that had he been less secretive, she wouldn't have put herself into such an invidious position, but when it had come to it, he had come to her rescue. The important thing was she wasn't hurt, much, and her father's killer had been caught and punished. That it was beneath the hooves of a horse and not a hangman's rope seemed fitting.

This satisfying thought was followed by another, equally as sobering: *Riordan Maguire wasn't her father. He had never been.*

The carriage turned in at the Abbey gates and suddenly Flora felt very tired. Despite her repeated assurances that she was more shaken than hurt, her legs still shook and Bunny had to help her down the carriage step.

'It's most likely shock, however I think we'll let the doctor decide that,' he said as they entered the hall.

'Oh no, please don't send for Dr Fairbrother. I think I prefer his arrogant face to his apologetic one. I imagine my hip will be purple by tomorrow, but not much can be done for bruises, unless you have a bucket of arnica at the ready. Oh!' She released a gasp which turned to a laugh as Bunny swept her into his arms and headed for the stairs.

They were only a few feet away from the first stair, when the door to the sitting room opened and Jocasta came running. Lord Vaughn close behind her.

'What's wrong with Flora? Or is this one of your romantic gestures, Bunny?' She laughed, but as she drew closer, gasped. 'What's happened to your dress, it's all torn and filthy? And your hands are bandaged?'

'Rescue mission,' Bunny said, continuing up the steps, but halted halfway up at the sound of Lord Vaughn's voice. 'I saw William's carriage in the drive, then it turned round and drove off again.' Lord Vaughn said at Jocasta's shoulder. 'Where's William? Didn't he come back with you?'

Evidently they weren't going to get away with saying nothing.

'We'll explain later,' Flora said over Bunny's shoulder. 'I need to clean myself up first.'

'Are you sure you are all right, Flora?' Jocasta wrapped both hands round the newel post and stared up at them.

Flora didn't have the energy to speak, so waved vaguely one of her bandaged hands.

Jocasta and her father drifted back to the sitting room, whispering together but both with dark, confused looks on their faces.

'What will happen to Caroline?' Flora rested her head on Bunny's shoulder.

'I don't know, but she was his accomplice in everything but your father's death. She has some explaining to do, that's for certain.' He paused for breath on the half-landing.

'Am I too heavy?' she said into the soft hair behind his ear, though the question was perfunctory.

'Well, let me put it this way. No more cream cakes and biscuits for you for a while.'

'Hey!' She lifted her head and gasped, but he was laughing. 'Tease. I'd slap you if my hands weren't torn and bleeding. Now what was it you said about Caroline?'

'Whether there will be charges depends on how much evidence they have and how good her lawyer is.'

'In any other circumstance I would suggest you defend her, but not on this occasion.' Flora couldn't summon a crumb of sympathy for the woman who had known McCallum had killed her father and had poured her tea as if it was the most natural thing in the world. It was small consolation that she most likely hadn't poisoned it.

'I wouldn't even consider it. In fact this case might encourage me into the Prosecutor's Office.'

'I don't believe that for a moment, you much prefer defending the underdog.'

'William will tell us what happened when he gets back. I imagine we'll be required to give the police statements about what we found at the brewery, but that can wait until the morning.'

'I don't think I can face William.' Flora snorted. 'I wouldn't know what to say to him.'

'You don't have to say anything, just listen to his side of the story. It might surprise you.'

'Everyone appears to have one of those, a story

I mean. Along with a list of excuses for their lies and secrets. Apologies and justifications pall after a while.' She tensed, recalling McCallum's triumphant face when he told her not only who William was, but also that her father had known all the time. 'Do you intend to carry me all way up two flights?'

'Think I'm not up to it?' His glasses slipped down on his nose and he crossed his eyes. Flora obeyed his silent signal and obliged by pushing them back with a finger. 'Thanks.'

'You're welcome.' She was aware she wasn't shaking any more, but for some reason felt incredibly tired. 'I feel safe now. Thank you.'

'That's the idea.' He set her down outside their door, but kept his arms round her, his head bent to her hair. 'I thought I had lost you back there. When I saw you lying on the ground, I—' He choked back whatever he had intended to say next.

'You've already said that, and you didn't.' Flora planted a kiss on his forehead, then pushed open the door. Like contestants in a three-legged race, they limped towards the bedroom, laughing as Bunny tripped on the rug and almost brought them both down onto the floor.

'I don't believe Caroline knew about the fire in Richmond,' Flora said as Bunny helped her onto the bed. 'She was horrified when McCallum told her he was trying to get rid of me for her sake.' She declined the blanket he was about to throw over her. The room was stifling enough.

'Shall I have some tea sent up?' he asked.

'No, thank you.' Flora grimaced. 'I've had enough tea for today.' *Even though she didn't drink Caroline's tea, the mere thought made her stomach hurt.*

He removed the blanket and discarded it over the nearest chair, then clamped his hand onto her forehead.

'What are you doing?' Flora frowned.

'Checking for clamminess. Shock can be quiet serious, you know.'

'I'm fine, simply disoriented. It's unnerving to discover that at the age of twenty-four my entire life has been a lie.'

'Not all of it.' He lowered himself onto the side of the bed and took her hand in both of his. 'I'm steady enough and I'm not going anywhere.'

'You know what I mean.' *No divorce then?* A glance at the clock told her the dressing bell would go any moment. 'I don't feel up to facing everyone. Not yet. You get changed and go into dinner. I think I'll stay here a while.'

'Everyone will want to know what happened this afternoon, but if you aren't up to it I could do it for you.' He rose and patted her hand. 'You lie here for a while and think. I'll go and have a bath and come and see how you feel later. It's still an hour before dinner.'

The door closed with a gentle click, and she relaxed against the pillows. She recalled what McCallum was going to do to her and jerked upright as a rush of ice-cold dread flooded through her veins. The window stood open and a light breeze billowed the curtain inwards, while a lone pigeon cooed from outside and she reminded herself she was safe. She pressed a hand to her chest and forced her breathing to slow, and lay down again. He couldn't hurt her now. No more than the doctor on the SS *Minneapolis* hurt her when she had threatened his freedom.

The pigeon cooed again and a light breeze shifted the stifling heat of the early evening. Her eyelids fluttered closed and in the seconds before sleep claimed her, she wondered how she could ever look William Osborne in the face again.

Flora woke to a room bathed in soft evening light and Bunny's face leaning over her.

'Did you have a nice sleep?'

She yawned and stretched, then winced as her sore hands caught against her skirt.

'Hmm, what time is it?'

'After nine. Dinner is over I'm afraid, but I asked Amy to prepare some sandwiches as I knew you would be hungry.'

'How thoughtful, and strangely enough I'm starving.'

'I consider that a good sign.' Bunny retrieved a tray from the dresser and placed it beside her on the bed. 'Not very interesting, no ham or smoked salmon, but there is cucumber and egg mayonnaise.'

'Sounds lovely.' Flora nibbled at the corner of

an egg sandwich. 'I could do with a bath after this,' she said through bites of sandwich. 'Then a good night's sleep.'

'You don't fool me.' Bunny perched on the edge of the bed and regarded her steadily. 'You cannot put this off until tomorrow. The family are like a bevy of nervous cats downstairs, all vying to get their stories straight.'

'I don't care.' She dissected a ham sandwich and nibbled at a slice of pink meat. 'They've all lied to me for years. I've a good mind to pack my bags and go to the Belle Vue Hotel and leave them to it.'

'That would be cruel. Besides, I know you. You are dying to know every detail.'

'Then *you* tell me. The Vaughns appear to explained everything to you.'

'Not everything.' He moved the empty plate to one side and handed her a glass of milk.

She winced as the glass made contact with her grazed hand but the milk was cool and refreshing so she put up with the discomfort.

'Come on, let's get it over with.' He removed the empty glass from her hand and pulled her to her feet. 'You'll feel much better afterwards.'

She caught sight of her reflection in the cheval mirror, and groaned with dismay at the smuts of dirt on her cheeks and chin.

The hem of the skirt was torn and hung down to the floor at one side, the fabric stained with mud and what could have been blood from the scrapes on her hands but had soaked into the black bombazine. An inch-long cut on her forehead bulged slightly, the skin beneath it threatening to turn black at any second. Her hair had escaped its pins and hung in tangled chestnut curls down her back, while what remained of her soft bun lay in a wispy mess flattened on one side.

'I'm going to need your help to make me respectable.' She held out her hands, 'I cannot manipulate buttons or laces with these hands.'

After a frustrated fumble or two, mostly on Bunny's part, they removed Flora's gown and soiled petticoats, washed her skin and refastened the buttons, hooks and eyes on a clean black skirt and blouse. Manipulating a brush and hair pins proved a challenge, but Flora viewed the final result with satisfaction.

'You can throw that out too,' she said as Bunny retrieved her soiled black gown from the floor. 'I have no intention of wearing it again. And I'm not wearing that either.' She nodded to the corset that hung by its strings in his other hand.

Bunny eyed the item with mild dismay, but made no comment as he returned it to the drawer. 'Maybe I'll get you a lady's maid when we return home.'

'It's a lovely thought, but I don't usually have scraped palms or a sore hip to hinder me. Maybe it wouldn't be prudent until you are made a partner in your law firm?'

'Oh, I think we can manage one small maid before that happens.' He took her bandaged hand and tucked it beneath his elbow. 'Ready?'

'I suppose so.' Though his wry smile told her Bunny wasn't fooled. He knew as well as she did that she couldn't wait to find out what William had to say.

CHAPTER 27

With her hand in Bunny's, Flora inhaled a deep breath as she limped into the sitting room, a task made easier without the restrictions of a corset. Jocasta and Lady Vaughn occupied a sofa, while William stood awkwardly beside the mantelpiece, apparently having found something of acute interest in the ormolu clock that stood there.

Conversation stilled abruptly and all eyes turned towards Flora.

'Ah, there you are, my dear.' Lord Vaughn grasped both her hands and guided her to the nearest empty sofa. 'We all hope you feel better after your nap. Bunny told us all about your dreadful ordeal this afternoon. Who would have thought McCallum was—'

'Yes, yes, George,' Lady Venetia interrupted. 'Flora knows better than anyone what happened.'

'Even so, it must have been awful for you.' Jocasta planted a gentle kiss on Flora's cheek. 'William says you were almost killed.'

Warmth crept into Flora's face at the mention of William. She found she could not meet his eye and, instead, eyed the plate of petit fours on the table beside the coffee pot.

'Might I have some coffee?' she asked, recalling she had left an untouched pot in her room.

'Oh, of course, my dear.' Lady Venetia rose and moved to the sideboard. That she poured the brew herself drew Flora's attention to the fact there were no servants in the room. To protect their reputation, or hers?

'Have to say I never much liked the Mountjoy woman.' Lord Vaughn declined coffee but helped himself to brandy. 'When they are that flirtatious they can never be trusted.' He carried his glass back to his favourite wing back chair by the empty fireplace.

'Which shows how foolish I am.' Lady Venetia sniffed, her lips trembling. 'I quite liked her, despite her overbearing manners. I had no idea she had no money. When I commented on the state of her house, she said she planned to refurbish and was ridding herself of old furniture. I even encouraged her attraction to William. Had I not done so, none of this would have happened.'

'Venetia, dear, you're gabbling,' Lord Vaughn chastised her gently. 'Now give Flora her coffee.'

'Oh, of course, sorry.' She stared at the cup and saucer for a few seconds before handing it to Flora. Her empty hand shook slightly and she brought it to her mouth in silent distress.

'I doubt you can be held responsible in any way,

Lady Vaughn.' Bunny flicked up the back of his jacket and took the seat beside Flora.

'It's no one's fault but mine.' William stood with his hands at his sides like an awkward schoolboy. 'I should never have—'

'Please, stop this.' Flora replaced her cup in the saucer after one sip. 'Self-recriminations don't help, what's done is done. Mr McCallum said – some things, and I need an explanation.'

'One which is well overdue, Flora.' William fetched a straight-backed chair from the side of the room and dragged it into place in front of Flora. He perched on the edge, his elbows on his knees and head jutted forward. 'You must be angry and confused, but I hope you'll allow me to explain.'

'More lies and secrets?' Flora said, aware she sounded bitter but didn't care. She picked a nut from a Florentine biscuit tucked into her saucer and brought it to her mouth. She wanted to devour it whole but didn't like to in front of everyone. Not when they were all looking at her.

'I know you're angry,' Bunny whispered, easing backwards slightly, as if to give William space to state his case. 'Just listen to him.'

'That's why I'm here, isn't it?' Flora began. 'However, if you don't mind, I could do without hearing the part about my being the result of a youthful frolic with a maid. It's humiliating enough knowing everyone has gone to great lengths to conceal the truth from me all my life, including

414

the man I believed to be my father.' She blinked away sudden tears, unable to remove Riordan Maguire from the box in her head marked 'parent'.

'Are you sure you want an explanation, Flora?' Jocasta raised a sardonic brow at Flora. 'You seem to have worked it all out by yourself.'

'Quiet, Jo,' Lord Vaughn snapped, which evoked a sulky look from his daughter, who gave an apologetic shrug.

'It wasn't like that, truly.' William squeezed his eyes shut then opened them again on a sigh, which made Flora regret her casual cruelty. Perhaps he did deserve a fair hearing. She studied him properly, half expecting him to look different from the man she had always known as her employer's brother. If anything, Flora was the one who had changed. Her perception of herself had shifted and she no longer felt anchored to her old life. 'I've been irresponsible for too long,' William said. 'I've allowed others to cover up my mistakes, but I did try to make amends. I simply wasn't allowed to.'

Flora was about to ask what he meant but was interrupted.

'Is this absolutely necessary, William?' Lady Venetia demanded, a tremor in her voice.

'Of course it is!' Lord Vaughn joined the conversation. 'Now do be quiet, Venetia.'

Flora blinked in surprise, never having heard Lord Vaughn talk to his wife that way before.

Lady Venetia's bottom lip trembled and she

scrabbled for a handkerchief. Jocasta moved to her mother's side and slid an arm round her shoulders. William's soft voice became the only sound in the room as he relayed the story of his arrogant youth, where on the marriage of his older sister, his fortunes had taken a turn for the better, thus introducing him into company he had hitherto been denied. 'I thought I could have everything, including Lily.'

Flora winced and Bunny eased closer, and slid his arm round her.

'I want you to know,' William said gently, 'that your mother and I were deeply in love. She was no brief encounter discarded as soon as I discovered she carried my child. I wanted to marry her.'

Flora jerked up her chin. 'Then why didn't you?' But she knew the answer to that. For Lady Vaughn's brother to have married a lady's maid wouldn't have gone down well in the social pages.

'That was my fault.' Lady Venetia's voice came again 'When I found out, I made him cancel the wedding.' She continued to hover at the back of the room as if unwilling to be included in the revelations, but without the determination to leave.

'You had arranged a wedding?' Part of her wanted to demand they stop, go back to the way it was when she was the butler's daughter and not privy to family secrets and conflict.

'Yes, we had.' William dry-washed his face with both hands. When he raised his head again his eyes had clouded with anguish. 'I was weak and allowed Venetia to convince me it was the wrong thing to do. Thus when Riordan offered to—'

'Make an honest woman of her?' Flora raised a cynical eyebrow in his direction.

'Something like that.' William shot a hard look at Lady Venetia. 'I knew Riordan loved Lily, so I let myself be convinced it was best for everyone. The family sent me to America, and I might have drifted for a while, but no one was more surprised than I when I made a success in the railroads.'

'You have to understand,' Lady Venetia interrupted, 'I was a very different person in those days. Appearances were everything and a lady whose servants were out of control reflected badly upon the family name.' She let her voice trail off as the tension in the room stretched. 'At least, that's what I was led to believe.'

Flora recalled what Jocasta had said about her grandmother's behaviour towards the young Venetia. Suddenly she felt less critical.

'Wait a moment.' Flora held up her hand. 'If William was in America, what happened in the lodge house when I was a small child?' The scene which had been the cause of a lifetime of nightmares.

'I might be able to answer that,' William began. 'I returned to England when you were almost two, Flora. Lily had settled with you and Riordan in the lodge. I'm afraid that was like salt in the wound. I tried to avoid her, but I couldn't keep away. I went to the lodge one summer's afternoon and begged her to come away with me.' He shook his head in response to Flora's unspoken question. 'She refused. Lily said Riordan was good to her, that she was happy and she had a child she adored. She told me I should go back to my life and let her live hers.' He inhaled slowly and blew out a breath through pursed lips. 'I couldn't believe she had rejected me, so I tried to convince her. She stood firm, so to persuade her I picked you up. You were—'

'—playing on a rag rug in front of the range,' Flora said, recalling the scene in her head.

'Yes. A mistake, but I thought it would persuade her that we belonged together. Instead she panicked. Lily thought I was about to take you away from her. She lunged at me with something, a skillet I think. She caught me on the side of my head. Instinctively I brought up an arm to avoid it and you fell out of my arms. She staggered backwards and you fell to the floor, on that same rug you mentioned. Lily hit her head on the kitchen table as she fell and – well it was – chaotic. You weren't hurt but you screamed, and there was Lily lying on the floor with blood coming from her forehead.'

'Then what happened?' Flora summoned the scene again, but as always, the images stopped with her holding her mother's skirt and the coppery smell of blood.

'Patience, Flora,' Bunny whispered. 'He's trying to explain.'

Flora nodded. 'I'm sorry, but this has been a

418

shadow in my life for so long. Now there's a chance to put a stop to those dreams for good. Maybe your talks about Freud meant something after all.' She offered Bunny a weak smile that he returned.

'Riordan happened,' William said when she turned back to him. 'He must have seen my horse outside, or someone told him I was there. He came rushing in and threw me out. When I had made sure Lily wasn't badly injured, I went back to America. I never saw Lily again.'

'That wasn't the end of the story though was it?' Flora asked through a tight throat. 'Some time after that, my mother died.'

'Four years later,' William said. 'I hadn't set foot in England during that time, but Venetia wrote to me. She told me about Lily's work with Miss Sawyer and the night she went to Sam Coombe's house.'

'I thought,' Lady Venetia began and then faltered. 'I thought Lily had run away to be with William. That they had planned it and she had boarded ship for America.' She sniffed once into her handkerchief, then straightened her shoulders.

'I hadn't seen her, and there was no plan, because Lily made it clear to me when we last spoke that nothing would have come between Lily and Flora.' William took up the story again. 'She wouldn't have simply, nor would she have taken Flora away from the man she had grown up with as a father. When we were forced to realize Lily wasn't coming back, Riordan and I came to an agreement. He insisted you be raised as his child. You were all he had left of Lily. All either of us had.' He took her free hand in his, his touch warm and so natural, Flora left it there. 'I didn't forget you, how could I? Whenever I came back to England, I visited you.'

'I made mistakes, Flora,' Lady Venetia said. 'We all did. Even Lily. I only hope you may come to understand.'

'Understand why you took the coward's way out?' Flora split a look between Lady Venetia and William. 'You both did.' Her chest tightened at the thought she wasn't considered good enough then to be part of their family. Perhaps she wasn't now either? It was obvious what and whom Lady Venetia was protecting all those years ago and it was neither Lily, nor Flora. It was the Vaughn family name.

'Flora, can you forgive my mistake?' William asked gently.

'Which one? Leaving my mother with child when you were about to marry her, or attacking her when she wouldn't leave with you when you deigned to return?'

'That's not how it happened.' He closed his eyes briefly, and when he opened them again, they contained new resolve. 'Even so, I ask your forgiveness for all of it. Not that I haven't regretted every rash act since I met Lily. Everything except Lily herself. I will always be grateful I knew and loved her. I'm grateful too that she had you. There was always you and whenever I returned to England, I saw you in her.'

Flora's anger receded and tears pricked the back of her throat. 'I never suspected. Not for a moment.'

'Why should you?' Bunny said. 'As far as everyone was concerned, Riordan Maguire was your father.'

'My mother must have been a special woman for two men to be so devoted to her?' Flora said it with a degree of hope, but in her own ears she sounded cynical.

'Indeed she was,' William's smile gave truth to his words. 'Riordan and I always wished you had known her for longer. Six years wasn't enough.'

'So do I,' Flora murmured. 'What I do remember is vague, and fragmented. Her voice, her smile, but which don't seem real now.'

'I'm sorry that my actions deprived you of a more privileged childhood,' Lady Venetia said.

'I'm not ashamed of my upbringing, Lady Venetia,' Flora said, ignoring her condescension. 'Riordan Maguire was an exemplary parent who never let me down.' She levelled an accusing stare on William and when he flushed, she bit her lip. What right did she really have to criticize them? Then her throat burned as she recalled with a shock that the one constant person in her life was gone and she would never see or talk to him again.

'He was indeed an exceptional manservant. We'll miss him dreadfully,' Lady Venetia said, displaying her famous lack of tact, then compounded it.

'I'm only glad I sent Eddy back to bed after dinner. I don't want him to know about our family indiscretions.'

Jocasta silenced her with a look, reminding Flora of the lunch they had shared on the terrace.

'Jocasta?' she began. 'When I said my mother had married the father of her child, you questioned it. I didn't think much of it at the time but, well – you knew didn't you?'

'Jocasta?' Lady Venetia stared at her daughter wide-eyed. 'I did everything I could to keep it from you girls. Do Amelia and Emerald know too?'

'What does it matter now, Venetia?' Lord Vaughn snapped. 'Hasn't any of this told you what damage secrets do? Mrs Mountjoy would have had no weapons to use against us without all this subterfuge. Oh, not that I blame you, Venetia,' he said in response to the horrified look on his wife's face. 'The time for all that is done, don't you think?'

'Hear hear,' Jocasta said.

'I wish you had told me,' Flora whispered, mainly for Jocasta's benefit. 'Even if it was only gossip. Although I understand why you didn't.'

'I would hardly accuse my uncle of fathering the butler's daughter and make my mother a liar.' Jocasta wrinkled her nose in distaste. 'One doesn't talk about things like that.'

Flora sighed. Now Jocasta sounded like her mother.

'Now if you all don't mind,' William said, his tone

commanding silence. 'May I have a few moments with Flora alone?'

'Oh, yes, well of course you may.' Lady Venetia set about ushering them all to their feet and towards the door, her jerky movements resembling those of a nervous sheepdog.

'Will you be all right?' Bunny whispered. His eyes glinted behind his spectacles indicating he would stand his ground if she asked him to.

'I'll be fine.' She ran a finger along his jaw.

He nodded and rose, joining Jocasta by the door.

'I have to accept some culpability in this matter,' Lord Vaughn said, pausing on his way out. 'I capitulated more easily than I should have, for which I blame my own mother entirely. You see,' he tucked his hands in the pockets of his jacket and hunched his shoulders, 'my youngest brother was the result of a liaison between my father and the daughter of the local reverend. Thus we're hardly in a position to throw stones.'

'Uncle Henry?' Jocasta collided with him as he blocked the door, halted and stared as if she had been struck. 'I had no idea.'

'Of course not, Jo,' her father said, dismissive. 'As you said yourself, one doesn't bandy these things about. They wouldn't be family secrets otherwise.'

'Oh, really, George.' Lady Venetia's shocked face reappeared round the door frame. 'Whatever possessed you to repeat that story?'

Jocasta's voice could still be heard clearly from

the hall. 'Wait until I write to Meely and tell her that her favourite uncle—'

'You'll do no such thing!' her mother cut her off. 'The Astors are grander than we are. They would never understand.'

'Can't stop me telling Jeremy though, the only scandal in his family is . . .' Jocasta's voice receded into inaudibility as the door closed.

Silence surrounded Flora, broken only by the tick of the mantel clock, leaving her self-conscious and suddenly shy when William lowered himself onto the sofa beside her. What was she expected to say to this man who was little more than a stranger?

She looked down at the patterns the scratches had made on her hands, as if they didn't belong to her. 'What do we do now?' she asked in a voice that shook.

'I don't expect you to call me "Father", if that's what worries you. However, I would welcome an opportunity to get to know you better.'

'I think that's for the future.' Flora raised her head and looked into his eyes. Eyes she saw in her mirror every morning; a thought that unnerved and yet strangely pleased her at the same time.

She took a deep breath. 'For now, I need time to mourn the only father I've ever known.'

'I-I understand.' A shadow passed across his face which told her he had hoped for something more. Something she couldn't give him – not yet.

CHAPTER 28

Flora woke the next morning with stiff hip, sore hands and a sadness that dragged at her heart. It was as if she had lost Riordan twice, once to death and then discovering he wasn't a blood relative. Later that morning she would say goodbye to him forever, taking him even further away.

She and Bunny arrived for breakfast to find Eddy, dressed in black mourning and his hair still damp from his bath, tucking into a large plate of fried sausages, bacon and eggs.

'Can you believe—' he broke off to cut into a sausage. 'The maid brought up a bowl of bread and milk on a tray and said it was my breakfast?'

'How dare she? Bunny scraped back the chair and gestured Flora into it, his lips twitching. 'I wouldn't put up with that sort of treatment if I were you, young man.'

Eddy snorted a laugh, but didn't respond as his mouth was full.

'I'll fetch your meal for you, Flora,' Bunny whispered as he tucked in her chair. 'What would you like?'

'Eggs for me, please, and maybe a tomato.' Flora smiled up at him, grateful he didn't force something more substantial on her. She never could stomach cooked meat first thing in the morning. 'I take it you are feeling better, Eddy?' She arranged her napkin over her lap that kept sliding over the heavy black fabric.

'Much.' Eddy grinned, just as the door opened to admit Lord and Lady Vaughn and William. The latter greeted everyone in turn, his gaze lingering on Flora for longer than was necessary.

Flora dipped her nose to a cup of coffee a footman had placed before her. A night's sleep and a new day had not made the situation any more real, and as she watched William move round the room, she kept repeating in her head that he was her father, but the sentiment wasn't there, only words.

Lord Vaughn paused only long enough to wish everyone a sincere, but subdued, 'Good morning, before he advanced on the bain-maries on the sideboard rubbing his hands together. 'I'm famished.'

'Eddy!' Lady Venetia halted at the sight of her son. 'Why aren't you in bed?'

'Because I'm starving.' Eddy held up his fork which held a generous slice of bacon. 'I'm going to have another helping too.'

'Don't you think you should wait and see what that woman doctor your father insists will be returning today says about that? And why are you wearing your black suit? Surely you don't intend to attend the funeral?'

Flora hadn't considered this, though after one sweeping glance she realized that everyone was dressed similarly. If not in full mourning, then a more reasonable tribute of respect. Her heart warmed at the thought all the Vaughns were going to come, even Eddy.

'Leave the boy, Venetia,' Lord Vaughn returned to the table with a plate piled high with everything the dishes contained, even kidneys and kedgeree. 'He knows his own mind.'

'Indeed I do,' Eddy said between mouthfuls. 'I'd known Maguire all my life and I want to pay my respects. If he hadn't suspected the arsenic thingy, Flora would never have put it together and I might be dead now.'

'Eddy, don't!' Lady Venetia waved a hand in front of her face as if dismissing the thought.'

'Yes, well.' Eddy pouted. 'I miss him. It feels odd not seeing him every day.'

'Thank you, Eddy,' Flora's whispered, her throat burning with suppressed emotion. 'I appreciate it.'

He gave her a shy grin, pushed back his chair and headed for the sideboard.

'I just hope he doesn't make himself sick,' Lady Venetia nibbled at a slice of toast, and flushed when her husband frowned at her. 'Which reminds me.' She rose slowly to her feet, one hand brought to her lips, obviously distracted. 'Some of the flowers and wreaths have arrived here already this morning. 'I'll have to go and see to them myself now we're without a head butler.' She released a long suffering sigh and headed for the door, almost colliding with Jocasta who was on her way in. 'I might have to try an agency.' Her lips curled slightly on the last word.

'Poor, Mama.' Jocasta smirked, having apparently heard this last comment. 'She doesn't like change does she? I think she's more upset at what Mrs Mountjoy did than anything. Mama has few real friends, even superficial ones.'

Flora greeted her with a smile, noting Jocasta wore unrelieved black and had even wound black ribbons into her hair. She mouthed a silent 'thank you' as Jocasta passed her chair, which was returned with squeeze of Flora's shoulder.

Jocasta's smile dissolved into a frustrated sigh when she reached the sideboard. 'Eddy! You've just taken the last sausage,'

Eddy grinned at her as he darted past her and resumed his seat.

Sighing, Jocasta ladled food onto her plate while muttering under her breath that he would be more spoiled than ever after this. 'No one made this much fuss of me when I had chicken pox last winter.'

William hid a smile, and nudged him as they stood side by side filling their plates.

'It's not the same as being poisoned,' Eddy pointed out as Jocasta took her seat. 'I nearly died.'

'Does anyone know how Peter is?' Flora attempted to bring a halt to all talk of dying, picking at her eggs with little appetite at the thought of what the morning held.

'Still weak,' Lord Vaughn said, looking up from his plate. 'Dr Billings feels he'll likely be well enough to go home later today. She'll call in later and check on him.'

'I doubt Mr Griggs will be too enamoured of you running up a medical bill on his behalf, Papa.' Jocasta sniffed.

'I've instructed all her bills are to be sent to me, so Griggs doesn't have to worry.'

'That's most kind of you, my lord.' Flora looked up in time to catch his slight flush and deprecating shrug. 'Venetia is annoyed enough with me already about Dr Billings. She doesn't approve. Oh, and by the way.' He raised his fork in the air. 'Dr Billings doesn't think he's got consumption either, merely bronchitis which has worsened through being ignored.'

'Oh, I *am* pleased to hear that,' Flora said. 'And I rather like the name Dr Grace.'

'That's what I call her,' Eddy said as he tucked into another generously filled plate. 'She's nice. Comforting, like the school nurse and Flora rolled into one. May I have some of that coffee?'

'Don't push it, little brother.' Jocasta narrowed her eyes as she placed a glass of milk in front of him.

Eddy flushed but didn't argue.

An awkward silence ensued broken only by the click of cutlery, the odd cough and a snap of a newspaper.

'Isn't anyone going to tell me what is going to happen about Mr Scrivens? I haven't seen him since yesterday.' She hoped he hadn't got wind of what was happening and had bolted.

'Ah, yes him.' William returned to the table, having poured himself more coffee. 'When Bracenose came running out to tell us you needed help at Mrs Mountjoy's, Scrivens must have seen it. Knowing he was under suspicion he decided to make himself scarce.'

'So while we went off to rescue you,' Bunny interjected. 'William instructed him to find Scrivens and make sure he didn't leave the premises.'

'By any means he thought necessary, where his exact words,' William added, smiling.

'Did he find him?' Flora asked carefully.

'Indeed. He was packing his things when Bracenose located him.' William said.

'The police were still at Caroline's house sorting out the mess there when Venetia and I got back,' Lord Vaughn joined the conversation. 'I ordered Scrivens put into the cellar for the night. Constable Jones will question him later this morning.'

'He had better bring a police van with him, because Scrivens is going to jail,' Eddy said, evidently delighted with the idea.

'Pity it's September and not January. That cellar can get like the Arctic in the winter.' Jocasta spread

430

conserve on a slice of toast and took a bite. 'I suppose we can't have everything.'

'William and I confronted Scrivens together,' Bunny said. 'After a certain amount of persuasion, he admitted McCallum had paid him to do it.'

'What sort of persuasion?' Flora frowned.

'That's irrelevant.' Bunny waved his hand as if shooing the thought aside. 'Anyway, William found something interesting amongst his belongings. A train timetable for the London and South Western Railway Company.'

'He's not as bright as he likes to appear,' William snorted. 'He even underlined the Richmond times. There was also a dated receipt for the Petersham Hotel.'

'William convinced him he could hang as McCallum's accomplice, which shook him. After that it was easy. He made a full confession to Constable Jones.'

'And I missed all this?' Flora huffed a breath. 'How disappointing.'

'You were sleeping. But at one point Lord Vaughn had to pull both William and myself off him when he told us how he had started the fire.' She slanted a look at him and he added, 'no, we didn't touch him, though it would have been most satisfying to lay the man out. It appears Nancy was partly to blame.'

'Nancy? Our kitchen maid?' Flora recalled the girl's distress that she might be blamed, which seemed odd at the time.

He nodded. 'You were right about her protesting too much. He claimed to be a salesman and she left him in the kitchen while she went to get Crabtree. While he was waiting he slipped into the cellar and emptied oil over an old piece of carpet, lit the fire and left before Crabtree arrived.'

'Nancy wasn't to know he would do that.' Flora's hip began to ache and she shifted on her chair in an effort to find a more comfortable position. She was about to ask where Scrivens was now, but refused to pretend she cared one way or the other.

'He'll be gone by the time we return after the funeral,' Bunny said as if he read her thoughts. He covered her hand with his and glanced at the clock. 'It's time to go.'

'I'll have the carriages brought round,' William said gently, scraping back his chair.

Flora eased open the stable door and stepped inside, pausing to allow her eyes to adjust to the gloom after the bright sunlight outside. Gentle snuffles and soft snorts drew her along the row of stalls, which she trod carefully to avoid clumps of soft hay beneath her feet.

'Tom, are you here?' she called, frowning. It wasn't like Tom to leave the stables in a mess. She rounded the post and halted, startled as she came upon a couple in a tight embrace.

'Mrs Harrington!' Tom sprang away from an extremely pretty girl who took a step back, one hand raised to a riot of long, honey-coloured curls in an effort to pat them into some sort of order. A gesture less of shyness than pride, her vivid blue eyes returning Flora's look in amused challenge.

'I do apologize, Tom.' Flora's gaze remained on the girl. 'I thought you were alone.' She turned away, embarrassed. What Tom Murray did and with whom was no business of hers, though she couldn't help wondering who the girl was.

'No, don't go, Mrs Harrington.' Tom crossed the space between them. 'I want to explain.'

'You don't owe me an explanation, Tom. I only came to tell you Mr Harrington and I are due to catch the train back to Richmond straight after the funeral, so I came to say goodbye and to thank you for your kindness.'

'Miss Flora!' Tom grasped the girl's hand and dragged her forward. 'I want you to meet Betsy,' he said, his voice tinged with pride.

'Betsy Mason?' Flora gaped as she looked from him to the girl and back again. With everything that had happened she had completely forgotten about Betsy.

The girl's vivid blue eyes widened slightly in challenge as she returned Flora's look steadily.

'Well.' Flora leaned against the nearest upright. 'You caused quite a stir around here. All sorts of stories circulated about what had happened to you.'

'Nothing happened,' Betsy said, her voice low and musical. 'I simply needed some time to think.'

'I'm intrigued as to where you went, and why?'

433

Flora asked, then added. 'I'm sorry, I have no right to ask.'

'She's been with me,' Tom turned to stare at Betsy as if he couldn't believe his luck.

'Quite an improvement on a collie, Tom.' Flora raised a brow to the ceiling and smiled. 'And your eye is almost healed.' Tom fingered his face, and Flora went on, 'I'm guessing Scrivens was responsible for that?'

'Aye. He made a remark about Betsy which wasn't true.' He gave a dismissive snort. 'She wouldn't have had anything to do with him, but I couldn't have him spreading lies about her could I? Though I'm not as handy with my fists as he is.'

'That's a skill he may need where he's going,' Flora murmured, then louder. 'You don't have to worry about him. He's in no position to make your life difficult anymore.' Flora changed the subject. She didn't want to discuss the man now, nor ever. 'Why did you run off after the fête, Betsy?'

'Mr McCallum, well, he made me all sorts of promises.' She flushed and covered her mouth with her hand, but Tom didn't react at all. It was as if he knew everything there was to know about her and none of it mattered. Much like herself and Bunny.

'I know it was stupid of me to fall for his lies,' Betsy went on, 'but he made it all sound so wonderful. We would be married and I would go and live at the hall, and-.' She broke off and swallowed. 'It was all lies. At the fête, when I asked

434

him when he planned to announce our engagement, he laughed at me. Said I was stupid to
believe it was anything more than a bit of fun.
That I wasn't good enough for him I slapped him
and ran out.'

'No one has seen you for a month, where did
you go?' Flora didn't mention Constable Jones,
no doubt Tom would sort that gentleman out.

'I was going to leave, though I had nowhere to
go.' She shrugged her dainty shoulders, the gesture
on her somehow appealing. 'I told Tom telling him
how miserable I was and the trouble with Mr
McCallum and Scrivens. He's always been nice to
me, and I knew I could trust him.'

'We agreed she should stay in hiding until I
worked out what to do about Scrivens,' Tom said.
'If he knew she was here, he would have pestered
her again.'

'It was you I saw at the cottage that day, wasn't
it, Betsy? And you've been hiding above the stables
for all that time?'

Tom laced his fingers through hers and pressed
them against his chest. 'It's been grand, Mrs
Harrington. Like a holiday. Now Scrivens has got
what he deserved—'

'Yes, I cannot believe he tried to burn you out
of your house?' Betsy's eyes widened with as much
excitement as shock. 'I knew he was a sly creature,
but a murderer?'

'An unsuccessful one, thank goodness,' Flora
said.

'Anyway, Betsy doesn't have to hide any more, and we're going to ask her uncle if we can get married.'

'He'll give his permission, you don't have to worry about that.' Betsy looked up into Tom's eyes. 'Especially when he knows we've been living together this last week or so.'

'I imagine he will.' A smile tugged Flora's mouth. 'Many congratulations to you both.'

She strode back to the door and pulled it closed, then leaned against it, smiling to herself.

'What are you smiling at?' Bunny said when she joined him at the carriage.

'Do you recall what you once told me? That life is messy and not every question has a neat answer?' She held onto his arm with both hands and hugged him to her.

'A little profound for me I would have thought. Why?'

'I'll explain later, but it appears that not every mystery has an unhappy ending either.'

'Maybe, but I hope you'll be more careful in future. There are some unsavoury characters out there and you're too trusting.'

'You must rue the day you became involved in my complicated background.' She released his arm only long enough to climb into the carriage. 'Are there times when you wish you hadn't married me?'

'Absolutely not!' He slid into the seat beside her. 'I cannot wait to tell Mother that she'll have to cease her pointed remarks about governesses now my wife is an heiress and sister-in-law to a lord.' His smile faded. 'Have you made your peace with William yet?'

'Peace isn't quite the right word. William wants to get to know me, which seemed an odd request when he has always been a part of my life. I suppose I'm the one who has to adjust my thinking about him.'

'I expect he's well aware of that, but what do *you* want?'

'That's the point. I don't know. I'm still so angry that I was lied to all my life.'

'William had no choice, you must understand that. He wants to do what's best for you now. For both of you.'

'Too little, too late,' Flora murmured, then louder. 'That doesn't mean I can't let him sweat a little.'

Bunny slewed his eyes sideways at her, sighed and rapped on the carriage roof as a signal for them to leave. 'Now, are you ready to lay your father to rest?'

'He wasn't my father though, was he?' Flora's voice hitched.

'Yes, he was.' Bunny squeezed her hand as the carriage set off. 'In every way that mattered.'

Roy - N.P.
Ra/- Wei

Lees MW